Demorn: Blade of Exile

THE ASANTI SERIES: BOOK ONE

David Finn

DEMORN: BLADE OF EXILE

Interior Design by QA Productions

Cover design by Deranged Doctor Design

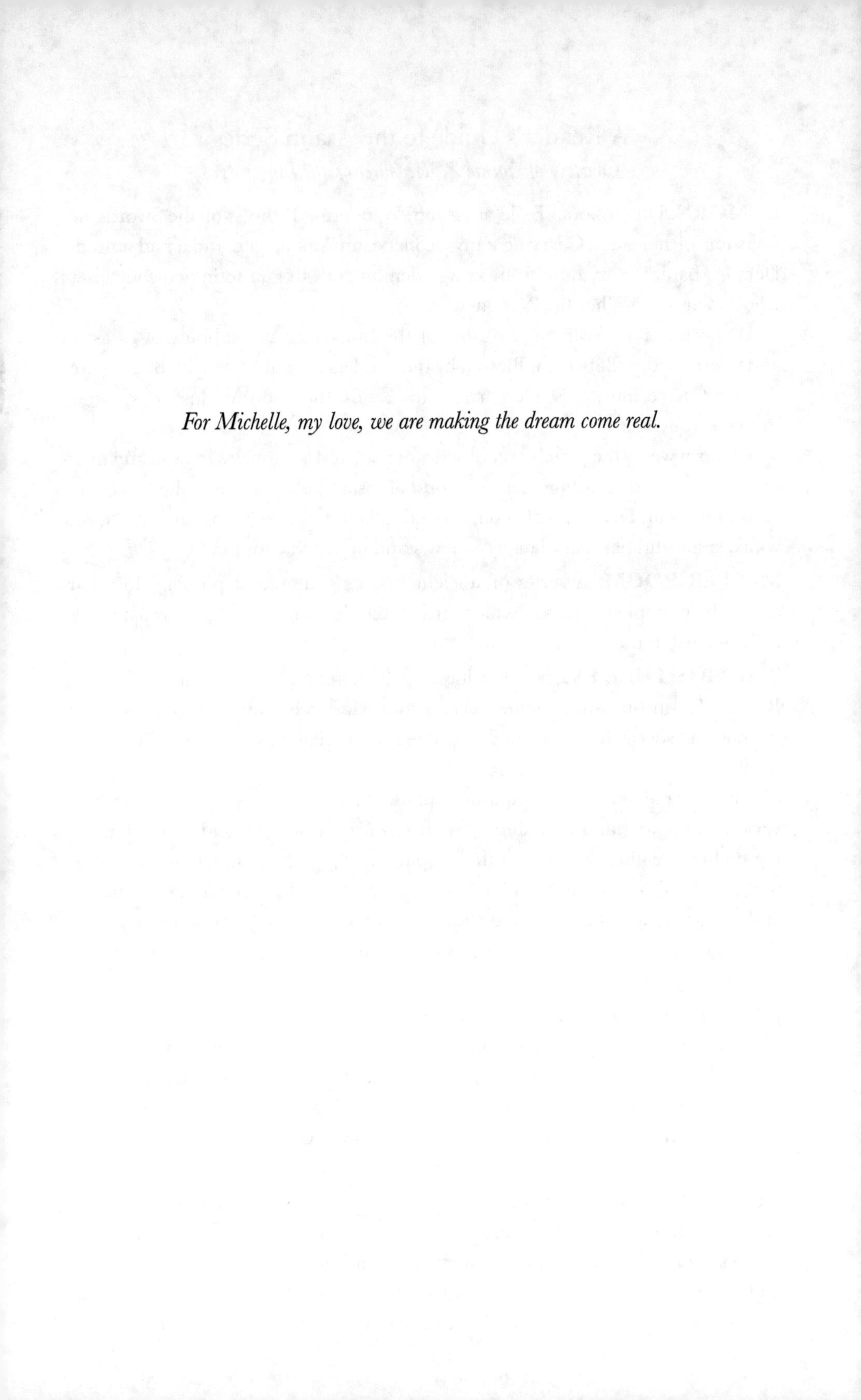

For Michelle, my love, we are making the dream come real.

A Reader's Guide to the Asanti Series

Courtesy of Jackie Z, Treasurer of the Innocents

DEMORN: Dimensional Exile of Asanti, Wandering Princess of the Swords, are just some of her titles. Carrying a mystic blade, an Athena gun and a bad attitude, Demorn battles everything from savage demon gods to gun-toting cowboy losers who run away with her boss's money.

Demorn is a high-ranking member of the Innocents, a Clubhouse of assassins and thieves within Babelzon. Blessed by the goddess Alodin Mars with blazing eyes that can pierce into souls, Demorn wields Xalos, the sword of Justice, spawned from her ruby heart.

Demorn wears the pain locket of a death god, and is a touch sarcastic and nihilistic. Determined to avenge her lost world of Asanti, obsessed over the loss of her girlfriend's soul, Demorn fights on, collecting bounties and killing creepers, quick with a smile and her scary laugh . . . few stand in her way for too long.

MASTER ROOM: A series of ancient Rooms scattered at pinpoint locations across the multiple realities in which ancient entities control and manipulate reality. Damaged in the Fracture Event.

THE FRACTURE EVENT: On July 17, 1968, in San Francisco, in the Primary Reality, Triton operatives gained access to a Master Room on Haight-Ashbury Avenue and successfully activated a Source Bomb, triggering the shattering of that reality.

The effect of this Source explosion splintered across the layers of multiple universes, weakening and breaking apart the concepts of time and place, imploding multiple realities into each other, wiping much of the population's memories through the Primary Reality. Cracks opened in the walls of multiple dimensions and savage demon gods began to claw against the Void Wall where they have lain dormant . . . This disaster is known as the Fracture Event. Demorn remembers it, one of a select few.

BABELZON: The sprawling, futuristic city where Demorn and her brother crash-landed in the Spire jump ship. Ruled by the Tyrant, home to over 100 million, Babelzon is surrounded by huge portals that are gateways to other worlds and parallel dimensions. Located adjacent to the Grim Earth, Babelzon is a key trading hub and many citizens live and die never leaving the city's walls. Legend tells that the Tyrant raised the city from the ground by the power of his mind . . .

THE INNOCENTS: The Clubhouse of assassins and thieves that Demorn works for, located in Babelzon. The Innocents stay below the radar, their base hidden behind laser forcefields in the Inner Sanctum. Their huge clubhouse, funded by Tony and the jobs they take, runs deep underground and accommodates a tight band of fighters, telepaths and killers. Membership is exclusive and every new entrant is screened by leading members within the Ruby Room, their layers stripped bare. The Clubhouse contains many secrets, a whispered myth among the populace. *You can pay for Innocence*, they say.

INNER SANCTUM: The most exclusive section of Babelzon. It houses the Council chambers and the Innocents Clubhouse.

SUB BABEL: A term for the outlying districts of Babelzon, out from the Hub, often used with derision.

ASANTI: The Mirror World of Asanti was an acclaimed lodestone of knowledge, famed across a huge network of parallel realities, located in a mirror pocket dimension. Asanti was destroyed in the aftershocks of the Fracture Event. A small segment of Asanti refugees including Demorn and her brother escaped on a Spire jump-ship as the planet exploded. Just a few Asanti survive, riding the storm.

TRITON: In the wake of the Fracture Event, aspects of dark demon gods infiltrated the time-stream, loosened of their chains within the Void. As they sank their savage teeth into reality, the Triton Corporation was formed, backed by agents of the dark gods, humans and aliens who fell under their sway. The Triton mega-corporation seeks to manipulate the present and future by infiltrating the time-stream. Demorn has battled Triton operatives several times across various decades and locales, seeking to avoid a colossal takeover of the present from the past. For all their power, Triton's grip on reality is tenuous and reliant on fear, much of their labor farmed out to mortal operatives. There is hope . . .

TONY: A mob boss who has risen to the City Council in Babelzon. Tony's network tentacle runs deep through Babelzon. He owns multiple business throughout Babelzon, legitimate and otherwise. Tony is close friends with Demorn, giving her many missions, mostly hits, sorting out problems he doesn't want to touch himself.

Tony had an Asanti wife, deceased in the Asanti Event. Tony and Demorn share a love for Frank Sinatra and Pina Coladas. Every Wednesday they dine together in the Jade Hotel, watching a clone Sinatra sing the hits. It's a life, Tony says.

WHITE LION: Tony's psychotic bodyguard and primary muscle in the house. Few trust him, and he trusts none. *A dangerous shark in a city full of sharks*, is how Demorn describes White Lion. They loathe each other.

ALEX: Demorn's beautiful friend and chief rival within the Innocents. Fastest gun in the Clubhouse. Most completed Tyrant runs out of any Innocent. Alex is a highly dependable assassin with few morals and a love for cash that outweighs even Demorn's.

GUARD DOG: Alex's bodyguard, ex-cage wrestler, a genetic "freak", fiercely loyal to Alex who rescued him. Low intelligence, highly suspicious of outsiders. Hates Demorn's flippancy.

TOXIS: Lethal Huntress of the mysterious and deadly Blood Clan. Soul sister of Demorn, and a telepath, Toxis is linked to Demorn by the Adolin Mars tattoos on their arms. She carries an enchanted ash staff and often aids Demorn. Toxis originates from the Firethorn dimension. She never stays too long in Babelzon, longing for the deep ice caverns and rolling green forests of Firethorn.

KATE: Demorn's ex-girlfriend, hurt long ago in Firethorn on a mission gone wrong, her soul taken by parties unknown. Her ghost lingers around Demorn, while Kate's physical shell lives on in LA, where she is a C-list actress, hustling for TV gigs.

FIRETHORN: The Fort by the Sea, and the entry point to an immense fantasy dimension. The Sisters of Firethorn hold the line against the forces who would seek to burn the Fort down. Demorn has been coming to the White Fort since she was ten, prior to the destruction of Asanti. Demorn has been unable to access Firethorn for almost two years, reasons unknown.

THE DEAD KING: A legend amongst the Sisters of Firethorn, a mythical King who inhabits the wild forest around the White Fort. They search for the Dead King in mad rituals . . .

THE GRIM EARTH: The term used by many Babelzonians to describe the remains of the Primary Earth, sections of which were untouched by the Fracture Event. Demorn often takes hit missions on the Grim Earth. She often holidays in Vegas with her friend and fellow comic fan, Suicide Sue.

THE TYRANT: Enigmatic ruler of Babelzon, possibly immortal, the Tyrant oversees all in Babelzon, feared and respected by the entire city. He does not appear in public, although Tyrant propaganda channels broadcast throughout the city. Many venerate him, but as with any ruler, there are pockets of rebellion scattered throughout Babelzon. Many myths and secrets tie back to the Tyrant.

THE TYRANT RUN: A hugely popular blood-sport competition held and broadcast throughout Babelzon. A series of death traps and challenge fights set the runners against each other. The winner is rumoured to meet The Tyrant, though most Runs end with all parties dead. The Run is the highest rated show in Babelzon, screening across thousands of channels. Alex is the most successful Runner in history. Many Innocents have entered the Run to eliminate targets and collect bounties.

ALODIN MARS: Patron Goddess of the Innocents. Every Innocent bears her mark upon their body. A Goddess of War, draped in red armour, carrying a holy spear. Every Innocent knows a little of her legends, but nobody knows everything about this mysterious Goddess. Quick to anger, but generous with her gifts, Alodin Mars is the fierce embodiment of the Innocents' ideal. Her motto, and that of the

Innocents, is *Straight sword, clean heart.* Demorn has remarked that Alodin is just one of the primary aspects of the Goddess. She has seen others. People are never quite sure how to respond.

MICTECACIUTAL: An ancient evil Death Goddess consigned to the Void. Demorn carries a locket with a piece of Mictecaciutal, which grants her healing power while flooding her with pain.

SMILE: Demorn's brother, tech wizard. Traumatised by the loss of Asanti and non-violent in nature, unlike his sister, Smile has struggled to adapt to life in Babelzon and the ways of the Innocents. Although he has a spare room in the Clubhouse and is close to his sister, Smile spends most of his time on the Spire constructing simulations and seeking to repair the vessel. Three years ago, Smile was snatched from the Spire and experimented on by a New Science cell based in Mexico City, before Demorn rescued him from their tortures. Smile is now only partly flesh and bone, much of his form is a virtual construct.

THE SPIRE: The Asanti jump ship which crash-landed in Babelzon, carrying Demorn and Smile. The crash has damaged and crippled the ship. However Smile is able to salvage much of the tech and is kept busy reverse engineering the tech.

PALE SUNS: An ancient race of corrupted sorcerers, normally human, who have studied and delved too long and too deeply into the dark arts. The dread power has fed back and ate into their souls, corrupting their bodies. These sick, lost monsters seek the moment of Emergence. Demorn hates the Pale Suns and hunts their kind with a passion.

THE GRIM EARTH: This is the term used by many Babelzonians to describe what remains of the Primary Earth Reality, sections of which were untouched by the Fracture Event. The vast majority of the Grim Earth population have no knowledge of the Fracture Event and the worlds beyond them.

THE GRAVE: A doomed dimension of animated skeletons and undead.

XALOS: The Sword of Justice, an ancient katana which spawns from Demorn's ruby heart, burning with purple fire. Demorn sometimes struggles to summon the mysterious blade. Xalos is driven by a deep desire to redress the wrongs and injustices done to others. Once the blood starts to flow, Xalos becomes insatiable, with Demorn barely able to control the fury and speed of the blade. Luckily, Demorn loves the taste of battle and imparting Justice . . .

JASON ALOQUIN: World-builder, designer of realities, moody teen.

FRANK SINATRA: The Chairman of the Board. One of the most famous singers in the 20th century, and Demorn's friend.

Part 1

1

Demorn's boots crunched across the ice roof, the pain locket burning on her chest. Her pistol glinted in her right hand. She was careful on the slippery surface, seeking the entrance to the lair. A Medusi sprang at her, turquoise eye-beams bouncing off the ice, pale skin marked with sun tats. Demorn flicked an energy star from her gloved wrist, slicing through the Medusi throat. Her gun hand followed as it gurgled into death, the body ashing out over the ice.

She tugged her leather jacket tight around her, blocking out the cold. The sun was a pale disc glittering off purple sunglasses.

Demorn's fingers found the grate and she overrode the primitive sensor alarms. She could feel the monsters beneath her, flickering at the periphery of her awareness. They hissed to each other through the ice, garbled translations through her implant. She heard a human scream inside the lair. The voice died out fast as the creatures ripped into flesh. Her fingers tightened on her pistol but it was far too late now. The invisible watch blinked on her wrist, a yellow grin on a blue face that only her eyes could see. Smile had been reliable. She had found the nest at last.

Demorn heard one of the creatures giggle, an edge of madness in the tone. An old, slow sad song started playing in the cavern, tenderly haunting as it came from nowhere. Staring into the whiteness of this frozen world, Demorn thought randomly of past loves, past lovers. Soft lips she'd kissed, a lilac perfume that had lingered in Demorn's sheets, clothes and heart, memories blazing suddenly inside the neon maze.

Demorn slid through the grate, tumbling down onto the ice, firing at the fast moving shadows as they howled with hatred and fear. Her pistol found the first one, disintegrating the Medusi body with a vivid purple fire.

It was as if she was back in some Sanctum Club, dancing with beautiful people, as the dark shapes fell and she spun through the air, in rhythm with the feelings of another life, before the hunting became everything. The Medusi screamed as they lit up in holy purple flames, beautiful turquoise streams of light haphazardly bouncing off the frigid cavern walls, snake hair thrashing as they died.

Nothing touched her as she cleared the room. All that remained was an exhausted peace of corpses and ash. The music had stopped. Another tune began playing sad and big, a dirge to the ice that clawed through her heart. She shot the stereo.

Demorn prowled through the room. Surviving Medusi hissed and cursed at her from shadows, wounded and scared. She threw down three sapphire blue jewels, lighting up the lair. Crystalline statues were scattered haphazardly through the room. She approached the statue of a young man. So life-like, frozen forever. Her gloved hand felt the glassy surface, the terror on his anonymous face which could never find peace. So many races and creeds, from so many cities, so many worlds. The Medusi had been down here for years. The trail to them had been long and hard.

The floor was slippery, coins strewn across it. Alien insignias mixed with more familiar human coinage. She left them on the ice floor. Her bounty was far more precious than a few coins. Her watch flashed, the yellow smile fainter. Her mark was still down there, deeper in the cavern. She heard the moan of a young girl, dying out. Without conscious thought, Demorn ran into the dark, away from the sapphire light that kept the monsters at bay, hearing that young voice as if it were her own, calling out from the dark.

She ran down through a long narrow tunnel, the sunglasses becoming her night eyes. A brutal wind blasted her, more bitter with each step she took. She saw three Medusi racing up toward her. She fired on instinct, killing two outright. The third ran up the wall, avoiding the shots, then flew past her, terrified. Demorn slowed down, every sense alert. She saw a young, teenage girl dressed in an oversized jumper and short skirt, huddled crying in a freezing corner of the tunnel. Her face was a blend of smudged pink lipstick, thick makeup across a pretty face. What Demorn always remembered were her hoop earrings, and a terrible sick whiteness that all the fake tan in the galaxy could never hide. The girl's eyes were black tunnels and her hands shook, expensive jewellery rattling on thin wrists. Demorn glanced at her watch but it was not flashing. This was not her target, this was not her payday.

She bent down, talking softly. 'How many were left alive?'

The girl murmured, 'Almost none of us, not now. They liked to play.'

Demorn felt Xalos stirring in her chest, the ancient flames of the vengeance blade. The old disgust rose up inside her, the familiar need to bring justice and make amends. For wrongs that were not of her making or design, but still her place to fix.

Demorn held her freezing body tight. 'Not anymore they don't.'

The girl's makeup ran with black tears. 'I don't think I'm alive, they killed me, they killed me too.'

Demorn could see through her, into the dark, cold tunnel. The girl was just a ghost, shimmering for a little while. She vanished in the wind, still crying, going to wherever the dead go.

The tunnel opened into a chamber laid with glass coffins. All the coffins were dark except for one, which shone with soft pink light at the far end. A large archway was lit up, opening to a mysterious darkness beyond. Demorn knew what lay in the coffins. But she still looked inside, she could not turn away. In each dark coffin a crystal statue clawed at the glass lid. Each haunted face wore a variation of private terror, eyes wide open to their awful fate.

Demorn reached the last pink coffin. A teenage girl lay sleeping in a foetal position, dressed in a black t-shirt, torn blue jeans, messy long, blonde hair streaked with green. She looked about sixteen with change. Demorn's watch sparkled with a big flashing green smile, rotating across the screen with the confirmation.

Rachel Kobayashi. She'd found her mark, Demorn thought with a sigh of grim satisfaction. She depressed the coffin lid, pink light bathing the girl, and lifted her light body out. Rachel slightly smiled, curling into Demorn's arms, her face tranquil in this dirty, frozen place. Demorn felt her dead heart stir a little. How had she survived?

Demorn pushed the girl's jumper up. *Ahhh.* The blue tattoo was there upon her wrist: Alodin Mars, the Goddess of the Innocents, resting on a glowing spear. Club Protection.

Rachel's eyes opened, ocean blue, framing a young face. 'You came.'

Demorn smiled, her watch sparkling a final time as the voice matched up with the logs. 'Yeah, Rachel. That's my job.'

'Who are you? How do you know who I am?'

Demorn took her glasses off. Her eyes were a blazing green. She raised her right hand, took off her glove. On her wrist shone the same tattoo, Alodin Mars glowing upon her pale skin.

'My name's Demorn. I'm an Innocent working out of Babelzon. Your father contacted us to find you.'

Rachel's face broke out in happiness. She tightly clutched onto Demorn's jacket. Her eyes were tender and full of something that Demorn used to have, now only recognised in others. It was the most naked trust, the trust you have when all else has been taken away.

'I'm in the Innocents fan club! Does this rescue mean I can be full-time now?'

Demorn set her down on the cold ground, smiling. She quickly took off her watch and pressed it onto Rachel's slender wrist.

'We'll see. It's set for the Clubhouse. Inner Sanctum, Babelzon.'

Rachel looked confused. 'What about you?'

'We're connected. I'm on a time delay. I've got something else to do here.'

'Like what?'

Rachel's eyes were big and filled with tears. Demorn impulsively kissed her on the cheek.

'Don't worry, I'll be okay. Grab a coffee and go chill in the Music Room.'

The girl snorted.

'You actually have a room that you call a Music Room?'

Demorn smirked. 'Oh yeah. Sometimes I go in there all alone and listen to country albums and get all sensitive.'

Rachel looked a little uncertain. 'My Dad hasn't talked to me in weeks, y'know. I hope he's not mad.'

Demorn was smooth. 'He wants you back real bad.'

White lines burst through the floor, forming tiny cracks in the ice.

'You're just saying that 'cause he's rich.'

Demorn slid her purple sunglasses back on.

'He pays well, that's true.'

Pure light blazed through the archway like a small sun. The ice coffins cracked and shattered. Rachel screamed in terror. Demorn held the girl close to her. From inside the white light, it called out their names with a shocking, cruel intensity, over and over. Demorn knew something cold and evil lay there, in the centre of the light. A bitter gust of wind blew through the archway into the room, horribly intense, laced with plague and death.

She felt weak, and the pain locket on her breast throbbed with power, clearing her mind with a burning focus. The Club portal opened and Rachel flickered away into nothingness, pulled back to Babelzon.

2

The scream repeated, filled with agony and hate. Sometimes it sounded like one man, then it was a multitude, a chorus of hate. The voices didn't ask for Rachel anymore, just Demorn. She walked through the archway toward the light, her glasses phasing to handle the intense brightness.

A strange thin man in a tight white suit stood in a cavern, a glowing cracked egg in his hands. The giant beam of white light spilt out from the egg. He smiled at her, displaying short black teeth that glistened in the light as she came through the archway.

A Pale Sun! Demorn whispered her surprise. His eyes blinked slowly, yellow, reptilian and lidded, as he examined the cracked egg. The light radiating outward ceased, sucked backward, absorbed into either the egg or himself, she didn't know. His figure blurred and Demorn saw a spectral after-image of a massive five-headed reptilian figure, echoing through the cavern, shuddering outside reality, vibrating through space, triumphant and all-consuming.

Her eyes snapped back to this world. Bodies of Medusi were littered around him, charred and burnt. The Pale Sun tossed away the ruined egg, now dark and charred. She realised larger eggs surrounded him, some cracked and open, many still unhatched.

'What is a monster like you doing here?' she said, raising the pistol at his head.

He chuckled. His voice was a dry rasp.

'So says the bounty hunter with a gun to my head. It's a funny life.'

She shot bullet after holy bullet into him. The Pale hissed as the bullets struck, tearing into his suit, spilling dark blood. She watched the wounds close, bullets pushing through pallid skin, dropping to the cavern floor. He caught one in his fingers, examining it.

'Holy bullets, how they sting.'

A forked tongue flickered across his black teeth. 'But that's all they do.'

He moved his white fingers. A venomous cloud took a crackling shape between his hands. Her instincts flared. The glasses knew. Poison, goddammit!

Demorn grasped the pain locket around her neck, murmuring the trigger word. An instant aching coursed through her heart and her hand clasped tight around the locket. She could feel the extra strength flooding into her limbs, as the fire of a death god burnt through her heart and into her soul. Demorn flew into the upper reaches of the cavern, the poison cloud spewing toward her. She caught some of the vapour trail, dry-retching, soaring upward. Of course I never bring my nose plugs, she thought with a dry disgust.

Demorn reached the upper limits of the cavern. Her magic eyes scanned the icy room, pain searing through her body every moment she floated in the air. She couldn't see anything but the frozen ceiling. This was a dead end. The only way through him was through him. Demorn pulled a red and green mask from her jacket, down over her face, the synthetic folds meshing into her glasses and skin, synching and enhancing her senses. Her sight became crystal sharp. Demorn could see the deep lines in his corrupt face.

The Pale Sun laughed below, voice rippling with contempt.

'A blessed gun and some accessories. That won't be enough! I'm a Pale Sun! I'm an Emperor of the Lost Sun!'

Whatever that means, Demorn thought.

He can be beaten.

The intense voice echoed through her mind, passionate and clear.

By Alodin! A telepath.

The voice echoed back through her mind.

He has not yet taken full form, we have no time! Attack with me now!

Demorn saw a red form flicker wildly through the cavern. The Pale Sun disappeared for a moment in the billowing black cloud which surged up into the cold air. Demorn could see him within the poison cloud, trapped in some lightning speed clash with the fast-moving figure. She focused her mind, tumbling down toward the fight, the mask and locket protecting her from the worst of the stinking poison.

As Demorn landed, she felt a surge of power flow from the Sun. A rumble of transcendental thunder echoed with lost wailing and oceans of tears from all the cities on all the worlds that would fall before the Pale Suns, preparing the universe for some horrible, unnamed entity that would come in their wake, the alien thing that clawed at the edge of her own dreams . . . now, before, after, forever.

Gasping, Demorn rejected those false visions. He was just another trickster, a mad killer driven underground with all the other sick creatures. The Pale Sun towered over a lithe figure in a dark red cloak striking him again and again, lightning fast, with a staff that burnt with insane fire.

Demorn moved into the fight. Demorn fired at the Pale Sun. The red cloaked figure turned. It was a young woman, she had a face of pure fire, a hunter demon carrying revenge from some deep hell, charred orange eyes that cut deep through the dark. The image reverberated into Demorn's mind, seared onto her soul forever. Seeing those bright eyes burn against the unspeakable void, Demorn felt her own doubts subside, replaced by rage against the Pale Sun. She felt a hunger for revenge which blocked out everything else, cleansing her heart utterly.

Demorn watched the bullets burn and sting as they struck the monster, shots refracting through reality, multiple faces echoing in the void. He howled in anger and frustration. The huntress struck home with her staff, the holy bullets by some miracle not touching her cloaked form as she flipped wildly in the cavern air.

Now!

Demorn sneered her scary smile, the mask curled around her features. Yes. It felt right. The demon-huntress swept upward onto the man's face, cracking the wood hard across his face, flying high into the air with an athletic jump, releasing a sharp metal blade, driving it down into the monster's neck.

The Pale howled, and for a single moment, Demorn saw the Sun as he truly was, stripped of artifice and cloaking spells. Both wonderful and revolting, a pure and complete evil, no real trace of humanity left in it anywhere. Inside was something far more ancient and far more terrible than humanity, a stain across blank white that flashed across Demorn's magic eyes and soul. She would never forget the inner workings of the Pale Suns.

Demorn blinked, refocusing. The creature had shed the human skin. But it lived. Solid ivory horns protruded from the monster's bleeding mouth, ripping through the flesh. Black scale was forming upon his skin. A long shimmering spear lay in his hands. Ignoring the spike embedded in his neck, the creature drove upward and caught the hunter as she leapt away. The monster cruelly twisted the spear, then slowly drew it from the chest of the huntress.

'I AM BORN AGAIN!'

'Get ready for the grave,' Demorn said, firing the pistol, but the bullets deflected from the shiny hide.

The creature snarled down at Demorn, and for all the blood split, she knew he would not be killed that way. She holstered the pistol on her leg, signalling with her left hand, smiling her cruel smile. Her heart beat true and clean.

'Come get me, behemoth.'

It charged at her, brandishing the bloody spear. There was a ripping and tearing in the air itself, and a huge pain in her chest. Demorn looked down, gasping at the hurt. Her t-shirt was soaked a vivid crimson, and a blazing katana burst through her chest. She moaned in pain. Xalos was spawned. Demorn grasped the katana handle. The pain disappeared, replaced with an exhilaration and light-headed rage as she swung the blade in a blazing arc. Xalos sliced past his black spear, and Demorn screamed an Asanti oath wrenched from the gutters of her heart.

She felt the jarring impact as the blade tore into the creature, hefting through the scale-black armour, thudding into flesh. Memories and information flooded into her, wrongs done by this evil entity, crimes committed, innocents hurt, victims sent to miserable, forgotten deaths. The deeper the blade sank into the creature, the more she ate into the evil, the more she knew of his crimes, stoking Demorn's desperate, wild need for vengeance, a measure of justice for haunted souls.

Xalos burnt viciously bright while the creature howled in miserable agony, row upon row of sharp black teeth glistening in his endless mouth of horrors. The burning blade was light in her hands now. Her purple sunglasses had been knocked away in the battle. His hands became talons. Demorn's green eyes sparkled with magical fire. Demorn struck again, cleaving Xalos into his neck, smashing the bones jutting from its mouth.

With a primal death cry and a final pulse of negative emotion, the creature expired. She felt his last evil wash over her and fade. The purple fire dimmed upon Xalos. The flawless steel katana lay in her hands. She felt light-headed, empty and exhausted. She cleaned the blade upon the scales and slid the blade into the scabbard upon her back. Both faded away. The monster altered back to a human man in a white suit, ruined and gouged by a blade, his neck half-severed.

She bent and examined the body. Even the teeth were no longer black, but normal, stained and chipped with age. He looked ordinary. He's no Pale Sun, she realised. He's just a man.

Spells cover the sun emperors and their servants.

The mind voice was intense. Demorn looked back. The hunter slowly stood up, hauling herself up upon her staff. Demorn could see her flesh healing beneath the torn red cloak, but the wound was very fresh. The girl's black hand was shaking ever so slightly. There was plenty of blood on her body.

Demorn moved toward her, but the hunter brushed her hand away in a dismissive gesture.

I shall heal. We can only kill the body. His soul has fled.

Demorn casually took out her pistol and shot him three times.

'Or nowhere. I don't always believe that stuff about souls, babe.'

Demorn pulled the mask off her face. Her face was flushed with intense excitement, her green eyes fiery and alive.

'Sometimes it's just cradle to grave, bones to dust.'

The hunter nodded, her blue eyes flickering as she saw Demorn's face.

I am Toxis of the Blood Clan. You have a hunter's instinct.

Demorn went to put her glasses on but Toxis placed an elegant hand upon her. She removed the red hood. Her hair was close-shaven and her skin was sheer black. Toxis looked with great intensity into Demorn's blazing eyes.

But you trust too much in the baubles of the gods.

'What should I trust in? The power of love and my witty remarks?'

Toxis looked at her with flames in her blue eyes.

You wear no crown. This is not the same legend I learnt by the campfires with my Sisters.

'I'm a bit young for legend status.'

Toxis looked thoughtfully at Demorn.

You have magic eyes and a strong heart. You always will, my Princess.

Demorn smiled, slightly embarrassed. She tried to ignore the soaring fire in her spirit, the haunting power of those charred eyes upon her. She had no idea what Toxis was talking about.

'My name is Demorn. I'm a bounty hunter, attached to The Innocents. I work out of Babelzon.'

The huntress nodded with strange reverence. ***The Mythical City of Portals.***

'Yeah,' Demorn drawled. 'That's what they called it, like a thousand years ago.'

Toxis slowly raised her fingers towards Demorn's brow. ***But you are not born there. I can see the signature upon you. Your aura is that of a tomb.***

Demorn smiled, catching the girl's hand.

'Like you said, I live in the city of portals. People come from all over to do business. Babelzon is home for as long as it pays. What about you? You're well trained and getting through my conditioning, not blundering around like most of the telepaths I've crossed paths with.'

Toxis spoke, her voice soft and heavily accented. 'Was this the first time the Sword has spawned, Princess?'

Demorn slid her purple glasses back on, losing the mood. She brushed her shirt, which was no longer bloody and torn. 'No, not the first time.'

Xalos is your fate and doom. You will see it more often, now that you tread this path.

Demorn ran her invisible watch over the face of the man, looking for an open warrant. What path, she thought.

'Do you know who he really was?'

He was as he said. A Pale Sun, an Emperor of the Lost Sun.

Demorn raised an eyebrow. 'Yeah. That didn't mean much when he said it either. I thought the Pale Suns were a terror cell.'

The scanner found something, flashing blue upon her wrist. A random newscast hidden deep in a small-time local satellite feed, a face flashing up in the air.

'... van Roberts, a mid-level gas mining employee with Triton Corp, missing and presumed dead since a Category A snowstorm swept the region four months ago—'

Demorn sighed as she shut down the scanner. 'What a bust. At least I got the girl. Her daddy's cash should keep this trip in the profit column.'

Beware the girl, beware Rachel. I journeyed deep through the

winter caverns to arrive here. I saw the idols and the skeleton dolls resting inside their coffins. Have no illusion. The one you sent away is a spirit bound to a dark path.

'Ah, c'mon. She was just a moody teenager. I prefer to look on the bright side of hostage rescue.'

In her mind she tallied it up, like always. Smile's tracers had found the ice cavern, but she had begun a continent away with a cold trail. The weeks of searching had been costly. Cash had greased the hands of multiple small-time politicians on her way to tracking the Medusi Hive, deep into the tiny ghost towns left after the ice-mining boom died out. Demorn stopped the mental sums before she depressed herself. It was always going to be a love job, she realised dryly. A run and a grab for the Innocents. Club debts.

Toxis was studying the cracked eggs and the maimed corpse. She drew some of her own blood, drawing an archaic symbol on the man's head, murmuring bizarre word strings. An intersection of angled shapes flew into the air, crystalline and complex, faces of great serpents with their dripping fangs.

Toxis looked up at her, her eyes urgent blue lasers.

Emergence!

The angled shapes rose into the air, turning and changing. Demorn saw the lidded eyes and the flashing teeth of great creatures, monstrous serpents and worms. She also saw weird symbols upon strange banners, glistening in the spinning images. She saw great golden cities and mighty kingdoms and great things gone to ruin, some perhaps to come. She saw a White Fort with a red flag flying high on a battlement, over a windswept ocean. Something flared in Demorn, an echo deep within her, a distant memory of childhood, until slowly it all seemed to lose form and fade away.

Demorn was fascinated. 'What are they? Angels?'

Toxis lay hunched over his body, her fingers pressed to his skull.

No . . . not angels. Old serpents, rising shadows from the void. Lurking at the corners of this world and many others, exiled . . . but chained to life with deep spells and contracts, as they gnaw at their bonds.

The hunter's eyes were glazed, her mind-voice drifting. Demorn placed her hand on her forehead, the skin clammy and cold with sweat. Demorn watched the circling spirit-shadows carefully, and her heart filled with something close to fear. And Demorn did not fear easily.

'Who bound them?'

Toxis spoke with a child's voice, light, almost silent. 'My ancestors. The Blood Clan.'

. . . they thrive in the hive of humanity, world-eating souls, so hungry, filled with the horror of the void. It will take so much more than Xalos, Princess. Your blade won't be enough, they are too cruel and too much has already been lost NO FUTURE NO FUTURE . . .

Toxis groaned, her blue eyes now dim. Demorn could see blood pouring from her wounds. Her mind-voice sighed wordlessly.

I am Toxis of the Blood Clan . . . scatter my ashes at Firethorn by the Wide Ocean.

Demorn seized the huntress's wrists and dragged her away from the man. The girl was suddenly weak and didn't resist. The wounds began to close again, but the effort had come at a cost. Soon, the huntress lay in a quiet sleep, huddled in Demorn's arms. The spirit images had gone.

Now that she so close, Demorn could see the huntress was much younger than she had seemed at first glance. Her dark, toned arms rippled with muscles. Across her legs and arms were the marks of old scars. This was a body was built for War and the Hunt. The memory of demon red eyes burnt through Demorn's mind, the image of some revenge ghost driven forth from the gates of hell. But how different is she to me, Demorn thought, looking at Toxis, as she felt her own chest which spawned Xalos, the blade of purple fire which drove her to ever more savage and frequent acts of vengeance.

Not so different, Demorn thought with a shrug and a slight smile. We are both at war, both hunters. And both so far from home.

3

Huddled against Toxis in the cold, dark cavern, Demorn could feel the natural heat radiating off the huntress. Demorn's red and green mask lay on the ice floor. She lit a small energy fire on the ground, placing Toxis by it. She searched the room.

Toxis groaned in her sleep, restless. Demorn's magic eyes searched for treasures but all that she could see were a few baubles, cheap costume jewellery upon the dead Medusi girls.

The Medusi were quite beautiful. In the stillness of death, the power of the serpents gone, she could see the pure beauty of their icy skin marked with intricate tribal sun tats. A flicker of something like pity went through Demorn as she traced her finger across the porcelain skin of one of the dead Medusi. She had killed so many of these creatures these last few weeks while she tracked them back to this nest.

Demorn turned away. Such thoughts led nowhere. She felt herself drawn to the far ice wall, and she could see faint shadows of red writing upon the ice. As she got close, the writing faded away.

On instinct, Demorn took off her sunglasses. Her eyes shone like green flames. The writing blazed in vivid blood-red neon, each line written in Asanti, the lost language of her dead world, a language barely seen outside of her dreams.

NO FUTURE ONLY ULTIMATE FATE.

NO FUTURE ONLY ULTIMATE FATE.

Demorn staggered back, the words hurting her eyes. Instinctively, her hands went for her pistol, firing at the shining wall. The stunning ruby-red form of a beautiful woman burst out of the ice, tearing through the neon words, armoured and magnificent. She moved like something from a fever dream. The bullets bounced harmlessly off a massive, reflective shield emanating across the woman's ruby body.

Demorn emptied her clip into the shield. She tried to place different shots into the ruby-red form but the shield blocked everything. *I can't hurt this thing.* Demorn stopped shooting and slid the pistol back into her holster. In the same moment, the burning shield vanished into the armour of the being. The armour vanished and she looked upon the naked core of an Asanti goddess.

'A True Goddess,' Demorn murmured, and her fingers automatically flicked the ancient signs from childhood, distant to her now, but still remembered. The Goddess smiled. Her face was many, within and beyond reality.

Not the old signs anymore, Princess. We are in the next world.

Everything was burnt crimson bright. Demorn saw the glistening pink oceans of her home world, the crystal sky that sparkled above the Towers of the Guard. Demorn felt her heart leave her, absorbed into the burning core of this being, every part of her dragged into her prism. She screamed Asanti oaths that she had not uttered in years, as if she still prayed nightly to the Mirror Worlds. Every moment she looked upon the creature she felt their bond go deeper. She saw Asanti exploding in memory, spinning untouched, both the nightmare and the fantasy reflected in the burning furnace.

Demorn felt drunk on the elixir of a thousand memories all at once. Her holy gun killed enemies and caked her in blood. Her gun was too late to save friends. Xalos danced on a dusty plain, a pale, dirty sun reflecting on the burning blade that dimmed to extinguishment, a slow cycle of dying and resurrection. Everything burnt away. She looked upon the goddess with cold eyes, remembering her formal training, slowly repeating a slow sequence of code to calm her mind.

'Long ago, I swore to bow to nobody, be them god, goddess, woman or man.'

Demorn ground her teeth against the temptation. If it was a spell, it was like no spell she had ever felt. Her words felt like cotton wool in her mouth.

The goddess spoke, her language perfectly accented Asanti, her hand holding Demorn's arm, her grip soft but secure as iron.

'Never kneel, never bow. Straight sword, clean heart.'

Demorn whispered, 'Asanti prophecy, Asanti speech. What are you?'

The Goddess smiled. 'Something imprisoned, now free. How long since you left the Mirror World?'

The Mirror World. Demorn's heart was racing. *Asanti.*

'Five years. My brother and I left on one of the last jump ships. Asanti is gone. A dead dimension. We watched it die and shatter.'

The fire of the goddess dimmed down to embers. Her form was graceful and voluptuous. She wore a thin robe over her body. The goddess had sad, wise eyes. And Demorn knew what she was.

She brushed her hand across Demorn's face, her touch tickling with faintly hot electricity. 'So many cast adrift, so many exiles.'

Demorn murmured, 'Not so many. So few . . . Alodin.'

The Goddess sighed. Her voice was light and calm.

'Well, of course you know me, though few would.'

Her ruby hand caught Demorn's wrist. The tattoo flared into intense burning, ink shuddering on the skin.

The Goddess laughed, releasing her hand. Demorn was blushing.

'You didn't think us real, did you?'

'I am kind of a sceptic.'

'Oh, it doesn't matter. Most gods kill themselves or each other. Eternity is too long. Prophets sell the corpse. I am Alodin Mars. I was their Goddess for centuries. We were so proud, we gave away our strength, reflecting across the galaxies . . . until the storm gathered and then broke us.'

Without thinking, Demorn whispered, 'We must gather it back, to make Asanti live outside our fever dreams.'

Demorn felt the torn, haunting gulf of loss in her chest. Her words and vow was that of all Asanti refugees, but she had not heard them uttered in many a year, even between her brother and herself. So many hopes had died, the vows along with them.

Demorn breathed, 'We must become the storm upon their shores.'

The ruby goddess dropped a final shield of perception. Demorn felt the magic in her eyes responding. Reality seemed to fall away. The goddess's body was a translucent red, covered with intricate, shifting burning tattoos, images of strange, forgotten beasts and people. How could have Demorn ever doubted this?

The Goddess touched a thin, long scar upon her taut belly, then brushed her finger across Demorn's face.

The ice cavern vanished. Demorn felt the heat of a burning desert, beneath a purple sky. She was deep in valleys of crystal, shining under an alien sun. She knew it was the homeland. Demorn looked up toward those sheer cliffs of purple-red crystal, and she felt herself soaring into that strange sky, higher and higher. Time shifted. Demorn saw Asanti explode again, like on the nostalgia stream blogs, like the news channels on all the anniversaries. The giant holo-screen in the sky when she was thirteen and it was only her brother and her, alone in the Babelzon slums, their jump ship dying behind them, beneath the merciless lights of a future city they did not know, where they did not belong.

Asanti kept exploding, again and again. She ached for it, she mourned it, everything that was gone. Then suddenly, things changed. Demorn felt a surge of power and rebirth flooding her mind and heart as they blazed back alive inside the empty places. She felt herself imprinted with vivid rivers of information. Every word and image inlaid with ruby red. The codes of Asanti. The libraries of Alodin Mars.

Demorn woke, huddled on the icy floor. Her mind still throbbed with the power of connection. The images in her mind slowly dimmed like a storm abating, fading with a final vision of a white fort above a lonely, golden ocean, a fire-red flag flying from the high battlements.

The ice wall was broken. The blood-red words were there, scattered and broken like fine china. NO HOPE JUST ULTIMATE FATE. She hadn't been dreaming, Demorn knew that much. She caught sight of herself in the shattered mirror ice. Her eyes blazed and burned with green fire. Her vision was so clear it hurt.

A long red mark was upon her right cheek. She brushed it with her finger. Demorn knew this was the scar of Alodin Mars. She felt strangely proud.

Toxis knelt beside her, still injured, but supported by her staff.

You are reborn, my Princess.

Demorn smiled grimly and got up. 'I don't know about reborn, I save that talk for bad guys who find religion. But I do feel different.'

Glancing at Toxis, her magic eyes saw more truly than ever. The skull of fire within the hood of the huntress was clearly visible. A soul desperate and alive with a savage need for vengeance. Demorn saw so much, almost too much of herself in that visage.

'I'm cold. We killed the boss, we saved the girl. I just saw something that's completely blown my mind. Let's get out of here and pretend things can ever be normal again.'

Demorn held Toxis close to her as they slowly left the cold cavern behind with all the dead. Suddenly the freezing dark corridors of the ice cavern seemed so confining and claustrophobic to Demorn that she could not imagine spending another minute within them. She held Toxis tightly as she brushed the locket, welcoming Mictecaciuatl, the decayed, death god herself, soaring through the cold corridors, eager to leave this den of Medusi and strange magic.

They emerged topside. Demorn breathed deeply in the frigid air, looking toward the sun, pale and thin in the white sky. Toxis cast off the hood. Her delicate fingers traced Demorn's cheek.

I can feel the god mark upon you, even though I can no longer see it.

Demorn was quiet. 'It's on my soul.' She paused. 'Maybe it's always been on my soul.'

Toxis stood up, leaning less heavily on her staff as she looked across the icy wasteland.

Most outsiders cannot hear my mind-voice. They think me a mute, stupid girl.

'It's their loss.'

You danced in the crystal graveyards of your Homeworld and you bear the mark of your Goddess. You spawn the savage, burning blade, but you do not wear a Crown.

Demorn looked carefully at this vengeful huntress. 'What do you know about it?'

Toxis spoke in her intense, low voice. 'I know the prophecies, spoken through the generations of my land. You come from the Mirror. You may remember or forget.'

Demorn looked at her curiously. 'Let's say right now, I forget.'

When we next meet, it will be as strangers. Perhaps with a blade at each other's throats. Perhaps as sisters, in my distant homeland by the sea.

Demorn felt a tired empathy flow through her. 'We can't really tell the future, Toxis. We're alive. Hunt well.'

Toxis slit the top of her hand with the blade upon her staff. She pulled her cloak away, and took a thick golden band from around her toned arm. She tore off Demorn's jacket.

This is my soul. I break it in two for you.

Toxis snapped the bracelet into two and placed it around Demorn's arm, blood slick on her fingers, blood across Demorn. It burnt savagely for a moment, melding tightly onto Demorn's skin, settling into a smooth coolness.

I pledge my Blood Clan to your cause, from First Dawn to the Long Night.

Demorn looked at her deeply. 'I am Asanti. Do you know what vows mean to us?'

Toxis nodded. 'We know the ways of the Mirror. This is my sacrifice.'

Demorn smiled. 'Okay. I take your burden, I split my soul for you.'

Toxis fitted the other half of the bracelet back on her strong arm. She looked up at Demorn with those clear icy eyes. Demorn lightly kissed her cheek. Her form flickered, vanishing into the wind.

'Thanks, hunter,' Demorn whispered to the empty air.

For a few moments she stood there, suddenly alone again. She wondered what her brother Smile would make of it all, back in Babelzon. As if in response, her wrist buzzed. Green dollar symbols scrolled down the display. She couldn't help but chuckle. There were more important things than gods and mysterious prophecies. Daddy had gotten his baby back, the cash had cleared.

A face icon appeared upon the video, the red smile flashing. A kill code. Smile had found something close. She watched the numbers rolling down the screen, in the higher ranges.

'Is no wilderness too deep and distant for you to find me, Smile?' she said dryly.

'Hey, sis,' a light voice said. 'Congrats on the retrieval! It must been quite a mission.'

She laughed. 'It had its moments. Are you calling just to sing my praises, brother dear?'

Smile's laughter reminded her of tinkling village bells.

'I'm the President of your Fan Club, it's my job to sing them. Now, what about a little easy money?'

'I'd prefer a lot.'

She saw one name all over the marker ad. 'Something for Tony?'

'He asked for you personally. Just a clean hit on the way back home, he said.'

She looked out over the ice, cracking her neck, thinking of the strange sights she had just seen. 'Ha. He said.'

The war was getting hot. Enemies and allies appearing and disappearing in thin air. She felt an unease about the Innocents and what lay back in Babelzon. It was a hell of a lot of angles.

'I'm suspicious of clean hits,' she murmured.

He laughed with a somber edge. 'I know, sis. But I'm suspicious of the noose around our neck. This last quarter everything we earnt barely paid the interest on your table Cage debts.'

Smile was shimmering around her, his face a flickering electronic shadow of blue and white. His light voice was touched with foreboding. She subconsciously flicked electronic pink glowing cards through her fingers, rippling from her black gloves. Smile's voice dropped a touch deeper, insistent.

'We *need* Tony on our side if things go bad.'

She brushed the screen with her finger. Mission accepted.

'Of course we do,' she said softly. 'It's my debt, after all.'

The target data started feeding into her brain. Her brother sighed.

'Ah, we all have our vices. But the Cage tables are cruel. Stay away from them.'

Demorn smiled, wishing that she would. She could feel the buzz of the cards in her implant, she almost never disconnected. There were decks being constructed and games in progress even as she stood here. There were deals surrounding her that Smile couldn't see.

'What's that on your cheek?'

Absently, she ran her finger along the smooth scar.

'Nothing. Just a souvenir. I'll speak to you when I'm back. Peace out.'

The connection ended and Demorn looked across the barren snow fields, the sun glinting off her glasses and the bitter wind howling in her ears. The cold tore through her body and feelings. She watched her ship come in on remote, blank inside, seeking only a moment or a memory where she had been clean, some place where nobody owned her. She wondered what she would do if she found it.

4

The Sands Hotel, Las Vegas. 1964.

Demorn emptied a chamber of bullets at the aliens, taking two of the insectoids down cold in the corridor, laser charge burning the air. The final one phased when her shots struck, suddenly upon her in the narrow doorway, cramping Demorn for room. The insectoid's spindly arms slashed out with a clawed hand which she barely dodged. Claws smashed into the wall.

She dropped, spinning a low kick into the underbelly, sending it back into the wall. It hissed, thrashing madly. Demorn smashed the alien's mandibles with her gun butt. She seized the hard slick body with an iron grip, no mercy in her as she beat it to death.

Behind her, she heard Sinatra swear softly.

When it was over, she slammed the door behind them, wiping a trace of gunk off her leather jacket.

'Nice moves, kid.'

Demorn looked across at him, sinking deeply in the couch. Blood splattered his tuxedo. His crisp white shirt was stained red.

'Thanks, boss. Sorry you almost got tagged out there.'

He shrugged with a casual air, looking at her with vibrant blue eyes.

'They're goddamn alien insects. It's unexpected.'

She laughed, nerves and some worship touching her as she powered the chamber back up. 'Kinda. But I've been killing them all week, boss.'

'You're really not from around here are you?'

'What makes you say that?'

He chuckled. 'The clothes mostly. You wear goddamn future combat boots.'

She grinned. 'They're functional.'

He waved his hand at the dead alien on the floor. 'And the way these things don't shock you.'

The room was small and tight, a backstage hangout for the classy talent. She realised everybody was screaming. Then she noticed the screams were cheers and they came from the TV. It was a mad airport scene, crowds of teen girls and guys going crazy as four mop-topped young men jostled through an airport crush. The blood from the insectoid girl had smudged the TV, green lines splattered across the screen, touching John Lennon's black-and-white TV face. The Beatles vanished into the limousine, the screaming behind them endless.

Demorn turned the set off. Sinatra poured a scotch, ignoring the Beatles as if they were invisible. He half gestured at the husk of the alien, the blood on the screen, these trappings of death.

'How many times now, Demorn? How many times have they come after me the last couple of weeks?'

'I've killed five in the hotel. More insects in the desert with the other guys. I've tried to stop it getting close to you.'

Sinatra nodded. He looked tired, suddenly older, all his 50 years.

'It's always close to me, been this way for years,' he murmured.

She moved in close to look at his wound. It seemed better. The blood was now dry. She'd noticed this resilience before.

'These things normally do more damage with their claws.'

He gently pushed her hand away. 'I'm happy as a clam, but we've gotta get back to the desert. There are secrets out there, things I haven't shown you.'

Fair enough. 'It was a good show tonight. They cut into your encore. I was looking forward to it.'

Sinatra laughed and finished his drink. 'I haven't done an encore in a year. I'm tired, kid. Let's get the Ruby Lady and get outta here.'

There was a single rap at the opposite door. Demorn's hand tightened on the pistol.

The Ruby Lady sauntered into the room, her skin shining and translucent, flashing ruby red in the room's soft light, looking and smelling beautiful. Her sheer gold dress barely covered her glorious body. She kissed Frank flush on the mouth, and his hand roved over her back and gently played with her long golden curls.

Demorn watched with impassive eyes as a dark triangle of power opened on Sinatra's palm and her shining form encased him. As the Ruby Lady drew away, the black triangle miniaturised into nothingness. He instantly looked younger, more alive, and softer.

The Ruby Lady turned to her, greeting Demorn with a sweet smile, brushing her lips gently over Demorn's cheek, her aura incredibly powerful and intoxicating, purple eyes so radiant and alive. Demorn had loved the Ruby Lady from afar for a month, now she could resist no longer. She brushed her mouth against those sizzling, exotic lips, letting warm fire into her cold heart, that place which knew so much vengeance. She felt a trace of Asanti-like power, something that lay dormant, awakening.

Sinatra was dryly amused. 'She's quite the kisser, isn't she, kid?'

The Ruby Lady laughed like tinkling glass, lips withdrawing. Her perfect hands slipped into Frank's. Demorn smiled cheekily. She felt a sudden heavy pressure on her right eye and forehead.

'Telepaths,' she hissed quietly, like a small promise of death. 'Angry ones.'

Her mind was layered with scars and years of conditioning and training. They wouldn't track her quickly, but she couldn't say the same for Frank and his Ruby Lady.

Demorn smiled her scary smile. 'This one might get messy. We gotta get to the car fast. Follow my lead.'

She pulled her mask out of her leather jacket. The glistening synthetic red and green material slid across her, accentuating her senses, melding to her face, charging her instincts and her powers.

She checked the gun charge and flung her body outside the door, shooting in the direction of the thoughts, gunning down a black suited government-looking type rounding the corner, his gun half drawn. He had a crown of thorns for a face, his true self exposed as the creature died in the hail of gunfire. The corridor was cramped, a backstage exit lane. There was a junction up ahead. She could see the flashing exit sign. She ran to the junction, Frank and the Lady close behind her.

Guns were going off back in the direction of the stage. Frank's boys in some holding action. She closed her eyes and stilled her mind. The Ruby Lady coughed lightly. Demorn glanced across. Blood ran from her perfectly formed mouth and nose. The telepaths had found their weak link.

The crown of thorns monster spasmed beside her, face shifting into nauseating shapes. Demorn let three energy stars fall into her left hand. She rounded the corner in a heartbeat, releasing all three stars, two hitting point blank range, charring and burning at close quarters.

Her pistol was firing as she rolled across the intersection, kicking away a small table to give herself room, the scent burning in the air, her heart beating fast. The telepaths' shots were haphazard, untrained, and impulsive. They were used to confusing their quarry with simple mind tricks. Those tricks could work.

But not today.

The exit sign flashed as she killed them all, shooting from cover, taking out both monstrous crown of thorns creatures. The pressure in her eye abated.

The Ruby Lady was slumped against the wall, Sinatra sheltering her with his own body. Demorn was down to her last few laz packs. She hadn't expected to spend more than a couple of nights in Vegas. Cleaning the insectoids' nests had taken some work.

She heard steps on the concrete stairway below. The pressure on her eye came back, far more intense. She heard the growl of a monster, something out of the darkest nightmare. She wasn't sure if it was in her mind, or real. Demorn knew with a grim certainty that another few minutes trapped in this club and they were all dead and the mission would be utterly lost. I deserve only the haunted, wailing underworld, if *that* is my pathetic effort, Demorn thought. She closed her magic eyes behind the mask, following the aura of telepathic energy. What was coming up the stairs was a different order of terror.

She heard the Ruby Lady exhale. Sinatra held her shaking form. Blood all over the carpet. Her skin had lost tone, she looked wan and translucent. She looked more human. Sinatra squeezed a couple of rounds towards the exit door with a snub-nosed pistol she'd never seen him use before.

Demorn glanced at the Lady, grinning. She saw one hand flash a deep ruby red. She motioned for Frank to stop shooting. Let the bastard come to us.

The exit door opened slightly.

Demorn flicked the Athena pistol to full power. 'Your friends are all dead,' she snarled, smiling. 'And I'm just starting to enjoy myself.'

Everything was quiet for a moment, a pause more disconcerting than the fight itself or the strange monsters plaguing them. A volley of bullets discharged through the gap in the door, shredding the corridor, missing her by a half moment as she dived out of the way. One long burst, semi-auto, without control, hitting nothing but pictures and wallpaper. Messy, sloppy work.

The clip emptied on the six second mark. Demorn fired her Athena pistol full charge into the exit door, blowing out a foot-wide hole in the wood. She heard the slam of a body crashing down concrete steps.

'Now!' she hissed, moving like lightning, kicking the exit door open, seeing the inert body at the bottom of the stairs. She sprinted down. He was human, dressed in the same black suit as the others, guts blown out from her pistol, already dead. His face was a shifting mess of thorns and paper-thin skin.

She checked his neck. A barcode tattoo: TRITON CORP. As she touched the letters, she saw a dimensional horror stirring in some death tomb, and she released her fingers as if burnt by fire. So the humans were in league with the demons. It scared her, but it didn't surprise her. Invaders always used traitors, no matter if it was 1964 or her own future time. Men had always prayed to devils. Her fingers rubbed across the barcode again, but the connection was blown. Whatever she had glimpsed hadn't emerged.

Sinatra said, 'Look at those bums, lounging all over my limo.'

Demorn looked out into the murky car park. She could see Frank's black limousine. Three muscle-men nervously stood over it, glancing around wildly, guns out, arguing amongst themselves.

The Ruby Lady shone behind him, making Demorn's back warm with the heat of her aura.

'They're just mortal men, not monsters. They're scared, their masters are gone.'

Demorn chuckled. 'Well, they won't have to wait too long to join them.'

The Ruby Lady sauntered out from the darkness, into the middle of the car park, under the low lights, strolling toward the three men.

Demorn tensed, holding Frank back. The men stood transfixed as the Ruby Lady ambled toward them gracefully, singing a slow show tune with her smoky voice, breaking into a soft shoe shuffle, performing a slow dance right in front of them. Demorn had to tear her eyes away. She knew it was magic of the deepest and most dangerous kind, but she could not stop listening to the song, she didn't want to. The Ruby Lady was so achingly beautiful.

'Oh brother,' Sinatra sighed.

The men dropped their guns. Demorn walked toward the gathering, the pistol in her hand, a wary eye on the men. Their eyes were glazed, they were long gone. She slid the pistol back in her leg holster, unlocking the limo's boot. She felt for the fake base, taking her katana from its hiding place. Slowly she slid the blade from the scabbard.

Demorn rolled her eye across the Ruby Lady, letting herself feel the song. In three separate sweeping motions Demorn beheaded the men, blood splattering across the car park floor, across her hands and mask.

The Ruby Lady didn't stop singing even then, she just kept going, dancing beautifully around their dead bodies on the concrete floor. It wasn't until Sinatra came up behind her, holding her tight, that the Lady seemed to return to some version of reality, and she stopped, huddling into him, her skin blazing red.

Using her blade point, Demorn traced the word *Innocents* upon the concrete floor, written in the blood of the dead men.

Demorn held the doors open. The couple slid into the backseat of the limo. Sinatra raised an eyebrow at the slashed heads, and the message written in blood.

'Touching message, kid. But what the hell does it have to with this?'

Demorn cracked her neck as she got behind the wheel and started the engine up. 'It's a club I'm in back home. I want the creatures to know.'

'Know what?'

'That we hunt them, wherever they are.'

'Who are they?'

'Bizarre creatures invading our reality.'

'Ah,' Sinatra said, dropping it, as she took the limo out of the hotel car park, onto the flashing lights of the Strip, heading for the outskirts of town, moving fast.

The desert night was cold. She was glad she'd worn the leather jacket tonight. They had parked off the highway. In the distance Demorn could see the road and the car headlights, but it was well past midnight and almost silent.

The Ruby Lady had wandered off on her own, humming some old

party tune. Sinatra was quiet beside Demorn. From out here, Vegas was a soft glow on the horizon, a shimmering mirage of lights and hustle.

'I don't know how you keep her out of the papers,' she said at last. 'She's so beautiful, I could never forget anything like her.'

Frank sighed. 'I don't *keep* her out of anything, kid. The Ruby Lady stays in Vegas, I'm here a couple months a year. She loves the parties and the pools and the hotels. She likes to do her little show, bare a little flesh, sing a little song, leave them panting and in love.'

'I never knew she could sing like that.'

He looked at her with his ice eyes. 'How do you think she met me?'

And then he smiled, waving the question away. It wasn't really a question. The Ruby Lady was desire, she was a beautiful fire. She didn't know how Sinatra could date her and not lose himself completely.

'I can't stay much longer, boss,' she blurted. 'I've cleaned as many Triton nests as I can, but you should be putting distance between yourself and Vegas. This whole time-line is becoming corrupted.'

He laughed. 'Screw distance. I want to show you something, kid. For keeping the insects and various maniacs from killing me.'

The insects were a local presence, a Vegas legend, he'd said. Her hits on their nests had been ruthless and precise. But it never paid to take things for granted.

'Don't relax too much. The baddies aren't all obvious monsters with thorns on their faces. There's plenty of human traitors in league with them.'

Sinatra laughed dryly. 'Oh, I know that, dear. That just makes them monsters, too.'

He didn't even seem injured now. He just seemed tired.

'I knew you were coming, kid. You, or something like you.'

With deliberate care, he took a pair of expensive, gold-framed sunglasses from his tux. They had shimmering purple lenses which burned low and soft.

'They're beautiful,' she said.

Frank smiled sadly. 'They were Jack's. I still remember him on Inauguration Day. Jets were flying over us. Everything seemed filled with hope. He asked me if I looked up to the stars.'

'Do you?'

There was heaviness to Sinatra's chuckle. 'I told him I'd spent my life in cities. I couldn't see the stars up there for all the lights around me.'

Demorn laughed. 'God! What a thing to say to the President.'

Frank laughed, pressing the sparkling glasses into her hand. 'That's what Jack said. Then he gave me these and told me to go out to the desert.'

Demorn put on the glittering glasses. The night sky changed to a maddened scene. Huge pregnant stars floated in the void. The desert lit up in negative, the desolation so empty and incredibly lonely and vast. For the first time since she had fled dying Asanti, Demorn could feel the Mirror, reverberating in the universe, still alive, not shattered yet.

Behind the purple glasses, her eyes scanned the void, following the murmur of the lost dimension. She could feel the dormant power inside her, igniting as it connected to something vaster. Her body of flesh and bones was a vessel to the Asanti Flame, the reflecting Mirror, everything outside just an echo, a ghost of what might be . . .

Then suddenly, the connection was lost, abandoned.

Demorn phased back to now, stunned by what she saw. An enormous burning crater had opened in the desert floor, the size of a football field. Inside the crater she saw the outline of a massive circular ship, destroyed in some huge crash, seething with electrical discharge and mini explosions. A swarm of the insectoid bodies littered the crater, petrified husks.

Demorn walked toward it. With each step the scene grew more active and alive. The screaming of the insects was loud and wracked with terror.

Sinatra put his firm hand on her shoulder. 'It's just death down there, sweetheart.'

Her tone was wistful. 'Death's what I'm good at, boss.'

Sinatra's blue eyes flashed. He held her chin with his delicate fingers. The desert wind blew cold.

'I'm not really your boss. You blew into Vegas like a hurricane. You've saved my life like it was your own. I just want you to know, Demorn. I know there's something funky in the Land of Nod.'

She laughed. 'The Land of Nod?'

He winked, lighting a cigarette. 'Oh yeah. Craters in the desert. UFOs. Glamorous broads who sparkle red. Thorny heads. Tentacles. Funky future boots. Things are real strange and it's all gettin' stranger.'

Demorn said, 'I can't argue with that.'

Sinatra paused, and then spoke, but it was like he was talking to a memory, not her at all.

'Jack called me two nights before the bastards shot him. We didn't talk much that last year or two. He's the President, I'm Frank Sinatra. Life gets in the way.'

Demorn noticed the present tense, the throaty nature of his voice, the way he would not look at her with those eyes that saw into everybody's soul. He absently took a drag of his cigarette. She wondered how the year had really been on him, since JFK got blown away in Dallas. She wondered if that was why he wasn't doing encores.

But she did not say anything, just stayed close to him, her slender body around his elegant suited figure.

'But that Saturday night, he called me up in LA, right on 2 AM. He knew I would be awake. Jack always had the personal touch.'

Sinatra sounded fond. 'Guess that's why we all loved him so much, the Irish bastard. He wanted me to go to DC, had something important to show me.'

Sinatra crushed the half-finished cigarette on the hard desert floor. 'I had a big show the next day. Who cares? I hopped straight on my plane, went right to him. I was in the White House before dawn.'

Frank's voice thickened into a growl. 'He was the President, kid. A year ago, that meant something. Not like the bastards running the joint now.'

Demorn softly said, 'I know. Did he give you anything else?'

Sinatra looked at her then. His blue eyes were not smiling. He loosened his bow tie and undid the top button on his white shirt. The bloodstains had completely gone. He carefully undid a thin gold necklace from around his neck. She saw him palm a small white gem into his suit lining. A small locket hung on the smooth necklace, engraved with an intricate marking of tiny thorns. The locket glowed softly in the night, purple shadows across his sharp, haunted face. For a moment she saw the ravaged face of a beautiful woman inside the locket, at once both so familiar and impossibly alien, but that slid into black nothingness.

'He got the locket in the War. Jack was around Berlin when it fell. It's something the Nazi's had stolen, something old. He gave it to me. Said he had kept it long enough.'

'What does it do?'

'He said it would give me some soul, maybe I could use it when I sang. Said I would know when to pass it on, too.'

Sinatra lightly tossed the necklace to her, locket and all.

'He was right.'

Demorn caught it with her left hand. Instantly she could hear the unquiet murmur of power throbbing in the locket, a hungry and urgent voice that whispered strange promises of rewards from the death-womb in exchange for sacrifice and worship. Her head throbbed.

'Be careful. It hurts to use and it takes as much as it gives. I can barely be bothered to sing if I don't wear it now. When I do, it's almost too powerful . . . the old songs hurt too much.'

She said, 'That's why no encores, isn't it?'

He sounded like a haunted man. 'They dig up bad stuff. It ain't my style. I'm a wreck after every concert.'

Demorn put the necklace on, smooth and cold against her skin. She looked out at the crater and the dead insectoids, charred and burnt. Demorn could feel an echo of heat, she could hear the crater calling. There was more than death inside it. She knew she didn't have a choice, she had to go down there. Sinatra looked relieved. A bit wiser, a little kinder.

'Something tells me you won't use the power to sing, kid.'

Demorn saw the Ruby Lady walking toward them in the distance, a sparkling red shadow. Demorn smiled, feeling cold promises mix and stir.

'I've got a horrible singing voice. It's really sad, because I always wanted to be a country singer.'

As the Ruby Lady came closer, the crater faded to a ghostly mirage, and the power of the glasses seemed to lessen. Demorn looked to the sky filled with swollen stars. She watched them slowly revert to distant pinpricks of light. She felt light and naked beneath it all. She was a long, long way from home.

Sinatra pulled her close. She had grown so fond of him this last month. It had become more than a mission. She'd enjoyed calling him Boss. She'd enjoyed saving his life. She'd dreamt about not going back home to Babelzon, back to the Innocents and the missions, back to a girlfriend she'd lost to runway shows and sleazy TV producers, but Demorn knew that was only a fantasy.

He brushed her long brunette hair softly as she nestled into him. He smelled of lavender. That's how Demorn thought of him, whenever she heard him singing in the long years still to come. Like a beautiful ghost in a beautiful life, drowning in lavender.

'Let me tell you a secret, kid. After a late night show, when I'm alone, looking out over the city, sometimes I feel that this is all a dream. The applause, the money, the fame. It all feels so fragile, just a lucky dice roll on Fate.'

He stopped, then softly added, 'Sometimes I wonder what Jack thought in the last second before the bullets hit him.'

Demorn caught his hand and looked into his ice eyes. She had her own past, her own loved ones. He seemed to know and understand everything. She closed her eyes. She was on the skeleton ship, surrounded by cruel, tall men with fleshless faces and threadbare black robes, searching for something she had lost, searching for somebody that she had failed.

Frank lightly touched her face.

Acting on instinct, Demorn grasped the locket. She felt brutal power flow through her. The raw pain clawed through her mind and heart, burning the soft parts of her, cleansing her soul of compassion, all the soft parts she had protected from the harshness of the world.

But no more! Mictecaciuatl, Mighty Pain Goddess of the Western Desert, surged through Demorn. The goddess was just a shadow of her true visage, shrieking in maddened triumph, to be unchained in a pure Asanti vessel, the power flowing without any form of tenderness into the very core of Demorn.

Demorn let it sear through her, only her Asanti mental training keeping a final, strained leash on the rush of power, controlling it barely.

Exhausted, Demorn smiled her scary smile as the Pain Goddess quieted, the horned image slowly dispersing from her mind.

'What do you know about those guys in the black suits at the Sands? The crown of thorns squad.'

He held her tighter, not talking.

She whispered, 'I'm trying to save us all, boss. Believe me. *Tell me.*'

Sinatra murmured trade secrets.

'Jack hardly ever got past tipsy, but he was three sheets to the wind that night, real shaken up. He had a service revolver in his hand and old war photos all over the desk. Pictures of guys from his unit. Lot of them crossed out in red. He just kept saying, "We're compromised, Frank, we're riddled with Triton, we're fucking compromised."'

Triton. Like the barcode.

Sinatra took a long drag of his cigarette. His voice was thoughtful.

'I didn't know what he was talking about. I thought he was going batshit crazy. Our President. Going nuts with his finger on the big red button.'

He took another long drag, staring into the empty desert. 'I mean, what the hell is Triton? I thought they made cars. They're buying up signage in Vegas now.'

She knew. They littered the future where she came from. The Pain Goddess was bouncing around inside. Demorn was twitchy and anxious.

'It's a shadow from the future. A corporation. God knows what they *don't* do. They've started coming here now. Stamping barcodes on the necks of the goons. Buying up muscle like cattle.'

Sinatra looked at her slow. 'The future. It's all coming out now, hey kid?'

He was slightly shivering. He stilled himself, pulling a thin envelope from his tuxedo's inner pocket, passing it to Demorn.

'It wasn't till he gave me the glasses that I really saw the photos.'

His voice was raw and ripped with feeling. 'Those bastards at *Time* magazine can never know.'

She opened the envelope, a series of glossy black-and-white photos. Jack with his brother Bobby in the White House; Jack somewhere in Asia with his chief of staff; Jack at a gala with Jackie. Young, beautiful Jack in WW2 with some soldier buddies; teenage Jack at college; Jack on his inauguration with absolutely everyone. The pictures had perfect clarity, he looked stunning, he was JFK. But something stirred in her eyes.

She put the purple glasses on. She saw the truth. Tears welled in her eyes and a shiver ran down her back.

'Oh no . . .' she murmured. 'Oh, Goddess, no . . .'

The photos almost fell from her shaking hand. But she kept looking. She watched the faces with Jack morph into strange sickening creatures, far larger than those at the Casino, pulsating and moving in the photos.

She saw the Five-Star General standing with Jack on Inauguration Day change into a sick monster with thorns upon his wizened head. His mouth opened through dislocated jaws to multiple rows of spiked mouths. His form wavered in the black-and-white photo, growing larger and larger, darkening the photo.

Nausea clogged in her throat. Demorn felt the cold shadow of death fall over her. She flicked to the next one. Jack and Bobby together on a boat, side by side, proud and smiling. She turned to the next picture, Bobby and Jack in the Oval Office, perhaps a year later, and Bobby's face was lost to the monsters, his hands were clawed, clamped to the edge of the desk, as his evil, twisting visage leered into the camera, a mesh of tentacles issuing from his head.

Photo after photo, Jack was surrounded by these creatures of evil, twisting and turning inside the photos. Their eyes were deep, dark pools of malice. They gazed out from the photos like horrific, time-bound gods. Black-suited crown-of-thorn minders were omnipresent through the photos. They seemed to shield the larger creatures. There were so many, so many.

Demorn quickly gathered the photos back into the envelope.

She tore the purple glasses off her face. She fought a maddened impulse to smash them into the ground. Slowly, she brought her breathing under control. She thought of the message she had written in their blood with her sword. That brought her back to this moment. She was alive. The Innocents lay in the future. They hadn't lost yet.

'Who else knows?'

Sinatra shrugged. His voice was gruff. 'I don't know. I flew back to LA the same night. Jack was dead in Dallas a couple of days later. I've tried to keep moving.'

Sinatra was caught in the shadows of a complex world.

'His wife was one of them, y'know. She's not even hiding it that well. Jesus, I think they got the whole family. Whatever the hell *they* are. Tentacles, tusks, goddamn psychics, it's like something out of a fucking comic book.'

He shivered suddenly, and she couldn't resist nestling into him. Nothing seemed to warm him though. His body was tense and cold.

She said, 'They're dark gods and aliens from the future. They can hide in the past. But I never imagined 1964 would be crawling with this many.'

Sinatra whistled. 'Jesus. Dark gods. I don't like the sound of that.'

Demorn gestured to the golden necklace around her neck.

'They were drawn to the locket by the way. It contains a strand of hair from a Pain Goddess. Mictecaciuatl. She was part of their Order once, before she was betrayed and slain.'

'You make it sound like a war.'

'Where I'm from that's exactly what it is.'

Sinatra kissed her absently on the forehead, laughing softly. 'Where you're from. The goddamned *future*. I knew it, kid. It was that or outer space.'

Demorn laughed. How about both, Frank, she thought. The Ruby

Lady was beside him, gleaming in the night. Her presence seemed to feed him hope. She felt him start to relax.

'Don't feel too bad, you play the mysterious angle well. Just my normal bodyguards don't have laser guns, and they scare a lot more easy.'

Demorn softly kissed Sinatra. 'Stay alive, boss.'

His eyes touched hers for a second. Sinatra had played this game for a long time.

He asked, 'What made me special?'

She paused, glancing at the flashy silver watch on her wrist. This far back in the time-line, it didn't shield itself.

'There's a prophecy. You're not crucial to it, but you living past tonight was. At least to the people who paid me to come.'

He looked at her closely. 'The people who paid you. You don't seem the type to believe in prophecies.'

Demorn smiled wryly. 'I'm the type to believe in money. The people paying can believe in whatever they want.' She paused. 'Plus, I wanted to hear you sing. So I took the mission.'

He brushed his face with his hand. The ruby pinkie ring he always wore sparkled with an insistent fire.

He said, 'You're up for sale, aren't you?'

'Kinda. Depends who's buying. I try to be good. Sometimes have to settle for halfway.'

His eyes were kind. 'Ain't that the truth.'

She had never found it so hard to end a mission. 'Where will you go now?'

'Vegas is blowing way too hot. I'm going back to LA with the Lady. Maybe book a studio, put my guys at the door, try to sing a few new songs. Screw the politics. I never trusted Bobby anyway, even before he grew a praying mantis for a head.'

'OK,' she said, giving him a last kiss. She had to let go. Demorn walked into the crater abruptly, leaving him with the Ruby Lady shining in his arms, two figures against the darkness.

Sinatra murmured something soft to the Lady that she could not hear, was not meant to hear. They were such a beautiful couple. She loved both of them so much. Demorn had no knowledge of what happened to him. She didn't know if the monsters from the photos got to him, the perverted agents of Triton Corp. She didn't want to know. She wanted to believe that Sinatra's connections and his Ruby Lady had kept him safe.

Without even realizing, Demorn's hand had gripped the locket in a vise grip and now she rose into the air, moving faster toward the UFO, the heat growing intense. The locket took full hold, pain erupting through her body, seeping into every pore, sinew and bone. Fevered waking visions overtook Demorn.

She saw the damaged craft plunging from the sky, torn apart from the strain of its long journey through distant dimensions and space, plunging without control into the dusty desert on a mysterious planet, charring and burning, metal exploding around her. Everything was noise and horror. Around her, the insectoids were suddenly alive, howling and screaming in their high pitched squeal, trapped in a death replay, terrified, as their ship burned and exploded around them.

The creatures were somehow aware of her as she glided amongst them, her body flickering in and out of existence. She felt the cold, unmistakable cruelty of nothing space with its barren, lifeless gods. Then came the hissing of the insects, speaking in their root, guttural language, words of jealousy and bitter hunger and hate, everything lit up by the burning. Underneath it all, her mind throbbed, the locket filling her with whispers of undying glory, raining Asanti justice upon her many enemies, her blade wielded in the god wars of forever.

Floating, she came to the metal surface of the craft, a shattered mess of broken tech. The insects looked dead again but the screaming still filled her ears. She looked up but she couldn't see the desert anymore, just a shimmering wave of energy. She turned back to the ship.

Demorn saw a strange green smile painted on the metal wall, slowly spinning on the metal, clockwise to counter-clockwise, and back. Her watch synched with the rotating smile. *Home.*

Demorn placed her hand on the smile. Sharp teeth bared. Demorn felt everything shift, the stars in the sky long gone, and a brilliant wave of cold energy pierced her and the screaming of the insects ended.

5

Time — Current
Location — The Memory Garden

Dazzling purple sunglasses covered her tired eyes, feeding where and when she was. The air smelled of sweet jasmine. Demorn looked up to a crushed blue velvet sky. Twin moons hung in the ether. A white falcon flew past on fast wings.

She looked over the meadow. It seemed to go forever, long green grass, yellow flowers. In the far distance she saw a tall pyramid structure. On the edge of her magic vision, the gentle blur of mountains on the horizon.

Her brother was playing some bizarrely complicated game inside a maze of holograms, red light from the screens staining him. He was very thin, skin pale as a ghost, a neon red smiley face clinging to his black body-suit.

'Hey, Smile,' she murmured.

Smile turned to see her awake, his face lit up with golden flashing teeth. The smile shifted to *Asanti Pride* in delicate white lettering across his mouth, the game vanishing as he rushed to her.

'You made it back, Sis! I thought you would never find my marker!'

She staggered up and hugged her brother hard, didn't want to let go, his slender body filled with a hot warmth.

'Yeah, I went deep. You know how I love Vegas. How long?'

'You were out for almost a full day.'

'The marker was hidden in a UFO crash. Filled with insectoids, of all things.'

He took the purple glasses off her, polishing them on his sparkling form, before handing them back. They glittered in her hands. He looked at her, batting his eyelids.

'Insectoids? Nutty. How was the past, Sis?'

'Heavy on the pretty girls and the catchy songs.' Her tone darkened. 'But it's as we feared. Ultimate Fate rolls backward in synchronicity. Triton was *everywhere*, Smile, insidious. They have infiltrated the grid, weakening the barrier, so the virus will crash through in the end . . .'

She trembled. Without even thinking, her hand slid to her katana and she withdrew the blade from the scabbard, energy dancing upon the metal.

Smile laughed softly, his fingers brushing against her hand. She relaxed, letting the blade fall back.

'Wow, you sure are blowing hot, Demorn. You weaken the barrier yourself by going back in the first place, y'know.'

Smile's voice tinkled. She found herself looking into the azure sky, strangely vacant. Ghostly pyramids floated in the blue, inscribed with patterns of white symbols.

'Now you're drifting inside the Garden of Memory, lost. You're replaying and adjusting the past, treating life and time like a movie you can edit.'

Smile's electric finger ran along her invisible scar. Dreamily, she caught his finger.

'It's not all fixed. Sometimes the UFO isn't there. And the insects are cultists and demons.'

Smile laughed dryly. 'Transition points. Details and tricks, some of them mine to get you back home.'

His fingers pulsed along the side of her brow.

'It's been *years* since he gave you the glasses and the cursed locket. What do you hope to gain by going back? He's just a singer singing old songs.'

Demorn was sharp. 'Enough, Smile.'

She adjusted the necklace which burned hot beneath her thin shirt. 'The locket is blessed by the spirit of an angry pain goddess, not cursed! There's a difference.'

Demorn ran her hands across her face, waking up from old memories and dreams. She could feel the magic feeding back across her eyes. She flicked a pink face card out of her gloves and caught it. The Bleeding Queen. She let the image burn before she slid it back into the deck.

'What is so important about Sinatra anyway?'

'It was a Red Morning mission, charged to me personally. I backed a hunch. He had trinkets. Take your goddamn pick,' she said with heavy sarcasm.

His face glittered impenetrably. Smile carefully placed the sunglasses back on her face. His teeth shone with a generic, cheesy smile.

'Fair enough, soldier.'

Demorn got up and began to walk through the short-cut grass. She left her leather jacket on the ground. She loved the peace inside the Spire, strongest here inside the Memory Garden, miles and miles of electronic grass. It washed away the blood.

She felt the faintest hint of burning from the golden band on her left arm.

'I almost forgot we had two moons.'

Smile walked beside her, gently taking her hand. 'Mother took us to the Memory Garden on Asanti, didn't she?'

She squeezed his hand. 'She did. Just before the end. It feels like so long ago.'

His body became like a purple wave of fire, tingling through her arm from his hand. She was always fascinated when he unlocked the secrets of the Spire in a way she never could.

'What other trinkets did your widely inappropriate old man crush give you?'

Demorn laughed, her fingers brushing the golden necklace. 'Small things.'

Smile's image darkened to that of a black mirror. She saw the burning Goddess reflected in the mirror, a burning image of pain and fear, searing her own soul.

His eyes flashed purple. 'The Pain Goddess stirs! By Asanti!'

At the mere mention of the dead world's name, the locket's raw, violent power awakened, surging through her without reason or compassion. The ground rumbled beneath them. She saw the blazing image of the Pain Goddess rise to die in her black mirror, the name reverberating behind her eyes. Mictecaciuatl, Mictecaciuatl, Mictecaciuatl, an urgent throbbing power slowly subsiding . . .

'Now that *is* something special,' he said thoughtfully.

'Asanti was alive back in Vegas. I could feel the Mirror Worlds spinning above me.'

He shrugged. ‘But they live in isolation, doomed to commit the same errors which led to their end.’

‘How can you say that about our homeland!’

His glittering face turned to her. ‘Because it happened and it’s true.’

Smile rose into the air, diagrams and images of planets spinning around him, connected to his digital mind and the gigantic database he was plugged into. It didn’t make much sense to her, the multiple versions of worlds and universes that circulated in those diagrams, shifting as she watched, collapsing and folding in on each other, only to split and divide again. As she watched, many of the globes charred and burned.

‘I spent the first twelve months after we crashed accessing the Spire systems, playing out scenarios of Asanti being resurrected.’

Around them, the vast grassy meadow vanished along with the blue sky and the twin moons. They were in Smile’s lab. Sheer walls featured with Asanti codes and diagrams sealed them in, complex banks of machinery and screens. He waved his fingers, the walls shifting. She stood in a giant staging area, one of the vast hulls of the vessel, the size of a city. Simulacrums of animals and monsters were penned in behind tight electric fences. In the air around them, programs ran thousands upon thousands of visual routines. The maze of data and information blew her mind and semi-creeped Demorn out. Smile floated through the information flow. Corporate Asanti logos plastered the walls and floated through the air. Advertisements for dead corporations from a dead world. Inside the Spire, she could believe that Asanti still lived beyond the Mirror. Here, Xalos burned so brightly in her chest that Demorn felt that she could almost *will* the resurrection of Asanti. She could see flashing visions of the goddess Alodin Mars; she felt she could hunt forever.

Demorn’s visions flicked between the meadow and the cemetery and the technological miracles of the ship. She walked toward a huge chasm in the center, a burning hole in the Memory Garden, smoldering like a pure volcano of light. This was the heart of the Spire unveiled, the core of the gigantic vessel that had sent them across the shattered Mirror into unknown, alien dimensions.

But Demorn’s eyes could see the rotten nature of it, the damage and the flaws riddling the structure. It was the horror of a vessel dislocated so far from the origin, abandoned. Each repair effort was a patch . . .

‘Don’t stare into it, Sis. You’ll be driven mad.’

Smile gently took her hand, leading her away. He had become barely visible, a purple flame amidst the circling worlds burning out around him. It always unnerved her how connected he was to the Spire, in a way she never could be.

'You were right about the synchronization. Something major happened in that date period in Vegas. But I could never tell if it was just bleed-back from events happening later on. That's why I agreed with Red Morning to send you back in the first place, even though the energy cost took about a year off the Spire's life.'

Demorn said, 'The Spire is still dying?'

'All this is just life support. The Spire is mortally wounded. Nothing we have done has done more than staunch the bleeding. Pushing back that far, using time markers to find your target, ate serious energy.'

Demorn repressed a slight shudder, thinking of the cold of the translation, the evil within the frozen space, those slow moments between death and living when she had journeyed to 1964. Many horrifying secrets lay in that abyss of nothing.

Smile studied the photos, absorbing them into himself and the machine. They blew up big in the air surrounding them. The generals standing with JFK in Vietnam, hideous corrupt crown-of-thorns faces barely beneath the surface of the skin, Jack smiling so perfectly, his aviators on. Bobby standing with Jack in the Oval Office, his slick suit and big smile so at odds with the writhing, tentacle mass erupting from his head, while his brother was so blind to it. So blind until the midnight truths with Sinatra.

'Was it worth it?'

Smile sorted through the fragments. 'Yes, but it's puzzling, Sis. We know what happened, complete infiltration. Did it bleed back from our future? Or does it start there, and bleed forward? Both theories are viable. Is this what happened to Asanti?'

Demorn snapped, 'Well, I'm sorry that the dark gods and insectoids weren't giving interviews on how they came to control the goddamn world, Smile.'

He was droll. 'Nobody ever accused you of being a detective, Sis.'

'I've solved crimes,' she said defiantly.

'You've *killed* people who did bad things, Demorn. That's punishing crimes, not solving anything.'

Smile switching topics.

'You know what is in that locket, don't you?'

'Yeah. She was a Pain Goddess.'

'Such a pretty term. Mictecaciuatl was a raw spirit born on god torture worlds. Synthesized pain. She fed on souls and desperation and pain. As does whatever fragment of her that still exists inside that locket around your neck.'

That fit, Demorn thought.

'But the glasses he gave you . . . they've unlocked something deeper in you. Something in you that we will need to survive the Storm.'

'Are you turning into a prophet, Smile? Because I've never trusted their promises.'

Smile laughed, embarrassed. 'Not at all.'

His mind was opaque, barely visible. Flashes of red danced through his digital form, blurred and indistinct. Suspicion flared in her. Instinct. She grabbed him by the waist. He grew murky and filled with shadows, almost disappearing. But he couldn't escape from her firm grasp.

'Tell me!'

Smile became totally clear for just one single moment, his entire self transparent, every secret he held cast in neon. He opened his hand and she saw the image of a woman in it. She touched it, and the scene blew large in her head — the woman spread-eagled on a city sidewalk, long, greying dark hair splayed out, her body wrapped in a long red cloak.

An elegant pistol lay in her hand. She was slumped at the base of a gleaming city tower. Her body was twisted, broken. An intricate, familiar marking was carved into her left cheek.

No! NO! Demorn's grip grew tighter on his arm. She morphed further into the image, saw the woman up close.

She breathed, 'Red Morning . . .'

Her skin burned as the golden armband seared her skin with a savage, sweet pain. She saw a lithe figure merging into the crowd, fast, quick to vanish. She knew the kill codes of the Blood Clan. She had hunted with them, feasted with them, fought beside them. They were friends, many of them Innocents.

The image vanished.

She *felt* something rather than heard anything. Demorn's eyes blazed as she turned. Like a blood ghost, Toxis the Huntress stood in the shadow of a dark portal.

'You killed her?'

The soft, intense voice flickered through Demorn's mind.

It was a punishment.

'What charge?'

Treachery.

A cold rage stirred in Demorn. Smile silently flickered away into nothingness. He knew better than to get in the middle of Innocent affairs.

Toxis stepped out from the half-light.

Demorn said, 'Speak fast, Blood Sister. Or die fast.'

Toxis's red eyes sparkled.

She betrayed us all.

'Not good enough!'

Xalos burnt brighter than Demorn had ever felt, blazing forth from her chest, power leeching from the confines of her soul. With a wild, barely controlled stroke she slashed at Toxis, only to see the blade blocked by her staff, moving like a whirlwind. The effort of stopping an Asanti blade was written over the face of the Huntress. A small sliver of blood dripped from her nostril.

The purple flames curled around the blade. The red hoodie had been cast back from the face of the Huntress, and Demorn gazed into her soul with all the raw power she held. There would be no hiding place from her reckoning.

And then she saw the awful truth. She saw what Red Morning had become. She saw what their leader had hidden underneath the robe and mask. The purple fire dimmed, responding to her own doubts, troubling Demorn.

'You are my Blood Sister,' she breathed. 'She led us for twenty years! Why did you not come to me!'

Toxis held her gaze, eyes blood red.

I don't know how long she consorted with the Pale Suns.

Demorn lashed out with a vicious kick, striking Toxis in the face. The flames on the sword blazed high, and she brought the Sword down for a killing blow.

In a red blur, the Huntress tumbled to the portal exit, the blade hissing and burning at the air behind her.

I don't know if you have betrayed us too.

'You fool!'

Demorn flung a series of energy stars into the portal, watching them shatter, exploding in empty space, a moment too late. The Huntress had gotten away, her final words echoing in Demorn's skull.

'Well, wasn't that just a waste of throwing stars.'

Despite her fury, Demorn had to smile at Smile's laconic attitude. Her brother operated at a different vibe. She slowed down before she could look him.

'Red Morning sold her soul to the Pale Suns.'

Every word was like a death-knell. Smile was a reflective ghost.

'Toxis found out. Executed her.'

She heard a deep bell tolling inside her mind. The tattoo upon her right shoulder burned with an uneasy fire. 'Can you hear it, Smile? The Cavern Bell?'

He was unsurprised. 'No, I don't hear any Bells.'

There was tearing in the air beside them. The portal opened, a swirling energy mass that slowly widened, revealing a barren stone floor. The bell tolled deeper and more urgently inside her mind.

Demorn's eyes glittered. 'The Cavern is calling to us for a reckoning. A new leader must be chosen.'

'Something tells me it's not a democracy where everybody gets an equal vote.'

Demorn smiled her scary smile. 'You're funny. It's a battle to the death.'

'Sounds like the worst and most violent thing ever.'

Demorn chuckled. 'That's because you aren't a sworn Innocent.'

The portal opened farther, tearing open the air inside the Spire. Miniature skulls circled the portal entrance. The silver lake was glistening and steaming.

'It's so damn ominous and down to death now isn't it? No wonder I prefer to stay on retainer,' Smile said softly.

Demorn growled affectionately, 'Don't worry, I'm a survivor. What are the chances of repairing the Spire?'

'Slim to none, we're grounded. I'm scavenging from half-busted tech to build our arsenal for what will come.'

What will come. Demorn looked at him with blazing green eyes.

'You know as well as I do then. Ultimate Fate is ahead of us, and Triton behind us. We will make our stand upon this world, in this City, and wreak vengeance upon our enemies.'

He shrugged. 'I guess I just don't understand why they're *our* enemies.'

She flicked her hand in a warding gesture. 'It's the same Goddess our people worshipped, the same dream. The same War. Can't you see that?'

He was silent for a while. 'I've delved deep into the Spire archives. I can't forget what happened to our people when they fought in God Wars after the Fracture. They were ravaged and beaten. We were left alone. Asanti is dead!'

Smile was trembling and she saw electronic tears upon his face. His face became a deep, dark mirror. She could see the burning husk of their world, charred and broken, refugees screaming all through the Spire, as she held her brother tightly, when the scarred Spire ship was flung into hyperspace, through the shattered Mirror, exiled forever, while their world exploded and died and died and died.

She laid upon his shoulder and whispered in Asanti. *'Not alone. Stormwinds carried us to this harbor. Don't doubt me.'*

He nodded. His hands moved in a shimmering Asanti gesture, one of obedience and loyalty.

'Don't die.'

Demorn brushed his face tenderly. 'I won't die, brother.'

Smile's face slowly glowed and she watched the tears dry and steam away. He looked up at her suddenly. His face lost the digital mask and the cybernetics beneath it. For a moment he was just her brother again, flesh and bone, as he had been, before the scientists had gotten to him. His warm, electric fingers brushed her face, and he picked at the electronic mesh over and beneath her skin.

'Your mask is all used up, Demorn.'

'I've killed too many monsters with it.'

He laughed, the yellow icon waking, glittering and spinning across his face.

'Ha! You've always been so sentimental about that old mask! You've worn it for years.'

'Three years to be exact. It kept me light and fast. But things change.'

The worn red and green mask barely glimmered with power anymore. Smile peeled it off her face.

'I need something for the death matches to come. I can feel it in my bones.'

Smile's face cut to instant arctic white with one single black outline.

'If it's truly down to life and death, there's one I've been saving for you.'

He walked into the purple flames, phasing to a blue ghostly form. Finally he came out of the fire, holding a cruel metallic mask, writhing with twisted black and silver bones. He tossed the bizarre mask to her. Demorn's face blazed with a blinding white when the mask opened, a frightening mash of skeletal magic.

She closed her eyes, letting her face soak in its cold lethal embrace.

'It's a Soul Mask,' Smile said. 'I've been growing it for you.'

Whose soul was it, she wondered. The metal slid easily over her skin, feeding a strange, wild blast of strength through her.

'Think of something good, Sis. Something pure to you.'

She felt urgent, old laws surge inside her, chilling her blood with their raw finality, a lack of any kind of mercy. Then Demorn knew what the mask carried. It was the souls of dead Asanti, warrior spirits interlaced in the dark skeletal power, riven through her blade and heart. It was her soul, bone and pain laced through it. She felt the inside of graves, the wasted spirits of those she had slain and would slay. Demorn felt the joy of vengeance, her green eyes flashing through the night, Xalos a wild purple flame that would never go out if she kept wreaking vengeance in the name of the goddess.

Suddenly she remembered Kate and the Winter Park and her ruined heart. The Soul Mask gripped and suffocated, fitting perfectly and horribly to her face. Demorn was staring at the portal and the floating skulls but all she saw was fragments of the dead past.

The stylish apartment lay far above the harbor. Thin red curtains filtered the morning sunlight. Kate floated above Demorn, her gorgeous pale body naked from the waist up, striking some quasi-meditation pose, blonde hair loose and free.

Demorn's magic eyes sparkled as she traced the outline of Kate's body, close to a dangerous kind of love that had no boundary or end point. Saturday morning cartoons played on the TV. A huge, muscle-bound man in a torn black-and-red costume was smashed against a broken city building, collapsing it. A hideous creature with innumerable heads towered above him, indistinct features shifting horribly, the heads twisting and clawing through the air.

The cartoon picture became live action, horribly realistic. News feeds scrolled across the bottom of the picture, feeding death quotas and blinking emergency numbers and data about the National Guard, encoded bursts of barely concealed electronic panic. The beaten-up super-god flung himself into the air, his face smashed, good looks gone. He expended a series of huge energy bursts upon this entity that seemed to have little or no effect.

She looked beyond the creature and saw buildings burning and the sky was thick with grey, charred clouds like blank slate. The super-god was smashed back to the ground, his body now weak and brittle, burnt out like a mini-supernova.

'What is this?'

Kate looked at her with cold blue eyes, something almost like loathing in them. 'It's the future, dear. It's the terrible future.'

It was awful, the honesty in those blue eyes. Demorn felt a strange dreadful chill, as if somebody had walked over her grave a million years hence.

Demorn turned the TV off. 'I don't get it, Kate.'

Kate drifted to the floor, and touched Demorn's face. Her hand was cold. 'We're only half here, most things are an illusion. We cast shadows, both forward and back.'

Kate lazily covered herself with a thin pale blue cardigan over her full breasts and body. She's so fucking beautiful, Demorn thought. She's all I ever want. With the TV off, the noise and images gone, she began to feel more relaxed.

'C'mon. It's just cartoons and silly stuff.'

Kate's hand drifted to the remote. 'Oh, you're so sure of that? Do you want to watch more of the show?'

Demorn slid the remote away from her. 'No. I feel weird. I'd rather just watch old movies. I don't want to think about the future or scary cartoons.'

Kate hand drifted to Demorn's body. It felt good. Demorn let her caress her. Kate whispered, 'Don't think about tomorrow, these are our summer days, babe.'

I know they are, Demorn thought, with a vaguely bittersweet dread. I feel like I have already lived and lost them. But she is here with me now, Demorn thought, as Kate slowly kissed her neck. She brushed the curtain back. A deep harbor shone in the near distance, midday sun reflecting off the waves. Demorn felt an incredible yearning. A single tall tower stood by the shoreline, rising high above a small cluster of yachts, casting a long thin shadow upon the water.

The Jade Hotel. Something like dread filled her heart for a moment. It was Wednesday. Tony was waiting for her in the Hotel. Her car was just outside. She could leave now, be having lunch and cocktails with him within the hour.

Yeah. It wasn't going to happen.

She tried not to think of the monsters on TV. She just wanted this fragile peace to last through the day. She just wanted the song on the TV to last forever. But it always ended.

Kate whispered, 'You can stay here as long as you want,' her breath soft and sweet. Demorn's heart was taken, no longer wholly her own and never would be again.

The old life flashed away as a searing montage of jarring memories in vivid neon. It all felt far away, like it belonged to somebody else. Soon there was nothing but the sense of haunting loss. Only Demorn's extreme sense of self-control stopped a primal scream erupting from the depths of her being. Vaguely, she knew she had slumped to the ground. Smile's arm was around her, and slowly his warmth brought her back.

'Thank you, I love this mask more than anything.'

Her green eyes blazed from beneath the tight mask. She could see the intricacies of the machine around her, the lasers in the sky, the basic machinery of the Spire, the energy fields tying everything together. The meadow shifted into the grey walls of the lab. Visions still flashed of the Memory Garden, deeper and darker than ever before. The death-skull mask had sunk slowly beneath her skin, leaving Demorn's face pale and intense. Everything felt sharper than ever before. More real.

Demorn picked her leather jacket off the ground and pulled it tight around her. She took the gloves from the pocket and slid her glasses on, and ran her hand through her long hair. She felt younger, restored.

The Cavern Bell tolled through her mind.

'How do I look, Smile?'

Her brother was soft and filled with light.

'Like somebody about to kick everybody else's ass.'

She smirked. 'Well, I should be fine, just as long as I don't have to solve a goddamn murder mystery.'

Demorn half-stepped through the portal of skulls, the magic cold and foreboding around her. Her brother was a blue ghost. She held onto that as the screaming began to start again, louder than ever before. Suddenly she didn't want to remember Chicago. She didn't want to remember Kate and what they had lost. Demorn walked through the floating skulls, vanishing from the Memory Garden.

6

The air was cold. Steam rolled off the water. A small group of Innocents were gathered around the lake. The portal closed behind her, tearing at the air, miniature skulls falling to the ground. Demorn caught one in her gloved hand. She studied it, an alien skull that crumbled almost instantly in her fingers.

The group turned at the noise, mostly familiar faces, a collection of Innocents.

'Nice catch, Princess,' a tall blonde in a gorgeous white bodysuit said. Her voice carried more than a hint of sarcasm.

Alex. Her own portal was still flashing out behind her, purple waves rippling around her attractive, curvaceous form. Leather holsters on each of her long legs held a pair of elegant pistols.

'Hey Alex. I'm surprised this is your kind of thing.'

Alex fake yawned. 'Mostly I prefer killing for money, but this could actually be fun. She's always been a flat out bitch to me.'

Demorn felt that familiar mixture of suppressed desire and mild loathing for Alex. They had fought often over the years. Each wore scars from the other. Regardless of what Alex said, both had been close to Red Morning the last couple of seasons, racking up the missions and the kills, hanging close to the Glass Throne. But fighting wasn't all they did, Demorn thought, her eyes quickly rolling over Alex's body and intense blue eyes.

'Just be a good girl and don't shoot anyone, Alex.'

'We'll see.'

Alex wandered to the group by the water. Demorn followed, keeping her distance, hand lightly brushing the handle of her blade, studying those who had arrived. Alex's bodyguard, Guard Dog, stood in the shallows, his massive cartilage-ridden body no doubt benefiting from the steaming, magic waters of the silver lake. Even Demorn could feel their healing properties working on a score of cuts and bruises upon her own tired body.

Alex lightly called to him, and the Guard Dog slowly surged out of the water toward her, his grotesque body holding and lifting Alex in a tight clasp. He half growled in Demorn's general direction. As always, she kept a respectful distance.

Two Innocents with black cloaks thrown over their features and bodies stood by the lakeside. Near them, a blurred image faded in and out. She could smell a faint whiff of burning. Someone was using old school shields.

The water began to surge and boil. A silver cage emerged from the churning water. A red cloaked figure slumped inside, facing the group with an awful, insane intensity. Demorn ran to the water's edge. Inside the cage was Red Morning, her face pallid as a ghost, the red symbol of the Blood Hunt carved upon her cheek. Caught in some horrible middle point, she looked neither dead nor alive.

She felt Alex beside her, drawing a pistol, swearing an obscene oath, but not firing. The hooded figures retreated from the shoreline, hands shaking with warding gestures. The cage rose farther out of the deep lake. Still, the pallid face stared at them. Demorn saw lights reflecting from the Cavern's ceiling high above them. She glanced up, every sense on alert. On the cavern roof, she saw trace outlines of moving shapes. Her mind froze, gaping in wonder and fear at what she saw. Time itself seemed to freeze, the air like pure ice.

Demorn saw gods walking. A great shining female figure, a writhing head of snakes upon a long spear. Roughly drawn figures of tall armoured men and women surrounded her. Some held standards of their kingdoms or their lords, some held axes and swords. But they all let her pass and they did not walk with her or challenge her. The longer Demorn looked upon the images, the closer she felt to them, the more sense these line drawings made, glistening on the Cavern rock, telling stories of the gods. The Goddess shone, becoming real to her eyes. *Alodin Mars.* Everything was vivid. Many of the men surrounding her wore faces of the skeleton. Heavens were burning, death was eternal, a stain that followed a spirit into rebirth.

Priests did not know their own gods. Prophets were mad liars.

Demorn raised her hands to her lips. Without realizing, she had whispered this in Asanti.

The Goddess drifted upon the water, but she was not there too. Silver light flowed from her body. She turned to Demorn, her image glistening with power and possible futures. She was partly no more than a silver outline. Within this, the Goddess was a great warrior carrying a dead Medusi, while another part refracted in a space beyond time and space, an essence that no simple vessel of flesh and bone could hold.

Truths imprinted onto Demorn's mind. The oaths she had sworn to the Innocents, the blood she had spilled on foreign battlefields, the souls and bodies that Xalos claimed . . . it was for some vast God War that played over eons, across the gulfs of time. She saw pyramids through a million heavens, pulsing in synchronicity, while around them a sea of corruption flowed beyond the barriers.

Demorn looked closely at Red Morning. The woman looked older in living death. She had a strange, grim wisdom about her; her fingers lightly rapped the silver cage bars. She spoke, her lips barely moving. The voice was thunderous, almost painful, penetrating the minds of the Innocents as much as it hurt their ears.

'So this is my Fate, Alodin Mars? To be dragged as a slain ghost before my peers?'

Red Morning had always been a woman given to casual cruelty, quick to sarcasm. It was almost amusing, to see that even in half-life, with her enchantments stripped back, her age and her weariness obvious, she maintained her pose.

The two cloaked Innocents disappeared into their portals, vanishing back to the Clubhouse. Demorn sneered. Lightweights. Hoods or not, she had a good idea who they were. They couldn't see Alodin Mars, but they knew her name—it was inscribed on the souls of all Innocents. They were terrified of the legends of their birthing.

Demorn felt a small flood of empathy for Red Morning. She could see the horrible weight inside that cage, crushing on her soul, the despair within Morning's pallid gaze. The mark of the Blood Huntress burned vividly on her skin while the Silver Goddess rose to the cage. Red Morning screamed, holding both palms out, exposing the twin red suns inscribed into her palms.

Alex's expression was one of detached curiosity. Her portal flickered behind her, purple shadows. Guard Dog was gone, suspicious of magic and gods. Demorn's glasses could see energy coalesce in the sun-tattoos, raw and dangerous. For the first time Demorn saw the limitations of that wild power Red Morning held, that raw, death magic which had leveled townships and torn cities apart. She could see inside the soul of her fallen leader, so much of it already passed beneath. She could see the lack of any true or lasting power — it was just magic tricks and cruelty, an obsessive goal to lead that had become routine greed. Demorn saw the dirty secrets, what the Pale Suns had given Red Morning, small increments of power stretching over years, pathetic against the deep power of true magic, which were the silver bars and the silver lake of the Cavern.

'It's so disappointing,' Alex said, taking her hand in an unexpectedly kind gesture. It was true. In here, their minds mingled.

'Can you see the Goddess, too?' Demorn asked.

Alex nodded dreamily. 'Vaguely . . . but I can see enough. Wow, that bitch *really* did betray us. I thought that intense little hunter friend of yours was just playing throne-room politics.'

Demorn laughed absently. 'Toxis doesn't care about politics.'

'Probably wise. What happens now?'

Red Morning's burning palms were intense beacons of twin light, energy rippling down her arms.

'We get to see if she can break out of a God Prison. If she does, it's up to us to kill her.'

Alex's laugh was a growl.

But the wild sorcery of Red Morning, learnt so long ago in the back alleys and drug dens of Babelzon, was going nowhere. It seemed nothing against the Cavern's true power. But anyone who had ever led the Innocents had something special. Against the tide of the dampening, a raw heat of red energy swept out from the twin red suns upon her palms. Red Morning was riding a last wild power surge, laughter pouring from her pallid form. Her joy turned to a snarl of horror, the energy going nowhere, feeding back into the silver cage, searing Red Morning inside a bubble of pain. The woman howled and screamed, issuing deranged threats of damnation on everyone and everything.

Without much compassion, Demorn watched her die again, eaten alive by raw destruction and flame, the same sorcery she had wielded with such dread power in life. Unquietness murmured in Demorn's chest, a whisper of Xalos. She wondered where her own path would lead. Many times she had fought when Xalos spewed forth, delivering justice and retribution upon her enemies. Demorn had lay at the center of an inferno, harnessing the power of death, caring nothing for what message she sent or whose judgment she served.

A least she was no traitor. Hissing last sighs of hatred upon her own, Red Morning died again, the mark of the Huntress upon her face. The silver cage descended into the lake, water slowly calming.

Demorn could see the water was filled with skeletal figures. They chilled her to look at. Some of them retained a vestige of humanity. She glimpsed the tail of the Serpent rising in the water. She averted her eyes. There were some forms of evil and endings that Demorn did not want to know.

A silver crown emerged from the water, hanging in the air, blood and burning marks still upon it. A sliver of passion ran through Demorn. She cast her eyes toward Alex, who flicked her hair with contempt, looking like some gorgeous instrument of death.

A bell rang through the Cavern, loud and solemn.

'I heard that, and it's damn eerie,' Alex murmured.

Lightning smashed through the roof which was suddenly open. Rain fell, pure and cold. The silver image of Alodin Mars pierced Demorn's thoughts and dreams, casting away well-trained mental shields like rice paper. Demorn had instantly drawn her burning blade, but under the sheer power of the Goddess she sank to her knees, the flames dying.

Alodin Mars laughed. Demorn looked up. The Goddess held Alex by the throat. A gigantic Medusi head writhed on the Goddess Spear, glittering eyes open. Alex uttered a small cry but she was already stone. Alodin Mars dropped her to the ground, a statue.

'She is the best killer you have. But she is not the one I seek.'

Demorn found her voice, avoiding the gaze of the writhing Medusi through the very limits of the training.

'Am I?'

'You might be. But the one I seek has NEVER kneeled!'

Alodin Mars hurled the spear, and Demorn rolled on instinct. It shattered earth and rock.

Alodin Mars withdrew a thin whip from her gauntlet, cracking it across Demorn's face, cutting the right side of her cheek almost to the bone, along the path of the old scar given long ago in the ice cavern.

Demorn hissed in pain, blood across her face, swinging the fiery Xalos in a vicious arc, rage flowing through her.

'Stop this sick game of the gods!'

Alodin Mars parried the blade of Xalos with her gauntlet, her whip lashing out to catch Demorn's hand, and then driving the katana into the ground, shattering it.

Alodin caught Demorn in a loveless grip. 'A game? So what if it is a game?'

Demorn sneered. 'Makes me wish I'd been right when I said I was an atheist.'

The laughter of Alodin was a light breeze of distant childhood meadows.

'The race of Medusi were beautiful women, born in hot caves. They were hunted into near extinction for their magic blood. Hunted by humans with their swords and small minds. You killed many, didn't you, Demorn?'

Demorn grimaced. 'It is your spear she lies upon, Alodin. Not my sword.'

The goddess smiled, her teeth sharp.

'So she does. I killed many in the God Wars. They are vain, fickle creatures.'

She pointed a finger at Alex and the rock cracked around her white jump-suited form. Alex lay gasping on the ground.

'*That* one is more ruthless than you shall ever be. One day, she may even surpass you in my affection. But not today, Mirror Child. You are the one who has carried me in dreams from distant worlds.'

She released her grip. The whip snapped back to her gauntlet.

Demorn got up from the ground. The cut healed fast, but a thin white scar remained, glistening and burning like wildfire.

Alodin Mars spoke. 'It is best you remember the fate of your last leader. She screams as a ghoul in Hades. I will never let her up. I can break the weapons that I give.'

Her silver image floated in front of Demorn. She tore the purple glasses from her eyes.

'And I can smell another Goddess on you, an old thing, as I smelt it in the ice cavern years ago. It has grown stronger now. I smell ruination, the death-womb, worms crawling in her barren belly.'

The eyes of Alodin Mars were multi-layered prisms of light. There was no escaping that hall of glistening mirrors. She outshone everything in Demorn, filled all the emptiness inside. She lit up the hollow spaces. With burning lips, Alodin Mars kissed Demorn with a lusty passion. Demorn had no defense, no hiding place before this blazing, undimmed soul.

Alex retreated into her portal, color flooding back to her face. It was just the two of them now. The silver lake was quiet. Steam rolled off the water. Alodin Mars put her glowing white hand upon the locket.

'She's in here, isn't she? Oh yes! She's in HERE! Come to me, Mictecaciuatl, fight me!'

Alodin Mars laughed as savage pain flared up from the locket, burning Demorn's chest, and Demorn was dragged along, knees hitting the rocky ground. Power and anger surged through Demorn. Her left hand became a metal fist. She swung into the face of Alodin Mars, striking clean. The goddess tumbled, loosening her hand upon the locket.

Demorn's mind was crystal clear, haunted by visions that were not her own. Distant conflicts on old lands. Quarrels between Queens and Emperors who gambled kingdoms and subjects, with everything beneath them a pawn. Demorn swung again, feeling the death, the rotten curses that lay upon the steel.

As she smashed her fist into Alodin Mars, her right hand became a steel fist, and she struck again. Alodin laughed, her multicolored eyes dancing, as she wiped translucent blood from her chin.

'You really want to dance, don't you, Mictecaciuatl? You want to die again?'

In a haze of passion, Demorn picked up Xalos, reformed from shards when her hand touched the handle. Purple flames licked dangerously across the metal.

Alodin Mars' eyes glinted. 'Oh, you do have a *fine* blade to reckon with, Mirror Princess! There is a reason I haunt your dreams. THERE IS A REASON I PROTECT AND GUIDE YOU.'

Demorn spoke like a puppet speaking through a puppeteer. Her voice was jagged, suffused with something rough and bitter. Her chest was laced with pain. It was hard to remember who she was.

'The girl's mind is stained, Alodin. She is corrupt as rotten fruit. Her world is a tomb. Why have you taken an orphan as your hero?'

Alodin smiled. 'You sound older, Mictecaciuatl. Desperate.'

Mictecaciuatl's laughter was a cackle threaded with insanity. *'I know oblivion as you never have. She is a cold mistress.'*

Alodin cracked the whip across the rocky cavern floor, energy glinting off the sharp thread. She floated across the floor. Her words flowed as energy waves, reverberating through Demorn's ears.

'I dance naked with my warriors, I run with the black wolves, I ride the dragon over the Endless Sea by the light of the twin moons. I AM BEYOND YOU, GODDESS OF PAIN, GODDESS OF THE DEATH WOMB. I choose Demorn because I can!'

Alodin's hands shone with pyramids of power as she floated high into the air. The cave drawings became moving images, shadow creatures of immense power colliding into each other, containing a powerful malevolence, glimmers of the end, drowned in the blue light of absolute infinity. Alodin Mars shone like a blinding northern star. Behind her, there was a score of ancient dragons. Mighty creatures with lion heads rode the dragons.

'In this deep Cavern, I swear sacred vows with my Innocents, sharing things that other gods would never share, fighting battles you lost, wars you abandoned. All for the love of our family and our people and their memory!'

The Cavern ground trembled slightly as Alodin's voice grew louder and more full. 'This was my birthing place in the ancient eons. Why did you think you could come here and challenge me?'

Mictecaciuatl spoke through Demorn's lips, her voice clogged and strained. *'I speak from a cold void. I survive on shreds of power. I exist in the screams of the torture, you fat, complacent whore . . .'*

Alodin's whip thrashed around Demorn's neck, winding tighter and tighter, drawing blood. 'Abandon your vessel, dead god, leave this cavern.'

The pain goddess flickered through Demorn's mind, an object of destruction, shadows of renewal from the flames, echoes of the God Wars, the refracted dying of thousands. Demorn shuddered as she saw the black sea of decay beneath everything. She wasn't sure who she was anymore, filled with the hideous knowledge that these gods took a piece out of everyone.

'Leave us, Mictecaciuatl! Or I shall destroy every last trace of you!'

Demorn cried out in futile rage, the pain blazing through her, a final wild wave. She pulled on the whip, her fingers cut by the sharp thread. She sliced upward with Xalos, cutting into the body of the goddess, opening a red rain of blood.

The katana sliced upward. For a tiny moment, Demorn saw the spirit of multiple Alodin Mars, scattered across universes in time. Then she saw that she was mistaken. Alodin Mars gripped the katana in her shining hands. The universes collapsed back into one. The goddess raised her left hand. A single triangle of power glowed beneath the red blood. The same mark as upon the Ruby Lady and Sinatra, years ago, in Vegas.

As Demorn watched, the wound was healed. She realized the truth then. She never forgot it as long as she lived to serve the Innocents.

'The blade is yours,' Demorn breathed in astonishment. 'It comes from you.'

Alodin Mars laughed richly, her sharp perfect teeth glinting.

'Yes.'

Alodin Mars pushed the blade into her flesh. It shimmered with energy as it sunk deep. Slowly, the purple fire died, withering away. Her visage trembled with vicious energy.

Alodin Mars' multilayered eyes glittered. 'And to me it shall return. When you are nothing but a sweet thought in the Memory Garden, with your brother weeping for you, and the people who prayed to you left behind. Remember *that*, Princess of the Swords. The path of vengeance leads to a grave.'

She withdrew the sword from her stomach, throwing the burning katana into the lake. Demorn watched the slash in the goddess's white stomach fade to a red angry scar, then a white line, then nothing but shimmering perfect skin.

Demorn felt empty, burnt out. The pain was gone. She brushed the locket with her gloved fingers. It was inert and vacant.

'Where is she?'

Alodin Mars laughed. 'Banished. All the foul remnants of her.'

Demorn fingered the locket suspiciously. She didn't know what to say. 'For how long?'

'Days. Weeks. That last, little part of a dead god is very resistant.' Alodin Mars glanced at her sharply. 'You still wear the fist of steel. You don't lack bravery, Princess, bringing totems of Mictecaciuatl to my domain.'

Demorn looked down at her left hand, still coiled in the fighting fist. She relaxed her mind, feeling the flesh come back to her, memories of brutal old fights slowly fading out. Her heart felt lighter.

Alodin Maris took her hand, leading her into the water. The armour of the Goddess fell away, leaving just a thin black dress. She looked younger and less severe.

'We were sisters once, you know. Long ago, before the Fracture.'

The water was hot. Demorn felt all the wounds fading away, except for the lingering cut across her cheek. That never fully healed, even when it was invisible. She could see its ghostly presence reflected in the now still waters. Alodin Mars brushed her cheek.

'The mark will be unseen to anything but the most magic of eyes.'

Demorn looked into the water. The reflection of the Goddess carried a glistening golden glass crown. Her armour was studded with arrow marks and the greaves upon her arms were scored with battle damage. In the reflection, the serene face of Alodin Mars was stern and older, marked with a lifetime of burdens and fighting in distant wars, campaigns far from home.

'I can live with a few scars, holy one.'

'Good,' whispered the shining figure. 'The God Wars have lasted eons, infected our havens, scarred so many worlds and destroyed countless hopes. The Fracture burnt through my family and my worlds and those of countless others. I am no saint, no feeble god demanding love. My armies have eaten cultures who opposed me. Some worlds called me the Devourer, as I slayed their champions.'

Demorn moved her hands in a warding gesture. 'In Asanti, you were called the Moving Storm.'

'How I loved Asanti!' Alodin Mars cried out, her hands suffused with lightning. She flung a huge, searing ball of energy across the pool, striking the rocky face, lighting up everything. Demorn saw a mighty silver glass throne on the other side of the lake. Her mind vibrated with the strength of it, the power, calling to her.

She felt a strong hand upon her shoulder. The face of Alodin Mars had grown terrible and spectral, vibrating at the edges of space and time.

'I am a storm in a violent sea. When Asanti died, I could not take corporeal form for years. Many of my temples lay there.'

Demorn asked, 'What happened to you then?'

'I was a wandering ghost, whilst Ultimate Fate stalked my dreams as a wolf with a hideous face.'

Alodin Mars stared into the water. Images of battles shifted through the reflections.

'Do you wish to lead them, Princess? These Innocents?'

Demorn was quiet. 'There is nobody else left.'

The goddess laughed; electricity danced through her fingers. 'You think that alone gives you the right?'

Demorn smiled. 'No. But I came to fight for the throne. Loss was always the void for me, no matter what. Let me fight.'

'Very true. The wailing of Hades is a mortal's fate.'

Demorn waded through the hot water, toward the silver throne.

'I knew your father once, Sword Princess.'

Demorn turned, her eyes sharp.

'He's dead.'

'Not when I knew him.'

Demorn sighed. 'On Asanti, before the end?'

Alodin's cool gaze held an unmistakable trace of pity.

'No, not there. When he ruled in Firethorn, an eon ago.'

7

A giant roar echoed through the cavern, untamed, naked and pure. Demorn's magic eyes scanned the deep water. Alodin Mars became a silver outline, fading back to the Cavern Walls. The memory of her faded in Demorn, becoming just the memory of the Club Goddess again, her secrets buried in myths and whispers, and she forgot the name of Alodin Mars.

Underneath a layer of darkness, in the horrible cold at the bottom of the lake, Demorn saw the great Serpent coiled, unmoving, a lidless eye open. Her heart was chilled.

'There's something in the water, a reptile,' she murmured.

A whisper ran across her like a light breeze. 'Yes there is, but nothing you could defeat. Forget the Great Snake, unless you seek utter destruction.'

Demorn felt a pain in her chest, then a holy fire as Xalos spawned again, erupting with a pure flame. The blade was light in her hand. The roar echoed again through the dark. The Goddess was utterly gone. The cavern was colder. Demorn felt more mortal. The Cavern roof was open. Cold stars lit up the walls. There were no more drawings.

Demorn felt she was seeing into the past itself, when lizard-men had walked the earth, a warmer, older time. Her mind phased with the visions. She saw the building of ornate stone pyramids, hordes of priestess moving in unison, sacrificial rites in hollowed out tombs. Flames guttered from massive fires in the ground. She smelled the searing flesh of enemies, sorcerers concocting strange recipes, the hatching of gods in humid birthing chambers, swearing compacts inside the very fissures of the universe.

'What is this?' she asked in a cold voice.

A huge, lumbering form reared out of the shallows on the other side. A great lizard reared upon thick hind legs, his neck in thick chains, an enormous spiked club in mighty hands.

The chain was released. The creature leered at her, moving with disturbing speed towards her in the shallows. Demorn grinned, arcing the blade in a fast balanced position, taking attack form. She was perversely glad the pain locket was burnt out, happy the Pain Goddess did not offer assistance.

His giant form reared out of the water, and she could see the holy madness in his eyes, anger at his forced submission, and all the ways that made him slow and impulsive. The creature swung his mighty club wildly. She avoided with ease, backing out of the water. Enraged, he catapulted toward her, saliva dripping.

Demorn's blade stuck home, the fire tasting his hide, filling Demorn with hot pleasure as she slashed through the obscene hide, dark blood stinging her skin.

The water behind him boiled. A swarm of creatures emerged from the water, smaller, faster lizards, maddened by the humiliation of their king, hissing ominous sounds of death and hate.

She howled Asanti death chants, her mind filled with battle joy, the death soul-mask surging onto her face. She fought the spawning horde, feeding her dark, powerful energies through the long hours it took to kill them all in the shallows of the magic lake.

Demorn swam through the hot water to the shoreline, the blood washing off. Her arms ached and her eyes glittered. She had killed so many, given not an inch of mercy. The Cavern seemed lighter. The throne was close now, silver light shining. The floor was polished.

A staff smashed in front of her. A soft voice purred through her mind. ***There will be no Crown for you, sister.***

A dark foot smashed across her face, almost snapping her neck. Fast hands deflected the second blow. Demorn rolled away, surging out of the water. She could hear the Throne calling, undercurrents of power and promise. Toxis stood there, sheer red cloak over her powerful dark body.

Demorn went to grab her blade, but the ash-black staff moved faster, smashing into her shoulder, stunning her with a mighty crack, her whole right side stunned and paralyzed. Demorn ducked the reverse swing, and with everything left in her, she swung with her left hand, striking Toxis flush across the face. The cloak hood was knocked back, and the staff tumbled from her hands across the rock. Demorn smashed her again, sweeping her leg. Demorn put her foot on the hunter's throat, slowly adding pressure. Toxis' eyes were blood red, poisoned by anger and hurt. Demorn's mind trembled with passion and fatigue. Her knuckles were bruised. There was no steel spell strengthening them. She didn't want to kill her friend. She beheld the spirit of the huntress, as she had first seen it years ago, a pure spirit of rage which knew nothing but the Hunt.

'Why, Toxis?'

I CANNOT TRUST THE INNOCENTS. ANY OF YOU MIGHT BE THE TRAITOR.

Her words echoed with sad anger. Demorn kneaded her shoulder, slowly bringing feeling back. Sadness flowed through her.

'We are Sisters. I have hunted with you in the wastelands of the North, we have saved each other. Xalos will not light for you, Toxis. Something in me won't let it.' Demorn slid the katana out the scabbard with her good hand. 'Must I really kill you like the rest?'

The Silver Throne hummed a transcendent tune behind them. In the corner of her eye, Demorn could see images play upon the throne, the dark shadow of a mighty king who had once ruled, achingly familiar, but now forgotten.

Toxis closed her blood eyes.

Tell me. Do you even remember Firethorn, Princess? Do you know it as more than a name?

Demorn paused. The name stirred faint memories, shadows beneath the surface. The Goddess had invoked the word. Faint visions of hot jungles, a white fort by the Sea, a red flag flying, jigsaw pieces of a dream.

'Glimmers.'

Toxis dry, sarcastic laughter echoed through her mind.

My land remembers you, Princess.

Demorn felt lost. The magic in the air was heavy. The undercurrent of power from the Silver Throne was almost irresistible now. She glanced at the Throne and she could see the Dead King. His features were haunted, his rugged face gone pale. He wore thick chain mail, ripped apart by blades, and she could see the deep mortal wounds. His eyes were dead. His mouth moved soundlessly, but she could not tell if he was some cheap conjurer's trick.

The Dead King calls to us! LISTEN!

Demorn abruptly sheathed her blade and took her foot off the hunter's throat. 'I can't hear what he says, Toxis. If you can hear him, help me.'

Toxis rolled away from Demorn, springing to her feet. She carefully put the ash staff across her back. Demorn saw a series of burning insignia along the neck of the Huntress, glowing with strange, foreign symbols. The same symbols burnt along the Cavern walls. Demorn felt a mixture of dread and anticipation. Toxis placed her lithe hand along Demorn's neck. Her fingers burnt, Demorn's tattoo catching aflame upon her wrist as she reeled away.

Toxis eyes were pure blood.

Do you remember NOW?

'I remember . . . more.'

The King's dead eyes came alive. A fang glinted. His rugged face lost any pallor. He looked powerful and dark. Lightning crackled in the air above them. The Cavern seemed vast and empty. Unseen creatures howled loudly in the darkness.

Toxis knelt before the Throne, head bowed. Demorn sat beside her. Her green glittering eyes were wet with tears. Memories flicked through her mind. She could remember standing on the White Fort, overlooking the Sea, Toxis by her side, and she could not tell if it was the future or the past.

His deep voice rumbled. 'Firethorn has fallen to evil, the bonds of the Clans are broken. Toxis hunts Babelzon for traitors. You have deserted your Sisters. Why?'

Demorn looked up, angry. 'I have to explain myself to you? I barely remember you as anything but a phantom dream. My life is outside this Cavern, dead thing!'

'In Firethorn, I was your King.'

'Firethorn was a child's dream. A game I played with my brother while we fled Asanti.'

His face came out of the shadows, partly wild beast, partly human.

'A game you played as you fled a tomb. A game that was not a game.'

She could see him struggling to hold on to his humanity, forcing his words out. 'Gods plague your life like insects.'

A strange dread flickered in Demorn. Her hand grasped the katana. Her fingers flicked in a warding gesture against his words. From the tombs of her mind, she knew she had some relationship to this creature, but that didn't assuage her fear. Xalos came alive, purple fire searing from the blade.

'Leave this Cavern! You are no Innocent, witch creature!'

The Dead King shook his head slowly, his dark eyes flashing.

'I am no Innocent. Just as I am no voodoo horror from the witches coven. But I am still your King, reborn from beyond the Dying.'

Demorn dropped the blade, hearing his voice clearly, as he seemed to master his animal nature, and his features humanised. His armour glistened. There was blood on his hands, holding tightly to the Silver Throne. Desperation and wild hunger moved through his eyes.

Toxis was utterly silent, her eyes on the floor.

Demorn knew suddenly and without doubt that this half-monster was what become of her King. His chain mail was torn. She saw the open wound in his side, bleeding out.

'How do you live?'

He grimaced and his face grew wolfish. He chuckled with a throaty rumble.

'It is a twisted half-life. I linger outside the Halls of the Dead. I hear the wail of the Underworld in my dreams.'

She was solemn. 'I've heard it is a place of shadows and fear.'

The Dead King shrugged. 'All things must pass beneath, my Princess. The ground calls to me, but the Pale Suns have stolen my bones. They use them in dark rituals to call their masters.'

His voice faded away and she could see he was in great pain.

Pale Suns. Toxis screamed. ***How my King! Our bravest warriors guard the cemetery walls!***

He snarled, 'Because Firethorn is lost! And the bravest warriors lie dead, while the Princess of the Swords has forgotten her land!'

Suspicion flared in Demorn. More than ever, she felt adrift, assailed by phantoms and rumours, while Red Morning drowned in the magic waters.

'We have problems of our own, Dead King.'

He clambered off his throne. She could see the effort, blood spilling with each step. A terrible golden crown lay upon his head. A huge two-handed sword lay in a mighty scabbard by his side, soaked in enchantments, both good and evil. Demorn knew instinctively that to fight him here would be true death. Even in the Cavern of the Innocents, she was no match for him yet. The inscriptions on the rock walls around her sang holy tales of his reign. She didn't know what to believe.

'Tell me what you want, King.'

'I need you to find the Bones, Demorn. The Pale Suns have hidden them in the land of mortals, upon the Grim Earth.'

In a blur, she sank Xalos deep into his chest, piercing the metal links, making sure the katana plunged deep. He showed neither surprise nor pain, the barest of snarls upon his face. She breathed an oath of protection as she slowly withdrew the blade, for she did not know what he was, a spectre or some ancient curse of the Cavern.

'I can't allow you to live, it's evil,' she whispered. The Dead King said nothing as the light fell from his eyes. The gold crown tumbled from his head, bouncing upon the ground then vanishing.

Toxis screamed behind her, primal and insane.

Demorn turned, already swinging the katana, but the Huntress was too quick, dark skin blazing with red symbols. She dodged, a blade springing from the ash staff, slashing Demorn, and her sharp teeth savaged Demorn's neck.

Demorn smashed her away, but the huntress only smiled, crazed, wild laughter echoing madly both within and without her mind. Demorn staggered back, throwing Toxis away. Around them, lightning struck, electrifying the lake, smashing into the rock walls.

The roof was gone. The universe lay above, wild and open, howling and icy cold. Demorn looked up and she could see the mighty castles of the gods. Blood pyramids upon the sands. She glimpsed their mighty war machines, momentous actions strung over eons. Demorn could see the chains around the Universe. She glimpsed the terrible power of Ultimate Fate, beyond anything the Club could stop. Or so it felt.

Looking into it, Demorn's heart became ice and was never the same again. Without realising, she had climbed onto the Silver Throne.

Toxis turned to her. There was no fury in her piercing turquoise eyes.

You lead us now.

Demorn felt light-headed. 'You just bit me in the neck like some goddamn vampire. And now you wanna elect me?'

Toxis laughed softly through Demorn's head. She took the red hood off, revealing her face. She was striking. Beautiful and intense, her face flawless, pearl studs in each ear. Intricate ink tattoos ran down her dark neck. Her mouth held the hint of a smile.

It was just a kiss, Princess. We hunt together, sister.

She placed her hand on Demorn's burning tattoo. The air felt charged.

In Firethorn you lead us. You fight for the White Fort. But here, you forget.

A shiver ran down Demorn's back. She felt older, more vulnerable. The connection flickered at the edge of her mind, as it had for years, through so many blood-stained missions, so many hits.

Firethorn. It was a distant dream to which she longed to return but never could. Demorn whispered, 'I know it's real. I know it.'

Toxis looked at her, her dark face spectacular and beautiful. ***The storm is almost upon us. Our towers begin to topple.***

Xalos glittered. She got off the throne, her gloved hand brushing the Cavern walls, veins pulsing with energy. She saw Innocent faces impressed into the stone. Proud and furtive. Old and young. Boys and girls. Women and men.

'They haven't toppled yet, Toxis.'

The longer her hands touched the Cavern wall, more Innocents, living and dead, appeared on the walls, a lineage that had passed down generations, from world to world, through refugee camps and slaver cells, from the highest Inner Sanctum tower to the gutters and the shadows of unknown cities.

'I pledge us to this War. As long as I live and lead the Innocents, I pledge us to this War.'

The cavern changed, becoming a magnificent throne room. Golden statues filled the room. A shining pool dazzled with crystal waters. She saw the goddess reflected in the waters. A spiked golden crown lay upon her head, and her eyes flashed with a terrible pride and power.

She looked out the vaulted window. The city was hers now. Beautiful minarets atop lofty towers dazzled under a blinding sun. Elegant towers stretched through multilayered canals. She saw the flags and standards of many nations. She saw her face upon many of them. Her heart filled with hope and happiness, and pride. The warm sun washed her face.

She trembled with power and the promise of a future where they won . . .

Instinctively, she felt Toxis beside her. She closed her eyes. The curtain drew back and the golden city was no more.

You did not have to choose this war.

Demorn's laugh was a growl. Past and future flickered in her.

'Oh, something tells me my mind was made up long ago,' she murmured.

I will meet you in the White Fort. We will stand together.

Toxis's golden armband glowed.

'Yes, Sister.'

The huntress vanished. Demorn's arm band burned in compulsive sympathy. She felt suddenly tired as she looked over the Silver Lake.

The golden throne room bled back to the stark Cavern rock walls and the steamy lake. The silver throne felt cold and horribly lonely as she sank back into it.

Demorn said, 'You can come out now, Tony. I know you're there.'

There was a low, good humoured laugh. Tony's relaxed, corpulent form appeared, perched on the edge of the Glass Throne, careful not to rumple his expensive grey suit.

'Sorry for staying lo-fi, kid. I got invited to a lynching, but now I'm completely confused.'

Demorn was good natured. 'Join the club, boss.'

Tony was a good fit for her. Old school Babelzon, a player agent and a club owner from Sub-Babel who had hustled his ass all the way to the Council seat. He knew her basic beats. She gripped his hand, feeling some warmth upon the cold Throne.

'I just don't understand how you even got *in* here, Tony. One, you're not a goddamn Innocent. Two, you're a *huuuuge* atheist. You don't believe in anything, let alone a fucking Goddess.'

Tony chuckled smoothly. 'But I *do* believe in money and contacts. That's two things Innocents are good at understanding.'

He flashed a thick red ruby ring upon his left hand, sparkling with fire.

'Entrance was by virtue of marriage, of course. I don't see everything you see. I don't need to. Maybe it's because they didn't put a chip in my brain, who knows.'

His voice was light and his smile vacant of malice. He might believe what he said or he might not. That was Tony, hustling angles.

'Who's *they*?' she said, in an old ritual.

Her lips brushed his cheek, staying only a moment, never too long.

'Oh, *they're* far too dangerous to know or name.'

The space around them phased. Demorn felt the Cavern magic subtly slipping away. The soft darkness become light, and the harsh contours of the silver throne became a plush armchair. She heard the purr of air conditioning. Demorn opened her eyes. She was curled up next to Tony, in his flashy bright office up in Jade Tower.

'Weirdest funeral ever,' he said.

8

Expensive leather couches, stark white walls with bright abstract paintings. A panoramic window overlooked the cityscape of Babelzon. The only sound was the distant chatter of Tyrant Run death-match commentators.

She said, 'They never shut up, do they? I don't know how anybody thinks.'

He guffawed. The sound cut out.

Tony smelled of expensive perfume, radiating warmth and money. He kept it light, but there were depths. She liked that she could feel his gun beneath the suit. No matter how high and perfect his office was, Tony was a hustler. She glanced again at the ruby glistening on his finger.

'Sure is a good looking ring.'

His voice was soft. 'She sure was a good looking woman.'

Tony's smooth voice had an edge of something else. 'Let's not talk about the dead, kid.' He held Demorn's hand tighter for a moment. 'Ah hell, let's dance across the edge of darkness. Apart from us, all the cool people are dead. Red Morning included. Not that she liked me much.'

Demorn giggled despite herself. Tony got her, he liked to mix light and dark. Nothing seemed to worry him too much.

'Did you *really* meet Sinatra?'

She nodded, coy. 'Sure did. It was trippy. The magic made me forget for a while but the Garden retrieved it.'

'That's quite the fucking blast.'

Tony was contemplative.

'I can't believe you made it back intact. People told me it was just about impossible.'

She fished a playing card out of her jacket, rolling it through her fingers.

Tony was grinning from ear to ear.

She was droll. 'But almost impossible isn't impossible. It's just hard.'

She flicked the card to him. Tony caught it in his fingers. It was hot. He held it close to his face, examining it, turning it over. One side showed a series of interlocking triangles. The other was emblazoned with a single, shining word. TRITON.

Tony stared at it for a while with hungry eyes.

'I thought these cards were a legend.'

She looked at him almost shyly, crossing her legs.

'They are. That's why you paid me so much money to go back in time and get one.'

Tony's smile was a hungry leer as he drained his drink. 'How did you *do* that again, Demorn?'

She loved the surprise in his voice.

'There was a Five Star General in Vegas who just *loves* a long, slow drink with a sultry brunette.'

Demorn leaned in and took a fresh glass of diet cola. Her perfume was stronger than he remembered.

'I can play sultry.'

He fumbled in his suit pocket. The card was gone, back in her hands. She rolled it back through her fingers.

'Do you really want it, Tony? Do you want to be the guy in the suit, played by the hot body in the corner? They say you either Rise or Fall.'

Tony relaxed back in his chair. His expression was unreadable.

'Maybe I do want that.'

She laughed her scary laugh. Demorn really didn't care. Whenever she thought she just might, she remembered the void, sucking everything into the dying. Where all the brightness of all the stars turned into the swollen blackness. Who could care when it all led there?

Demorn tossed the card in the air.

'It's a Trinket card, Tony. One of a set. They're blessed, cursed, whatever. Mortals should be scared.'

Her green eyes blazed. Her fingers unconsciously brushed the locket beneath her shirt. Tony didn't miss much.

'You're mortal. Why aren't you scared, Demorn?'

'I'm a professional. I'm an Innocent. I've got a defense.'

Tony chuckled, leaning across to his mini-bar, getting her a diet cola with a cherry twist, sliding it across the desk to her.

'Sure you do. Such a good girl scout.'

Taking the drink she pressed the card back into his hand. It was hot in his palm, almost painful. For a moment he kept looking. His expression was unreadable.

'Be careful, Tony. Triton was all over the past like a plague. They lie. They promise false things. Don't trust it.'

'Oh, I'm careful,' Tony murmured, carefully placing the card into his suit. The red ruby ring lit up on his finger. The windows shifted electronically to total black.

'We're doing this now, Tony?'

Tony smiled. 'All part of the service, isn't it?'

'Ha. Well, you do pay the best, and you *did* marry Asanti.'

She clicked her fingers slowly, in time with an old song playing through the office. The world went away. Tony looked eerie and malevolent in the red light of the ruby ring, his features heavy-set, the lightness gone.

Demorn got up, slow dancing. She took off her leather jacket, giggling, throwing her gloves off too.

'I always feel like I'm about to strip for you. But I know you prefer blondes with much bigger tits.'

Tony guffawed as she poked her tongue. A white shadow flickered and danced in reality behind him.

'You're such an old man that way.'

He watched the hypnosis take full effect, the red ruby magic taking Demorn through the layers. She sank deep into her chair, at first restless, then growing still, until finally her green eyes glittered in the darkness and red shadows.

The card was burning in his pocket. He could feel the white shadow towering behind him. Tony seized the card from his suit, and turned it over. The insignia was gone.

FALL

There was an abyss inside the picture, a piece of nothing that promised nothing with a vicious howl. He couldn't see into the abyss, couldn't see beyond it.

FALL

Tony knew that there were legends and myths about this place. But as

Tony gazed into the picture, into the card, he knew the legends were empty, too. They were created by dead people who gave everything, dying frightened, bereft of real answers.

Shivers ran through his body, flooding his bloodstream. He wasn't supposed to feel so much. He wasn't supposed to give so much. He wasn't supposed to keep looking at the card. He was just a club owner who fought people and killed people and traded people and bought people and tried to be kind to a tiny few. He didn't understand the abyss, so real, so hyper-empty, so utterly vacant. The chasm didn't care about his dead wife, it didn't care about the club-girls, it didn't care about blow-jobs, it didn't care about Demorn, it didn't care about the nights he couldn't sleep, it didn't care about anything.

FALL

Tony blinked. He put the card back in his pocket. His hand trembled for a moment. He waited till it steadied.

The white shadow towered behind him. Just empty. Everything around him was just empty.

FALL

Demorn was a mirror, glazed and utterly vacant. He loved her, Tony knew. She loved him. And suddenly, Tony knew he wouldn't see her alive too many times. He didn't know why or how.

FALL

His hand stilled. The slow song was playing.

This was still his office, perfectly air conditioned and quiet. Demorn's purple sunglasses lay on the desk, near her fingers, restlessly shifting in their own rhythms.

Tony turned away, throwing his drink into the pitch-black window. The glass smashed into a thousand pieces. His hand was bleeding. Tony didn't care about that.

He said, 'Where is the Dead King?'

Demorn stared absently into the electronic black curtains that blocked out the brilliant sea view. She sipped slowly at her drink. She touched her face. Her pale finger caressed a long white scar that glistened down the side of her cheek.

'You always ask me this, don't you, boss?'

Tony said nothing, but after a while, he repeated, 'Where is the Dead King?'

Interlude 1 — Somebody, Somewhere

Demorn smiled, listening as the Sinatra clone toyed with the expensive dinner crowd, snapping through his monologue. She leaned against the glass window, brushing her pale fingers on the cold surface, looking down at the beautiful white clouds and the sparkly blue ocean far below the Jade Hotel.

She closed her eyes as he started crooning “Close to You,” soaking in the melody of his voice. Images of beautiful girls and boys filled her head. Soft feelings filled her heart.

The cute guy beside her suddenly caressed her face, murmuring something low and throaty under his breath. Absently, she slapped his hands away. The hands came back, and she twisted his fingers sharply, glaring at him with cold, angry eyes. Dark green sweater, pressed tan slacks, tan loafers. He looked like he belonged on a fucking yacht in the middle of the fucking ocean.

Demorn said, ‘Don’t touch me.’

He pulled a sulky face. ‘But baby, you look so lonely, and Frank is singing for young lovers.’

She almost had to laugh. ‘We might be young, but we aren’t lovers. Hands off.’

Sneering, the boy snapped, ‘You’re a cold one. That’s what they all say. A real fucking ice princess.’

‘Of course they do,’ she said softly. They always said that, all the wandering hands, all the people who wanted her to feel one way, be one way, and be somebody that she wasn’t.

His nose started bleeding. She watched, quietly amused as it dripped on his cashmere sweater. The boy looked terrified, his eyes reddening and glazing over. Demorn gripped his wrist to stop him falling to the floor.

She waved her fingers. 'Enough, enough.'

The sea of beautiful people seemed to part when Tony entered the room and came toward the booth, his large form easy and cool in an expensive suit. As Tony sat down at the table, the boy's nose stopped bleeding and he ran away fast, looking terrified.

'What is with you and new people, Demorn?' Tony said.

Demorn shrugged easily. 'I think it's just that a lot of new people are assholes, Tony. But I didn't make his nose bleed. That would be *your* pet.'

Tony grinned, holding his hand up, ordering them a drink. 'Well, you got me there, gunslinger. The Lion doesn't like new people much either.'

A slim, youngish man in a stylish white dress shirt moved smoothly in Tony's wake, collar wide, two buttons undone to show a smooth, tanned chest. His delicate purple eyes flickered across the crowd, looking for anybody not scared enough of Big Tony.

Demorn watched the Lion take a spot in the booth, the barest of winks acknowledging her.

'Hi,' she said with a half-smile. She liked this strange creature; there was something cool about his impersonal style. That didn't mean she trusted him at all.

Tony guffawed, his gold chains glinting. He looked richer every week. 'Me? I'm all about bringing people together.'

Sinatra reached the sad crescendo of his tender song, belting out the chorus while the mirror ball spun. She stopped listening to Tony, looking through the room for a snapshot of instant cool, in this exclusive hideaway so high in the sky, where life was an air-conditioned surface slide, and nobody got hurt as they floated across a minefield of elegant parties and drunken nights, where the secrets everybody had, everybody shared, and then forgot.

Demorn looked at the beautiful, anonymous, nameless women clustered on the dance floor and by the bar. Thin, tall and tanned, platinum-blonde will-o-wisps, mixed with a fair scattering of amazing brunette variants. She wondered where they would all go, in a year's time, in five years . . . would they still casually drift like lonely goddesses through these elegant soirees? Or would they become ordinary, falling to earth alongside the lesser mortals, where the parties were less beautiful, the strangers stripped of mystery, hungry for their flesh and fading glamor.

Sinatra ended the song, the stage lights flashing. He took a bow and walked off stage to the crowd's rapt applause. Tony was on his feet, clapping loudly.

'He's so good, he's so goddamn good. I got him booked all over!' he gushed. 'I'm gonna make Sinatra big again, just like when he was alive.'

She let herself believe it was true and would happen.

'How much was he?'

Tony sighed. 'Too much, kid. The developers are fucking robber barons.' He shrugged. 'But they know the punters *love* a real flesh and blood clone. They can really sell the song. It beats the hell out of those tinny cyborgs they have singing in Downtown.'

Demorn looked out to the wide open blue sky, wondering how high up they really were. The city was covered by clouds.

'Downtown has its charms,' she murmured.

Tony smiled, looking closely at her. He held out one of his big hands and took her pale hand across the table. 'Of course, kid. We *were* Downtown.'

He glanced at his flashy silver watch. 'Meantime, my clock tells me its 2 PM on a Wednesday, which means Innocents is the official order of business.'

He held his drink up. 'Salute! To our brave Innocents!'

Demorn raised her glass slightly and drained her piña colada.

For whatever reason, it was the only alcohol she liked, and she only ever drank it around Tony. He was a good time guy, he paid a lot of bills, he supported the club.

'First item, where the hell are we on the Pale Suns? 'Cause I got people on my ass *and* my assets about this thing. I heard Council members talking about it. That makes me nervous, given our connection.'

Demorn fished something out of her jacket, and slid it across the table to him. Lion stirred in his seat, then relaxed. It was a large, yellow, rotten tooth in a small plastic bag.

'I got this off a contact. He was working the Cult. I made it to the meeting.'

Tony picked up the bag, examining it closely. 'What did you see?'

'A bunch of idiots praying to a shrine with a tooth on it,' she said smiling. 'Seriously, that's what I saw. Maybe the tooth belongs to somebody important. Maybe it's just a cultist who should have gone to the dentist more often.'

Lion's voice was ice. 'The contact?'

'He's dead. Usual story. He had sympathies on both sides of the fence.'

Tony's corpulent face showed a mixture of complete disinterest and slight puzzlement. 'Double agent?'

'He liked my money. He wasn't really a believer. But there was a girl, and she was pretty, and she did believe . . .' She paused, looking deep into the glass. 'They're all dead now anyway. No trail. Just a rotten tooth.'

Tony asked, 'Do you believe it? The legend?'

Demorn could feel Lion probing hard at her mind. Real hard. She hoped the shields Smile installed and her Asanti training were solid enough. She didn't want or need Lion opening up a crack. She was honest with Tony about the things that mattered. Everything else was compartmentalized and separate.

Demorn tapped her forehead. 'Tell Lion to stop. He's been in here once, he knows what I saw in the Ice Cavern. I don't need him reading my love letters and personal fucking diary.'

Tony waved his hand at White Lion. The pressure relented on her skull. 'I trust you, kid. Things are just getting big on us awful fast. We're nervous.'

She put her glass down hard. 'Good. You should be. Because the cavern was years ago and the Suns keep manifesting here and down on Grim Earth. I've caught images in the mirrors of these cult-infested crack dens. I'm not worried about whether cult legends are real. I *know* they're real enough. I *know* it's a trans-dimensional threat. What we need is a way to stop it tearing Babelzon apart.'

Big Tony had stopped smiling and there was darkness on his face. He leaned back in his expensive suit.

'And us with it. A club on top of the Jade Hotel, the Seat on the Council, a whispered word in the Tyrant's ear. It took a lot of plays for a Downtown boss to get this far.'

He looked moodily out of the window, toward the beautiful blue sky.

'This Pale Sun thing is a tremor right now, deep down in the bowels of the city. I wonder if this will be the earthquake that fractures everything, sends us all crashing back into the waves? All the traitors and all the loyal soldiers, crashing down together.'

She didn't like this heavy mood. Demorn spoke quietly, 'Get earthquake insurance. Red Morning is gone. Don't waste your time thinking of traitors. I lead the Innocents now. You need us, we need you. I will personally kill anybody who tries to take you down.' Demorn grinned suddenly. 'I'm going to put it in the Club Charter and everything.'

Tony winked. 'I know. Be a good girl for me.'

He pushed across an envelope stuffed with notes. She quickly placed it in her jacket, weighing automatically. This would keep the Club afloat for another year.

'Thanks, boss. That's some serious Jacuzzi money.'

Tony looked at her a second longer than usual, his typically loquacious expression touched with a weight of sadness. The ruby ring flared into being on his finger.

He said, 'Where is the Dead King?'

Demorn stared absently out at the wide, empty sea. She sipped slowly at her drink.

'You always ask me this, don't you, boss?' Her eyes surveyed him, almost lazily.

He nodded. 'I can't see that Goddess you're so scared of.'

Demorn touched her cheek. Her pale finger softly caressed the long white scar that glistened.

'Whatcha think? That I'm the type to knock myself around?'

'Oh, there's something out there,' Tony purred. 'Pulling the strings on you all. It tells you to fight wars and worship it. But that doesn't mean I trust it.'

The room seemed colder. White Lion seemed to phase in and out.

'Lucky Town Casino,' she said abruptly. 'I think his bones have been there a while.'

Demorn seemed to wake up. She realised she was wearing her purple glasses and she wasn't sure when she had put them on. Demorn slowly took them off and threw them on the table. She looked at him very closely. Tony's hand slightly shook. He stilled himself. His ruby ring shone brighter for a moment.

She was still under the spell, but she was a creature of total impulse. Tony knew that. If Demorn wanted to gut him with Xalos, she could.

She turned her glazed eyes to the dance floor, empty and darkened. The Sinatra clone was a distant memory. A spectacular crystal chandelier reflected the dying reflections of the sun. It wasn't 2 PM anymore. It hadn't been for a long time.

Tony spoke carefully, focusing on letting the ruby ring slowly bring her to the surface, watching her eyes slowly lose some of their stunning fire.

'I'm right beneath the Tyrant's Eye. You know how much I hate magic. I don't trust it. But Babelzon was built on Source Stones. There is a fucking *necromancer* on the Council now. Real creeper. Turns out it isn't all sleight of hand and rabbits out of hats. I had to buy a ridiculous black coat. I feel like a Cult member. I'm waiting for the day we have to sacrifice a virgin.'

Demorn laughed lightly, almost abstractedly. 'Good luck finding one in this city.'

'If I don't have an angle, I'll fall fast.' There was a plain edge to his voice that she didn't recognise.

Demorn sighed. 'Fine, I'll be your damn angle. I want my rates adjusted for danger pay though.'

He threw out a casual question. 'Do you remember Sparky?'

She did. An annoying little jerk with electric powers and a punk attitude. She'd never let him step foot inside the Clubhouse.

'Yeah, one of your minders, before Mr Lion. Didn't you get let him go?'

'I had a bad feeling. We turned off his electric.'

Tony beamed out a small light-show from his fingernails, and she watched an insane young, thin superhero tearing apart a squad of men in black suits with guns, crazy electric streams disintegrating their bodies.

'Turns out, maybe not. We pulled this out of Texas.'

She smiled. 'Looks like things really worked out for him.'

He waved his fingers and the holo vanished. 'That footage is twelve hours old. I should have put a bullet in the back of his head.'

'I'm happy to do it for you. So, Texas?'

Tony nodded, his eyes lifeless, dark.

'I'm a shadow in Texas. I stay low down there. I want to stay that way for now.'

'So get in, turn off the electric, walk away?'

'Exactly. But meantime, find out why your magic keepers want you to go to the exact same low-rise dump casino.'

Demorn raised an eyebrow. 'You're kidding me.'

He held his finger up, the ruby ring sparkling. 'That's what you told the ring. Bones of the Dead King. Lost in Lucky Town, Texas.'

She rubbed her hand across her forehead. 'Nobody has told me anything. I haven't been back to Firethorn in years.'

'That you remember. People lie. They play games. They implant ideas in the minds of impressionable young people. Why not these things you call gods?'

Demorn's hands moved involuntarily in a warding gesture. The perfume of Alodin Mars was still on her. There were some Fates you didn't tempt.

Tony smiled. 'Don't worry, your Goddess can't get into my buildings. She can't hear what I'm saying. Demorn, I know you're not some blind worshipper. You saw what happened to Asanti. Your people survived the main event only to be swallowed by a Fracture aftershock. Where was your goddess then?'

Demorn's heart went cold. Her eyes flickered. As his corpulent face smiled, the window behind him showed Tony dressed in a dark robe, flames burning behind him, flickering on strange temple walls filled with intricate scrawls. These waking visions danced and vanished like mirages. She had so many terrible suspicions.

Tony's smile was absent of warmth. His hands gripped the couch. White Lion had vanished.

'You know what I really think?'

She looked at him calmly. 'What do you really think?'

He drained his drink. 'I think it's all a junk virtual reality. Something they cooked up to keep you passive and off their trail.'

'Who are *they*?'

'The Pale Suns. The beings that helped destroy Asanti and kill my wife. The creatures that hide in the portals. The monsters that you kill for money. They could even be the same scientists that got to your brother.'

All she could feel was cold. His words continued but in her mind she was replaying all the people in the facility she had killed to save him. Her eyes glittered like stars. Demorn smiled through her private terror of remembering the past.

'I killed them. All of them.'

'Nobody could kill them all. We have too many enemies for that, Demorn.'

'What are you saying?' she murmured.

'That I'm a businessman who understands the forces that control you.'

She could see his sweat, a taste of something desperate and sincere that wasn't normally there.

'I rent you, to kill people and get me things. But *they* buy you. They throw you a crown in a mythical land. They *like* you to be that wandering sword that so appeals to your ego. *They* wipe your mind clean. They keep you just random and dangerous enough.'

Demorn looked at him with cool amazement. 'Is this what the card burning a hole in your pocket said?'

'It doesn't matter.'

She smiled her scary smile. 'Oh yes it does. It means everything. Show it to me.'

Tony threw the card onto the table.

Demorn's eyes flickered over it, glittering. The chasm lurched into view. For her, the abyss was different. She watched it fill with the bodies of those she had slain. She saw them often. She knew those which Xalos had judged worthy of death. She knew those for whom the Sword did not burn, and she had torn them from life with her own will.

She saw the abyss fill with those she had loved. She saw it fill with all the forgotten, faces like dolls, lipstick smiles and sadness scrawled over porcelain. Demorn didn't fear such things especially. She could see much further than Tony, she could see into the base of the chasm. She could see what flickered in the depths, churning energy spirals without end. She saw the bones of those she truly loved. In the end, she had to turn her eyes away.

Demorn took the card off the table. His eyes followed it all the way to her jacket pocket.

'I told you this was a dangerous thing to covet, Tony.'

On impulse she turned back to the empty sea, leaving the couch, pressing her face against the club window, pressing the card into the glass. The twilight sky was blue and cloudless.

She saw the huge fire in the atmosphere, the sky darken with a slow inevitability, a mysterious and total terror that only she saw, extinction just for her eyes, the clouds torn apart, the water boiling, as the huge burning comet burnt and tore through the atmosphere, killing everything, a noxious cloud choking the city and the world—

'I don't know what is real. I don't think this is.'

Tony caught her as she fell, his strong arms comfortable and secure.

She pressed her body into his, kissing him on his cheek. He held her close. His expensive cologne mixed with her perfume.

As they held each other, Tony whispered in Asanti, '*May the night bury your storms.*'

She murmured back, '*And the harbor you find be a safe one.*'

And as she watched, the comet left the twilight sky, which no longer burned, and the wide sea was placid.

'This is just a waking dream, isn't it?' she said.

'It's real enough,' he said, his lips brushing her brow. 'Your dream is very shallow.'

Tony whispered in Asanti, '*May the night bury your storms.*'

She murmured back, '*And the harbor you find be a safe one.*'

Demorn looked at him closely as they parted and sat back down. She could see emotion in his eyes. Those were traditional Asanti pledges to loved ones.

'I haven't spoken Asanti since she died,' he said, the words plain and direct, not his normal smooth way.

Impulsively, Demorn kissed him again on the cheek, feeling better.

'You should speak it more often. Even if just to lose that big ol' Babelzon backstreets accent.'

Tony's laughter was a slow rumble. He laughed, starting to say good-bye. The heavy sadness was gone. He suddenly looked big and confident and rich again.

'Let me kill this Sparky punk for you,' she said slowly. 'If I get my hands on the bones of the Dead King, it's bonus back slaps all round.'

'You're right, Demorn. Do this thing for me. Then we need a night out in Downtown, get drunk at a show, throw money at some topless girls.'

She laughed. It was so comfortable, his expensive cologne mixed with her own perfume. In her mind, Sinatra was singing down on the stage again.

'That would be fun, I miss our nights out.'

'Give me the card, Demorn.'

Demorn gave him a slow mock salute, her burning eyes close to his. She passed him the card, tingling through her fingers. If she wanted, Demorn could see so much deeper. She could see his soul, a compromised and murky place, flames guttering out in the dirt. But she knew he would have hated that. Something was definitely rattling Tony. This was bigger than one ex-bodyguard going cowboy down in Texas.

Her fingers flicked imperceptibly as the salute finished. *Do you still trust me, Boss?*

His fingers moved in unfinished rhythm.

Totally BUT Be careful of Lion—

White Lion was standing, his slender frame against the glass windows, delicate purple eyes on fire, assessing them. He touched Tony's shoulder lightly. Tony paused, his attention drifting. His fingers didn't finish the sentence.

Lion glanced almost shyly at his seat. Lion never drank a drop at these meetings but he always fidgeted and sometimes scribbled notes. She saw a crumpled napkin on his plate. She scooped it into her hand. What she saw written in spidery writing made her heart turn a little cold.

I've almost finished the key to get back into your head.

She looked up fast and could see a cruel, slight smile on Lion's lips that vanished to nothing. The napkin flared and she dropped it, it was ashes by the time it hit the table. For a moment his smile was hideous, flaring brilliantly in her mind, pushing her defense right back to the scars.

You're not really here, Demorn.

She smiled her scary smile. 'Oh, I'm here Lion. Get the fuck out of my head.'

Tony was already moving away, a king shark in an ocean of baby sharks. Lion walked behind him, a dangerous, fickle white shadow. Suddenly Demorn didn't like that impersonal style any more.

She thought about the secrets that she knew, the dark alleyways and forgotten back offices of Babelzon, where the lights didn't shine on the dirty deals Tony had left in his wake and did not want to remember. Tony pretended he still knew the street, but he was a long way from her kind of action. His soldiers played out their roles in little wars and the end result didn't touch him.

Just knowing that, Demorn felt sadder than she had felt in years and for just a moment, utterly alone. The houselights dimmed, the crowd let out a hush. Sinatra walked back on for an encore. Demorn sank back into the booth, suddenly in the mood for sad songs. She whispered for her brother on her invisible club watch. Smile answered instantly, his yellow grin flickering unsteadily in the video display. He knew she wasn't messing around when she called this soon after a meeting with Tony.

'Where are you?'

'The Jade Hotel,' she murmured. 'We've got a problem.'

'Who?'

'The White Lion is onto us.'

Smile swore viciously. 'The psychic hit man!'

She shrugged. 'And whatever else he is. Who knows what they grew in those vats.'

Smile's yellow icon spun like crazy. 'They grew just about *everything*. How long do we have?'

'A week. Tony ordered me out of town. He's obsessed about Pale Suns and Dead King rumors.'

The Smile icon turned upside down and blue. 'Dead King? That's Firethorn Mojo. What does Tony know about that?'

She could hear her brother thinking, playing angles. Every step since Asanti died and they wound up in Sub-Babel had been a calculated risk.

'Tony is getting lost. What does he know?'

The two of them had played the angles together. She would take a bullet to the heart before she let anything tear them apart. She wasn't about to start lying to Smile.

She said, 'Lion got to me one night. I was a bit loose, my defense was down.'

'How long? How much?'

Demorn brushed her brow.

'The asshole got about five minutes in my head. Whatever he got, it was too much. Now he wants back in.'

Smile sighed down the line, sounding young and not as cocky. 'Well ain't that just fine and dandy.'

Sinatra hit the chorus. People in the audience were crying.

She breathed out. 'Tony had a lead down in Texas. It could lead back to Firethorn.'

'Is it that good? Firethorn is dangerous and about as predictable as a video game.'

Demorn laughed. She could feel the coldness rising in her, the dice rolling in her soul. 'Are you really scared about dangerous, baby bro?' she asked softly.

The mirror ball lit up the faces of the beautiful people. It seemed like Frank sang to a sea of makeup and glitter and windswept big hair.

'Because Babelzon will get real goddamn dangerous if I don't have something solid by next week.'

'Okay, go be brave. Who you gonna take to Texas?'

'Maybe it's time for a solo run.'

'What do I tell the Innocents?'

'Tell them the world might end in a week. Use the most serious mission code-word we ever invented. Be enigmatic and mysterious.'

He laughed loudly, his energy flowing through the connection with a sudden richness. 'That I can manage. How long are you staying in the Jade Room?'

Demorn slid her purple sunglasses back on, curling into the couch. She waved subtly at a stunning blonde waitress for another piña colada.

'Until Sinatra finishes his set.'

'You and long dead lounge singers . . .'

'Attached at the hip, I know. We might all die tomorrow, after all.'

Demorn clicked off, taking her drink off the stunning blonde. Sinatra kept singing and she let the tune carry her heart a little while, take her somewhere different, where feelings were softer and not everything was stolen. She brushed her fingers through the ashes, strewn across the purple sun logo on the tablecloth. On impulse, she got up and went to the window. They were up so high she couldn't see the City or the Sea. It was just blue sky and white billowing clouds as far as her magic eyes could see.

'I'm not here. I'm not really here,' she murmured. She didn't know to whom she spoke or why.

End Interlude

9

Demorn woke with a gasp. A moment of confusion. She was in a red chair in Tony's dark office. She let herself fall back through levels of normalcy, regulating her breathing. Tony's hefty form was slumped over his desk. His ring was faded, a barely visible sparkling rock on his finger. White Lion stood over him, fingers pressed to Tony's forehead. Blood ran from Tony's nose. A shining crystalline pyramid rotated in the air. She felt tired and hypersensitive, mind vague.

'Get your hand off him!' she growled. The pyramid crashed onto the desk. Tony stirred.

White Lion smiled his awful smile that held no kindness.

'She wakes.'

The black electronic curtains lifted to a horribly bright sky. Rows of metallic towers like glittering castles. The office slowly revolved, revealing the gorgeous expanse of the wide ocean, that alluring empty promise of freedom.

She gulped down the last of her cola. It tasted flat and stale.

'Damn right I'm awake. What are you doing to Tony?'

White Lion withdrew his hand from his forehead.

'What is it to you, little killer? You have your instructions.'

On automatic, Tony spoke, 'You're going to Texas.'

He slumped to the desk. His office was quiet. Distant lounge music played somewhere outside, filtering through the stark modern office.

She kept her eyes fixed on White Lion. A vision of ashes. A world of the dead. Horrible futures playing out in her head. And his dreadful voice for he was talking. As he did the visions faded.

'We tricked you, stupid little killer. Into the past you went and like some errant thief, you carried back the tool of your own destruction. And now the curse has infected the soul of your patron. He will fall and so will the parasites that feed off him.'

Demorn smiled her scary smile. 'Oh, the past. I'd forgotten about the past.'

She held a finger to her right eye. 'Easy to do when you look to the future.'

His purple eyes were sick. 'What do you see?'

'Just a little bit. It's a party trick I picked up on the road.'

She took off her purple glasses. Her eyes were stars. Magic laced through her.

WHAT DO YOU SEE!

'For you? Death and/or torture mostly. In the end, the Triton lose patience with you. You're too random and too cruel. It isn't good for business, and like all experiments you had to be ended someday. Tony isn't in the office when they come. Maybe he's with me. The Triton take their time, and I don't blame them, not for that anyway.'

White Lion backed away. She could see spirals of energy uncoiling off him, sharp and dangerous.

Arrogance tinged with a hiss. 'You don't know the first thing about me.'

Demorn's laugh was sad. 'You're right. I only know the end, where you crawl through the office with a ruined body and mind, choking on blood.'

His skin ripped and a jagged claw tore through the air, wild and coated in barely controlled energy. At the last moment her blocking arm caught the energy claw, cutting her. His purple eyes danced insanely. The claw dug into her leather jacket, burning. Demorn focused her mind. With great effort she expelled the energy claw. The projection died out, the claw sailing back into his ruined face with the glacial smile and cold eyes.

'You're weaker than you think, Lion.'

He drifted up from the floor, the body just a puppet now, like it always had been somehow, jerking like a broken thing, bones snapping. The energy projections formed around him, animalistic and savage, his purple eyes coalescing into a series of multilayered lids in the belly of this strange beast. He spoke and it was through her mind again. She could hear distant wind chimes in his voice.

YOU WILL NOT SURVIVE YOU WILL DIE YOUNG NOTHING HAS BEEN WRITTEN ALL CAN BE CHANGED.

Demorn laughed, but there was no hope or humour in her. Xalos sprang from her chest, a warm, almost comforting pain. The blade danced with intense purple fire.

'Oh, it can change, but not by much, and not for you.'

She grasped the locket hard and felt the power surge through her. Her hand became a fist of steel. Hate clawed through her.

'Come try kill me, monster, come try kill me.'

The energy creature that was White Lion was everywhere, her mind dancing off a thousand reflections that became ten thousand, and that again, exploding close but not quite to infinity. Her sword tore through the air in tight circles, and she was dressed in the dark kimono. Slick blood ran down her arm. He was not one thing, he was many creatures, filled with lit hungry souls, some terrible sick darkness, and her blade killed so many of them.

They sang to her mind, not wholly evil, some corrupt, some imprisoned, some old things wanting to die. But the Lion was not weak and he did not want die. The energy claws and the teeth struck her countless times, although she did not feel much, lost in the savagery. The longer she fought, the more the locket overtook her. The pain and the wounds upon her body fed her, making her invincible, almost utterly evil in her soul.

Demorn had only the barest grip on who she was or had been. Her heart beat like ten thousand drums, and her eyes blazed like stars. The name of the mighty Goddess of Pain who had controlled the fate of nations thundered through her.

Mictecaciuatl, Mictecaciuatl, Mictecaciuatl. Slayer of cities, world killer. The gigantic energy animal soul-screamed. Lion's multi-layered eyes all gazing at her, hypnotic and poisonous.

YOU SHOULD BE DEAD YOU SHOULD BE DEAD MICTECACIUATL FLOATS IN THE VOID WITH THE CARCASS OF THE LOST GODS.

'I'm not dead, I'm not dead, I'M NOT DEAD!' Demorn cried, focusing on the flames and the pain, slashing at the white energy claws that thrashed around her. Ice blood ran in her veins. Pain almost blinded her. Through everything, she saw the creatures that lay inside the Lion, in all their hideous glory, the energy construct that fed through the gaps of the fabric of reality via the experiments of Triton, filling the hollow shell.

Demorn screamed in Asanti, holding onto her own mind, as she slid Xalos into him. The energy filled her mind, they were bonded, Lion's thoughts bleeding into hers. The chimes under his mind-voice became music that was the backdrop to everything. It didn't matter about good and evil, not with the universe being so big, swallowing up her tiny point of view, those few insignificant wishes and hopes she had left. An infant's scrawl on the walls of infinity. Her eyes filled with tears. No matter what cruelty had been done to the White Lion, the music and the power of the beings who possessed his shell were magnificent and elegant.

Then it was over. Her sword lay in the belly of the beast, jagged energy spirals pouring around the terrible wound. Lion's mind-voice died to a quiet whisper of rage, then nothing. As it faded, she felt a strange flicker, a connection to a whole reality die out. It would be many years until Demorn fully forgot the feeling of empty loss that pervaded her, a door to a series of possible universes closing.

White Lion lay on the ground, his white suit covered in blood. Slowly, she realised most of the blood was her own. White Lion was curiously undamaged. Cuts and stab wounds covered her.

She grasped the locket, pain laced her heart. Instantly much of the blood dried, her wounds and cuts closing and healing. She saw his mind was utterly destroyed. The wounds upon his mind and soul were gaping areas of huge loss. Empty ruined spaces where once had lay conduits to dark gods. That his physical body was unmarked made it more horrible.

She fought the urge to throw up.

Lion's eyes opened, weak pale purple. 'You know what I am, then.'

Demorn put her boot upon his throat.

'*Were.* You're nothing anymore.'

Lion went to speak. She clamped her foot down harder on his throat, holding her finger to her lips.

'You never built a key for me, did you? It was just a bunch of dark spirits floating around in your head, and you getting me drunk one night. That's so lame.'

He was starting to choke. Demorn barely resisted the urge to crush his windpipe, releasing her foot.

Tony woke up, disorientated and unsure. He loosened his tie, looking at the office, which showed signs of the disturbance, a broken chair, one of her throwing stars in a painting.

'What the hell happened in here?'

Demorn helped White Lion up from the floor. He was light, almost weightless in her hand.

'Lion and I had an exchange of views.'

Tony looked at his ruined painting. 'Somebody could have woken me up to act as moderator.'

White Lion looked at Tony desperately. He seemed lost and distracted. The infamous mental pressure was absent.

'She's crazy, Tony! She's possessed by—'

Demorn slapped him viciously across the face with her steel fist, sending the slender White Lion crashing onto the desk, back down to the floor.

'Stay out of my life and stay out of my club.'

White Lion ran from the room into the outer office. Watching impassively, Tony flicked a switch under his desk. Lion hadn't even made it to the foyer before Taser waves ran through him, and he dropped to the sheer white floor. The drop was silent, but she heard a distant psychic wail.

Tony leaned back in his chair. His eyebrows raised. 'Could you at least put the sword away and pull up a seat, Demorn?'

Demorn slid the katana into the scabbard, chuckling as she sat down. It faded from her back.

'You didn't even ask for his side of the story, boss. I could be lying. He could be innocent.'

'Lion's never been innocent, and I've never trusted him. And you don't lie Demorn, not to me.'

There was a moment of soft silence between them. The office revolved, revealing the dazzling ocean view at sunset. She always looked out at it with longing. Somewhere across it lay freedom. Tony leaned back in his chair. The soft lounge music from outside was soothing.

Tony's gaggle of employees went back about their work, deliberately ignoring Lion, still twitching with the electricity pouring through him.

'What a weird day,' she said.

'It's up there, kid. I obviously missed a few plays.'

'Sorry about the painting. Lion tried to kill me, if that counts.'

Tony sighed. 'He's kind of a prick like that. Did we even have the Wednesday meeting in the Jade Room?'

She shook her head, 'Nah, Lion has been doing some weird mind control juju on us. The last meeting was all in our minds. We were in this room the whole time.'

Tony poured them fresh drinks, cola for her, his usual scotch on the rocks. 'Well, at least that explains why my ass feels like it's been dead for three days.'

'In case you forgot, you promised me a raise on my next job,' Demorn said, taking her cola.

'How fortunate you remember that. So, you're not possessed?' He pointed to the hand resting in her lap. 'But you *do* have metal fists?'

She laughed, slowly flexing her hand as it became normal skin again.

'I got a locket on my adventures, Tony. It belonged to a pain goddess. I tap into her powers. I can *get* metal fists.'

His face was totally blank, just like when he signed the cheques. 'A pain goddess? So, it's really, *really*, safe then?'

'Sure it is,' Demorn said, wearing her scary smile. She put her jacket back on. 'I'd get so mad if this was all just an excuse to make me strip, y'know.'

Tony smiled back, despite his complete exhaustion. 'I vaguely remember something about a card . . .'

She held his gaze. Visions of Tony danced through her mind, futures, possible and dead. She saw him in the office covered in blood, Triton torturing him. She saw him in the Temple, the rest of the Council hanging in the air around him, evil power leeching off the ceremony of the damned. She saw him walking through a beautiful garden, older, at peace, no more blood on his aura.

The visions faded, all of them. It was just regular Tony with his dark suit and the distance in his eyes.

Demorn said, 'A high level totem card is currently burning a hole in my jacket. It could ruin you or it could save you. Do you want to see it?'

Tony shrugged. 'Who knows what I want? I've been in this office all day. I wonder when we ate last.'

'No idea, but I'd *kill* for take-out.'

'Well, call me the Dreamweaver. I can get us great Italian and prevent a homicide.'

Demorn laughed. He buzzed his receptionist with the order. Suddenly it all seemed so silly. To act frightened when you weren't. To not grasp onto each living day. To run from love, when it was so short a span. It was all so short. While the world turned burning.

'How about we take the afternoon off and listen to Beatles songs?' she said. 'We can let the music decide how we feel about totems.'

Tony's laughter was a slow rumble of surprise. He took her hand. 'What a fantastic idea.'

Demorn reached into her jacket and put the totem card face down on the desk, where it trembled with power. She felt her heart throbbing, blood pumping through her body, in synch with the totem's power and heartbeat. The Triton pyramid shone a savage green. Tony grasped the pyramid, his face lighting up with the hazy glow. Her hand was wrapped around his. An electric power flooded them both.

The Beatles were playing the *Revolver* album out of nowhere. The room darkened as the sun sank fast into the wide ocean, dying just to be reborn. She looked at Tony and he was twenty years younger, his face lighter under the glow. Mini pyramids of power floated in the room, ripe with potential untapped. The sun was rising and falling into the ocean. Her magic eyes saw the glistening connections between the pyramids. She saw tomb worlds, extinction events. She saw source worlds, radiating with the hunger of beginning. In the corner of the office, Demorn saw the familiar shadow of a blonde girl turning away. She felt her heart tremble. She knew that haircut, she knew that face.

With her free hand, Demorn turned the card over. It glistened golden and burning.

ARISEN

She looked at Tony, gazing down at the same card. He was lost in his own fantasy and she wondered what he saw. Were they all lost in their private universes, tumbling through infinity? The pyramids span. The blonde girl was floating in the air, mediating, partially nude, totally beautiful.

ARISEN

Demorn knew her name. She loved her, and she remembered her name. The Beatles sang. Softly Demorn felt herself rise into the air, away from Tony's grip. He looked at her with tender eyes that were filled with hurt. She smiled, the world frozen and slow.

ARISEN

Then she was next to the blonde girl, and they were holding each other, in this strange magic place with the power of the pyramids searing into them. And there was nothing more to say. Just a beautiful blonde girl who kissed her with all her soul. There was nothing more to say. She was a killer who had been bled empty, filling back up with feelings.

ARISEN

Part 2

1

The short red cloak of Toxis rose high on her gleaming muscled legs. A red veil covered her face. Her eyes were blue lasers. The agency lobby was as frozen as a spring midday under the haunted blue sky. The pretty receptionist cast the huntress another in a long series of wary glances, as he pretended to check things on his computer. Toxis enjoyed catching his eye every single time, making him slowly more terrified.

Demorn moved smoothly through the sheer white office space, her business with her boss done at last. Toxis fractionally bowed her head in greeting. Demorn ran to the hunter, greeting her with a tight hug. Their golden armbands burned orange red.

Toxis mind voice was urgent.

I was woken in the dawn by the Blood Sisters. They say you have found the trail of the Dead King.

'I've caught a scent. How long was your sleep?'

Many weeks. My wounds were deep but the River has healed me.

Demorn slid her purple glasses on.

'You really are in the wars back there, hey.'

Firethorn has been at War my whole life.

Demorn laughed. 'My life too.'

Toxis was puzzled. ***No, you ruled over much peace. And will again if we defeat our enemies.***

'Well, just a day would be nice,' Demorn said. Her voice dripped with sarcasm. They vanished together.

The pretty receptionist breathed a sigh of relief. These weird visitors who didn't take the lift put him off his lunch and made him think of questions he never wanted answers to.

• • •

The two of them phased into Sub-Babel. This was at the very top of the tower. The glass roof and windows above them swirled with purple Source energies. Demorn could see the city beyond like a strange mirage, Babelzon becoming a distorted mirror of itself, shifting to bare desert sands.

Toxis dropped her red veil. Her hair was longer than the last time Demorn had seen her. A tattoo of a flaming sun lay upon her dark cheek. Her body was muscled and tight. Toxis's lithe fingers unconsciously drifted across a thin scar across her hard abs. She looked suspiciously into the depths of the machine.

Demorn said, 'I did that, y'know. The wound. I'm sorry.'

Toxis was looking into the purple storm, with intense blue eyes that held no anger.

I assumed it was so. Xalos cuts deep.

'And you don't care about why, or how?'

Toxis shrugged, such things were very boring to her.

The River washes away much, Sister. Our short battles belong to another life. I was reborn with a clean soul. It is the way of the Hunt.

'How very Zen,' Demorn murmured, curious. 'That's an impressive tattoo.'

Toxis sneered.

It is the price paid to keep our peace treaty with the Swords of the Sun.

Demorn glanced sharply at her. 'A branding?'

In return, the Swords wear the Blood Clan crest on their faces. Such is the deal struck in desperate times. Rather this than the Swords burning the White Fort while we fight the demons in the ice caverns.

'Are things in Firethorn that rough?'

The ice caverns teem with waves of our enemies. My Sisters hunt in packs through dead, forgotten cities, seeking to turn the tide. In the Deep South, the Swords fight death-worms rising from the very bowels of the earth. And each time I cross to this world the day is shorter upon my return to the White Fort. Night will fall soon.

Demorn brushed the golden armband. 'I had no idea. I haven't been back in years. I feel distant.'

Worry not. If our kinship was severed, and the Fates had died, we would no longer wear the armband. I would not remember our bond. We would pass by the other, strangers into darkness.

'You make it sound so simple.'

Toxis spoke aloud, as she so rarely did. Her voice was a soft whisper.

'I have journeyed to the forbidden Oracle and I have seen the future if we fail. It is worse than either of our deaths, worse than the white walls of Firethorn falling to the hordes. I saw a nightmare world where the dead cry to a dead god. A grave world where the exiled ones have eaten what is left of the universe and still hunger. And so they come back, questing through time, to eat again, when the world was ripe and thriving.'

Ice went down Demorn's spine. The exiled ones traveling through time. What she had seen in Vegas. Triton. She forced herself to speak with a casualness she didn't feel.

'I don't even remember what the prophecy says. I barely remember the Oracle. It's covered in mist. The longer I stay here, the more it feels like a TV show with hot girls and shootouts.'

Toxis looked at her with bloody eyes.

The prophecy says you are a wandering vision of death who will come only in the most urgent hours of need. The Sword Princess who will save the White Fort and win back the Glass Crown.

'I've always liked that version,' Demorn said.

Toxis was quiet for a moment. ***There are many prophets. You have come before, you will come again.***

Demorn laughed her scary laugh. Together they watched as the Sub-Babel energies churned, phasing around the dome. She put her hand against the glass roof; it was warm to her touch. The Portal opened, glistening in the sky, an open wound bleeding silver.

Toxis murmured a strange curse against the gods. The purple clouds dispersed. The tear in reality hung there, transfixing them both. There was nothing inside the tear. No sky. The stars had died. For minutes that seemed like years they hung in the twilight lands, beyond what was real and what wasn't.

Demorn gently took the hand of the huntress. 'Babelzon lies at a distant axis from most other realities. The translation is just taking longer than normal. It's nothing to be scared of.'

Toxis groaned, doubling almost in pain. Her dark hand gripped the ash staff, sliding it off her back.

Can you not see the machines of suffering?

The glass was shivering. Demorn looked back over the enormous cityscape far beneath them, eerie and ghost-like. At the edge of her awareness, she saw great millstones, a giant, churning engine, moving within this reality and outside of it, connected to the fabric of everything. Grey metal wheels, spiked and very ancient. For the first time, Demorn saw the chains of the Universe. She was filled with an overwhelming sadness as the spiked engine slowly turned, a complete sense of loss for which there was no name, deep with raw tears, ravaged of any kindness or blessing. But she couldn't name what made her feel so alone, so bereft of love or kindness. She couldn't remember anyone, nothing sweet, nothing real. Just the fog of nothingness, this wasteland of oblivion.

'They say not to look into Sub-Space,' she whispered.

Demorn tore her eyes away with a visible effort that left her shuddering. Images of the blonde girl she loved flickered through her mind and she held onto that. She looked at Toxis. Her eyes were blood red and tinged with fever.

Could the King lie inside the wasteland of the machine?

Demorn shook her head. 'The Dead King hangs onto the world of living. But out there . . . is a soulless place of no name, a ghost of reality, not even a reflection. Nothing truly lives inside it. Pay it no further mind.'

Demorn clicked her fingers, blackening the windows. The Dome felt vast and lonely. Nothing was easy and light anymore. Would it ever be again?

Toxis had drawn a protection symbol in blood across the window that burned like fire. Upon the wall, two pods flickered, disgorged from the machine. Toxis took a small, ornate wooden box from her red cloak.

My Sisters gave me this. It is the token of my crossing.

Demorn opened it carefully. Inside lay a small beautiful doll, dark brunette hair on an icy porcelain face, spread-eagled on the satin lining. She wore a short red and black ballerina dress. Small pointed teeth glinted behind the full red-painted lips.

'A vampire doll!'

Toxis' voice was unusually sad and poignant. ***It is a Blood Icon of my Clan, gained at great cost.***

Her fingers felt across the light scar again. Toxis looked at Demorn with a blank hunger, exhaustion upon her face.

Feed the doll your blood. She will tell you secrets, Princess.

Demorn laid Toxis down in the pink-lit pod, the Hunter curling into slumber, as the passive lights swept across her. Demorn closed the pod. Then she held a finger over the box, nicking her ring finger with a small blade. A droplet fell upon the doll's tight black dress. The doll animated, reaching out a small, graceful finger, taking the droplet from her dress, swallowing it. She began to dance slowly, seductively unbuttoning a layer of her clothes, losing her top as an electronic hum came from the box.

Demorn's heart quickened as the box began to play a grinding club tune, and the dancing of the doll became frantic, on the verge of no control, thrashing against the sleek walls of the box, lights bouncing off the walls, her white-ghost skin glistening, every move more vivid as the doll was lost in the tune, becoming it. Suddenly it was over and the vampire doll was spent, looking with red eyes up to Demorn. Her dress was discarded and torn, her long black hair a mess as she sank into a long couch that appeared from nowhere.

'What vacant lonely eyes you have,' drawled the little doll. She hitched her dress and adjusted her lacy black bra. 'What do you want, sweet Princess, while I'm here, all breathless, sated by your lovely bittersweet blood?'

'I seek a way back home, to Firethorn. I am exiled.'

'Ohhh,' the doll murmured, striking odd words. 'That's *where* we are *then, when* the King is dead, and the gates to Firethorn are closed . . .'

The Ballerina twirled absently, continuing soft and dreamily. 'He's in a dark room, a long way from this place. A light is blinking on and off and he has a cold heart. Why do you want him?' she asked absently.

Is she even talking about the Dead King, Demorn thought in frustration.

'I can see the Glass Crown shining upon you, as in bygone ages, I can see the blood upon the tall spikes. You are ascendant, you are the Princess of the Skulls and the Sword and your legend ECHOES—'

'Hush!' Demorn said severely.

The doll stopped, almost puzzled, seeming to consider different versions of the story. She half-sang lost ditties and sipped on the blood. Her attention wandered. She held a small vanity mirror to her pretty face, playing with her hair.

'It's such horseshit to say vampires are invisible in mirrors. How do they think we do our hair?' She yawned, tossing the mirror into the corner of her box. 'Everybody knows I'm obsessed with appearances. Goodnight, Green Eyes, dream deeply in a shallow world.'

The vampire doll drifted to sleep on the long couch, limbs akimbo. Demorn felt slightly like a voyeur and she closed the box. The soft tune cut off. She opened the other glistening pod. They were deep inside the Portal. The windows had opened again. Murky creatures that might not have been real drifted through the clouds. The deeper Demorn looked, she could see echoes of old movies. Dead TV stars, pop culture junk memories.

Demorn slid her purple sunglasses on, turning her implant on, letting the songs inside her head drown out the questions. She sank into the soft cushions, fingers closed around the doll box. The pink glass slid across her face, nerves tingling with anticipation.

The silver wound tore open above them, exposing a gaping blackness where the sky should have been. This was the Void, a whispering dream of horrors. Memories danced, eyes wet with tears, Demorn's hands grasped tightly against the pink cushions of the pod, no longer sure what was real or what that meant.

She saw a beautiful girl again, she saw Kate, long blonde hair shining in the sun, pretty face laughing at some joke, flashing a golden bracelet around her thin wrist. It was the same dream, Demorn realised, the same one I always have. Her last thought was of Kate, she cared for little else.

Interlude 2 — Pop Songs

Demorn was inside the ice cavern, underneath the layered tombs, hideous visages and ceremonies of death. She was covered in white body armour, slick red stripes. The pain locket was gone, skin raw across her throat where it had once lay. She couldn't remember much of what happened before. The taste of blood was on her lips.

The cavern was completely dark, no external light. Her burning magic eyes could see deeply in the blackness. Operating on instincts, Demorn's hands flickered over the sarcophagus. She found the code and punched it. The coffin swung open.

Inside, Kate lay frozen, eyes closed, face blue. She was older now, touching early twenties, her blonde hair very long, covering a gorgeous body. As Demorn gently took her from the coffin, Kate lightly coughed, drawing fragile breath. Her body quickly gathered warmth and Demorn's magic eyes filled with tears, because it was suddenly so horribly real.

'Demorn! How did you do it?'

She laughed with an edge. 'Persistence. I never give up.'

She gathered Kate, her gun hand drawn, as they started back up the ice tunnel. She glanced at the layered tombs, filled with frozen people. No time to save them. No profit. She heard movement close by. The audio channel in her helmet caught garbled trader speak. Her name. Haggling on price.

The pearl-handled pistol shuddered in her hands, laser burst lighting up a small group of shadowy enemies. They moved fast, but she was faster, cutting them down inside the tunnel. They fired back, rapid fire spray. Demorn hustled against the tombs to take cover. They weren't clever or fast enough. The fight went on for a few minutes more. When it was over, Demorn kicked at one of the corpses, draped in weird black leathers.

It was a cloned young boy, his data code ripped into his neck. Merc scouts. She even knew the model type. She'd even known the boy they'd based it on, but he was dead now and he'd been a lot better than these cut price rip offs.

Kate breathed quickly, her body warm and tight against Demorn.

'I like your new perfume. It's fresh.'

'Thanks. It feels like we're forever doing this.'

Kate's lips brushed her armoured face.

'Have we even been introduced formally?'

Demorn's laughter was a throaty chuckle. They kept moving. The taste of blood stayed on Demorn's lips.

End Interlude

2

The portal hung above like a purple scar in the night sky. A sleek black Jag was parked on a dead side street.

Everything on the strip was rundown and seedy. Neon billboards for entertainers well past their prime covered the storefronts. A neon ghost-town, empty of real people. Across the road from the Jag a flashing sign flickered red and blue on the side of a squat, ugly casino.

ROLL THE DICE AT LUCKY TOWN, flashing red to blue, blue to red. ROLL THE DICE AT LUCKY TOWN.

A man exploded out of a window near the top of the building, shattering glass onto the empty road. He smashed down on the street, grunting heavily when he hit. Three arrows stuck from his side, shimmering faintly red.

He moved slowly across the ground, hurt, not dead. He was clad in a cheesy and cheap looking silver suit. Demorn soared out of the same shattered window. She landed cat-like on the neon-lit street, and she spoke from the darkness.

'At least you missed my car, Sparky.'

Demorn stepped into the neon light, her purple sunglasses sparkling. Her katana was drenched in blood. She wore a cartoon skull t-shirt, tight black jeans, black boots.

'Now where'd you hide his bag of bones?'

Sparky sneered up at her, all three-day stubble and crazy eyes. Clearly hopped up, Demorn thought.

'You look even more like a teenage whore these days,' he slurred.

She gave him a hard, fast kick across the face.

'Well, at least I'm keeping my looks. Meanwhile, you look like an underfed rat, Sparky. And you were one of Tony's most handsome boys.'

She pointed the katana at him. 'Don't make me cut up what's left of that pretty face.'

Sparky spat the words at her. 'I'll never tell.'

Demorn smirked. 'Oh, you *want* it the hard way.'

He snarled, holding his hands up. Electricity flowed from the neon signs and the street lights, fed directly into his fingers. Sparky slowly dragged himself up, energy crackling into his body. The arrow wounds began to heal.

Demorn raised an eyebrow. 'Man, that is a really *terrible* costume! It's like you haven't read a comic since the early '80s and think supervillians actually dress like that.'

Sparky looked self-consciously down at his clothes, a cheap-looking silver Lycra suit with a great big red lightning strike across it. Grinning, Sparky held his right hand out, shorting out the big casino sign, leaving just the word LUCKY.

'The clients love it! They tip BIG!'

He really is a cheap little punk, she thought. But a punk who'd always had a few extra volts in him. Already he looked much healthier, though still batshit crazy. The arrows burned, breaking off his body. The sign spluttered, totally burnt out.

'You wouldn't be so tough in a blackout,' she said dryly.

Sparky's manic eyes flared. 'You're gonna FRY now, bitch!'

He charged forward screaming, hands pulsating with raw energy. Demorn sneered, rotating in a vicious spin kick, striking Sparky hard, smashing his face, breaking his nose. The kick knocked him backward. The katana swept through the air, blood arcing out of his chest. Demorn landed on graceful feet.

There was a single, long bloody gash cut across the lightning bolt and the lame silver suit. Sparky looked pathetically surprised. In one motion she cleaned the katana across his suit and then sheathed the blade in the scabbard on her back.

She could think of a lot of one-liners but they all felt mechanical and too petty. She pulled the pistol from her leg holster, pointing it at him almost casually.

'Final chance, Sparky.' She shot into the sidewalk, both sides of him, the bullets ricocheting away. 'Any death-bed confessions?'

Sparky looked away, shattered.

She pumped a round into his leg. He screamed. She let him.

'Play with me. Where'd you hide the bones?'

But Sparky just screamed weak abuse, his fingers outstretched, clawing for distant energy sources, seeking to heal his shattered body. Traffic lights on the next block exploded, feeding him a trickle of power.

Not this time.

'Tony says go fuck yourself.'

She discharged the pistol into Sparky's chest, three shots point blank. The bullets slammed into him, the pistol flash reflecting in her purple glass-es. Her face showed no emotion or movement. She felt nothing, just a cold determination to get the job done.

'For the Dead King,' she breathed in Asanti.

Princess.

Demorn looked up to the window. The locket around her neck sparkled and she flew up to the broken window, gracefully landing inside the casino. Looking at it with fresh eyes, Demorn couldn't help but notice the run-down decor of the place, a dated Western-themed faded glam.

It was the kind of place it was hard to put a decade on, somewhere that was always twenty years back. Ten bodies lay scattered throughout the room, scattered on tables and across the bar. They all had a single arrow sticking in them. Most of the corpses were sleazy businessmen in suits. A couple of heavy-set bouncers and two dead, busty hookers completed the pack. The job had been thorough, professional, unsentimental.

Toxis was crouched on the bar, her red cloak riding high, hood and veil pulled over her face. A long bow was slung across her back. Her dark sleek hands held the final bouncer; she snapped his neck. She turned to look at Demorn, coming in through the window. Flashing blue eyes through the hood. A trickle of blood ran from her lip. Toxis wiped it away with one sleek finger.

They are all dead, Princess.

Toxis jumped off the bar, showing off her muscled legs. Demorn looked at all the dead.

'That's some quality shooting in a tight spot. Well, I turned Sparky's lights out. He didn't have anything to say, though. We aren't much closer to the Bones or those Pale Suns.'

She took a sceptical glance at the decor, all wood panels and TV screens playing minor league baseball.

'They wouldn't be caught dead in a crummy dump like this.'

She looked at the trickle of blood on Toxis's finger.

'Thirsty?'

I am celebrating the Hunt.

'Well, rock on.'

Toxis took something from her cloak.

He was wearing this.

She flicked it to Demorn. It was a silver ring, with the face of an old man upon it. It seemed both cheap and priceless. As she turned it in her palm, one eye of the old man glistened while the other pulsated with black.

'An Odin Ring.'

She closed it in her fist, looking at the crappy bar and the dead businessmen.

'The Ballerina was right then. How did these mooks get hold of such heavy mojo?'

She looked at the cards scattered on one of the poker tables. She shuffled through them fast, the cards flicking through her nimble fingers. Demorn took off the sunglasses and put them on the table. She felt younger with them off, softer somehow. Her eyes were a very bright green as she dealt the cards face up across the deck. Instead of standard house playing cards, they were tarot cards of Death, twisted variations of the King and Joker cards.

Toxis placed her hand softly on Demorn's shoulder.

I sense dark magic here, Princess. I would not keep the holy glasses off.

Demorn was far away as she gazed at the Death and Joker cards. Her eyes suddenly caught aflame.

'The holy glasses give me a headache. Even killing that loser fed me back some energy.'

She glanced around the room, instincts flaring. The house stereo started playing. The TV screens on the wall all switched to an old hobo looking guy in a cowboy hat singing some old song about damnation. One of the dead businessmen staggered to his feet. Rock started to surround him. His face morphed to rock, then his entire body, as stone pushed through and past his skin.

'Gross,' Demorn murmured.

Toxis fired an arrow into him but it shattered on the rock forming over his old skin. His suit burst. The transformation looked painful. The eyes of the dead man glowed bright red when his whole face turned to rock. Toxis flung herself at the rock monster, her staff-spike out. But lightning fast though she was, the monster caught her in his great hand, and tossed her across the room. Toxis landed on her feet, like a tossed cat, bruised but unbroken.

A massive burning sword appeared in front of the rock creature which he grasped with both hands. Terror flared in Demorn. It was Xalos. He carried Xalos. Demorn felt weakness and the intimation of loss. But she quieted her fears.

The monster rumbled, 'I do not come for you, Toxis of Firethorn.'

The sword was inscribed with glowing, arcane symbols.

'I come for the Princess of the Swords. I bring Justice for her crimes!'

Demorn pulled her katana out, and went into a crouching fight stance.

'You missed a memo, Rocky. One, that's my sword, I've been looking for it. Two, I'm the one who supplies the Justice.'

She waved a thumb at the dead businessmen. 'They were the bad guys.'

He was even more rock-like now, totally inhuman. His voice rolled out like thunder, undeniable and true. 'You are soaked in the blood of innocents. Justice must find the guilty.'

Demorn grinned, alive and happy. 'I'm soaked in blood but I don't know about innocents.'

Toxis laughed quietly in her mind. ***Your sins are mine, Princess. We fight, live or die.***

In unison they leaped at the rock monster, Toxis with her staff whirling, Demorn with her katana blade gleaming with the light from the slot machines and faded western glam. Xalos smashed into her katana, parrying her cut with a wall of iron and fire. It shuddered through her arms and a wave of heat passed across her.

Ignoring Toxis, the monster punched Demorn with his massive hand. She dodged, her head evading the main impact. He struck her shoulder, sending her tumbling to the ground.

The rock monster raised his arms, holding the massive Sword, preparing for the final kill blow. Flames glowed upon the huge blade, reflecting in her eyes, the inscriptions flickering and promising a death and darkness which she would almost welcome.

'Justice is BLIND,' the monster intoned.

From the ground, Demorn sneered at him, weary of it all, the drama, the bravado. 'Have I shown you my ring, Rocky?'

She pointed the Odin ring at him, closing her eyes and focusing her mind on the pure white fire. The monster moaned as the rock in his face crumbled and split. Demorn jumped to her feet nimbly. The creature staggered back. She saw pieces of flesh reappearing. She moved fast and slid the katana into the spaces between the rock.

Demorn whispered in his rock ear as she dug the katana in. 'You actually talk about Justice mid-fight? You're like a bad late night courtroom drama.' The blade seared into his flesh slowly, and then she cut up. 'Slow and BORING.'

As the red eyes faded out, the TVs went to blank static and then to black. The hobo in the cowboy hat singing country songs faded away, his low, slow drawl a few beats behind the pictures.

'Man, I loathe modern country. Give me Johnny Cash any day,' she said dryly.

The rock covering the monster had almost fully crumbled now. His face returned to human, just another sleazy, overweight businessman. As the magic of Xalos left, the combined wounds from the arrow and the blade grew too great. He gasped, dying. With a trace of something like sympathy, Demorn held his body from falling.

'Why,' he rasped. 'Why do you keep killing me?'

Demorn brushed his grey, almost undead face with her hand, tenderly.

'You did my kingdom wrong. I am revenge.'

He choked out a response. 'I have a family in LA, a wife and kid, I was a good man for years . . .'

Her face went cold. Demorn sliced the blade up into his body. 'It's not how you died.'

The last of the rock vanished. She withdrew the katana, wiping it clean, pushing his body to the ground with her boot. The ghostly image of Xalos had disappeared. Demorn felt vague and distant, looking over the ruined gaming room. Toxis flashed across her mind with the Innocents' chant.

For the Dead King. For the Dead King.

Demorn looked across the room. Blood was all over the table, staining the cards that showed the Joker and Death. She brushed her gloved hands over the cards and every card was a nightmarish variation of the King and

Queen. They wore vaguely familiar faces on the cards of people she had known long ago. She flung them back on the table. Sometimes, her eyes saw too much.

'It's for somebody I guess.'

Suddenly all the screens on the TVs changed again, reflecting a simple graphic. Two words, in a language she did not know in orange and white lettering. It was on every screen in the room, glittering for a second.

Demorn braced, waiting for something to happen amongst the fresh dead. But nothing happened. Except the code that kept rhythmically flashing. She saw a few candles lit in the deepest shadows of the room, flickering in the glow of the poker machines.

Demorn brushed the expensive suit jacket of the man she just killed. She took his wallet from the inside pocket, finding a small, sharp black claw icon within a series of money clips.

Demorn rolled the black claw through her pale fingers.

'We've come in the middle of a summoning. And Mr Innocent, with the trophy wife and kids, he was their Claw, their Head Mojo.'

She played with the claw a little, then tossed it with a sudden anger, breaking up the candles scattered in this corner of the room. It was just a token now, robbed of power.

What do they summon?

'The usual, no doubt. Evil cultists aren't that original. A minor league demon, a wandering poltergeist, echoes of real horror. Creatures they thought they could put on a leash.'

Demorn thought of the Rock Monster, bursting through the human's skin, blood and skin everywhere.

'But they're always wrong about that, when the bill comes due.'

An action figure lay on the ground in the middle of the small black candles. She examined it, a hyper-realistic and colourful superhero in fight mode, clad in red pants with a bare, ripped chest. Strange blue tattoos were laid into his skin. A giant wrecking flail lay in his hands.

Demorn looked up at the glowing words on TV screens, phasing in and out, in tune with her memories of long ago. Slowly the code words deciphered.

WRECKING BALL WRECKING BALL WRECKING BALL

She murmured an old prayer, her fingers warding protection rituals.

'Wrecking Ball. He was a character in a video game I played years ago. We played it on the Spire, fleeing the ruins of Asanti.'

Was he evil?

She laughed wryly. 'I have no idea, it was a fighting game. It was every man and scantily-clad teenage girl for themselves. He had a mysterious back story. He was kinda hot, and he carried a huge, over-powered wrecking ball that he liked to kick ass with.'

Demorn casually flung an energy star from her wrist sleeve into the biggest TV in the room, blowing it up. The energy blast arced out and took out all the TVs.

'Now someone is invoking him here. I'm not ready for that kind of crazy yet.'

Demorn smiled, seeing a big roll of money Toxis had gathered from the tables and the patrons. Distant sirens sounded.

'Let's cash our chips and split, babe. We've done what Tony wanted. And there's something lame about being in a casino on a Tuesday night.'

3

The black Jag gunned down Highway 61, crossing a highway bridge, playing classic Cream songs loudly.

Demorn was driving right on the needle, had been since they'd left Memphis city limits, fighting the urge to really open it up and let the car roar. Toxis was riding shotgun. The Huntress didn't wear her hood or red veil in the car. Her head weaved slightly to the sounds of the music, her gold bracelet tinkling as she rapped lightly on the car window.

Questions had been bouncing in Demorn's head every mile they got farther away from the trashy casino.

'You've stayed longer than normal.'

We haven't fought the last battle tonight. This Hunt isn't over.

Demorn smiled, feeling a little sad. 'It must be nice to know when the fighting will be over.'

She flexed her right arm, massaging out some tenderness. 'I was kinda hoping we could push on to Red River. I'm looking forward to some sleep, maybe play a game. I always keep a console in the car.'

When we kill all those we hunt, I find release. Then you can rest and play your games, Princess.

As they crossed over the end of the bridge, Demorn found herself looking toward that distant, dark horizon in the night sky. The world seemed like a wasteland belonging only to the dead.

'Do you ever wonder why?'

We hunt because our revenge is right.

It's so simple for her, Demorn thought. So black and white.

'I always thought so, too. But it's been a year since I could spawn Xalos in this world, on the Grim Earth. Tonight, it was wielded against me. It's enough to make a girl ask some questions.'

Distracted, she found herself looking at the small music box hanging from the mirror, the delicate skull-and-bones emblem carved upon the wood. She deliberately knocked the box, making it sway almost hypnotically. It tinkled quietly under the sound of the song on the radio with sweet delicate chimes. She imagined the Ballerina was grooving inside.

Looking in the mirror, for a moment Demorn saw the blood upon on her face, half in the shadows, half in the endless highway lights, blood splattered across her face.

'I've been on the road for too long.'

Toxis laid her elegant hand on her shoulder. Demorn's armband burned in response. She almost felt like it would happen, the magic would come, and she would be able to leave this dark place and join the Huntress in Firethorn at last.

Princess, you're clean.

Toxis rested her head on Demorn's shoulder. Demorn looked back in the mirror. The blood was gone but she wasn't fooled.

'It's been two years since I've seen Firethorn. I do cash hits for Tony and the Innocents and it doesn't worry me. I'm anything but clean, babe.'

This late at night, it was common for Demorn to have fever visions. The image was often the same. A tiny white house on a cliff, surrounded by a forest of green trees. Rain softly falling, serenely beautiful. The misty image flickering in her mind showed her in a red dress, standing in the garden of the white house. There was somebody next to her but Demorn could never tell who it was, they were blurred and instinct. She was gazing out into the beautiful blue sky and the gigantic river that rumbled far below the cliff. Everything in her longed for the freedom she felt there. The images faded away, as they did every night. Demorn knew she was close to running on empty.

'I want to escape this wasteland. I want to lose myself in the deep wilderness.'

Toxis was holding her hand gently, an unusually sensitive move for so ruthless a personality.

Come to Firethorn. Leave this soulless land, my Princess.

Demorn changed the song on the radio. She put the pedal down. 'When the Pale Suns are all dead, when I have the bones of the Dead King . . . then I can be free.'

The Jag roared down the highway.

• • •

They sat on the car's hood in a lonely car park outside a local Alpha's Burger joint. The light from the cheesy restaurant lit up a Highway 61 sign by the exit.

It was late night now, long past midnight, that strange, quiet time when the songs on the radio get a bit more classic, the DJ a little more personal. Everything got a little bit less fake. Demorn threw Toxis a couple of Alpha cheeseburgers. The huntress caught them, smiling her rare, lopsided smile. Toxis had a real weakness for cheeseburgers.

'I withstood a store full of drunk assholes for these, so eat up and enjoy.'

Toxis had her red hood pulled back on. She looked enigmatic and sexy in the half-light. Her voice was soft and accented.

'You have doubts, Princess.'

The slow music made Demorn thoughtful. She looked at the Highway 61 sign, flashing by the exit.

'I used to love songs about the highway. I used to love these missions. But now, they are just making me lonely.'

We are close to vengeance.

She shrugged. 'Maybe. This doesn't feel like vengeance. The King has been a long time cold in the ground now. What if I've already killed whoever murdered him? No flashing lights, no writing in the sky. Nothing to tell me that vengeance has been satisfied.'

I saw his body. The marks of a Pale Sun were upon him.

My beloved King. Sire of the White Fort. It used to be a punch to the gut, now it's an old wound that I navigate, she thought.

'I've killed so many henchmen,' she murmured almost dreamily.

Revenge is what the Dead King taught. You will know when the final blow is struck.

Demorn smiled her mysterious smile. 'Maybe. Hope so. Anyway, I'm loving the deep chats. How long do you think you will stay?'

As long as Fate will let me.

Demorn held her Odin Ring up against the neon sign glow.

Fate . . .

Her voice was quiet. 'I just knew Odin fought giants, y'know. My brother likes legends, the pagan gods, Ragnarok, the End, all that. I remember when I saw that rock monster produce my Sword. It's probably all that saved me. Luck, Fate, whatever. That's how close we are getting to the bottom line now.'

Xalos is powerful, and belongs to nothing but itself. Only the true and very strong can overcome its flames.

Or cheat them, Demorn thought. But she didn't say the words, didn't want to drag the mood down. She couldn't fool herself. The longer she was incapable of bringing forth Xalos, the more she questioned her path, what was right and wrong. Each mission she grew more mortal, more reliant on the pain locket and a bright steel blade. Farther and farther from the White Fort.

Toxis put her hand on Demorn's leg. She glared with her haunting blue eyes at the idiot punk guys in the window at Alpha's Burgers.

We are Sisters, the rest can all burn.

Music started playing from the box sitting between them on the hood. Slowly it opened. There was a soft pink glow coming from the box. Demorn lowered the ring, the blue glow upon her face. She gripped hard on Toxis.

'You feel it so raw.'

There is only fire then darkness.

The hood slid off Toxis's head. She was impossible to resist, Demorn thought, impossible, when she said cool stuff like that. They kissed once, passionately. Then again, sexy, close and friendly. Toxis smelled of the burning spices that grew in the valleys of the Far North, where her tribe came from. Neither of them wanted the moment to stop. The power of their bond meant they so often met as strangers, flung together in distant and desperate lands.

'You don't normally get to stay this long.' She nodded at the glowing music box. 'You've helped me enough tonight, huntress. I can go solo on this next one, whatever it is, whoever I have to kill.'

Toxis smiled that rare smile again, her blue eyes so powerful. She clicked her golden bracelet against Demorn's armband. The jewellery glowed and the huntress shimmered like a red ghost.

Meet me in the morning forest, magic eyes.

The huntress faded away like a ghost into the night, transported back to where she came from. Reflective, Demorn picked up the music box, glowing on the car hood. The interior of the box was soft pink. The Ballerina span inside the Box, dressed in a tight dress, sassy and hot in miniature.

'Where to now, dancing girl?'

Little black love hearts surrounded the tiny ballerina's head. She winked at Demorn, her voice light and skittish. 'Alpha Burgers, by the howling, lonely Highway. Go stop the Shark Gang.'

Demorn looked inside the burger joint again, more closely this time. She saw the same gathering of young men, but suddenly her magic eyes flashed and she saw they wore Shark heads, circling the room like hungry animals who smelled blood. Concerned, she got off the car hood. Hidden amongst them, she saw a young girl sitting in a booth, surrounded. She was no more than twelve, wearing a pink parka and blue earmuffs. She looked scared.

'Not far then,' Demorn murmured.

The Ballerina curtsied and the music box closed, the cute dancer grooving slow and sexy. Demorn slowly walked to the restaurant entrance, white fire burning in her heart.

Demorn walked into Alpha Burgers, holding the katana in a scabbard. The gang filled the floor. Their faces changed to shark to human to shark. One of the biggest Sharks looked at Demorn, sneering, his lips curling, showing savagely sharp teeth. Rough prison tats covered his leathery snout. He snarled abuse. The pack closed in around the girl. She was crying, frightened now. She was crying, holding tightly onto a white teddy bear.

One of the smallest, meanest looking sharks upended the girl's milkshake into the her lap. She jumped in her seat, hollering in fear, tears sliding down her face.

Demorn withdrew the katana from the scabbard, letting the sound of the metal upon leather be drawn out real slow. She spoke very deliberately. 'Let her go and I won't kill everybody.'

The punks in the gang turned, stunned. Their shark heads reflected in her blade, mirroring their ugliness back at them. She wondered if all of these boys even knew what they were, hiding beneath their contempt and their hate and their bling. They were monsters.

Demorn gestured to the girl. 'Come to me.'

The girl ran to her, slipping through the circling sharks, her small, shaking body pressed hard into Demorn's black pants and muscled legs. The bracelet around the neck of her teddy bear glowed.

Demorn stroked the girl's hair softly with her left hand, her eyes fixed on the gang. She palmed her keys. Her voice was a warm whisper.

'My car's in the lot, kid. Black Jag. *Go*.'

The girl ran out of the burger joint into the car park.

'Last chance. On your knees, boys.'

The gang hissed and snarled at her. She saw a ghostly flash of a white figure in the centre of the gang, draped in a long white cloak pulled over its head. A true Pale Sun. This time it did not vanish instantly, like so many others on this long trail where she had hunted them. Instead, it sat statuesque amongst the sharks, chalk-white hands clasped together in the folds of the cloak. Demorn examined the pallid, stretched skin over old bones, fingers glistening with archaic rings.

The Sharks seemed oblivious to its presence, but her heart flickered with unquiet as the Pale Sun viewed her through the depths of its cloak without the slightest movement. She held the gaze, not willing to give into fear. Slowly the Pale Sun vanished, leaving just the Shark Gang and their bitter snarls. The biggest Shark growled, raising his claws and pointing at her with a long, jagged bone knife. The title HEAD SHARK was stencilled in a tattoo upon his shark fin.

'Fuck you, dyke whore!'

A small, stocky Hammerhead ran at her, screaming and brandishing an unwieldy chain, swinging wildly. She cut him down with a fast, merciless slash of the katana. His shark fin was sliced off his body, lying on the floor. He looked young and thin and stupid. On the cut fin in red writing: DRUGGIE.

Demorn pulled her lips into a tight, scary smile. Her blade was slick with blood.

'I'm going to kill every last one of you.'

The Head Shark screamed obscenities, gripping the jagged knife, and hurling himself through the gang to face her. Demorn rushed forward, katana raised, a vicious smile on her face, her blade slicing through the air like a song.

• • •

Out in the car park, the girl cowered inside the Jag, peering out the window. Screams echoed in the night, short and loud, before they were silenced. The girl peeked out and witnessed Demorn slice through two gang members with a single stroke, spraying blood over the windows of Alpha Burgers.

She cowered back into the seat. An eerie quiet settled over the lot. Demorn walked out into the half-light, softly closing the restaurant door behind her.

She wiped the sword and sheathed the katana as she came over to the car. She was totally fine, a trace of their blood across her face. The girl squealed and ran out to hug her protector. Demorn smiled as she embraced the crying child.

'Thank you. I hate them, I hate them so much!'

The girl's body was shaking and shivering. Demorn held her hard.

'It's okay, babe, they're gone, no more Sharks.'

The girl pressed close, the teddy bear pendant glowing in the half-dark of the car park. 'All gone . . .' she whispered, looking at the windows covered in blood.

Demorn kneeled down to the girl, brushing away tears. 'Yeah, all gone. It's what they deserve, sweetheart.'

The girl stopped crying and happiness lit up her face. 'Never leave me.'

Demorn grinned, looking at the highway sign. 'Let's hit the road, kid. This place is gonna get cop hot real soon.'

'But we were in the right!'

Demorn winked.

'I know, but the real cops don't play by the rules of the old cop shows. They prefer the new ones where it's all paperwork and not letting stuff slide.'

Despite everything, the girl laughed, sucking in her breath madly, her head light and euphoric, as Demorn slid into the driver's seat. She gunned the car, and the Jag roared away.

She drove fast, putting Alpha Burgers in the rear-view mirror. Demorn passed an eye over the girl gobbling up her burger, one arm still clinging to her teddy bear.

'Where's home, kid?'

The girl looked at her, edging away on the seat, distant.

'12 Evergreen Street, Chicago.'

Demorn raised her eyebrow. 'You're a long way from 12 Evergreen Street, Chicago.'

The girl avoided her glance. 'What do you want me to say . . . *everything's dumb*. Where do you live?'

Demorn shrugged, eyes on the highway. 'The road, the Jag . . . a Holiday Inn room playing reruns.' She smiled. 'Wherever.'

The girl squinted her eyes, thinking. 'Um . . . is the Jag your car?'

'Yep.'

The girl's face lit up. 'You're like some magic nomad with a sword!'

Demorn pulled a crazy face, joking around. 'From big scary sharks!'

She held her hand out to the girl, across the car seat. 'I'm Demorn, I work for the Innocents. Restless, wandering sword.'

The girls shook her hand, giggling, nestling in close. 'It's cool how you're so strong.'

Demorn looked in the mirror. Her face was clear then suddenly she saw the blood again, covering her eyes and her visions, so that both the present and past were layered with the red rain, before everything flashed back to normal, and it was just her lonely, tired eyes in the mirror.

'In Alpha, did you see anything apart from those boys?'

The girl sighed, sounding sad. 'Are you talking about the Tall Man?'

Demorn kept her eyes on the road, saying nothing, letting the girl tell her own story.

Her voice was quiet. 'He follows me everywhere. Turns up at weird times, weird places. He just watches me, and not in a nice way . . . I hate him, he's such a creep.'

She looked up, tears in her eyes again. She's so damn young, Demorn thought. The Pale Suns take them so damned young.

'Is he your friend or something?' the girl asked, with a vague tremor in her voice.

Demorn's voice was stern. 'He's not my friend, honey.'

'I could see they were real Sharks, that's what scared me. I see everything like that.'

Her voice changed. The girl was older on the seat, a teenager now, looking out into the darkness. Long blonde hair fell down her shoulders. She has the magic eyes, Demorn realised. Just like me. With a sudden haunting chill, Demorn wondered if she could see the blood that covered her face and soul.

'What happened to 12 Evergreen Street, Chicago?'

'Everything's gone, all burnt away. I've travelled these parts for a long time now.'

She sounded sleepy and distant, looking out into the wasteland. 'It's just me now, drifting in the dark.'

The girl held the glowing pendant which had hung on the neck of her teddy bear. With a solemn expression, she swung the pendant in front of Demorn's eyes, the white beauty drawing Demorn's eyes, entrancing her. She saw the shimmer of a White Fort that she had forgotten, she heard and smelled the sound of a turbulent sea, crashing upon rocks.

Demorn reached out with her hand, clasping the pendant. It was cold to the touch, almost burning her palm for a moment, then just blank. The girl smiled with a distant friendship. She wasn't young anymore. She was a beautiful young woman around Demorn's age. Those ice cool blue eyes held a faint trace of boredom as layers of misdirection blew away.

She pressed the pendant into Demorn's hand.

'My name's Kate. You rescued me. We dated. We fell in love. I died. You might remember me now.'

The night air blinked orange and white and red, washing over both their faces inside the car. The Jag roared through a wasteland of charred earth, broken buildings, and burning cars. The landscape around the highway was lit up under a blood red sky. Demorn brought the Jag to a skidding halt by the road side. A huge series of enormous pyramids hung floating in the fire red sky, immovable, massive, somehow malevolent.

In all her travels, Demorn had never seen anything of this order or magnitude. She felt naked before the strange power of the gods. Kate seemed indifferent to the bizarre sights outside the car. Her fingers were warm as she brushed Demorn's neck.

'You really love this crazy, magic stuff don't you?'

Demorn released her hand and clasped the pendant tightly. She glanced at Kate. Her form was ethereal and her face shimmered with a golden energy. Flames flickered through those ice blue eyes, promises of dreams and haunting lies, a mirage of victory and defeat.

'12 Evergreen Street, Chicago,' Demorn said simply, feeling sad, remembering the address, remembering a first date a long time ago.

'You might have lived there once, but not for a long time, Kate. Where are you really?'

Kate was smooth, almost detached. She brushed a finger across the music box and the radio started singing an old song about Paris.

'You know where I am. Lying in bed with a producer full of promises. My head hurts. I'm asleep, but only lightly. I've been dreaming about us. Wondering what happened. There's been nobody like you since.'

'What do you want to hear, Kate? You broke my heart when you left. But that was years ago.'

Kate smiled, pale blue eyes shining. 'Rubbish. It's barely been a year. Not all of me went to Paris. A ghost of me is still in your ridiculous fantasy land.'

She pressed her hand against Demorn's heart. The white pendant shone in Demorn's fingers. Demorn looked deeper into the flames dancing in her golden aura. Kate looked ghostly, mysterious. Through her, Demorn could see the highway was filled with the burning images of people she had known, their homes and their houses scattered across her past, glittering faces of family and friends, and so many shadowed strangers who she did not know or had forgotten.

'You've started to forget me, too,' Kate said. 'I think you do it on purpose.'

Demorn laughed so as not to cry. Looking in those blue eyes, that savage knife to the gut began to twist. There was no comfort, no escape from her own feelings. This was so much worse than killing people.

'Jesus, Kate, it's just called getting over somebody. I don't like to think about the past.'

The images danced on the desolate highway, burning in the desert air. Demorn longed to know more of these strange waking dreams but they scared her.

Kate kissed her slowly on the neck. 'I don't think we're quite over each other.'

Demorn murmured, 'How are you here?'

Kate smiled dreamily. 'A huge part of me still wants us. It never goes away. It's very lonely in Paris. Strangers are so cruel. My agent just talks about vehicles and franchises. I walk through the city because it's beautiful, but I only see the greed and the machine. Underneath, everything is empty, most of all, me.'

'Why stay?'

Kate pouted. 'I've got the modelling contract and a nice enough ass to cover the bills. Maybe I do want to be a cog in their big ol' empty machine! Is that so bad?'

Demorn laughed ruefully. 'I kill people for money. I keep my judgement relaxed, Kate.'

Kate was light. 'People like you don't relax. Look how tightly you're holding the gem.'

Demorn smiled with a strange bitterness, tossing the pendant into the air, catching the gem, keeping her fingers curled around the silver chain.

'How close are you to what you want, Kate?'

Kate looked hungry and fragile. 'I'm close enough to tell myself I'll do anything.'

'That covers a lot of territory.'

Kate looked at her with ice blue eyes. Her voice darkened and was cruel.

'I wish I'd never died in Firethorn. I didn't want to die in your stupid fantasy world, Demorn. I wish you'd saved me. It meant you only had the real me left, no more fantasy. And I'm just not good enough, am I? I'm just a slutty, working girl actress who fucks for C-list roles and looks a lot like somebody—'

Demorn opened her hand and let the pendant fall to the car seat, not bothering to catch the chain. Kate disappeared in a crackle of electric static and the pendant vanished from the floor. Demorn slid the death soul mask across her face. Everything was blank and dead in her heart. The radio was playing some country song about wild, bad love. She felt a couple of tears mesh with the terrible cold. The stormy, dark sky was lashed with orange lightning, erupting into a blanket of vivid colors and spirals of wild energy. The tear in reality lay beneath the chaos like a scar across the night.

She ignored it all.

Demorn gunned the car, accelerating along the highway, letting the chaos swallow her utterly. She felt her personality burn, past the masks and the constructs. She sang softly along to songs she didn't know, had never known, her memory destroyed, green eyes blazing, feeling nothing but an overwhelming sense of loss and a terrible need for vengeance.

4

The Princess of Swords was pressed against a tall tree, on the edge of a small grassy clearing in the forest. She was in a slightly ripped black kimono. Her long brown hair was splayed out, the blade gripped tightly in her right hand. Blood lay upon the metal. There was a thin cut along her right cheek, stretching from below her eye to her chin. Her feet were bare. She felt dreamy and wild. The golden armband burned on her bare, muscled arm.

The forest lay everywhere, in all directions from the clearing. It was crystal clear twilight, a heartbreakingly beautiful blue sky over the thick green carpet of the forest. Her green eyes blazed and the katana blade caught the glinting of the twilight sun. On the very crest of the hill rising above the clearing, a large white fort sparkled in the dying rays, a red flag fluttering from the parapets in the breeze.

'Firethorn. I am home,' Demorn breathed.

Her heart beat fast, filled with many emotions. She looked around, memories and vivid images assailing her in a disordered jumble. Her last thoughts were of battle and the crashing of metal on metal.

A barbarian Varangian lay at her feet. His massive, jewelled axe broken and silent, his leather armour pierced clean by her blade. She felt his neck and the skin was cold. He had been dead for hours.

HOWWWWWLLLLLLLL.

The eerie, weeping howl like that of a hound from hell echoed from deep within the forest, trembling down her spine.

Demorn looked back up the hill towards Firethorn. Black-grey smoke drifted from the white fort, covering the red flag, a stain on the crystal sky.

Firethorn was under attack.

Demorn pressed a bloodstained finger onto the white poplar tree. 'I will not desert you,' she swore.

Then she ran into the forest, sleek and fast, holding the katana. The blood remained on the white poplar tree.

Demorn ran through the forest, obeying her instincts, finding the quick paths toward the Fort above. The twilight sun was mottled and shadowed, cutting through the canopy of lush, green trees.

She heard the hum of the water before she saw it, and slowed down to a soundless walk across the foliage. A thin, electric-blue stream trickled through the trees. A body lay against the small riverbank. It was the shattered remnants of a girl in the soft blue robes of the Ocean Clan, the body twisted at a bad angle. Her face was doll-like, barely more than thirteen, perhaps only a couple of seasons into the Way of the Ocean Clan.

Demorn saw the deep rending wound in her side, blood still pouring into the water. She pressed her lips on the forehead of the dead girl.

What new terror has come to Firethorn, Demorn thought, that my sisters should die like this, in the very shadows of the fort.

A snarl ripped through the forest leaves. Demorn twisted around, holding the katana in defense pose. A huge beast erupted through the foliage, snarling and growling, horns ominously glistening in the half-light. She leapt back, amazed.

It was massive, its muscled skin covered with glistening green plate-armour, huge fangs caked in blood. Ivory horns came from the scaled head. A demonic symbol was inscribed in glowing red writing upon the creature's side. A Devil Cat. *Corizan sorcery!*

The old thrill of battle ran through Demorn.

'Die, Devil Beast!'

The beast lashed at her with its great claws. She lithely dodged in the air, spiralling her body in a compact arc, landing gracefully on bare feet, the grace natural and fluid. Working fast, Demorn swung her katana and sliced the beast's leg, drawing savage green blood from ripped muscles.

The Beast snarled viciously, slashing again even more brutally. The jagged massive claws tore at her black kimono, hitting her left side, sending her flying back into the foliage, slamming into a tree. Her shoulder exploded with the pain of dislocation. Demorn grunted. With a stubborn acrobatic grace she caught hold of the tree trunk, her good hand barely holding onto her katana.

Her mind went sharp and fractured and clear as she ran into the forest, coming to the edge of the tree-line, a rocky cliff top exposing a canyon below. A blue river flowed far below at the base of the ravine, dazzlingly and distant, running toward the Endless Sea.

Back in the forest veil, the Devil Beast roared over the body of the dead girl, owning the carcass, desecrating it with that dreadful howl.

Demorn snarled as she wrenched the shoulder back into the socket. Her katana was ablaze with red symbols. She crouched by the tree-line, on the edge of the cliff, her right arm extended, no fear in her. A strange perfumed wind blew past her ears, ruffling her long hair. Her mind was completely detached and icy, weirdly rational.

The creature roared again, rearing up in the forest, horns and fangs dripping with blood.

I smell my death, Demorn thought with a smile. Crouched in defense pose, she saw behind the Devil Cat a beautiful horse emerge from the shadows of the trees, lightly dancing in the leaves. The horse stepped into a ray of light, and she saw a rotten, skeletal beauty, parched skin over white bones. A staggeringly beautiful crystal horn came from the head, untouched by the rotten stench of dying.

The Unicorn, she breathed, the Unicorn! And Demorn was filled with a savage joy to see such a magical thing.

The Devil Beast crashed through the foliage toward her, a brute uncomprehending of magic or wonder, spurred on by the vile wickedness of Corizan sorcery. She took a half step toward the cliff edge, every sense alert, her body taut.

The last battle is so pure.

The blade slashed across the Beast's huge forearm, drawing a flow of green blood that splattered across her face.

So desperate.

Demorn smiled with a savage, sheer energy.

I have seen so many last battles.

The great beast charged at her, head bent, wholly crazed, the great horns glistening in the twilight sun.

I have dealt death so often.

She weaved past the horns, but the great beast had much power, and it struck her injured shoulder heavily, forcing her to the ground. The taloned feet barely missed her head as she rolled away. Her blade struck at the underbelly in desperation, slicing through soft, pink-grey flesh unprotected by the plates.

And in a single, last movement she dodged the hurtling force as it tumbled from the short ledge, carried by momentum. The beast's sharp curved tail grabbed her leg, with all the uncanny intelligence of beasts, cutting painfully into her naked flesh.

After so many wars, so many daring escapes.

She cursed when the tail wound itself completely around her leg, wrenching Demorn from the cliff face. As it dragged her from the edge, she looked up, into the pure, free eyes of the undead unicorn, standing at the edge of the forest, and she saw all its sad, tragic love as it turned away, the sun glinting on bones.

It ends . . . so simply.

The Beast and she fell together into the vast ravine. Demorn strained as the monster sought to crush the life out of her, mouth dripping with blood and saliva, claws digging into her bleeding body. With desperate effort and a gambler's lucky left hand, she pushed with all her remaining strength on the katana handle, sinking the sword into the beast's gut. They tumbled from the ledge, every inch of mad effort filling her arm and shoulder with pain beyond belief. She realised she did not wear the locket. It was gone, vanished in the crossing.

I am a clean fire burning through the forest.

Her blazing green eyes saw the sun falling into the river and the thick forest spinning.

Burning to the end, I am nothing but the flame.

The Beast's demon-tinged eyes came into full view, inches away, blocking out everything else, drenching her in foul stench, blood and gunk from the creature's body soaking her as they fell and fell. Demorn twisted, pulling the blade, a cruel, mad smile across her face.

The devil sign burned out like a siren, before vanishing completely from the creature's plated skin. The red stain in the beast's eyes seemed to fade but she wasn't sure if she was just imagining everything. In the last moment, she kicked free from the Beast, a final heartbeat before the river.

I love Death, she intoned, *I am nothing but the flame.*

They crashed into the water, Demorn first, the Beast smashing after her. Blood foamed in the water. Everything went quiet.

The wide river kept flowing on toward the Endless sea, impassive to the petty affairs of women, men and beasts.

The water rolled on, deceptively peaceful. It was close to night, the air humid and sticky. Long grass reeds lay on the riverbank. Beyond that lay the thick forest. Smoke drifted across the twilight sky.

Demorn burst from the water, her black kimono torn all over. The katana lay in her hand aflame. Her green eyes blazed like stars. The creature rose out of the water behind her, its horns glistening. She saw the enormous wound from her blade, noxious green blood dripping down the plated hide.

As it rose from the water the wounds healed over. The beast roared, echoing and reverberating through the ravine. Resurrection power flowed through Demorn's veins. The devil sign was gone from the monster. With her magic eyes, she could see directly into its soul, raw and pure.

The beast snarled viciously at something in the long reeds. She held out her left hand. The undead unicorn flashed through her eyes, all white bones and thin skin, strange magic holding things together.

'Be calm.'

They had gone downriver with the current. The Devil Beast quieted down behind her, obeying its new Mistress.

With her cold magic eyes, Demorn could see the silhouette of five blurry red shapes in the weeds. Blood Clan.

'I will not kill a Sister without warning.'

Demorn focused on the central figure, a red cloaked woman, holding a long bow, ready to fire. She tensed, ready to dodge. The image blurred, then reappeared deeper in the reeds, her arrow trained on Demorn.

'But just a single warning.'

A soft, intense voice echoed through her mind.

So you can see us . . . Corizan witch.

The first arrow hummed from the reeds, which Demorn barely dodged. Everything moved slow motion, ballet style. She could smell a noxious liquid on the arrow shaft as it cut past her, into the river. Everything exploded into action. Her katana cut down two more arrows fired from the undergrowth.

In an instant Demorn crossed the distance between herself and the red silhouettes who fired, running over the grass tops, slicing their chests as she ran through them like the wind.

The girls fell into the long grass. Demorn dropped silently to the ground, half shrouded by the reeds. The Devil Beast was pinpricked with arrows, the last one thudding into its body and cutting through the plate armour, even as the monster tore a red clad girl in two, rearing high in the air, pricked by the poison arrows, defiant to the end.

The lead Blood Clan member, a lithe, fast figure, fired three more arrows into the Beast at close quarters as she spun like an acrobat with her bow. The Beast slumped to the ground, dropping the girl from its fangs. The broken girl looked beseechingly at the lead figure, mouthing words she could no longer say.

Mercy finds you.

Toxis fired an arrow into her neck, killing the woman instantly.

Demorn stood behind Toxis, her katana wet with the blood of the two other Blood Clan. The river ran beside them. Demorn saw a stunning purple butterfly flutter in the sky and she wondered how so much violence and wonder could blossom this close to the other.

It was a moment of quiet silence before a battle they could not avoid. The wind blew through their hair, that faint trace of perfume.

'I don't want to kill another Sister.'

I am Toxis, Leader of the Blood. And you are not our Sister.

'I know who you are. And you have often called me this.'

Toxis was calm, her head slightly turned, her blue eyes pure and haunting. The huntress was not troubled by death. Three more figures in red cloaks appeared in the green grass behind Demorn, circling them.

Demorn chuckled dryly. 'Ah, come now, Toxis, this is our fight.'

Toxis's eyes sparkled icy blue as she glanced back at Demorn. Her mind-voice was like the whisper of a ghost.

You have such pretty dreams, outsider.

Demorn was transplanted to a dark concert arena, cavernous and vast. Pink and blue laser images splayed everywhere in the sky, bouncing off a huge silver disco ball high above. She was slightly older, the hair a more layered Californian blonde, her purple Elvis sunglasses on. She felt happy and high. People were everywhere. Demorn looked up to the stage, where a perfect Vegas '70s Elvis clone sang "Suspicious Minds" in an electronic dream, holding a golden microphone with bejewelled ringed hands. He sang it to her and all the thousands gathered in the arena. His eyes were purple-blue, and he had a magical look. In the sky above, one sign shone vividly in red laser.

THERE IS NO DEATH HERE, SWEETHEART

Toxis smashed her across the face with a wooden staff. The staff cracked into Demorn's hand. Her katana fell into the grass. The vision was shattered.

Weak outsider.

Demorn staggered like a cheap drunk, the dream vision utterly broken by the stinging pain of the staff's blows.

Your Sword is silent.

Demorn blocked the next staff swing with a quick hand, lashing out with her feet, striking air.

'That was another life . . .'

The staff struck her face again.

Firethorn is burning while you daydream!

Toxis hauled on the staff in a mighty effort, flinging Demorn through the air.

THIS is your life, traitor!

Toxis leapt after her, her red cloak flying up high, exposing her dark, toned legs.

FIGHT FOR IT!

Demorn flicked out a vicious, graceful kick that slammed Toxis in the face, hitting the Blood Sister with a rapid two-punch combo. In response, Toxis back handed her across the face hard. The huntress grabbed her long, brown hair and wrenched her neck, savagely biting into it, teeth glistening as they broke Demorn's skin.

Enraged, hurt, Demorn broke the hold with a karate chop to her throat. Toxis staggered back, glazed and drunk from the blood that was spilling from her mouth. She looked wildly happy.

You taste of sugar . . . and happy music.

'So what? I've got a sweet tooth.'

Toxis eyes were misty with red blood lust. She charged in a blur.

Die smiling, witch!

Demorn soared into the air, curling up into a tight ball. Her quick hands went to a tiny sickle woven into the legs of her black kimono, threaded to a thin metal chain. She swung the chain down, gliding it with skill around Toxis's neck, wrenching the hunter from her path of blood lust. The chain wound twice around Toxis's neck. Demorn glided around her, her bare feet dancing briefly on the tall grass.

The chain wrapped tighter and tighter around the huntress's neck. Demorn pulled hard. Toxis's icy blue eyes widened with shock as the sharp sickle sank deep into her flesh, and Demorn held the chain tight like a leash.

'I am no witch, Sister.'

Demorn snapped the chain back to her wrist savagely, the sickle coming from the throat of the Huntress.

'I am the Princess of the Swords, and I have returned to save my people.'

Toxis fell to the ground, pale eyes bewildered, blood streaming down her dark neck, her slender fingers staunching the wound.

I can see your crown now, Princess. I can see your Crown . . .

Demorn caught her before she fell. She took the red bandana from Toxis's forehead and wrapped it around her own head, speaking the ritual words as she did so, releasing the body of Toxis in the river.

'Midnight claims the Blood.'

Toxis vanished into the water. The shadows of the remaining Blood Clan members shimmered in the long grass. Their kimonos shifted from red to jet black. She was their leader now. A light weight fell upon her heart, shadows of distant memories and unknown prophecies.

On instinct, Demorn looked to the forest, seeing a flash of a crystal white horn, sparkling in the trees. *The Unicorn . . .*

Slowly it emerged into the Sun, its rotted visage clear in the last rays of sunlight, the skeleton moving beneath the shreds of flesh that were left. Even in this corrupt condition there was a graceful nobility about this creature that could never be denied. The three Clan Sisters dropped to their knees, the grass bending to reveal their full forms.

Demorn threw open her kimono robe, tossing it into the river. She kneeled in the water facing the Unicorn. Her breasts heaved as the Unicorn walked slowly through the water toward her. The tattoo of Alodin Mars shone. A single, translucent scar lay upon her pale body where Xalos wrenched itself from her flesh, lit up by the sorcery of the Unicorn.

Unlike the girls who cowered terrified in the grass, Demorn did not avert her eyes. The creature looked upon her with sad, wise eyes. Her heart welled with emotion as she looked upon this desecrated, magical creature, filled with more soul and love and beauty than she would ever have.

The Unicorn came closer, nuzzling Toxis in the water gently with its crystal horn. Demorn looked down at Toxis, floating in the river, dead by her hand, like so many others. Time seemed to slip away. Memory too. The face of the Huntress was vaguely familiar, as if from a dream she had woken from, but she could not place where or when she had ever seen Toxis before. Her golden armband burned.

Everything seemed to start in the forest clearing. So much death, with the sky stained with smoke from the White Fort. There was no sunlight now. Twilight had become true night.

The Unicorn neighed wildly and she was filled with hope. A new sun rose in the sky, risen from the ocean. The sky blazed with pink and gold, bathing her face. The new sun was massive, burning bright red and filled with craters and spiked towers.

It cast a searing shadow across her. A giant red lightning bolt seared across the sky, striking Demorn flush in the heart. Demorn cried with a lusty freedom as the bolts hit her, saturating her body. The massive blasts echoed through the canyon. Thunder rumbled in the air.

She looked toward the great red sun. Energy from the bolt lingered in the air, and across the pulsing lightning were huge fiery letters.

LIVE FOR VENGEANCE AND LOVE
LIVE FOR VENGEANCE AND LOVE
LIVE FOR VENGEANCE AND LOVE

Slowly it all died away, the messages repeating in her mind, soaked up by her magic eyes. Her hand was holding onto Toxis, and the power of the bolt was spasming into the dead girl in the river. Demorn's hair was deep brown and longer. She felt younger somehow, less travelled. She was wearing her leather jacket again, a black comic book t-shirt underneath, blue jeans, black military boots.

She got up from the grassy bank. The river around them was suddenly a pinkish sparkling blue, as the undead Unicorn frolicked in the churning water. Demorn smiled, feeling a brief, light joy. Her eyes could see the magic still inside the creature, healing the last phase of decay. Her mind was blurry on the memories, but nothing mattered. She was reborn.

Toxis floated in the water, in the world of the dead. A silent, cold place. She felt her bleeding stop. Far below her, she could sense the chasm, electronic, filled with loss. There was no pain in her, no more hunger in her, just tiny flickers of rage . . . she couldn't see the Ice Dragons which plagued her dreams and nightmares, with their crazy, deathly flight.

Toxis opened her eyes to see the magnificent, horrible undead Unicorn prancing, its crystal horn reflected in the magic red sun. Her eyes were freed of all blood lust, icy blue again. Her wounds were gone and clean.

The Unicorn galloped wildly away into the forest.

A young woman with long brunette hair and huge, wide green eyes stood above her in the water. She held out a strong hand.

Toxis saw a golden crown floating over her head, cruel spikes glittering. She saw the universes splitting. She saw two girls, one of this one world, one of another. The clothes shifted but the magic eyes did not. She saw the chaos and the light each brought with them, reflections of both the saviour and the destroyer. The Goddess tattoo burned with a blinding fire upon her right arm in both worlds.

Toxis was humbled. She knelt in the water, limbs shaking.

Forgive me, Princess! I did not guess . . .

Demorn smiled. 'There's nothing to forgive, Toxis.'

She breathed deeply, savoring Firethorn, back at last.

'We will meet as sisters, or as strangers with a sword at our throats.'

She tossed Toxis her ash staff. Demorn pointed to the forest, rising far above.

'Enemies hold the White Fort. The Sun has risen from beneath the Sea. This is where vengeance begins.'

Toxis turned to the kneeling black robed figures.

Run, Sisters, awaken the Clan! We attack in the dawn.

The Sisters ran like the wind into the distance, black robes vanishing.

My Sisters . . . they no longer wear the red robe.

'They are Midnight now. That's the price.'

Toxis fractionally bowed her head.

Fair trade.

'But not you, Toxis. You will always be Blood, this world and the next.'

Toxis looked into the Forest. Some of her natural diffidence reasserted itself in the steely gaze she cast back at Demorn.

There is only the Hunt. Until the last darkness which embraces everything.

'It sounds so very dramatic.'

Demorn looked at the corpses, of the Devil Beast, so briefly freed of sorcery, of the young women still in their red robes, those the Unicorn didn't rise. It made her sad in an absent-minded way.

'Ask the dead about the darkness . . . So lost that they cannot lie. Red Morning told me that once, when she found me on the streets of Babelzon.'

She wasn't certain how she knew that. But she remembered that first neon glare of the portal city like the hazy afterimage of a dream. Then it was gone and the smoke hung in the glow of the red sun which burned above them, coloring the night.

As Demorn watched the white fort was suddenly encased in a gleaming crystal dome.

The crystal comes when the Red Sun rises.

Demorn pointed upward. 'There is a great evil up there. Who has taken the Fort?'

Varangian raiders. Aided by powerful witchery. She flicked her fingers dismissively. ***Corizan.***

'Varangians! Firethorn was never so weak as to fall to them!'

Toxis barely smiled, her look dripping with contempt. She pointed up toward the crystal encased fort.

You have long been absent. They have grown soft behind the white walls. Those in the Fort have forgotten the ways of War.

'And you?'

Toxis's laughter was soft and low.

The Blood are always at War. Our ice caverns are not littered with pretty things. We hunt in your name, in the land of the night sun, where Ice Dragons soar. We do not forget.

With that, she turned and melted into the tall grass reeds. Demorn walked slowly behind her, each of them soon swallowed up by the dark green forest trees.

5

Deep in the forest, Demorn felt the spirit like a cold breeze down her neck. They had been walking for over an hour. Her hand gripped the katana handle just as Toxis vanished in front of her eyes.

She was alone under the forest eaves. Demorn heard the echo of a distant song, weirdly familiar at first, then suddenly she felt sad because it was something from childhood. A small clear pond lay in front of her.

'Reveal yourself, phantom.'

A young male's voice whispered in her ear, subtle and soft.

'You play it so straight in Firethorn, don't you, Sis? I bet you use Old English, to make it sound especially serious. Do you actually say thou and art?'

She laughed despite herself, memories lacing through her. Demorn looked deeply into the reflection in the water, seeing his glittering smile, suspicious of ghosts and spirits. She almost knew who he was, and what he meant to her . . .

'No, I don't say either of those things.'

His smile glinted like an advertisement, empty and full. Cold fingers touched her brow, those of a wandering spirit.

'You don't quite remember me, do you? You go so deep into this world, you dive right beneath the surface. It's very dangerous.'

Demorn sighed, looking at the perfect glass-like pond, which grew larger and larger, into a small lake. Her feet were in the water. She was barefoot and in the black kimono again. Things felt dreamy. Talking with him, fatigue came back, hints of a life and concerns beyond the White Fort and Firethorn and raiders.

'I'm just so tired. Real or not, I'm just so tired.'

A cold hand brushed her forehead. With quick hands she grasped it.

'Who the hell are you!'

A slightly scruffy boy in blue jeans and a baggy t-shirt materialised close to her, by the water, smiling slightly, as her hand gripped around his thin throat. Instantly, she let him go. Recognition was flooding her.

He was like a shadow, flickering in and out of her sharp eyes.

'Smile?'

'Yeah, I'm the one who reminds you it's all super-real. I'm your brother, silly.'

She opened her mouth but said nothing. He brushed his ear, as the music seemed to fill the air around her.

'Hear that? Does that sound like the backing music for the naked dancing girls of Makeresh, or whatever wonderful delights you dream up in this fabulous land of mystery and magic? Or does it sound a bit more like the fucking Beatles?'

Demorn tilted her head. She knew the boy with the glittering smile told some weird twisted version of the truth. She knew the song. She knew there was more than the savage clash of sword on axe, there was a world beyond this forest and the white fort. She released her hand from the katana.

'It does sound a bit like George Harrison.'

'Well it is.' The boy held a small black box in his hands. 'Don't go too deep, don't forget where your real home is.'

Demorn ran her hand through her hair, thoughts shifting and synching into place. 'Maybe. But not yet. I have to save Firethorn.'

Smile was insistent. 'So many people need saving, Demorn! But life and time eat up everything and we can't save them all.'

He ran his fingers through the water, and the words ULTIMATE FATE glistened in gold.

Her fingers joined his in the rippling water. *Ultimate fate,*' she whispered, *no future just ultimate fate . . .*'

'You know that, Sis. You know the Innocents need you.'

Her face was sombre as she looked at the golden letters, and suddenly she remembered everything, memories and truths imprinted on crystal, refracting back to the start. Asanti burning, monsters shattering through dimensions, burning swords in terrible battles, lonely highways stretching to the horizon and blood all over her past, blood everywhere.

Then everything passed away. All that was left was the image of her and a group of young girls and guys, sitting in a grassy park, with a fire blazing, as they sang and slowly grooved in some kind of medicated Cartoon-Network happiness. She saw the pink network of shields over them, cloaking them, inside the huge future metropolis where their trails had led.

He reached out and took her hand. Demorn looked at her brother with sane, clear eyes.

'I don't give a damn about anything or anyone except us and the Innocents.'

He smiled. Everything dazzled. Her heart went warm as he kissed her cheek softly. 'Well, that is kinda our code, Sis.'

She looked up toward the hill in the darkness. 'The White Fort holds a lot of Innocent souls. It's important I protect them. In my moments of clarity, I know that's probably what draws me back.'

He waved his hand vaguely, his eyes peering at her katana blade. 'Okay, but just don't forget reality. I don't trust this fantasy stuff. I keep thinking a dragon is going to come eat me. I prefer to play it all on computer.'

She smiled at the cautious way he scanned the forest. 'Go home, the dragons might come. Tell the Innocents I'll be back soon. Make sure they don't cancel Singing Sundays. And *don't* play too much computer, you massive geek.'

He nodded, looking slightly less concerned, gone with one last beautiful grin. Suddenly there was just his glistening smile on the water and he was gone and Demorn was standing alone by the small pond in the deep forest, the soft wind dying slowly around her, her brother's voice echoing in her ears. A great loneliness filled her heart.

Alien stars twinkled in a clear, beautiful sky. Demorn looked up to them. They were so perfect, it all seemed wondrously fake. She felt like it was a million years ago. She felt like she was sixteen and she knew who she was. She was singing softly to the Beatles. Things slowly slid away from her mind, memories slipping away like rain down the steel towers of some future city she barely knew.

But there was no rain, just the stars. After a while, it was all gone and she felt calm and empty and fine. A campfire was burning in the middle of the clearing. The Huntress's sharp teeth sparkled in the firelight.

Demorn finished marking a nearby poplar tree with a sharp stick, then drew a series of similar diagrams in the dirt. Thin lines of orange fire burned across the white tree, forming strange dog and devil designs.

Toxis looked warily at the burning symbols.

You said you were no witch.

Demorn smiled. 'I'm not. They're protection symbols. Long ago, I studied with a Corizan sorceress. She taught me many things.'

Few trust the Corizan.

'Ha. They trust even fewer. Our travels were wide.'

Toxis idly flicked her staff through fast fingers.

These woods are wild. Few outside the Blood would travel in them after sunset.

Demorn shrugged, looking past the boundaries of the burning markings. 'What was Death like? I've never really died. Not properly.'

Is that why life is a game to you? I heard your mind as you fell. I can hear it now.

'Did you reach the Kingdom of Hades?' Demorn asked, shy.

My rage grew quiet. I touched an empty cold. I felt nothing else, saw nothing.

Toxis ran her hand across her heart in a ritual gesture.

The Red Sun and the Scarred Unicorn were above me when I woke. There was nothing else. Perhaps there is only the empty.

Demorn sat back down by the campfire. She looked into the flames, her expression solemn and mysterious.

'Yet here we are, this is not the afterworld. Something brought you back.'

Toxis nodded imperceptibly.

'There are things beyond death,' said Demorn. 'I've been haunted by them my whole life.'

Toxis reached out, her lithe hands brushing Demorn's cheek. Her mind-voice was tender and sad.

In our deepest caves I have seen images of you hunting the Ice Dragons, back at the dawn of our time. Your legend is known to all Blood. You wear the same scar. You carry the flaming sword. But your mind . . . it is a jumble of bright colours and noise I cannot understand.

Demorn was restless, could not sit still, smiling bitterly. 'I have lucid moments. Some nights I will wake and know who I am, and I remember . . . almost everything.'

Demorn pulled her katana from the scabbard. Power ran through her soul as purple flames licked the blade.

Do you remember everything now?

Demorn laughed, raising the katana toward the night sky filled with alien stars. 'Some things, never everything. I know that this sky, and that star, are reflected in another world, the images distorted so that we may not recognise it at first glance. Events blurred. Time rearranged.'

But this other world is not real, it is a dream?

Demorn smiled her scary smile.

'Oh, there's no one real world. That's a lie people tell themselves. We live in universes made of mirrors, cubes reflecting upon themselves. Some of the mirrors are broken and cracked, infected and polluted. Others lead toward the Source, refracting into the infinite.'

Toxis had gone very quiet. Her eyes were huge red pools of blood.

Demorn laughed lightly. There was hint of danger in her.

'Long ago on my home-world I studied such things. I know it's a lot to take in. I remember telling a girl I loved in Babelzon all this, years ago. I said it was a Quest to find the Source, all my travels here.' She chuckled uneasily. 'Although it was late and she was pretty, and I was probably just trying to impress her.'

Have you found this Source?

'No. I'm not so sure anymore. I don't think there's much to find in the end. Just ghosts of yourself and the people you left behind.'

Demorn looked at back at the fire. Her burning eyes were glassy. She felt exhausted.

'But some people are reflected almost perfectly through the Mirrors. Twin souls. They can feel the other. It's very rare and special.'

Demorn's voice trembled. 'You can kill one in this world just to hurt the other . . . that's what they did to Kate. It was very cruel. It's why she sails in a ship of the dead, it's why she can't forgive me.'

Demorn voice was fast and infected with pain. Kate was a model in Paris, Kate was hustling for a TV show, Kate was on a skull ship, sailing away. She's still a mirror of herself, Demorn thought with a tight desperate sadness.

Do you have a perfect copy?

Demorn laughed. She spoke with a lightness she didn't feel. 'Not me, huntress. I come from Asanti, a mirror world in a mirror universe. My universe was ripped apart by a monster. Asanti is dead. I was flung through the Mirrors, connected to the memory of a tomb world.'

Demorn saw fragile images inside the flames. Flashes of a purple crystal blinking on a desert floor, the howling of a future god.

'I'm not alone. Most Innocents are exiles. We take our pleasure in the work and what the money buys us.'

Toxis rose silently. Her lithe fingers touched Demorn's brow.

But have you filled the empty place?

Demorn closed her eyes. She saw the Clubhouse of the Innocents; she saw her vast, lonely bedroom; the huge night city flashing outside darkened windows. She saw herself killing the Shark Gang in the fluorescent lights of the burger joint, mixed with blurry images of kissing a lover in the numb frost of a Chicago park in winter, a sudden bittersweet ache flooding through her. Oh, Kate.

Demorn opened her eyes, looked away from the flames. The images faded away. She felt tired. She didn't want to look at these alien stars. She didn't want to try and find the glitter of distant, lost Asanti.

She brushed Toxis's hand away, smiled wryly.

'I remember . . . more than usual. Does that make me less empty? Then the fog descends and I'm just a wandering sword upon a highway that never ends. I've just got echoes.'

Demorn raised her flaming sword toward the heavens, sweeping it above her head, encompassing the stars with her burning blade.

'Fools curse the mirrors, they curse their twisted reflections. They imagine themselves free somewhere else, beneath a different sun, a different sky.'

And you don't, Princess?

Demorn smiled, walking toward the burning signs upon the poplar tree. Her fingers brushed against and through the burning symbols. Her green eyes blazed with the promise of a terrible future, and Xalos burned with purple fire.

'We are all reflections. Spirits chained to flesh. I remember singing to the Beatles, I remember drinking bad coffee and trying not to be lonely. Right now, I'm alive with a magic sword, trying to save everyone. That's enough for me.'

Toxis watched with huge blood-filled eyes, as her mind grew silent. She saw the Glass Crown flickering over Demorn's head, ghostly and so dangerous. This saviour could kill them as easily as save them. This saviour was a violent, empty vessel.

6

The fire flickered, burning low as Demorn kept watch. Toxis was fast asleep, draped in her red shawl. Xalos rested in the scabbard, laid over Demorn's knees. The stars shone bright in different patterns. Things phased, the universe shifting.

Demorn changed as she looked up at the sky, becoming younger, a teen in a blue hoodie and comic t-shirt, listening to music through her earbuds, bobbing her head to the tunes. She wore tight blue nylon pants with a red star emblazoned on them and her eyes burned like stars.

The signs on the trees lit up in vivid lines. Demorn walked to the edge of the clearing and touched one of the blazing signs. White fire burned in a perfect circle around the symbol and her hand.

An explosion roared around them, the choking scent of burning filling the air as the ground shook. Demorn saw trees torn from their roots. Red burning light spread across the sky as waves of energy poured from the Fort. She heard crashing. The elaborate crystalline dome was shattered.

Demorn shifted back to her black kimono, the purple blade alight in her hands. She spoke the command word; the flames lowered and she leaped across the boundary. An animalistic howl came from the forest. Tempting her, calling her.

Demorn looked back at Toxis through the magical flames, still curled up, sleeping. Demorn ran fast into the dark forest. The sky burned violet. She was filled with a pure urgency. Giant, hungry eyes of unknown creatures glistened in the night but nothing stopped her.

Demorn ran on instinct, upwards, across a high ridge, out of the forest, onto a rocky outcrop, and beyond that, the open Endless Sea. Lightning flickered across the water. Two creatures fought, ghastly silhouettes against the blood red sky. She moved closer. A bestial monster was raining huge blows upon on a tall rake-like figure in a colourful blue navy coat. The monster's back rippled with muscles, maxed out to a primal intensity as it punched and punched the taller figure. There was something strangely robotic, almost mannequin-like about the thin body being struck. It flailed aimlessly and crumpled jerkily with the blows. The huge creature turned, baring savage teeth at Demorn, fangs jutting from an enraged mouth.

Her eyes flashed, piercing the soul. She saw the suffering spirit of a man trapped deep within. Every inch of the beast held a violent power. Demorn approached slowly, her senses wary.

An Admiral Skeleton lay within the uniform of the beaten figure. Magic bones shattered as they were hit again and again, defenceless against the barrage of fists. Each time the bones were shattered they repaired, knitting together. The fists rained down without mercy. Dark sorcery.

Suddenly the Admiral Skeleton laughed insanely. It jerked and floated away from the monster's grasp, eerie and resplendent under the blood sky. The Admiral's blue coat had incongruous buttons on it, mainstream stuff mixed with bizarre vaudeville acts from the forgotten long dead past. It yelled out to Demorn, words floating weirdly in the air, white blocky letters issuing from his skeletal mouth, all some crazy, savage cartoon born into real life.

I AM THE BONE KING AND YOU ARE ALL DOOMED!!! YOU ARE ALL DOOMED!!!

The Beast grabbed the skeleton, dragging it back to the ground. The bone creature turned with sightless eyes at Demorn, the face a smiling mockery of life. The skeleton waved one bony hand, beseeching her.

'Save me, Princess of the Skull, O Princess Save me . . .'

Then it cackled, the voice a sad mockery of real need. Demorn sneered in disgust.

'I serve the Swords, not a skull. Go away, dead thing.'

The creature drove its fist through the Skeleton, shattering the death-smile face. With a brutal lack of mercy, the creature snapped off the head and threw it soaring from the cliff top, far into the ocean. The rest of the Skeleton fell broken and useless to the ground.

The beast roared in anger at the light pouring into the sky from the broken dome over the White Fort, his massive form outlined against the sea.

Demorn stepped closer. The creature bared his teeth, horribly human-like in its anger, infected with an immense animalistic possession. But Demorn felt no fear, her path was clear and straight as an arrow. Xalos blazed red in her hand, the purple fire changed.

'Begone, death.'

The creature slowly faded away, howling. For a single moment, she saw a proud, good looking man with a square jaw and a penetrating gaze, a truth about him . . . and then it was all gone.

She went over to the Admiral's coat, examining the rich blue uniform. She picked up the hat, old fashioned, out of some distant century, electric blue with gold trimmings. She twirling it in her fingers. Underneath the brim KATE'S REVENGE was inscribed in large letters. The hat flared up, burning with a vicious fire, and she dropped it, flooded with shock and emotion.

The bones charred and crisply burnt, forming a wavering Skull Icon. The words KATE'S REVENGE floated ominously through the blue smoke.

'Kate,' she breathed. 'Oh, Kate.'

On reflex, Demorn reverted back to her younger self, in the blue hoodie and classic comic t-shirt. Old folk music played on her earbuds, something they had listened to on lazy afternoons overlooking a sunlit sea, when they were alone together. It was so long ago. The past was a dream caught within a dream.

Her phone started ringing with a cheesy cartoon ringtone. MY EX MY EX MY EX scrawling across the display.

Demorn felt apprehensive. 'Hello.'

The girl's voice was light, happy on the surface. 'Hey, Demorn, remember me?'

Demorn looked out through the smoky skull, toward the ocean lit up by the red sky. It still felt like a dream and she didn't know where she was anymore.

'Kate,' she said softly, as if talking to the past itself.

'The one and the only.' The giggle was light.

Demorn brushed her hair from her face, feeling young and nervous. She didn't know what to say. It was so hard to say the first thing after everything. It had been her own heart and head which had burnt out like a forest fire, with flames so ruthless and so vicious, cleansing pain and the regrets. Leaving only a terrible, clean place, stripped back to the naked core.

'I thought you were gone forever, Kate.' She took a breath. 'I thought you were dead in Firethorn.'

A tiny pause, the voice on the other end soft. 'Do I sound dead? I'm just waiting for you to come rescue me.'

'I . . . don't know if I can anymore.'

There was a long pause on the phone.

When Kate spoke next, her voice felt far away, quieter and sad. 'But you can save everybody else? Do you remember why we broke up, Dee? Do you remember why you weren't with me that day?'

Demorn looked into the ocean. But there was no answer in the rolling waves. But she felt she could see things, neon signs on those dark waters, flickers of that long, final Vegas weekend where things had burnt out. Her body trembled, touching shadows.

Demorn said, 'We got different. Sang different songs, liked different comics, movies . . . different everything.'

There was a silence on the phone. The girl laughed suddenly.

'Gawd, you got so deep in the off-season! I was just wondering if you've let your hair grow long?'

Demorn smiled shyly. 'Yeah, I have.'

'Cool with a Capital K. You always looked so beautiful with long hair.'

Demorn struggled to control her voice, raw with emotion. 'You don't know how much I wanted things to change and be different.'

Kate sounded sad. 'I know, hun. Just like I know the song you're playing. I bet it's cool and sad. Do you still feel the shiver we felt that day?'

Demorn's felt time and place suck away. She saw the Music Arcade. The gleaming, unforgettable cheesy sign in a cheap, sprawling strip mall. Kate was by her side, holding her hand, somewhere in their pasts, both of them young and thin and cold. There was nobody else around. Kate looked at her, blue eyes flashing, saying something, but Demorn couldn't hear her or remember what she said. From the Music Arcade came the overpowering pull of the vortex, a magic howl of need and love and hate and obsession flooding into both their bodies.

Demorn walked in, Kate behind her, their fingers brushing. Both of them were crying, and their eyes burned like stars. Demorn could see the vortex, she could see the machine, she could see the sorcery, she could see even see the sorcerers, it was so transparent and clear.

Kate pressed into her. Demorn could hear her voice now, she was saying, *give them my love, give them my love, give them all my love*—

The vortex swallowed them. A huge tremor, years passed. Demorn saw a huge white house, overlooking a sparkling sea that glittered in the sun. Ease and peace washed over her as she lay in the heat. Kate floated in the air above her, lost in meditation, the sun shining on her beautiful pale skin and everything was OK, nobody had died. She wanted to hold on, she wanted to stay in the moment.

The vision broke back to now.

The dark ocean had replaced that shining sea. All the lights went out, except for the foreboding red clouds above. Kate was dead and gone. Demorn was afraid to look at what floated above her.

'Of course I feel the shiver. It's like a dream now, so long ago it hurts to remember.' Her green eyes were wet with tears. 'Why are you calling me, Kate?'

''Cause I'm dead in Firethorn and you still haven't saved me.'

Looking out across the water, through the smoke, Demorn saw a ghost ship on the Ocean. A huge black sail flew from the ship, the Skull emblem emblazoned upon it, the words KATE'S REVENGE clearly visible.

Demorn raised her hand toward the ship, flickering ghostly in the water, half covered by mists.

'I'm so sorry, Kate.'

The ship faded, ghostlike and distant, like Kate and the memories of them together. 'I miss you so fucking much.'

'Then save me, silly.'

'How?'

Kate laughed lightly down the line. Demorn's magic eyes searched the Skull Ship with her far vision, but she couldn't see a beautiful blonde girl, just an assortment of skeletal guards.

'This is Firethorn. I was just a *visitor*. Sure I'm dead here, but I'm only a little bit dead. Do you remember the Mission of the Skull Rings?'

Demorn hadn't heard those words in years. She looked down at her hand, the Odin Ring glinting on her ring finger. That wise old deathless god. Sometimes it could barely be seen, and she could never remember how she found it, but now his dark eye seemed to glitter.

'We were just kids having fun.'

'But kids can know the truth. You've got an Odin Ring on your finger, Dee. It helps me find you, even here.'

Demorn gave a lusty sigh. 'You're not even dead. You're in Paris at some fashion show.'

'The part of me that belonged to you is. We can have it all back and I won't be hurt any more.'

Demorn was crying. The phone call was over. It always ended the same way. The same promises. So much promise that it hurt. The Skull Ship vanished into the distant mists. With the blue smoke encircling her, Demorn looked tougher, colder, more alone.

She bent down to the charred Admiral bones. Not much was left of the uniform. Just a torn piece of the hat, inscribed with KATE'S REVENGE.

'I accept the Mission of the Skull Rings,' she said softly.

The smoke encircled her as she knelt by the embers of the bones, seeping into her body. When the smoke cleared, Demorn wore her tight black leather jacket, nylon pants, and black combat boots.

Demorn looked back to the White Fort with the red light streaming from it. The crystal dome was still shattered. The visions of the Arcade were gone and all her love was dead. She laughed despite herself at the skull bandana in her hand.

'So damn cheesy.'

Toxis watched intently from the tree line, her staff in hand, a barely visible red shadow.

What was that?

Demorn walked past her, eyes flashing, the skull burning on her jacket arm. 'My past. We all have one.'

Toxis lip curled in a faint sneer at the change in Demorn. ***You wear the Skull?***

'You were asleep,' Demorn said.

Toxis put a quick hand on her shoulder. ***The Blood Clan sleeps light.***

Demorn flicked the hand away. 'Well cheer up, sulky, 'cause I've found Blood a new mission.'

Red swam through the eyes of the huntress.

Demorn turned her head sideways, smiling slightly. The shadow of a golden crown flickered above her head.

'And what's life's without a mission?'

Toxis nodded her head slightly.

Demorn threw her the bandana. ‘Have this back. Do what you like with it. I’m just a person, Toxis. I couldn’t care less about being called a Princess. Come fight with me if you want. Or stay here, talking tough in the fucking shadows.’

Demorn walked into the trees, vanishing into the forest. Toxis looked at the White Fort. The red light played upon her features, the broken crystal dome shining and huge like a swollen, pregnant star. Blood and hunger filled her icy eyes. She could hear the bells tolling. She could hear the bells tolling deep in the heart of everything.

Toxis understood with a hunter’s instinct that this Princess of the Swords held a loose grip upon the throne.

7

The white falcon flew across the Endless Sea, gliding in the wind currents, called by lures and the strange pink light spilling into the sky. The White Fort lay upon the sheer top of the cliff-face. The standard of a red fire-dragon on black flames was burnt and fraying in the night wind. The last shreds of the crystal dome were burning out.

The falcon soared over the Fort. There was a barely noticeable blurring in the air and suddenly the dark figure of Demorn dropped from the sky, perched high atop the battlements. She vanished quickly behind the castle walls.

She gestured a series of abrupt commands with her fingers and the falcon flew back over the sea, the binding spell broken, the bird released. Demorn kissed a single white falcon feather and it quickly burned in her fingers, the primitive magic done.

Varangians manned the battlements all around her. Two big guards stood close by, slovenly and hateful. They carried weighty crystal axes, looking suspiciously at the burning sky, murmuring in their native tongue.

A third creature moved slowly down the wall-walk, a mindless ghoul. The other guards shuddered in repulsion and she couldn't blame them. Demorn peered into the ghoul's sightless, bloodless eyes as it shuffled along. She saw the wounds upon its grey skin and wondered how powerful the necromancer was to animate this loathsome dead thing.

The Odin Ring upon her finger glowed faintly as the creature neared, the purple single eye of Odin upon the black iron. She could sense the ghoul's sluggish, pathetic knowledge that something was out there. Her hand clenched the katana. The purple eye flared once, but the ghoul turned away.

Her mind synched with the Varangians' speech.

'We fight with the damned. Odin will not spare our cursed souls,' one of the guards spat out. Demorn agreed with a savage bitterness. She soundlessly plunged from the high walls into the lower reaches of the invaded fort, her feet silent and fast.

The white walls of the Fort were scarred by graffiti, horrible things written on the sacred walls. What was pristine had been defiled.

Demorn snarled when she saw THE GODDESS IS A DEAD WHORE scrawled in pink spray paint on a courtyard wall. A thin, ragged slave had just finished tagging the message, bopping to some pop-punk tune on his headphones, his look vacant, drugged out, and sick. Her katana flashed, decapitating the slave boy, his mohawked head spinning across the cobblestones, the music still playing.

She appeared from the shadows, a sneer on her face, rage blazing all through her heart. She looked down at the t-shirt on the headless corpse, a cheesy goth-rock opera motif which showed lightning bolts and sledge-hammers.

These children are lost, she realized. The reckoning would be terrible. Forget mercy.

Angrily, Demorn tore the shirt off the headless body and smeared it across the wall, destroying the message. She couldn't care less who saw her. She wanted them to find her, charge her in some savage death match.

But the rage passed. She saw a green glow emanating from inside a nearby archway. Cautiously, Demorn entered the half-familiar gate. Her memories were blurry and distant. Inside the grotto archway, a steaming green pool shone, filled with three bodies. A beautiful naked blonde woman. Two Varangians floated face down.

A huge Varangian laughed by the pool. Giant ceremonial horns curled from his helmet. He carried a bloody battle axe, electricity flickering over the crystal. His face was scarred and bloody.

Anger trembling inside her, Demorn looked at the diagrams on the walls, icons of the Goddesses and Lost Sisters of Firethorn. Broken statues were scrawled with glittering graffiti and blood throughout the grotto.

She leapt out of the shadows, almost invisible in her midnight garb, wrapping her gossamer-like chain around his neck, choking the Varangian before he could even draw breath. She cracked the chain viciously, killing instantly.

They ruin everything beautiful, she thought. The naked woman floated in the pool, pale skin translucent. Her hair was a luscious platinum blonde, her face turned away, half hidden in the steamy water.

But only half hidden. Demorn brushed her face with a strange tenderness that surprised her. She knew this beautiful woman, had fought both alongside and against her, in multiple dimensions.

'Alex. My favourite enemy.'

Demorn kissed her chastely on the lips. It was like kissing a ghost, the past itself. She had never thought Alex would really die. She always forgot Alex was an Innocent. She always forgot Alex was in both worlds. She forgot how alike they were. She ran her hand through the dead woman's hair.

'How could you die?'

A tiny sigh.

'How could you actually think she was killed off screen?'

Demorn eyes caught alight. She saw a small fast girl dressed in tight black clothes, almost invisible, swallowed by the shadows of the grotto. She was *a part* of those very shadows, flickering in and out of them.

'What?'

The girl emerged into the green light. An unmarked statue lit up. She was pale and young, shifting with the moments, something unreal about her. Her hand rested on a curved dagger slung around her waist. She sliced her hand across her neck in a slashing gesture, looking at the Varangians. She spoke playfully, energy washing over her face.

'It's off with their head and ask no questions, isn't it?'

Demorn looked at her curiously. 'I'm not looking for answers.'

'It's all so macho, so bloodthirsty. You're so angry. You kill with such relish.'

Demorn had been in this courtyard when it was a place of protection, not a defiled grotto. Everything was shattered and gone to the wild.

'Of course I hate the intruders. Don't you?'

The girl shrugged, flicking tiny dice across her lithe fingers, numbers glistening, the cubes disappearing back between her fingers.

'I'm not chained to rules, Sword Princess. The road is full of plunderers, fighting over coins and worthless women. Why should I add to them?'

The girl smiled and looked around the ruined courtyard.

'This is just a scene in a movie that never ends. They just keep shooting.'

Demorn rolled her eyes. 'Ah, you're a philosopher. And you like to pretend life's a movie. How exhausting. Not everything is meaningless, some people are worth something.'

The girl looked at her with sudden interest.

'Worth?'

She held up a red die, gazing through the prism of colour at Demorn.

'Whose worth do you seek to measure?'

Demorn looked at the other statues, defiled and broken, scarred by the Varangian brutes, then back at the single glowing icon of the girl.

'This is stupid, you're just some weird, amoral creature hopping on board whatever ship comes along.'

Demorn's fingers flicked in symbols of protection, but the signs felt vacuous and thin. This rogue goddess wouldn't be stopped or held by whatever simple spells she could cast.

The girl rolled a neat lipstick cube across her lips, making them a translucent ghost purple. Then she winked, magic eyes flashing and burning in the grotto. She flickered, and she was at the pool, holding Alex's hand. Steam seemed to pour through her. Her glowing lips brushed Alex's brow.

'I've seen far less attractive ships.'

Demorn watched her carefully, amused. There was power in this strange, flighty creature.

'Do you have a name?'

'Oh, my family calls me the Last.'

The girl dipped a toe into the water, dropping Alex's hand. 'But I prefer Melanie, it's less gloomy. It's what I write on tax returns.'

She looked at the other lifeless statues. 'But they're right, I am the last.'

Demorn glanced at the beautiful body of Alexandria in the water. Had she moved just slightly?

'So anyway,' the Last continued, 'we were talking about the Weight?'

The lithe creature seemed to slide into nothing, then suddenly her small hand was pressed against Demorn's breast, quickly whipping the locket from her neck, as she twirled away into the depths of the grotto.

Demorn gasped. It seemed something was sucked from her very soul itself. She felt the world blur, an empty ache all over her, feelings and images and memories falling out of her. The ache of the Winter Park, catching the L train over the bridge in the middle of a night, a Marilyn Monroe marathon on the cable channel, kissing Kate in a freezing apartment at midnight, perfume memories on a loop, fading in and out.

'A pretty little thing isn't she? Scrawled all over your heart,' the Last murmured. 'Part toxic, all gorgeous.'

In the mist an image formed of two girls standing by a sunlit valley. It was much more than a hologram, Demorn knew, it was a waking dream. Deep, green woods on every side. Demorn wore a tall spiked silver crown. Kate was dressed in a white parka and jeans. The two of them slowly walked through the valley for that seemed like hours, deeper and deeper into the woods, lost in some private chat, with private laughter and inside jokes.

Demorn reached out to touch the vision. She wanted that life. She had never really had that life. The Last tossed the locket back to Demorn. The reverie was broken.

'She hasn't left much of you, has she?'

The image of the sunlit valley began to fade into the mists.

Demorn's smile was sad. 'Not a lot. Even in my dreams, it's me who stays. She's just a visitor.'

The Last splashed her bare feet through the water and last of the visions vanished.

'Then walk away! Don't chase her, don't save her, don't fool yourself it will be some romantic quest to reach the edge of the map.'

Demorn looked at the shadowy figure. 'Why do you care?'

The Last laughed lightly. 'I'm a goddess of thieves, dear. I've had plenty of little scamps cry on my shoulder. Even the wicked have hearts. We all feel.'

She waved her finger at Demorn. 'But we have to keep our minds on business.'

She pointed at Alexandria. 'And our buxom blonde? Was she a lover?'

Demorn smiled, glad to be away from topics so close to her. 'Something more like like/hate.'

The Last Breath looked down at the naked body. She brushed her hand through the hot pool.

'I could hate her pretty easily,' the Last Breath whispered. There was a scary hint of hunger in her voice, some kind of need. Demorn realized this creature was not of any sex or species or gender preference. Her image was as lithe as her hands. The form she took flickered and rolled like a wave.

The Last looked at Demorn with a cheeky grin. Her eyes were light and her smile was razor sharp.

'She's breathing, y'know. Death lingers, but won't stay.'

The grotto grew hotter. The Last Breath become almost a wisp, a presence amongst the mists. She was very slim, older. As Demorn gazed at her, she saw this dark creature slitting throats on a battlefield, pilfering for coin, amoral and unbothered.

'Why did you give your soul away?' asked the Last.

'I didn't have much choice. It was either that or death.'

The Last raised an elegant eyebrow.

'Death. Are you frightened by it?'

'Back then, maybe. Not anymore.'

The Last Breath was in front of Demorn suddenly. Her eyes were golden. She ran an ice-cold finger along Demorn's face. Blood dripped down her cheek.

'You're still scarred. Alodin Mars must have liked you. To never withdraw her mark or her patronage.'

Demorn brushed the scar self-consciously. The Last pressed her hand upon the locket.

'Alodin Mars and her kin gouge into frail mortals like vultures, obsessed with wars reverberating through reality. She's fickle with humans, they're less than cattle to her normally. What makes you so special?'

Demorn shrugged. 'It was our deal. She left a little part of me.'

The Last Breath smiled but her eyes were dark.

'Which part? Your aura is a burnt-out shell. She left you mostly empty.'

Demorn brushed the hand away. Her cheek healed instantly.

'I still like music and good movies. I still like kissing and nice girls. It just means nothing too serious.'

'Hah.'

Demorn smiled. 'Ask anybody, I was never that deep anyway. My soul lies in my sword hand.' She flexed her hand. 'And there is a reckoning.'

The Last Breath drifted away from her, her shadowy form indistinct in the air.

'I don't fight in their wars, you know. I don't carry their banners and sing the marching songs. I wish you had prayed for me, not her.' She looked at the broken statues. 'But nobody does. I'm the Last, the sweet kiss to a culture before it goes under the earth with the worms and the skeletons.'

She glanced at Demorn, who was lost looking into the steamy grotto pool. There were tears in the Last Breath's eyes.

'I would only have stolen your soul for a little way, Sword Princess. Not the whole journey.'

She always wished she could see Kate again, be alone with her on that mystery holiday into the woods she could never remember finishing. The dream lay on the edge of her conscious mind, soft green falling rain by the white house, a lover's hideaway. Soft music playing all summer long, as it passed toward fall. Then that was over, leaving a blank beach with pebbles looking out to a grey, unmoving sea. She was sitting on the rocks as the white waves crashed around her, wearing a black hoodie with the words THE WORLD WON'T LISTEN *emblazoned in stark white letters.*

The murky spires of Babelzon reared up in the distance, shadows of a troubled future. It was all too hurtful and too awkward, the diaries of a teenager found in adulthood. Above the moody sea, the sky was filled with electric blue letters that screamed—

Demorn broke out of the spell, electric words buzzing on her mind. The Last Breath was against her body, laughing wildly. She was like a porcelain doll, purple lips, black eyes with a golden spark. Her scented perfume was familiar. Power trembled through her. She sprang away. Her black eyes sparkled with lightning, piercing and seductive in her glance.

In her lithe hands the Last Breath held a small purple reddish star. She pulled a thoughtful face. 'I like you, Wandering Princess of the Sword, always have. I've got something special for you.'

Demorn glowered at this lighthearted, foolish spirit.

'Is this where you ask me for my soul?'

'I already told you. I'm not in the soul business.'

She looked up at Demorn innocently. Her eyes sparkled with orange fire. Demorn suddenly realised the Last was wearing the skull insignia, the colours flickering and changing upon her forehead, neon bright.

Demorn reached for the katana upon her back, but her hand grasped empty air.

The Last giggled. 'They call me the goddess of thieves, so sue me.'

She drew the katana from her dark clothes. It blazed with a savage white fire, burning with a vivid heat, far more powerful than Demorn had felt or seen. The purple star licked the Last's hand and she fed it into the great blade. White-orange flames leapt higher, heat bathing the grotto and Demorn's face.

Demorn breathed, feeling the clean fire wash through her body and mind, wiping through doubts and lies.

As the flames of Justice burned higher and true, the veil of mystery passed from the Last Breath, leaving her face clean and clear. She had striking features and carried an imperial, alien pride. Her hair fell long and glistening black and her eyes were black and golden. The Last grinned, teeth glinting, tossing the blade through the air. Demorn caught it gracefully.

Demorn ran her hand across her face, feeling the soul death mask seep into her skin.

'It really is my soul, isn't it?' Demorn asked, feeling the heat from the blade turn cold as the flames turned purple.

'The last flicker or so. The bit that matters.' The Last Breath winked. 'I like my scamps to keep a little bit of themselves.'

The Last put her white hand against the wall of the grotto which shimmered with multicoloured energy shields.

'Can you see clearly with those magic eyes, Princess?'

The colour of the walls dazzled and burned Demorn's vision. She looked at Alex, floating in an isolation neuro-bath, her body punctured with bullet wounds, nodes pressed against her face, slowly healing, as she screamed against confinement, cursing unseen captors. Suddenly the hulking dead Varangians strewn across the grotto were not truly Varangians from some distant shore. They were men and women meshed with cybernetics, twisted flesh inside metal constructs. Much was illusion. Their images flickered and it hurt her brain to focus on it. She saw Triton's corporate marking upon their thin stretched flesh.

Demorn looked back at the Last Breath and saw just a sinister shadow with no face. A shiver ran through her as she saw the purple burning heart at the core of the shadow. She felt she glimpsed some mystery of life. Pyramids hung in the sky, turning. The White Fort burned.

'What does it all mean?' she murmured.

The Last Breath's voice was a smooth, kind whisper in her ear.

'It doesn't mean anything. Except survive and win. Maybe one day ascend, join the dancing gods, chanting over mirrored worlds.'

The Last's lips brushed her cheek lightly. Her perfume was that of rotting things, wet blood and fresh money. Demorn caught the Last Breath with a fast hand. Her green eyes blazed into the dark, shadowy goddess.

'Has Triton bought you?'

The Last Breath brushed Demorn's hand away with ease. Her mind opened up for one terrifying moment, showing the glistening Mirrors, multiple worlds and universes linked to each other by gossamer threads. The reflections in the Mirrors were ghastly and monstrous, while shadow gods danced to insane songs about nothing, howling for nobody, dead as they were born. It was the mad reality of that which Demorn had studied as a child, a kind of truth that pushed back at versions of sanity. As quickly as the image appeared, it disappeared, wiped clean, leaving emptiness.

'Demorn, don't you realise? *This* is the hostile takeover. This is the virus killing all of us who haven't accepted their terrible solution. This is Triton coming for the Fort, for Firethorn, our dreams and fantasies.'

She was the girl again now, younger than Demorn, very tired, not really making sense.

'Imagine you beat them, imagine you stop the rot of this entire sequence of realities. What do you want the end to be?'

Demorn felt an incredible sense of trust, an uncommon feeling in her. She didn't feel this way with anybody outside of Smile.

Demorn said, 'I warn you, it sounds really lame.'

She laughed at herself. 'I always wanted to just go with a friend to some rustic coffee bar, maybe high up in the mountains, maybe hidden deep in a city I visit, laugh about how silly our lives are. I can picture it, strong coffee, old school records playing, maybe Johnny Cash and Bob Dylan, something incredibly mysterious and beautiful. We chill through the morning sun, joking about how grim and serious we act, shooting all these bad people, wearing these death masks, when all we want is peace and quiet, space away from all these people who want to think of us as monsters. And that's just the start of the most brilliant day ever. We do loads of other stuff.'

Demorn paused, open. 'But hardly anybody wants that, do they? It isn't much of an end, more of an interlude.'

The Last's eyes were golden and kind.

'I love interludes. They're all about the quiet moments.'

A chill darkness fell across the grotto. The young girl vanished, her flashing purple heart the last thing to go. The Last Breath flickered back to the evasive statue of the trickster, almost but not quite invisible to the naked eye, her true face hidden beneath a web of intricate protection spells, difficult to focus on, impossible to remember.

The longer Demorn stared at the ruined statues on the wall, hidden by the greenery, weathered and rotten by time, the less she remembered of a girl made of light shadows and sharp savage grins. The emptier she got, the more Demorn realised she had to kill the Varangians. She had to reclaim the White Fort. There was just the War. Just the War.

8

Slowly Demorn came back to reality. There were no turning pyramids in the sky. That was just stupid, the by-product of witchery, no doubt.

Her head hurt.

She was gazing at a cowled, marble statue, covered in moss. She didn't know why. She barely remembered anything but the moment. The marble was icy to her fingers. A thin gossamer thread lay upon the statue. Demorn lifted it up, the grey thread winding tightly around her hand. Her hand shimmered, fading to vague nothingness.

With deliberate care, Demorn took the shawl, winding it around her leather jacket. In the pool, Alexandria smiled, her beautiful body still only half covered by the steaming water.

Demorn heard stirring in the water. The Varangian lying in the Pool begin to reanimate, lurching awkwardly from the hot water. With her blazing katana she beheaded him viciously. She drove the blade through the second undead, as it too stirred. Their dead bodies floated upon the water.

Lightning blazed through the sky, permeating the grotto, shaking the entire sky for a single moment. She found herself gazing at the lightning with a wistful heart. It seemed to soothe and sing to her soul.

I'm not afraid of anything, she realised. I'm not afraid to live or die.

'Zombie Varangians? Now *that's* a party, Demorn.'

The woman's voice was touched with a slight, familiar note of sarcasm.

Demorn turned around with deliberate care. 'Alex?'

Alex looked beautiful and sexy, her body lying seductively in the water, skin glistening. Demorn watched life and beauty came back to Alexandria's face, lips reddening, and her platinum blonde hair acquired a single streak of pure black.

Demorn felt trembling, mixed emotions. Desire and caution. The blade's burning dulled to a faint orange glow. Demorn brushed the edge of her katana along Alexandria's white neck, touching the delicate Japanese script running down the skin, to the curve of her full breasts. She really was so damn beautiful.

'You gonna go zombie on me too, Alex?'

The stomach wound was healing before Demorn's eyes, becoming a jagged scar, fading to a faint red outline, and then just smooth creamy skin.

'Doubt it, honey, I'm just waking up.' Alex yawned, her hand brushing her tight white tummy, covering her full breasts.

Demorn thought of all their little battles, their brief little treaties. Good times mixed with hurt ones, cheap funny jokes in between fast bullets. A strange friendship that survived despite themselves and what they did for a living.

Demorn slid Xalos into the scabbard and impulsively kissed Alex flush on the mouth. Alex gripped the back of her neck, meeting the kiss with a hunger that Demorn didn't try to resist. They broke it off at the same time. Demorn moved on instinct, catching Alex's hand with a small knife in it, inches from her gut.

'Too slow, Alex.'

Alex smiled luxuriously and released the blade. 'Ah c'mon, you know I just wanted to leave a tiny little flesh wound. It would only be fair; you got a free kiss and saw my tits after all.'

Slowly Demorn got up.

'You're too good for me to be saving your enormous ass. Are you getting sloppy in your old age?'

Alex dropped back deeper into the hot water, laughing a deep throaty laugh, the water covering everything but her head and wet, beautiful hair.

'I'm a working girl. I was in the Clubhouse, I took a job, then I took an axe to the gut.' Alex grinned savagely. 'Not my finest moment. Maybe I was distracted by all these big, hulking he-men.'

Demorn looked at the beheaded bodies in the grotto, their crystal axes smashed and scattered. 'They seem like boring oafs.'

'Ah, but boring oafs with huge, ripped muscles and crazy rock-god hair have their charms.'

Demorn laughed easily.

'Well, it's nice to have you here, Alex. You don't visit enough.'

Alex's laugh was lazy. Demorn wondered where the truth lay. Alex was a cagey one, you might as well expect straight talk from the Sphinx. For a moment it felt like fast laughs in the Clubhouse. But they were a long way from the Innocents and Babelzon. Whatever protection and calming spells were inlaid within these grotto's walls was being eaten away even as they spoke.

Alex spoke from the depths of the pool, her voice vague and sleepy, but determined to have the last say.

'One thing, Demorn.'

'Yeah, babe?'

'It's been black magic all job long, real voodoo shit. That's how they got me. The witch at the centre of all this, she knows our secrets. Where we come from, who we are. The lot.'

Demorn went cold. 'She's an Innocent? She remembers Babelzon?'

Alex's voice was soft and dreamy. 'Don't know if she's an official, card-carrying member, we never had a heart-to-heart. But she's walked inside our Clubhouse walls, that's for damn sure.'

Demorn's eyes arched in surprise but even as she opened her mouth to ask more, the grotto steamed up and Alex was gone. Oh, perfect. She glanced at her wrist and saw the yellow flashing icon of Smile upon her watch. Alex had been recalled home. Smile had handled the teleport back to the Clubhouse as soon as he'd picked up a heartbeat on Alex.

Smile wouldn't find Demorn that way. She had turned off her recall button years ago, after one of the first missions, and her brother had never convinced her to change her mind. Demorn kept looking at the empty grotto pool where Alex had been. Sometimes she wanted to turn it off for all of them. To see how they would fight when there was no easy way out, no backdoor, just the desperate need to keep fighting.

Demorn would have put serious cash on Alex disabling the recall, too. Maybe Alex really was a sphinx. Maybe Demorn didn't know her at all. Maybe Alex doesn't have the same death-wish as me. Maybe Alex has something or somebody to live for.

Lightning blazed across the sky, thunder crashing in response, rolling from the ocean. The graffiti glistened on the walls. Everything felt like blood and lasers. A clean rage soared through her heart. Demorn left the grotto running with fast, silent feet, the burning katana light in her hand. She knew she was going to end this, end it all.

9

The battle for the White Fort raged around the huntress. Toxis took cover in the colourful laser maze, the bow curiously light in her hands. An electric arrow was strung tight, the loaded charge hissing softly as she released. Her eyes glittered full blood-red; sweat glistened on her dark face. The maze changed around her, flickering with stunning red and green mirrored constructs.

The pane in front of her shattered as a massive battle axe spun through the grid. Toxis dodged out at the last moment, barely avoiding the spinning blade sailing overhead into the flashing red mirror maze wall behind her, shattering it, then rebounding back through the laser wall to the wielder.

Toxis winced. Her red cloak was singed by the crackling laser. Her arm was burnt by the wall. But she survived.

The maze shifted again. A great albino Minotaur charged at her, axe glistening, reflected on every mirror around her. On instinct, she tumbled back-flipping through the maze, leaping over the multicoloured walls, firing electric arrows, her fingers dancing as the mirror images of the Great Bull were shattered again and again.

The maze flickered to nothing, the mirrors and illusion gone. She was on a thin stone walkway above a dark valley. A giant steel tower reared above her, black and angry against the violent sky.

The Great Bull swayed with drunken movements in front of her, his gigantic albino form laden with her arrows, the shafts sizzling with electricity. Bestial eyes locked upon Toxis, snarling as the Great Bull tried to wrench the arrows from his hide.

Toxis heard the air itself hiss as she smashed into the huge beast with a wild roundhouse kick, sending the Bull flying onto an electronic maze wall surging into life. The Minotaur roared and howled in anguish. His skin was charred and burnt upon the electric wall. Toxis seized the wooden staff upon her back and pressed it into the creature's massive chest, holding the creature against the laser wall, her hands vibrating with the power of the maze's electricity.

With no trace of mercy or pity, she watched the Bull die. Many of her sisters had fallen to the savagery of the Bull. He had hunted and killed them on battlefields stretching across seven continents, in their beds, their boudoirs, their homes. Toxis had followed in the wake of his corpses for years, driving him deeper and deeper into the wilderness. He had become a figure of old nightmares, something to scare the young children with, a barely real myth, an almost too comfortable race memory. It was abhorrent to Toxis that the Bull had made it into the White Fort itself, the very heart of the Clans. She did not take her blood eyes off him as he died, his monstrous strength nothing against the electronic wall and her vise-like grip. Eventually, the Bull was burnt out and utterly dead.

And so this Hunt is over, she swore. Toxis murmured her hunt tribute, releasing her staff, the body of the Bull slumping face first onto the bridge.

Such a cheap death for so ferocious a Beast, who massacred so many.

The Great Bull had grown old. His skin was loose and the muscles smaller than the pictures of lore. Her keen blood eyes noted the markings on his skin, intricate tribal carvings, and then more recent rougher signs of witch-work.

A sudden fury overtook her as her mind screamed: ***Did you sell what remained of your soul to foul Corizan in the end, Great Bull?***

With a savage fury Toxis kicked the giant body into the cold, unwelcoming chasm. It toppled and fell away from the narrow bridge. Toxis looked over the edge into the abyss, an evil, icy wind pressing against her face. She drew the red cloak around her body. A small pink fire lay in the depths of the abyss, the pinprick of a tiny star. A warm glow so at odds with the terrible bitter cold in the wind and her own heart.

Don't jump Hunter. Don't jump Hunter . . .

It came as a voice on the wind, a soft girl's voice. She gripped her staff, instincts ablaze. As she did, the laser maze suddenly blazed up again. The chasm and the black tower vanished beneath a reflection of vivid, colored images.

The mirrors glistened and she was penned inside a laser box, her own image reflected bizarrely multiple times. There was now a haunted image of herself staring back, her face decayed and rotten, the red cloak dirty and tattered. Eyes that were empty husks gazed out of her ruined face.

Zombie . . . said that voice in the wind, a whisper dry as death itself.

Toxis looked to her left. That shimmering reflection was herself in a jet black kimono, that of the Midnight Clan. Her eyes were pure blue. She held a bloody katana. Rain fell behind the image, an electronic mist of blue.

This can be you, nobody's slave . . .

Toxis pushed her staff against the laser wall, and it shuddered in her hands. The Midnight Sister held her katana to the wall. The Zombie's hand burned and charred.

A massive energy blur smashed through the box, the mirror images refracting, splinters of her everywhere. The blur slammed into Toxis with the speed of a hurricane, lifting her up, bouncing her body off the laser maze, burning her arms. Toxis spun in the air, using the staff to rebound off the searing laser wall. She flipped to her feet, stinking of burnt clothes and flesh.

The blurring figure attacked again, knocking her off her feet, slashing her face wildly with a buzzing knife. She couldn't see properly, blood coursed from her eye. She heard a girlish giggle and sneered, focusing her mind past all the distractions and the laser wall and the strangeness of everything.

There was an eerie silence in her core.

She could feel the rush of the wind, the metallic click as the laser wall shifted. She could see without seeing the invisible blur and where it would be.

There was a single moment and her staff stuck home. She heard the electro knife scatter on stone.

She foot-swept the blur's path, and she pinned the moving force. She opened her blood eyes.

A teenage boy was captured perfectly in her hold, splayed against the stone. He was tiny and thin, desperation and panic in his eyes. He sneered at Toxis. His eyes were glazed and he reeked.

Speed Patrol?

'YEASO WHAT?? WE PICKED A SIDE, BITCH!'

Toxis slapped the boy. She felt pure hate in her heart. Her thoughts blazed into his mind, each word a ring of fire.

You swore to protect Firethorn. You swore to the Goddess in the temple.

The boy looked pathetically lost. 'The temple burnt. Things change-FAST in Speed Patrol.'

Toxis caught his wrist, turning it quickly and cruelly. It was littered with small puncture marks, surrounding the tattoo of the Goddess which the Clans wore.

Who did this?

The boy cackled. 'SlowDUMB Idiot . . . I did!'

The speed-boy squirmed in Toxis's grip. She slapped him hard across the face again.

'I had to stay FAST!'

He blurred, fighting the hold, vibrating fast. The two rolled to the edge of the maze. Something pressed against her tight stomach. Toxis looked down, to see him slide a smaller electro knife fast into her stomach.

Gasping slightly, Toxis chopped the hand away, and held the boy up by the searing energy maze. She felt nothing, no pain, no fear, nothing but the white fire within.

You're so slow.

The boy twisted to no avail. Toxis seized his trembling face, forcing the boy to look Toxis in her single blood eye.

How many traitors? How many helped Firethorn fall?

He spat in her face.

'Everyone, BITCH. ALL OF THE SPEED GUARDS. You can't beat Evolution you can't beat Revolution—'

Toxis bared her fangs.

You haven't beaten the Blood.

'Cowards hiding in a fucking cave! Their time will COME!'

Toxis bit deeply into his neck, her savage ritual. Her mind-voice was soft and terribly intense.

Traitors find no Mercy from the Blood.

Blood ran down her chin. She threw him into the laser maze and watched the energy burn him up. There was true wildness in Toxis. Her red eyes did not turn away until she knew he was dead.

The maze faded away again. The charred body fell onto the narrow stone bridge. Blind in one eye, blood leaking from the shattered socket and her torn gut, Toxis felt bizarrely triumphant and light-headed.

The axe of the Great Bull flickered in multiple colours upon the walkway. She took his axe, heavy in her strong hands. She wondered if it still carried all the souls it had taken.

The pink light increased from beneath the walkway, like a rosy sea flowing deep below. The tower in front of her suddenly cast off its cloak of steel and shadow and blazed white and pure.

Toxis placed her hand in front of blood eyes, away from this blinding light.

A shadow fell across the white light. She felt a terrible, ancient cold invade her bones. Her eyes shone red as she looked up.

Lightning and silver flashed across her blood-filled eyes. She looked into a void of blackness laced with flashes of thin white lightning.

The lightning formed a face. She saw one voodoo skeleton dressed in the red robes of a king. The bones grew flesh. He was a kind looking man with longish brown hair and sad eyes.

Her mind hissed, filled with suspicion. *What dark magic is this?*

He smiled, the light from the tower blazing in the background past his ocean of lightning and void.

'I am no shadowy trickster. I am not hiding from the Sun.'

His face flashed to the skull, all flesh gone, a magnificent, bejewelled, steel crown upon his head. 'I am the Bone King.'

The silver lightning backdrop became images of people, flickering against the blackness. She could see the dancing images of enemies, strangers, Sisters, comrades, both those living and dead. And so many that she did not remember anymore.

Then Toxis saw the dancing skeletons, the hordes of people that she had killed and killed and killed. A fierce pride filled Toxis. For the victims to her Hunt outweighed all.

He reached out with a tanned hand. Upon his finger was a perfect silver skull ring. His fist uncurled. A single blood rose lay in his palm.

Toxis knelt before him.

'Long you have fed me with your Endless Hunt.'

His ring sparkled a stunning silver, lighting up her dark, injured face.

'Now drink from my cup, wild one.'

Her lips brushed the cold metal. She felt the silver light soothe and bathe her, healing her ruined eye.

His voice was deep and friendly. 'Your Princess cannot take this ring, not till every world where I thrive is swept to ruin . . .'

My Princess, she thought with a cold passionless loathing. My Princess that kills my Blood Sisters. My Princess who is so careless of her own legend. She looked at the golden bracelet around her arm. The bond between us.

And then?

He looked at her with those sad, quiet eyes. 'I thrive like a wild rose in desolation.'

Toxis looked up at him. Her eyes had cleared to an icy blue, just like those of the Bone King.

Why do we fight you?

Her Princess armband started blinking purple, calling her, needing her. The Bone King grabbed her wrist. The skin covering his hand became a claw, brittle and icy.

'Because you are the slave of a selfish master.'

Her form started to flicker away, in answer to the call of the armband, but the icy bone hand pulled her back, kept her on the stone bridge.

I know. Can you free me?

'Yes.'

They were jerked from the bridge, not following the purple star, but into his silver lightning haze which covered the void.

The Bone King walked through a beautiful green garden, filled with black roses. He was dressed in a long black cloak. Silver lines ran through his dark hair. His face was young and kind. Toxis walked with him, her hand lightly in his.

She had no markings, no wounds, no sad thoughts, just the dreamy jasmine scent of the garden. She wore her red cloak, her long dark legs glistening. Toxis studied a stunning black rose surrounded by sharp thorns.

'Look at the Sun.'

She looked at the sky. A Black Sun hung there, a hungry, bottomless void in a wide open blue sky. Things shifted and the sky suddenly filled with shining white stars. But she could feel the gnawing emptiness beneath it all. The stars shone down on the Bone King. His face was phasing from skeleton to flesh and back. His blue eyes spilled real tears as he looked to the sky, and the tears upon his skin were black.

A massive Ice Dragon flew across the sky, the scales and skin glistening, no wings, a huge black worm slithering across the sky, so graceful and so evil.

'We are always so doomed, so doomed . . .' he said quietly.

She could not stop staring at the creature, framed against blue and the white stars. It called to her.

It feels so pure.

'It's your Death, wild one,' he said softly.

Such a clean way to die.

He put his bony hand on her.

The ice of the skull burned into her breast through the red fabric.

'What do you carry inside?'

She looked at him coldly. ***I carry the Blood.***

He shrugged. 'Once you did. You were so clean, so wild and free. But now . . . I can taste the garbage, the junk and the clutter.'

He grabbed her cloak and roughly seized Toxis toward him with his freezing hands. She struggled, but his grip was iron.

His low voice rumbled, 'You stink of fake feelings and compromise. Hunts half complete.'

Her eyes went blood red.

You know nothing, savage King of Bone. I am vengeance.

He laughed cruelly and his grip tightened on her throat.

'What of those you did not avenge, Blood Sister? Twisting in their shallow grave, forgotten by their Huntress. What of the monsters you let live, imagining yourself some sort of saint, while you play nursemaid to a spoiled Princess?'

His face flashed from bone to flesh in a hideous blur.

'What of them!'

She refused to die a coward. Her burning mind fought against his merciless cold.

Even a Hunter . . . must know Mercy.

'Mercy is not yours to give!'

He kissed her full on the lips, frost on his tongue. She felt the black ice enter her, frigid and unmoving, obliterating everything warm in her body and mind and heart. He withdrew his cold lips.

'It really isn't, wild one. Such weakness in the strong saddens me.'

As the ice ate into her soul, Toxis knew there was brutal, total truth in his unforgiving words. The Hunt had become corrupt and routine and weak. Young Blood hunted with blunt spears, more fond of their songs and silly games than the essence of the Hunt itself. So weak that they were now ripe to become victims themselves. In her soul Toxis hated them and their pretty, vapid uselessness. It was why she Hunted alone. It was why she had come upon the Princess in the ice caverns so long ago. Why she wore the armband.

The Bone King released her.

In agony, Toxis staggered to the ground, by the black roses. She could feel every arrow and blade wound from past battles, scars open and fresh again, blood pouring from the markings of a lifetime spent at war.

The Bone King bent down and gave her his skull ringed hand.

'Does it hurt? It has to hurt.'

Toxis looked at him with gritted teeth and blood eyes. She gave the barest nod.

It hurts, my king.

'Shed everything, Blood Hunter. The junk, the shallow love for fake friends who do not deserve it. Shed everything but the fire and the blood. I want just that. I do not need the wreckage of the weak.'

Toxis whispered with her real voice, so low and quiet she could barely be understood. 'I have never been weak.'

His face was the true skull. He wore a glistening silver crown. He gently stroked her face on which there were no wounds. His black death eyes glistened with an intense orange hunger at their core.

'But so many who travelled alongside you were.'

The Bone King reached into her mind with his claws and took what he sought.

The great wind howled through the frozen waste. A tight cluster of girls travelled through the wasteland, carrying spears and staffs, dressed in light animal skins.

One of the girls looked towards the green grassy lands far away. Beneath them, a huge mammoth rolled across the tundra. Her eyes flashed red as she looked wistfully at the great creature.

The image blurred back to Toxis in the Garden, his claw around her throat.

Leave me, reaper. The secrets die with me.

He smiled with his skeletal face, letting his hand move slightly from her throat.

'Yes. They do.'

The Bone King kissed her again, and this time, she kissed back harder. Her mind spun again as he seized her.

—they were in the Caves of the Blood. The Ice Dragon was there, a roaring, giant black worm in the darkness, black fire spilling from its round, teeth-filled mouth.

A horde of Blood Sisters attacked the creature, and it ripped at them with a nest of sharp teeth as they struck with long spears.

Reality shifted and she was staring out at an empty car lot at night. The blaze of a nearby diner was the only light. Mellow rock music played that she did not know and did not like.

Demorn was in a tight leather jacket, laughing, sitting on the hood of their car. The Ballerina of Dying danced across the car hood for them, pirouetting and gyrating like a crazy thing.

She didn't understand this restless, smelly world, with the guns, a Princess who reeked of the perfumes of this alien place, covered in blood. Toxis looked toward the diner, saw the markings of blood on the windows. Everything was dark magic, in their car, in the diner. Demorn was cleaning her gun while she giggled and told shallow stories. Toxis looked down. Her own hands were caked in blood. The Princess placed a loose arm around her.

Suddenly her arm burned and the armband glowed and she was gone—

The Ice Dragon was dead in the cavern, the insides splayed, spears sticking out of its glistening hide.

A coven of the Blood Clan knelt around the Dragon, worshipping and feeding on the corpse, drunk on the intense, rich blood. The women danced in drunken, crazed patterns over the dead Ice Dragon, rich in triumph and lust. She sang with triumph of the kill.

The visions passed. She trembled with their power.

The Bone King said, 'The world is so filthy but you are so clean.'

He wrenched his hand from her chest. A gigantic burn scar was left from his skeletal hand, every finger perfectly formed upon her cloak, burning into her dark skin beneath.

He whispered, 'So many times you have saved her. Your master. Your captor.'

All Blood protect her, since the Dawn.

He smiled with an eerie intelligence. 'Oh no, Huntress, that's just the lie of the White Fort, to make you die for them, again and again and again.'

Her mind went all red, no more control or thought. Savagely, Toxis attacked, clenching his thin flesh with her razor teeth. He stumbled, and she locked onto him in a death roll as he fell back into the Garden, feeling his weak skin tear and rip.

The Bone King struck her with his skeletal hand. Toxis was flung into the black roses. She snarled. She had scratched his bone with her teeth.

She flipped her body up into a karate pose. Part of her longed for the staff. But this was clean. This was a clean death.

I vowed to protect her from birth to dark, nothing will ever change it!

The King smiled sarcastically, and performed an elegant bow.

'And so you vow and you bow, Huntress . . . so deeply and so utterly. It's almost convincing.'

She rushed him in a blur. He caught her with uncanny reflexes, gathering her close in a death grip. She did not make a sound as the ice crushed through her body, choking her, starting to kill her slow. His hollow eyes glowed with the reflection of her fire. He placed his hand over the burn wound, aligning his skeletal fingers perfectly with the mark.

'You've so much to learn. You protect her, you save her. You take her bullets and her kicks and her spears . . . but you're stronger than the Princess. Where is she now? Where is she when I kill you?'

A tear of rage fell from her eye, no sadness, just hate.

NO MATTER HOW DEEP THE HELL I WILL RISE JUST TO SLAY YOU.

He turned his blank, dark eyes away.

'It's just like those cheesy movie villains always said. In life, the strong must cull the weak.'

Her blood vision faded as the ice ate through her entirely, no escape, just a gasping eternal pain, making her body a dry husk. He kept his power flowing through her corpse until the bones showed and there was nothing left, just a dead body in his cold grasp. He whispered to himself, no longer to her.

'They kill until all the weak are dead and only the monsters are left . . . fighting for a charred world, beneath black flags.'

He dropped her corpse. As he did so, he saw something on the huntress that hadn't burned. He bent down.

It was the golden armband she wore, untouched. The insignia of the Goddess was clearly visible, glowing purple lines on the clean metal. As he reached out the armband blurred purple and the body of Toxis vanished.

Sighing, the Bone King stood up. He was alone in his Black Rose garden. He absently picked a rose, the thorn nicking a piece of his fleshy fingers, a tiny bit of blood falling over his fingers. He looked out toward the Ocean.

His form flickered between his modes of being and he felt the world turn in a cold and distant way, his fingers feeling the shallow marks she left upon his bones, not caring if he would ever heal.

10

Demorn chopped down two zombie Varangians with a sweep of Xalos, silencing their last battle cry. The place was crawling with undead. The golden armband burned on her arm. Toxis was nowhere. The connection between them felt fragile.

She pushed through the half-open doors of the Great Hall, noting the foul skull graffiti had been marked into the vivid red fire-dragon symbols engraved into the thick stone doors. She touched the engravings with her hand, feeling cool power beneath the hideous graffiti scars.

The Great Hall was vast and filled with dark smoke, obscuring her line of sight and stinging her glittering eyes. The smoke billowed upwards, towards a open roof and a sky she could not see.

Cloudy orange torches lay upon the walls. Somebody had been lighting small self-made fires upon the stony ground. She saw strange diagrams of witchcraft laid into the ancient stones, drawn in what looked like dried blood. Her fingers instinctively wove small protection spells learned as a child to guard against the Corizan witches.

Demorn could not remember the last time she had come to the Great Hall, so long had it been since she had come to Firethorn. But she knew this was all very wrong. It had been a place of sun, not foul darkness.

A low guttural snarl came from the smoke ahead of her. She sank into a low battle stance. A Devil Beast emerged from the smoke, with red savage eyes and open putrefied flesh. Froth bubbled from the mouth of the creature.

Sweet Goddess, nothing could save this creature. The Devil Beast had become true undead.

A thin woman in a black robe sat astride the undead creature. Her skin was covered in blood symbols, and her eyes were as red as that of the Beast.

Demorn's heart grew cold. The woman was a true Corizan Witch.

'Does nothing stay dead?' Demorn asked.

The Witch smiled upon the Beast. There was no kindness or sanity in those red eyes.

'Not for long, Princess. This is my kingdom now. AND THE DEAD SHALL NEVER REST.'

The stone doors slammed with a sonic boom. The witch moved her fingers and three war-women leapt from the shadows. None of them touched the ground as Xalos cut through the air, taking lives mercilessly.

Demorn looked at the faces of the women. All were zombies starting to decay, their cheeks crossed with a single red sign of Corizan sorcery. Beneath that vile marking and the rot of the half-death, each face was distantly familiar to Demorn, fallen comrades. She knew that somewhere in life, they had all been Innocents once, citizens of the White Fort. They had been friends.

But no more. She flicked the gossamer thread from her wrist and wrapped it around the fingers on her left hand. Endgame, she whispered. Everything felt clear. She heard choruses of half-remembered songs echo in her head. A knife of bitter pleasure ran through Demorn.

'You love killing your sisters, don't you?' the Witch hissed.

Demorn was grim. 'Traitors forfeit mercy.'

The Witch looked at her piercingly. Demorn did not look away. Spells did not frighten her. Her mind was a clear place.

The Witch spoke almost like a song. 'They are mere puppets on a string.'

Involuntarily, the glittering green eyes of Demorn flashed through the death magic and she saw the mind of the Devil Beast beneath the unholy yoke placed upon it. The creature's former mind was gone, shattered by the excruciating journey from life to death and back. Her eyes phased back to the rotting face of the Beast. Was it just her imagination that she caught a glimpse of something mortal in those ruined eyes, a begging for a true end?

The Witch spoke in a low hiss. 'Most fought before they fell.'

But Demorn was not listening to the lies of a Witch. The gossamer thread whipped from her hand, ripping across the face of the sorceress and caught her neck, cutting her to bleed.

The Witch was dragged downward. The Beast reared and bucked wildly.

Demorn sprang upward, ripping the woman toward her blade.

'Then I free them from the rope!'

Her blade sought blood, but at the final moment, the Witch pushed her body backwards into air, snapping the gossamer thread. She soared into the blackness of the Hall, away from the magic sight of Demorn, foul smelling smoke covering her escape.

The Devil Beast screamed and roared in final, hideous anguish, the spell link broken. Demorn danced across the putrid flesh in a single step, leaping away as it crumbled to dust and bones beneath her feet.

Then she melted into the darkness, following the injured Witch.

Toxis was back on the walkway, wounded and in pain, staring into the blazing darkness, the lightning bolts flashing in the midst of the vortex. The lightning exploded around her, a pulsating mini Big Bang.

Blood came from her ruined eye. On both sides of the walkway was a swarming mass of dead Varangian Warriors, some rotten, some freshly dead. A legion of the damned. Toxis curled her lips in a ferocious smile. She swore her heart to the Blood Clan and the sacred altars of the Goddess, deep in the ice caves of her homeland.

She glanced at her arm, it was bare. She wore no golden armband anymore. No yoke, no chain, no tie. She was free to die. A legion of undead. Too many for even her. A vicious current of pleasure ran through her.

A hunter's death.

Toxis snarled as she got up, taunting the horde, screaming into their foul, rotten minds. ***YOU WANT TO KILL ME? COME KILL ME!***

The Varangians rushed her and Toxis leaped, striking with both legs, feeling no pain, her staff cutting in a circle sweep, destroying the first wave of zombies, throwing many off the walkway. She kicked and pummelled with her staff.

Blurred shapes flitted in amongst the fight. Corrupted Speed Patrol members, she guessed. They moved inside the wind, cutting and slicing across the air, buffeting her body, taking out her legs, sending Toxis to the stone, her staff cracking and snapping on the cold walkway as she viciously swung, trying to read desperate patterns in their insane rhythms. From her knees she lashed out with punches and kicks, sending several blurred shapes over the edge into the abyss.

Toxis regathered and bounced to her feet, her fists bleeding and cut, the red cloak ripped, dark flesh visible, blood and scars all over her.

There was an ungodly roar, and she looked up to see a massive ice giant, laced with zombie bones, mindless and yet inhumanly strong, smashing through the crowd. Enraged, it threw skeletons and Speed Patrol members out of the way as it thundered down toward her.

With her last effort Toxis wrenched her shattered staff from the floor and leapt towards the giant, bodies clinging to her on both sides.

She charged with a nimble running kick into the creature, swaying it, and then she shoved the broken staff into its huge body, releasing the blade within. Her hands went bloody when the blade cut her, too, messy in its work through the frozen skin.

The giant howled, swaying wildly, clawing at her body. She pushed hard and desperately into his icy hide, crying out in unholy triumph. Green blood spurted from the creature, onto her body, the blade driven deeper and deeper into some sick combination of ice and flesh. Below them the horde of undead struck at her body and the giant and each other, a sea of chaotic motion that knew no rule.

They toppled off the ledge, Toxis spinning from the ice colossus, leaving the broken staff in his chest. She tumbled toward the light, deeper and deeper into the electronic chasm, merging with the pink glow, becoming invisible to the naked eye, a single thought flowing through her. Everything felt free, and she felt a sliver of pleasure as the pink light became an ocean of pain and color, eating through her body, stinging her skin.

In her last moment her face caught aflame and Toxis screamed in pleasure, the Huntress stripped to her core, every instinct alight, feeling nothing but a blind, wild pain and a single thought.

A perfect death beats a perfect kill a perfect death beats a perfect kill . . .

The small ground fires lit the way across the Great Hall and she moved like the wind through the smoke, light and deadly.

Demorn came upon the Witch kneeling at the base of a dark wooden throne, holding a sinister death-head skull, surrounded by Corizan bewitchments on the stone ground.

The sorceress turned to snarl at Demorn.

The woman's face was no longer young and beautiful, but that of an old hag, and the black robe was not fine, but in tatters. The Witch's tattooed face was marked with long sores, burnt by the gossamer thread.

'I guess this proves spells don't hold back the years,' Demorn said as she circled the witch's circle, keeping her mental defences up, her mind repeating protection vows.

The Witch grinned, displaying rotten teeth, caressing the white skull marked with the strange Corizan symbols. 'Oh brave, precious Princess . . . so proud, and so well taught.'

The Corizan intoned something in her foul sorcery language, and held the skull high. 'But many have studied with the masters.'

The death-head eyes glowed ominously purple in the smoke. Demorn could feel the power vibrating and leeching from the skull. She kept her voice light.

'Was that your teacher? Your special magic coach? A trinket you can't separate yourself from, even when he's six feet under?' She smiled viciously. 'That's damn weak.'

The hag features softened again to a young woman with pretty black hair and a stylish black dress that revealed just enough to want it all. Her eyes were kind and cute, no blood signs, no dark magic.

The horrible skull was now a simple pendant on a silver chain, which the dark haired woman fitted around her pale neck, a black opal glistening.

'Oh, Fair Princess, you were so young, so open. I wanted to make you in my own image.'

'You?'

'Oh yes, don't you remember now, dear? As we walked along the white beach with your Daddy. What a gorgeous summer it was, just lovely . . .'

Demorn was taken someplace else, far from the Great Hall, far away from the blood that had drenched her hands and her body and her soul. She heard the fresh sound of crashing waves in the surf, smashing rhythmically against the shore, a fresh, clean counterpoint to this corrupt witch's den.

Feelings and scents came back from childhood, a childhood she did not truly know. She was young again, she was barely fifteen, dressed in tight blue jeans, looking out across the wild sea. The wind blew strong and free through her long hair.

Bones rose from the stained and dirty floor, and began to encircle her head.

'And do you remember the Fall?'

Her Daddy walked across the pebbles on the beach. His arm was around a small woman with black hair. The woman turned to look at her, her eyes flashing red. Everything felt fake and fragile. The witch's hand clawed across her Daddy's huge back. Demorn felt that cold horrible finger brush her face, as the witch's voice flowed over her mind.

'Fables tell of a cruel stepmother and a misunderstood, neglected girl. But I loved your Daddy so much, so very much. And you were just the wreckage from his former life, the shadow to his sun, a girl who would not learn her magic lessons, a girl who would not do as she was TOLD!'

Inside the Great Hall, Demorn staggered before the throne, almost totally lost in the spell. The bones spun fast around her head. Cobwebs covered the great wooden throne. Smoke cleared slightly to reveal how dirty and corrupt the Hall had become.

Voodoo trappings and animal and human sacrifices were everywhere. Demorn saw the carcass of a Unicorn, rotten and open, filled with flies and maggots.

And in the centre of it all, the Witch, holding her withered, ancient hand over her chest.

'Oh dear, how he loved you, my Dead King . . . . He was so sad the day I told him I needed his daughter's soul.'

Demorn winced with pain, half on the beach, half in the Hall, grinding through her words. 'My soul?'

'Yes. For his Kingdom to prosper.'

The witch cupped a white hand under Demorn's chin. Her nails were black and they stank. Her voice was cold and polite. 'It's what mattered most to him.'

The Witch kissed her Daddy on the beach. Her long, dark hair almost touched the pebbles on the hard sand. The black nails clawed into her Daddy's back. Everything felt like a nightmare. Demorn could see the past and the future and the present, and everything was corrupt, it was as if time itself pulsed with a dark heart.

Tears streamed down the eyes of Demorn, fifteen, on the shore, as the surf crashed down, and the music played and played in her earphones, and the loneliness went on forever, right out across the ocean.

Through her tears she could see the writing on the wild ocean waves. It said, I WANT LOVE I WANT LOVE I WANT LOVE

Demorn screamed. Her dreams had become nightmares. The letters in the sky smashed into the wild ocean waves. She had sunk to her knees inside the circle, with the candles burning high, and the skull shining pink light from empty eyes.

KABOOOOOOOOOOOOOOOM!

A huge colourful explosion rocketed through the sky, shaking the Hall, spilling the candles over, upsetting delicate enchantments.

The Witch looked up, surprised. The fire in the eyes of the hollow skull flickered and died out. In that single moment, Demorn woke, her mind painfully clear. She lashed out with a closed fist, smashing through the skull, shattering it from the Witch's hands.

The bones burned her hand but she didn't care. Her heart blazed with rage.

The Witch snarled within the broken circle, long dark hair whitening, her body becoming ever more feeble. She raised her thin, frail hands and began to cast some dark spell, but Demorn grabbed Xalos off the floor and drove the blade through the Witch's gut.

She held the red eyes that glinted from the pain of the steel blade.

'Screw you, lady. And your tricks.'

Gasping, the old witch tried feebly to push the blade away, to no avail. Blood began to pour from her eyes. She spoke in ragged, wheezy breaths. 'I can bring your Dead King back, bring him back for good . . .'

Demorn turned the blade in the gut. The metal caught sweet fire.

'Tell your lies to the dead, hag.'

She kicked the body of the witch and it slid off the blade, the tattered black dress soaked in blood. The sword glowed only a dull orange but she didn't care. She had needed a more personal vengeance; she had not wanted any help.

Demorn looked to the open rooftop which looked out to white shining stars. The sky was still reverberating with the last convulsions of the explosion, multicoloured lights sparking like fireworks.

The bracelet upon her arm burned away suddenly with a sting. She felt a sadness in her heart, and she knew with a hollow certainty that Toxis was gone from Firethorn. Maybe forever. Lost in their own battles, neither had come to save the other.

The smoke was leaving the Great Hall. The deep vastness of the room was suddenly apparent to her. The voodoo trappings began to vanish. The horrible carcass of the Unicorn faded away, and she could see spirits moving around that defiled creature. As the smoke disappeared, the stale stench that hung over the room cleared.

Demorn looked at the body of the Witch, which flickered, leaving only the torn black robe, still soaked in blood and evil blood symbols. Above the Hall the stars were clear pinpoints of light in the darkness. Despite everything, all this death, Demorn felt a strange lightness in her heart.

Demorn moved to look at the thrones. One was huge and black, adorned with wooden carvings. She saw the Fire Dragon upon it, carved into the chair handles. On the opposite handle lay a coiled Black Ice Dragon.

She saw an image of the Unicorn, her oldest avatar, glowing on the chair itself, soft and translucent. She breathed a soft prayer of peace, the chant unfamiliar, it had been so long. So long had she been away, covered in blood.

Her eyes caught the smaller throne, shimmering and shadowy behind the Wooden Throne, made of intricate designs of bone. Smoke still clung to this throne, close and thick.

Demorn knelt before the wooden throne, her head bowed. She threw her katana, still slick with blood, onto the ground before the throne.

Her green glittering eyes were wet with tears.

'Firethorn has fallen to evil things. My Sisters and my comrades have perished or betrayed us. The bonds of the Clans are broken.'

The empty dark throne sparkled with a flash of lightning in the sky above. Her voice was clear and aching with sorrow. 'I can kill everything and it will not bring you back.'

A large, dark shadow formed on the throne. A fang glinted the darkness.

A deep voice rumbled. 'Sometimes . . . you must walk the valley alone.'

Demorn looked up, startled. 'My King?'

'Sometimes, things come back.'

His face came out of the shadows, partly wild beast, partly human. She recognised the animalistic creature that had taken apart the Skeleton Admiral on the cliff. She could see the creature struggling to hold on to this aspect of humanity as his face grew clearer.

A strange dread flickered in Demorn, and her hand grasped the katana, even as she bowed, for she knew suddenly and without doubt that this half-monster was what had become of her King.

The Dead King shook his head slowly. 'I am no voodoo horror. I am still your King, even beyond the Dying. It is me, my child. Reborn from the wild.'

Hearing his voice clearly, Demorn dropped the blade. He seemed to briefly master his animal nature, and his features humanised. Impulsively, she rushed forward, hugging him tight. The Dead King hugged back, enclosing her, making her feel safe in his strong arms. For the first time in forever she could trust somebody with everything, she could relax. His body was warm and she could feel the safety like a real thing.

She saw a wound in his side. It was real, bleeding.

'How do you live, my King?'

He grimaced and his face became more animalistic. Then he chuckled with a throaty rumble. 'I linger outside the Halls of the Dead. I hear the wail of the Underworld in my dreams.'

She was solemn. 'I've heard it is a place of shadows and fear.'

The King shrugged. 'All things must pass beneath.'

She said, 'I don't want to pass under. I want to just keep running and never be caught, never be dragged under.'

He held her face. His eyes were sky blue, with no pain or doubt. In all the times to come, whenever she thought of the Dead King, it was his blue eyes she remembered, his blue eyes she turned toward, no matter what came afterward or would ever come.

'I hang to this life by a few wild forest spells, seeing each morning only by the grace of the Goddess . . .'

Demorn looked defiant and looked upon her bloody sword. Her voice was quiet and intense. 'The grace of the Goddess should be enough for all mortals.'

He smiled and she saw his jagged, fanged teeth. With a rough calloused hand he held her face.

'So clear. You are your father's child.'

He looked away. His powerful eyes gazed into darkness, glowering and fierce. For just a moment she was just his child again, no Princess, no hero, no wandering nomad killer.

He growled with a dangerous edge.

'But I am only partly your King anymore . . . most of me belongs to the wild, and the beasts.'

He hauled himself off the throne, his body huge, thick arms and muscled legs. She saw a black tattoo of a burning sun pressed into the hard flesh.

'The wild shall call its monster back.'

She looked up into his blue eyes but they were flecked with yellow hunger, restless, tense and uneasy.

Something old and cold crawled down her back, a premonition of the end, an instinct she could not ignore. Her sword burned strong, cleaning the katana of blood and filth, as she went into her attack pose.

There was an icy chill in the air, a sudden screaming and wailing surrounded her ears and mind, a horrible, hopeless cry of a multitude.

The Dead King fell to the ground, convulsing, his features turning beast-like. A great cry of rage escaped his body.

She looked up, and a tall white figure sat upon the wooden throne, restless fingers tapping across the dark carvings. The creature carried a white veil across his face, one red stain where the mouth was. Cold, yellow eyes were visible through narrow slits in the white veil.

Pale Sun, a Pale Sun.

The Pale Sun's mouth was open beneath the veil. She knew that was where the wailing came from. The Dead King looked at her, bestial now, in the claws of the Pale Sun. Her heart tugged with sadness. She could hear the crying and screaming of women and men. She imagined voices of people she had known, enemies she had killed, friends she hadn't saved.

The sane eyes of the Pale Sun were passionless ice. Although the cold creature said nothing, that cold yellow gaze knew everything.

Demorn's heart beat faster and faster, the screams becoming more intimate, closer to home, the desperate voices those of lovers and good friends, all wanting her help, to be rescued from their misery.

She wondered almost absently, is that the hell that is waiting for me? Demorn invoked a calming saying from childhood on Asanti, in those few years before the darkness and the troubles came, repeating *we are the storm to crash upon their shore*, the mantra of every Asanti exile, until her mind stilled to a frozen place, and she could speak without a tremor, despite the sick cloud surrounding the Pale Sun.

Understanding her place, and with a controlled effort against the feelings of hate, Demorn knelt on one knee before the Pale Sun.

It spoke. 'What rare control you have, Princess of the Sword. What would you ask of me?'

'I would ask you take the animal from the man, Shining Lord, as a sign of my victory over the Corizan Witch.'

The Pale Sun pursed his lips and the wailing greatly decreased. Presently he spoke, softly accented, a precise voice that revealed nothing.

'He is both animal *and* man now, Sword Princess, there is no difference, no turning back the clock. That was the price to fight the witches and the skeletons and many other things. He bargained with devils to keep his throne, as kings shall.'

She stood up, her green eyes icy. 'If you cannot grant my king this token, then I shall ask for nothing more from you.'

The Pale Sun smiled thinly and opened his mouth, the wailing as strong and mournful as before. 'All rulers ask for more, whether they sit upon these thrones a single day or ten centuries.'

Demorn said, 'My father was a brave King. So great was his passion for his people that he served as leader even after he had gone beneath, and the evil things clustered as cowards in his throne room. But now I claim this Crown, and I beg no favour, I seek no deal with the likes of you.'

'Good girl . . .' The Dead King spoke slowly, his voice thick, and she could see the difficulty he had in forming the words, the mark of the wilderness upon his soul. His face was tortured, a change was coming.

Demorn opened her mouth to say some last thing to the Dead King but nothing came out. They locked eyes. It was the last love, between a Dead King and his daughter. Her magic eyes saw so much, too much, they saw everything.

She saw the last pieces of him slipping away. She felt a cold wind blow, as cold as the wind that had blown when she was fifteen and on the beach alone, watching a Witch ensnare his heart.

'You are my King forever!' she screamed, and wild purple lightning arced through the sky, and Xalos erupted from her chest, from her very heart. She felt no pain, just a giddy, savage sense of exultation and victory.

The King smiled viciously, fangs showing, murmuring, 'Let the Blood hunt me! Let their Dead King be their glorious prey!'

Then he was gone, lumbering through the doors of the Hall, on his own dark way, his shadowy form growing ever more animalistic and savage.

With blazing hungry eyes she turned to the Pale Sun. It cringed away from the flames of her mighty Sword. She read fear and doubt in the yellow eyes.

The Lord raised his wizened hands, speaking quickly, almost cooing, as it rose slowly into the air, the skin tight upon its face, red cloak flapping in the wind.

'There is much you do not know, Princess of the Swords! The dimensions are in flux, *and we are as necessary as you are.*'

Her magic eyes saw the insignia of the Pale Suns branding the marble walls. She felt the pressure on her temple as the Sun tried to cloud and distort her mind. But it all felt hollow and a lie, and she felt like the rising morning sun after a long, cold night. Demorn waved her hand in curt dismissal.

'Leave now, liar, and mark my words. You and all your kind, are banished from my Court, while I still breathe.'

The Pale Sun twisted in rage, seemingly in agony. A light, blazing weight fell upon her head. Demorn knew she now wore a burning Crown, feeding into her power and her sight. The Pale Sun cowered before this fresh heavenly fire.

She cried out, 'Leave now! And the devils take your dimensions and your deals!'

Lightning rocketed through the chamber again, and she swung with the fiery sword. The Pale Sun vanished just as the sword smashed against the wooden throne, leaving a single thin split in the dark wood. Demorn caressed it with her finger.

Upon the wooden throne lay a single ring, made of fine icy crystal. The single eye of Odin shone a savage purple upon her right hand.

On instinct, Demorn slipped the ice ring onto her left hand. Instantly, the bone sent a sliver of cold deep into her, some savage message from the future. She knew then, that although a battle had been won, this War was long and far from over.

But it was not the time for sadness. The courtroom of Firethorn was bright around her, clean white light burning through the last of voodoo witchery, warming her cold face, cleansing the Hall and the White Fort. Sun poured through the open roof, dazzling onto the marble floor. All traces of the Pale Suns were gone, their markings banished.

Gone were the foul enchantments of the Witch. The Long Night was over. The sun danced on her clear blade and the purple flames upon it died away.

Demorn gave a shaky heavy sigh. She sheathed the katana and sat upon the throne. A simple golden-colored glass crown flashed above her head, as the astral shadows that she had carried since childhood coalesced into a solid, beautiful thing.

Warmth flooded her heart, soothing and calming her. Strength and energy poured back into her. She gasped aloud. She felt every scar and every wound heal. Even the long, invisible scar upon her cheek softened and vanished.

She could see the brilliant, clear images of the Goddess upon the throne room walls. Sun drenched her.

Demorn looked at the Skull Throne beside her, shrinking from the light, becoming smaller, more distant, like death to the very young, something that happened to other people like a myth. Until finally, that throne of bones was just a lined ominous marking upon the white wall, next to complex diagrams and hieroglyphics of the ancient cat gods and other legends of the lost past.

Three globes of light appeared in the air around Demorn, partly of this reality, partly somewhere else. One globe flashed white and cold, ash silently falling in a clear globe. One globe was as blue as the deep sea. The other was ruby diamonds and endless red fire.

With a quick hand she grabbed the perfect blue globe. It was light and cool. Demorn wandered through the white marble columns of the throne room to the fresh grass in the courtyard.

Skeletons were burning in the low green grass under the bright sun, leaving crystal armour and axes glinting in the hot sun.

The bodies of her Sisters were scattered throughout the grass. A final stand had been made here.

A series of wishing pools were arranged throughout the courtyard, leading to a great fountain in the centre. For just a moment, the ghostly white Unicorn pranced in the sparkling fountain waters, alive again, the ivory horn dazzling brilliantly. Her heart surged as the Unicorn reared high into the sky, neighing triumphantly.

She approached the fountain steps and brushed her fingers in the cold pool.

The water was so clear. As she watched, the word VICTORY flowed across the brilliant surface, red lights blending with her reflection. Her face seemed softer in this warm light.

For one brief moment she was alone and she had won. Demorn felt young and without her burdens. Her life before this, in Babelzon, seemed like a distant dream to which she would perhaps one day return, but not today, not soon.

The golden crown danced above her head and her sunglasses sparkled.

Gentle spirits slowly passed around her, and she could see the girls slowly stirring back to life. One of the Sisters that she had cut down inside the Hall walked across the lawn, her wounds healed and colour upon her face.

She still looked sleepy, as they all seemed, barely woken back to life.

Remember the Blood.

It was like a ghostly sigh in her mind, a whisper loaded with a lingering melancholy. Demorn glanced at her arm but the golden band was still gone from her skin. The place where Toxis had spoken to her, that familiar corner of her mind, had gone silent.

Is she dead now, Demorn thought. Or exiled beyond as I was?

She did not know.

Beyond the courtyard with its graceful white pillars and little wishing pools, lay the dark, green forest. To the east, beyond the sheer cliffs, lay the Endless Sea.

Her hands held tightly to the white walls of the Fort, as she watched the Sun rise over the morning sea, loving it, wanting it to never end, never fall. The Crown shone with a golden brilliance.

Demorn could hear her risen Sisters behind her, chanting her name and that of Firethorn.

She looked at the dazzling blue globe in her hand and released it into the air. Kate suddenly appeared in the glass, wearing a Spider-Man t-shirt that was too big and tight black leggings. She laughed, cute and full of hope, dancing in the apartment they shared so long ago, with the sea behind her and light in her eyes.

Demorn could hear the music in the room, soft, whispering promises to her soul. Tears streamed down Demorn's face, in sudden and unexpected release, as her hands gripped tightly to the battlements.

She didn't care that some of her tears were blood, for the way to victory had been sodden with it, filled with wars and vengeance and strife.

The chanting of her Sisters was raucous and savage, howling to the Sunrise. Demorn wanted the Sun to stay like this, always risen, triumphant in the early day. When her heart felt so open, and victory healed scars, reversing so much dying.

She ignored the dark clouds that suddenly filled the blue globe, and the lightning that arced across the glass. She saw only the face of the girl she loved so much it hurt.

The golden crown upon her head grew tall with terrible spikes. Her eyes became green flames. Still, she gazed at the rising sun, triumph in her heart as the red flag fluttered from the White Fort.

If not for the skull ring on her finger she might not remember the Bone Throne at all. But in her way, Demorn would always remember. The blue globe circled the Princess of Swords.

She turned from the Endless Sea, every sense alive. She walked through the throng of her Sisters, accepting their vicious kisses and blood-oaths. Demorn's visions meshed with theirs. Her eyes burned with the gushing fever of rebirth, the future pulsating bright.

Part 3

1

Two Years Later

The Skull Princess looked out at the red rain falling on sleek city towers. She was in an ultra-modern office, purple glasses on, wearing a tight leather jacket with a Spider-Man t-shirt underneath.

She looked at the skeleton beside her, long blonde falling down the bony back. Behind it, a small gang of Bones clustered in suits, avoiding their hollow eyes from her sun-glassed glaze.

Demorn pushed her finger into the blonde skeleton's black suit.

'This is my city. I'm the flesh. You're just the bone.'

She tugged at the blonde hair, just a wig, an affectation, a vanity. Skeletons weren't meant to have vanities, skeletons were meant to be six feet under. This whole world had gone crazy.

Her voice was soft. 'You want to make flesh, don't you?'

The Bone female nodded.

'Of course you do. So do as I say. Keep the scanner open, keep the electric on, keep the zombies and the psychos out of my City. And don't let anything get to my throne room.'

The skeleton bowed. Demorn could feel their sightless dread eyes as she moved from the boardroom down toward the hangar. It was blank death this world had bought, ever since Dead Day.

The creatures spoke and thought and did the simple things, but that was all they did, vague bad copies of what they had destroyed, machines on half speed stripped of originality or depth.

She watched the alien craft moving slowly through the polluted turgid air toward her tower. It landed in the hangar. It was pock-marked with the scars of conflict.

A female voice flickered in her head.

I hate this city, Skull Princess.

Demorn answered the mind prayer through her implant. It was good for short distance.

Who wouldn't? Call me Demorn. Let's go first name basis.

As she waited for the hatch to open, she flexed her finger, feeling the icy Skull Ring, careful always to stay in control and to keep her game face on. She never exposed her naked eyes to the Bone creatures.

Two men decked out in black combat armour clambered from the ship. They carried huge guns and had mean faces with big scars. They looked like they wanted to nuke the whole room. They looked across at her leaning on the wall, and she could feel their mixture of hatred and fear.

She could feel the idle crawling curiosity of the undead upon her, their savage, barely controlled hunger for flesh. She focused for a moment on the Skull Ring, tasting the ice deep inside her, letting it feed on her soul and feed back into the Bone.

In a single motion the skeletons exited the room.

They're gone.

Why do you keep the abominations alive?

The telepath didn't work with Bone. Demorn knew that much. She ran her operation all flesh.

They keep the city running — help me stay alive.

Until they break the leash. You saw what they did to the UK.

Fuck the UK.

The telepath laughed softly in her head. Demorn hadn't heard a real person laugh in months. It beat dead comedians performing stale routines. It beat old TV shows on endless repeat.

The telepath walked slowly down the ship entrance, an attractive Xaniath woman in a flowing green dress. Her skin was a light green, eyes a brilliant fiery orange. Her shorn skull was a mesh of electronica and the intricate stencilled markings of her distant people.

She sure was a long way from home. Demorn drew her shirt up and showed her tight stomach. She focused her mind and for just a second a red dragon form flared across her abs.

The telepath's fiery eyes became an inferno. Her voice whipped through Demorn's mind like a lash, smashing viciously on the implant's shields.

WHERE DID YOU FIND THE RED DRAGON?

Demorn flashed a casual peace sign. 'Oh, it's mine, hon, too legit to quit. I got in the Xaniath Hive. Full fledged Red Dragon Maze Conqueror.'

DRAGON MAZE CONQUEROR? But you are not even from the MOTHER WORLD—

'From Xaniath? No, not technically. But I saved the life of the Hive Queen. I earnt my stripes.'

Demorn felt a wave of languid sadness from the woman's mind. The Xaniath resumed walking slowly down the ramp.

Our Queen is dead. The Xaniath Hive is bereft—

'Yeah, honey, well in my world the Queen dodged that bullet.'

The telepath locked onto her eyes. Glittering orange met green diamond.

Is this not your world?

Demorn smiled, and stood up from the wall. She felt the pistol on her hip, wondered what an Athena bullet would do to the telepath.

'Different world, same city.'

She noted the flicker of confusion in the telepath's face, the dimming of the orange eyes. This woman was more desperate than she wanted to admit. She's probably wondering if I am just one more crazy in this screwed up grave world.

Demorn said, 'Honesty time, we both need each other. Come in and grab what you like.'

On impulse she dropped the mind shield. The telepath seized her like a demonic possession. For a single blurred moment the Xaniath knew everything, her searching gaze lighting up the secrets and the clean and the unclean places and the bitterness and the old, fond memories and the ice that lay throughout Demorn. She felt the woman scour everywhere, a bitter, searching fire from which there was no refuge. Then the fire was gone, leaving a quiet ruin in its wake.

The telepath's eyes phased back to normal. Demorn slid the shields tightly back in place, massaging her sinuses which ached after the intrusion.

She kept her tone light and dry.

'So now you know . . . I dig cute girls, old movies and long, hot baths. Can we still do business?'

The telepath was impassive, the orange eyes sparkling.

It's true then. You are not of this world.

Demorn smiled. The white bone ring glinted in the harsh lights of the hangar.

'I know, magic right? Come to my safe room, just you.'

OK.

As she walked down the ramp, the guards took places by the ship exit, holding their gun tightly. Nothing showed on their faces but belief and duty, even here, in this palace of cold and corruption. Demorn knew they didn't understand, not this city, not her. She wondered at the trust these guards had in the telepath, to come to the city of the damned.

Demorn sauntered over to the lift to her apartment. The interior was plush, with soft pink decor and nice cushions, a little luxury in the damned place.

They shot up to the heavens, higher and higher, to the very pinnacle of this hell.

Demorn mixed herself a fast drink from the bar she'd installed. She sank into a plush leather couch and ran her hand through her long hair.

The Xaniath woman looked uptight, the impersonal cool broken as her hands fluttered briefly around her face-scarf. By their standards, such movements counted as terrified.

'Relax, honey, we're safe.'

This is safe?

Demorn shrugged. 'Safe as the Grave gets. It must be cool, to have people who trust you.'

We saved them, they are grateful.

Demorn drained her club soda, casually eyeballing the telepath. 'Grateful? Is that the secret?' She drawled slowly. ''Cause I know a decent Xaniath telepath can make a human a walking meat puppet. I've seen it. Make us walk and talk and shoot. I don't care, but I know.' She shrugged noncommittally. 'And something tells me you're more than decent.'

The telepath did not move, her orange gaze fixated on Demorn, impassive.

Only the very weakest minds could be so controlled.

Demorn smiled her scary smile. 'Ah, but being weak is so much more common than being strong.'

The lift slowed and stopped, opening on a lavish penthouse apartment, at the very apex of the building. The room was shaded a delicate blue, softening the red reflections from outside.

Demorn led the way out of the lift and the woman followed.

The penthouse was an organised expensive chaos. TVs and monitors lined the walls, playing scenes from classic movies and beautifully pixilated computer games. Comics and books were strewn across shelves and the floor. Amongst the stylish leather couches was a beautiful throne, made from ivory bones, covered with a pink throw cushion. Exhausted suddenly, Demorn sank into the throne. The magic bones moved and adjusted for her body. A feeling of languid peace swept through her, and the ice softened inside her.

Ironically, the throne of bones was the warmest place for Demorn in this cold land, the only place where the icy burden from her skull ring eased.

The telepath moved lightly through the room. She removed the purple veil around her neck. In the manner of her people, the woman's mouth was covered by a bejewelled voice-box.

What happened to everyone else?

'Gone,' Demorn said vaguely, massaging her tired, sore eyes. 'Gone, gone, gone.'

The woman spoke softly, her physical voice synching and weaving in time with the psychic tone, a little bit sadder and more lonely.

'How long have you been alone in this nightmare, Princess?'

Demorn looked through the wide bay window to the City below , and absently ran her thumb across the back of the throne. This high up, the red rain looked almost romantic and you could forget about the skeletons, pretend that maybe it was just a beautiful twilight. But no city she knew had ever been so dark for so long.

She shrugged.

'It's been two years since Dead Day.'

That's a long time to be alone.

Demorn smiled, looking at the red rain. 'I wasn't alone at first. People died on me. But we all have dreams of escape. Don't we?'

Demorn withdrew a small, silver, coiled ball from her jacket. It glistened in her hand. Symbols glowed on the ball and a hologram materialised in front of them, showing a powerful young man in blue jeans with a grin spread across his attractive face.

He held a huge, writhing Admiral Skeleton in his hands. He threw the Admiral into the broken pavement of a city street, his hands glowing a sudden, vivid red.

A burning, spiked ball materialised in his hands and he smashed the mighty Admiral into pieces, the ball arcing out, destroying clusters of smaller Bones running toward him.

Wrecking Ball!

'Yeah,' Demorn said. 'He's a hottie.'

From the back of her wrist, Demorn flicked a shadow card through the holo, arcing across the images. The card snapped back into her fingers and Demorn felt some of that savage red energy feed and burn back through her like a brush fire. The hologram blinked away.

'He's a ticket out of The Grave.'

The telepath was motionless by the window, framed by red rain.

I have heard the thoughts of survivors, too. But he's just a video game myth. How can that rescue us?

Demorn laughed. 'Oh, Wrecking *is* a video game myth. Through more worlds than this dead one. He was in Babelzon. He was there when I was a kid in Asanti. He's been a permanent fixture in many a blissfully wasted youth.'

Demorn got off the throne, pulling the leather jacket around her, leaving her purple sunglasses on the ivory bones. She looked out at the soft falling rain, looking down at the passing ants far below with her glittering eyes, knowing they were not pedestrians and there was no use pretending they were. They were just sick remnants in a world gone wrong.

'Out there, beyond the city horizon, in the middle of the suburbs, before aliens and Dead Day . . . people believed in the Wrecking Ball.' Demorn's voice went soft. Her skull ring iced up cold, making her hurt inside. 'He was in LA last week. We got the holo off one of the satellite feeds.'

Really?? Los Angeles? But I thought LA was lost.

Demorn laughed. 'So poetic. Yeah, LA is lost. LA was always lost. It's got zombies, plague-carriers, and generic, gun-toting crazy assholes. Everything went bad there.' She winked at the telepath. 'But that's where he is, and that's where we're headed.'

We have flown over it, there is evil spread right across the sprawl.

Demorn's green eyes glittered. She suddenly didn't feel so dead or so worn.

'Who cares? Evil is everywhere. Evil was *always* there. Wrecking Ball is there. I need him.' Her green eyes sparkled. 'And most especially, I need the ring he's wearing.'

Why?

Demorn displayed her finger, the ice ring sparkling with a cruel brilliance. 'He's got one of these. I'm collecting the set. For me, the ring is OUT.'

You say we all dream of escape. What about the rest of us?

'How many is the rest of us?'

The telepath looked at her, fire eyes flaming hot.

Do you mock me?

Casually, Demorn wondered if she could kill the telepath with a bullet before the woman wiped her mind.

'No. I've had sidekicks, loyal kids who hung with me up here. We all swore we would protect each other. But it gets old. They all flew the coop to save the world. They all died. You can't save this world, it's gone.'

Do you blame them? This is a wretched place.

Demorn sighed. 'I tell them there ain't nothing left to save. It's not my world or yours anyway. So don't lie, to me or yourself.'

Demorn felt a wave assail her mind, a great ocean of turbulent flame and she was in a single white tower, feverish and alone, drowned out by everything. But the tide subsided as Demorn focused her mind, brushing her forehead with her pale finger. She opened her eyes.

'Aw come on, honey, I ran the Dragon Maze, I saw the Red Dragon. Let's play nice.'

The telepath closed her brilliant eyes. The ocean faded utterly.

You know of us but you could not understand us, brave Skull Princess. My copilot was wounded in the crash. His mind . . . was diminished. I was reduced to speech with him.

Demorn didn't know what to say. She could feel the almost overwhelming grief in the woman. For Xaniath telepaths to speak aloud between themselves was sacrilege. Such a thing was considered worse than death.

'The Hive is truly broken then,' Demorn said with a grim finality. This grave world had killed something else that was precious.

There is no true Hive here. He is gone leaving nothing but wreckage inside me.

She couldn't resist. 'You've got the humans with the big guns, don't forget them.'

Those brilliant orange eyes, open hunks of raw crystal. *Anyone who lives with me has chosen it.*

Demorn laughed lightly. 'Relax. I couldn't care less. I have Bones running my errands and keeping the electricity on. I only mention it because big brave soldiers with big guns can be very useful.'

She got up and poured herself a club soda from the bar.

'What's the worst thing about The Grave for you?'

The screams of the survivors. They call out to the cold universe, and only I can hear them. They all think they are alone or gone mad.

Demorn sipped her drink. 'You won't have that problem here, nothing lives in Bone City except me. And I'm wonderfully well adjusted.'

Dry mind laughter. *Yes, it's so quiet here. A void.*

Demorn was thoughtful. 'For me, I miss my favourite comics. I miss the late night shows; I miss the hosts doing their lame bits. It was the only news I ever bothered knowing. Everything is just a repeat now.'

She saw the telepath raise a single finger to the window, half turn away, eyes closed.

There's an emptiness in the other room.

'I told you. We're safe up here.'

The telepath gazed out the window absently, nonresponsive.

Demorn looked at the TV. Electro bombs rained down over the forest, in some greatest hits of a past jungle war pre-Dead Day. The silent blast rolled like a wave through the green trees, killing everyone in its wake, leaving the forest almost untouched. It was beautiful, so beautiful. The telepath's mind synched with hers perfectly, and Demorn felt the pristine quality of the Queen, laced with a terrible hurting sadness.

Your shields cannot contain everything, Skull Princess. I CAN FEEL THE EMPTY.

She forced her lips to move. 'Stay out. I don't want to talk about it.'

I know your heart was shattered but this is no answer.

'Stay out.'

You have to let her go, Princess. It's not her. ITS NOT HER IT'S NOT YOUR SOULMATE ANYMORE—

Demorn closed her eyes and gulped down the soda, enjoying the bittersweet tang, letting the terrible mind-whisper run through her, run through the shields, run into her. It felt like a disconnected dream. To trust and invite someone up here after so long, into this private place so high, where the nightmare softened, the first person not Bone. And they find out your secret and all they say is you have to let go. Let go of what? It felt like she had let go of everything. It felt like she was hanging onto sanity by her fingernail. If she let go anymore it would be a bullet to the brain and a note for nobody.

Demorn carefully said, 'You're good, like Xaniath always are. I know you're trying to help. But we all have our ways of coping.'

True.

The telepath spoke softly, facing the terrible red rain. 'This planet is sick. The plague was cruel to leave the few.'

A frigid pause, then a soft whisper in her mind.

Better for you to all have died.

Demorn turned from the screen as the bombs kept exploding, the air flashing with a blinding blue light.

'Amen to that, hon. You don't know how many friends I had to shoot with Athena bullets to make sure they stayed underneath.'

Demorn felt distant, from the rain, from the woman, from herself. She gestured to the dark city outside the window, just a few frail lights flickering.

'It's a haunted metropolis, it's not home. It will never be home.'

My ship can't make orbit. I need haven.

Demorn put a soft hand on the woman's shoulder. It was surprisingly strong and firm.

She said, 'Just trust me and I will get you off this rock.'

The woman relaxed into her hand.

In your world, did you really save our Queen?

'Sure did. It was a close thing,' Demorn whispered. 'The Hive was filled with traitors.'

She felt the woman tense imperceptibly, a wave of sadness wash across her mind.

The Queen died by the hand of her court.

Demorn chuckled. 'Well, I shot a lot of those hands. There are better worlds than this.'

Demorn felt her abs burn with the red dragon tat, a pleasant pain. Xaniath had been a long-range Innocent mission a long time ago. Cash in the bank. It was the mission that kept paying and paying. She'd been amazed when she learned they tried to build a Hive in this wasteland.

'Wrecking Ball is key.'

Key to what?

'To finding the back door out of this crazy dimension caught in a depressing end game.'

Dry laughter in her mind.

You have such faith.

'Not really, but I'm down to the last card in my deck.'

Demorn squeezed her shoulder.

'Do it because when you flew to Bone City to see the Skull Princess you knew it was going to be something dramatic like this.'

The telepath spoke to the dead city and to the Skull Princess. *I will help you.*

Demorn smiled. 'Never doubted you for a second, hon.'

2

Demorn sank back into the Skull Throne, looking on with interest as the Xaniath woman moved to one of the giant screens, fingers flicking across the war, the blue light of the bombs lighting her profile in the twilight penthouse room.

The screens cut from one war to another, jarring images of conflict. A single young black soldier ran from the blue light of the bombs, his faded green shirt torn, a single gun in his hand, eyes wide with fear as he ran through the undergrowth. The blue light exploded all around him and the soldier segued into a thin, teenage boy wearing a torn suit in a murky corridor, a silver pistol in his hand and blood running down his forehead. He looked scared and hurt. Lasers cut from the metallic walls and he was caught in an beautiful energy blaze, screaming.

The images de-synched and became a collage of exploding cities and a marching horde of skeletons and zombies, the total chaos of Dead Day, before it all collapsed into blue light.

She spoke through the voice box, her lilted tone curious and sad. 'Not everything is real. Some of these wars are pretend, Princess. Why?'

Demorn said, 'They are mostly just games.'

No. These people are real or becoming so. I can feel it even across the electronic chasm, I can feel them. As I can feel your brother inside the machines.

Demorn sighed upon the Skull Throne. 'Leave him out of it. Some things are personal.'

The telepath's fiery eyes clouded. Instantly, the big screens shorted out, with a blaze of orange energy and the blurry electric shadow of a spiked Wrecking Ball.

The woman shrank from the screen, her body blown back to the ground. Hellish laughter rang throughout the chamber. The bay window blew out. Demorn cursed.

The telepath's mind snapped through her like a whip.

This is the man you would have save us? He destroys more than he saves. He is so PROUD.

Demorn was rueful as she walked to the bay window, brushing her fingers against the glass, glistening with red rain droplets, looking into the falling twilight. 'Some things need destruction, they are beyond saving.'

All of us are proud, she thought, we few damned survivors left behind. She clicked her fingers twice and an old sweet love song played on the stereo. She made herself another soda.

'Tell your puppets to fire up the spaceship. I'll meet you in LA.'

The telepath touched her arm briefly.

Don't bring any monsters.

Demorn spoke, to the city, to the red rain itself, as much as to any Xaniath telepath.

'It doesn't matter to me. Of course I will come alone. No monsters.'

The woman walked to the plush lift. *Not even dead lovers.*

Bitter and sad suddenly as the lift doors closed, Demorn left the large room, slamming her bedroom door behind her. Tears stung her eyes and her heart was shattered, empty and hurt. She wished that telepaths could only read thoughts not feelings. Get out, she thought.

Demorn waited while the mental presence of the alien grew less and less, until there was just a faint trace left, and then nothing. She let all the shields slide back into place. Get out, stay out, get out, stay out.

Demorn drove the red Jag over the iron city bridge past the city limits, not caring about the shuffling skeletons and rotting zombies walking forever to nowhere.

She drove for half an hour in the early morning, farther and farther from the city, out into the suburban sprawl, half-burnt out wastelands, collapsing ghost towns. Cinemas that would never again play a new film, fast food joints that crawled with roaches and refuse, all that random apocalypse stuff.

She had taken this route more times in the last two years than she cared to remember. Demorn drove fast, playing upbeat songs to feel better, anything with a groove and a big chorus.

She found the silent parks and the empty malls the worst thing. A stillness that was mirrored in her, a lifelessness. She'd been alone too long. She kept driving.

Bone City was out in the desert, a sterile, small time, air-conditioned gambling town. It had been her girlfriend's home, somewhere they ran on Dead Day, one epic crazy road trip across the heartland.

Some nights Demorn would dream they were still out there on the road. Joking despite it all. The skull ring sparkled on her finger in the warm sunlight as she pulled the car over by the highway and hopped out.

The air was scented with the freshness of Spring, so wonderfully refreshing after the claustrophobia of the city, blowing out the cobwebs in her mind.

For a moment she saw Kate beside her, thin and blonde and beautiful, in a band t-shirt and tiny blue shorts, but the image faded, just ghost memories. Demorn kicked an old Coke Zero can along the highway side, smiling.

The city was so far away, a dark smudge on the horizon. This far out, she could pretend it was almost normal. Her watch buzzed slightly, invisible on her wrist. It faintly glowed with a pink half smile.

Jesus, she was so far away from her brother and the Innocents. These last two years she had almost stopped thinking about them.

Demorn wandered across low desert plain grass, following the signal, feeling the pistol on her hip.

The grass got dirtier and lower as the desert surface took over, pulling her closer to the ravine. The ground was cracked and now she felt it pulling her like a tide, calling in the old language, the language of a world she had almost forgotten, lost in this dead dimension. She hadn't been back here in years. She had forgotten.

Demorn reached the edge of the ravine. Cold wind flew up into her face. The chasm split into the earth, deep and severe. She looked down at the shattered Spire. Her spirit felt suddenly broken, like the metal of the Asanti craft below, torn and peeled, the organic super-charged heart exposed and corrupt. Burnt out and dying in this horrible, dead world.

Demorn sighed, taking off her purple sunglasses, slumping to her knees, her green eyes ablaze. Her hands pawed at the crumbling dirt. She was so alone in this world, so very alone.

The sun sparkled on the icy ring. Everything in her wanted to lose the Bone ring, send it tumbling into the ravine, walk away, face the deranged skeletons, go out shooting holy bullets, die not caring, so sick of living just to survive.

'Throw the ring into the abyss then, Skull Princess.'

Her hand flew to the pistol, drawing fast. She could see him, bouncing in and out of the sunlight, a thin man in a grey cloak, a shawl drawn around his face.

The purple laser on her pistol lit up. She could scan his body even as it phased back and forth from invisibility.

'This gun can kill ghosts, y'know,' she said.

His voice was amused. 'I'm no ghost.'

She traced his hidden face with the purple laser light. She could see evidence of wounds. His voice sounded vaguely familiar, but she couldn't place it. She was tired and had been alone too long. Her memories were empty places.

'Who are you, then?'

He seemed to suddenly become the sky itself, powerful and omnipotent, surrounded by an ever increasing number of mini-satellites that circled him, weaving through the air, seeing everything.

I WAS YOUR TYRANT. I WAS YOUR ONLY HOPE.

She shot again and again, bullets lacing into the flickering body. It staggered and twisted with the impact of the holy bullets.

Finally there was just a dead body by the ravine edge. The satellites disappeared as quickly as they had come.

She pulled the shawl aside. The man's face was barely recognisable, scarred and pocked with the markings of disease, but she knew the underlying features from propaganda posters in Babelzon and the giant statues throughout the City. She realised his voice had matched the subliminal ads pumped into Babelzon, night and day, reassuring, confident, amused.

There was not a drop of blood on his face. No true life in this little death. All the damage had already been done. She pulled his grey cloak away. His slender body was a mixture of robotic and synthetic flesh.

His eyes opened, a frighteningly clear blue. 'Oh, Skull Princess, how humbled you have seen your Tyrant.'

She got up, slightly disgusted.

'I don't follow politics. You were never my Tyrant. You're just a cyborg anyway, not the real thing, not really the Tyrant.'

His broken form tried to crawl away from the ravine edge. Her blue watch buzzed again. She had to get to the Spire. She looked down at the ruined ship, which seemed to whisper delicate Asanti hymns, rhythms and grooves lost since childhood.

'Strange things are here, Skull Princess. Terrible truths in this dimension, this dead world.'

A cold wind hit her.

She saw red clouds building on the horizon. The red rains would come soon, and that was death. LA could be death, too, a video game dice roll, chasing urban pop culture myth. The Spire could be death, bleeding at the bottom of the ravine. But nothing meant a lot to her; it didn't scare her anymore.

'That's why I called it The Grave. Everything's dead. You're a coward, Tyrant. It's why you sent a robot to do a man's job. It's why you hid, while this happened to the world.'

His laugh was electronic and pre-programmed.

'Jesus, you're a self righteous bitch. You really think you can save them, don't you?'

She laughed her scary laugh, looking over the empty desert.

'That's exactly what I *don't* think. This world is totally fucked.'

She looked into the vacant blue eyes of the crippled cyborg. Realisation dawned. She ran a hand across his face, feeling that mixture of ruined flesh and metal construct.

Her fingers rapped against his forehead.

'You're in there aren't you? The real you. This whole world fucking DIED and you're watching like some kind of jaded god!'

Filled with anger, Demorn tore the head off the cyborg Tyrant, throwing it into the abyss, hearing it rebound down the ravine.

'I'd love to do that to your fucking sky adverts,' she murmured bitterly.

Feeling sad and tired, Demorn pulled the soul mask from her jacket. It had changed since Smile gave it to her in the Garden. Back then it had fed her, nourished her, empowered her. Now it was a slick black skull, disfigured with pink and white claw marks, twisted by the environment, as her own soul had been stained.

Demorn put it across her face, felt the fabric eat into her, sucking at the marrow of her being, shredding the compassion that was left inside, taking everything soft that she had hidden, leaving just the mission and that irrepressible need to survive, to continue the mission, no matter the cost to herself or anyone else.

Demorn touched the locket and jumped off the ravine's edge, floating downward to the wreckage of the Spire, her invisible watch buzzing softly. She did her best to ignore both it and the familiar jagged pain that clawed in her chest.

3

Incongruous soft rock songs played in her implants when she touched the shattered hull of the Spire.

The shadows in the deep ravine cast a cold shadow on her, but the metal was warm to her touch. Her watch was flashing with a fully formed Smile icon.

Demorn slipped in between the torn metal walls, feeling loose, her heart beating fast. She brushed her forehead absently. Her Athena pistol glinted in the rays of the distant sun above.

Power still churned through the Spire; it hadn't completely died. She was a tough synthetic bitch, Demorn thought with a smile.

On the wall, an old video played brokenly. Some weird, stuttering ad for an iron-rations war gruel. It made her smile despite everything. On impulse, she slid the Bone ring off her finger, sliding it into her jacket pocket.

Beneath the death mask, she felt a sliver of ice melt, a dagger slide out of her heart. Everything felt hyper-realistic, the Spire suddenly not this torn, bleeding, dying thing, but alive, and filled with true power, a craft built to soar through the deepest heavens.

Her hand caught onto the side of the wall.

She heard Smile crying out to her, and a strange, woozy sense of unreality came across her. She tried her hardest to concentrate. She saw a bank of lasers light up ahead, heard voices of strange men. She ran through the half dark, lightly gliding and jumping over the debris of the Spire, the floor lighting up with odd symbols, seeming to wake as she ran toward his voice.

She came to an empty, narrow corridor, tightly closed doors, the only light a faint grey at the end. He was speaking from her watch, blurred and distant. She put it to her ear. He was talking gibberish, sounding in pain. Déjà vu. She'd walked this corridor before. Where had the men gone?

'Smile,' she whispered. 'Smile, are you there?'

A harsh voice came across the line, 'We've got him, you little bitch! Whatcha think you're gonna do?'

She was running up the narrow corridor even as he spoke, moving fast, barely keeping a leash on her anger and her need to rush toward the killing. She heard Smile cry again, close, his real voice mixed with the voice over the watch, another one in her memories.

The corridor blazed with trip lasers, burning and violent. A charred energy smell. On instinct, she desperately smashed herself against one of the narrow doors, busting it open. She heard them laughing.

It was some kind of crazy lab. Her brother was lying in a vat, his smile pierced with needles and alien goo, looking thin and terrified and too young. Dead looking bodies floated at awkward angles in vats next to him.

She shot at slow, fat hustlers and one white coat. One of them still had Smile's phone in his hand, his too-big gun never going close to pulling off a shot. There was no mercy in her, not a trace.

Smile looked like he had slumped into some kind of unconscious shock, but she could still hear him screaming in her head. She rushed to him. She slowly took him from the vat, burning her hands. Demorn knew she had done all this before, it had all happened somewhere before.

She looked into his glowing eyes. 'Is it really you?'

He smiled spectacularly, his golden teeth glistening, warming her, cheering her up the way he always did.

'It's me. But this is all a trick, Sis.'

He reached out and took off her mask. 'It's all just a movie I made.'

Demorn looked around. She watched the dead bodies of the hustlers fade away, the machinery too. Then the lab was gone, as if it had never been there.

They were in the White Room, miles and miles of snowy nothingness. A soft song played in the distance. The whiteness went in all directions. Faint outlines of couches and beds were hidden in the blankness.

She'd always loved this room. She'd made it their conference room back in the Clubhouse. Demorn lay down on one of the beds, breathing freely for the first time in two years. Smile sat cross-legged on one opposite, his purple cape drawn over him, glowing fitfully.

She ran her hand through her hair. 'I thought it was Mexico, I thought they had caught you again.'

'I know. But they can't catch me. You killed them all, Demorn. Even the big racist, awful ones.'

'Especially them.'

He smiled, taking off his cape. He wore an ancient, cool comic book t-shirt. His coloured eyes span like a kaleidoscope.

'I'm in Babelzon. It's a sunny Sunday outside, and the Innocents are turning a tidy profit. I've developed a serious caffeine habit and have trouble sleeping now you're gone. Meanwhile, our Fearless Leader is deep in the Grave, REAL deep.'

He wrinkled his nose and pointed beyond the white space. 'And you're not safe, Sis.'

'Tell me something I don't know. This whole world is crawling with undead. It turned while I was *here*.'

He averted his eyes, the spinning multi-colours fading to that of a very human looking boy.

'It's far worse than that. You're trapped in a box. The White Room is the only place I can reach you, this deep in the heart of the Spire. The ship can speak to itself through dimensions.'

He became animated, his fingers drawing a complex diagram with quick gestures, rotating planets, adjoined clusters filled with stars, an epicentre of galaxies that became a universe, rotating in alignment with other universes, some big, some small, some massive beyond reckoning.

'The whole dimension is isolated and becoming more so. Before too long, The Grave will slide outside of the framework, it will become a closed system.'

Smile's fingers danced across the adjoining universes, red stars now running like a virus through the stars, one tiny little universe growing bigger and bigger, red and swollen and sick, till suddenly she saw it separate, dirty energy churning and burning into miniature big bangs, a tiny balloon expiring and collapsing upon itself.

He spoke as it faded. 'I won't be able to reach you then, Demorn, Spire or no Spire. You must escape.'

She yawned. 'Oh please, not another lecture on dimensions and parallel universes and all that crap! I get it, there's Earth Z and Q and D and C. It's parallel universes like in the comics or old episodes of Star Trek. That's just the easiest way to think about it. We're Asanti, we're mirror people, this isn't news to me.'

He chuckled softly, still lost in the diagrams exploding across the neon whiteness of their private room.

'The easiest way. Maybe not the most correct way. My searches tell me these universes feed upon themselves. The consumption can take millennia, but currently it is speeding up, in constant flux, universes encroaching on each other, matching the mad prophecy of Ultimate Fate, swallowing reality itself, converging on an ever-moving point of temporary perfection . . .'

She placed a cool hand upon his head. He was burning feverishly hot, talking in Asanti. 'Enough, bro, enough.'

He quieted down. 'Why did you do it, Demorn?'

'You know. It felt simple. I was a lonely Queen in Firethorn. From my throne, I could see different worlds. Kate's still dead in Firethorn, bro. But she was alive here. It all seemed the same. It felt like we could start again.'

He looked vulnerable and lost. She took off the skull mask, revealing her face.

She said, 'I almost didn't pack my mask that day I came to visit her.'

Demorn spun the chamber on her pistol. 'Lucky I did. Chicago went Dead Day after our first coffee date. Ever since, I'm running on luck.'

He spoke quietly, 'Luck runs out fast when you don't care about living.'

The skull ring glinted from inside her leather jacket, both tempting and hating her. She didn't feel like inspiring speeches and waving flags.

Demorn smiled her scary smile.

'I've got an invite to LA and a possible escape route. Who knows what will be there anyway? It could be a death sentence. It could be one last final stand.'

His voice was slightly sarcastic. 'At least there will be people to share these arctic one-liners with, Sis. Better that than another year solo of canned food and sad songs and crying over your long lost ex. Who is STILL in Paris and STILL doing soft porn movies, just so y'know.'

Demorn couldn't help but laugh.

'Thanks! It was almost worth it, y'know. Some nights it was. On that drive out of Chicago, we said things we'd never said, we didn't hold anything back. She knew who I was. I don't give a fuck about models or cheesy movies or what she has to do to earn a living.'

Smile hugged her, and she felt his electric presence against her, his aftershave, his fast, intense brand of love.

'That's fab, but almost is almost and dead is dead. You can't bring her back, not all the way.'

He's probably right, Demorn thought with a sudden, sweet clarity which left her sad.

'Are you still doing Music Saturdays in the Clubhouse park?'

'Sure are. I make them squeeze in a country song, just for you.'

Demorn smiled, patting his cheek approvingly. 'Good boy. Hey, I got you something.'

She tossed him a package.

'Oh fucking sweeeeeeeeeeeeeet!' Smile exclaimed, his golden teeth shining super-bright as he opened up a game chip, the trailer constructing and playing in front of him, phasing into his system. The Wrecking Ball smashed through hordes of zombies, Bones and gun-toting looters with something approaching reckless abandon and murderous intent.

Demorn tittered at her brother's obvious, infectious joy.

He shouted, 'Wrecking vs. Dead Day! This is a bona fide classic, Demorn. This is LEGENDARY! This is not just banned, it's MYTHIC! How did you get it?'

'It was created by two gaming geeks in Firethorn. People I hardly knew.'

She watched as Wrecking re-energised his weapon, seared in a red blaze of light, the power rippling through his form, unceasing in his merciless destruction of the skeleton legion.

'It's so weird how they pretty much got everything right. It's kinda why I believe in Wrecking now.'

The trailer ended, and he turned to her, his cloak back, his face a pure white mask. The game vanished back into itself.

'So you do believe?'

She laughed. 'In all that stuff about universes eating themselves? Um, I hardly care. It's just another cool theory. But I *do* believe there's an exit in LA, and most especially, I do believe a big, bright superhero with a Wrecking Ball might help me get home. Now, brother dear, can we chillax and listen to the *White Album*?'

Smile's face glittered. He raised his hands and levitated off the white floor. The Beatles started playing.

'Of course, Demorn, there's always time for that.'

He drifted through the air, massaging her neck and tight shoulders. He wore no mask and his eyes blazed psychedelic purple and blue stars.

'It's good to see you without the glasses.'

Demorn smiled dreamily, so relaxed. She levitated off the white bed and sofa, and both of them slowly circled through the room.

'It feels awesome in here, it's like the only time I can be myself.'

She felt herself get caught up in the music, as she and Smile drifted together, lost in hazy mediation.

'Surely the Skull Princess rules this Land of the Dead?'

She half-smiled lazily. 'There's nothing to rule, there's no soul, everything is empty.'

'It sounds so unhealthy.'

She chuckled. 'I'm watching old horror movies by myself night after night in the penthouse, and I feel like my heart is filled with nothing except ghosts. Of course it's unhealthy.'

He brushed the hair out of her face. She looked at him, and he was fifteen, in his torn grey suit, a gash upon his face, like when she rescued him in Mexico, the only person who understood her completely. For a moment he was not smiling; the light spilling from his face was pure electric blue.

'Do you ever think about home, Demorn?'

'Every day, every night.'

Smile looked at a loss. 'Not just Babelzon. Our real home. Asanti. I don't understand how we aren't dead.'

'We survived the Fracture. We're lucky. The Spire crashed but we survived.'

His voice was distant, his form flickering, and he looked scared and lost and young. 'Sometimes, I can't remember Asanti . . .'

Demorn held her palm up, glowing. Smile held his up, too, and solidified back into being.

The Asanti symbol glowed between them, a multi-headed dragon with blue eyes. It seared on both their palms and she could feel his body and spirit as they flickered into each other.

They were back on the ship, young and alone, in the first moments after their world exploded — surrounded by crying strangers, their minds and spirits broken by the loss of their home-world, already starting to fight about what was left for them. Demorn saw herself in the reflection of a flickering alarm window, younger, a hard sneer upon her face, tightly holding onto Smile, no trust for anybody else, as the ship howled into hyperspace.

Everything merged.

She whispered 'we can make, we can make it' and his fingers gripped onto her jacket as the ship plunged out of the negative, hurtling toward the blue-green world.

Tremors and explosions tore through the ship and everybody was screaming but she clung to Smile and felt the white pure fire, everything exploding everything dying and birthing and rising and falling, perfumed graves, rotting mansions, snatches of songs and the sun shining upon them in a winter park, cold, and her heart beating and her brother's hand in hers, and Smile was laughing.

His flickering fingers touched her forehead. They both came out of the vision together.

'See, we didn't die, baby bro. We got out.'

He looked sad and confused, his famous smile dim. 'I hardly remember it, then in the visions it's so clear it hurts . . .'

She took off her mask. She brushed his fingers across her temple. 'It's the implant. They put mine in a few weeks before it went all went kaboom.'

Smile suddenly brightened. He could never stay down for very long, or fixated on one thing. Demorn loved her brother more than anything.

'Hey, I just remembered. A fish-head god gave me a message.'

He took something off a thin gold chain hanging around his neck. A tiny gold key lay in his hand, reeking of wild sorcery, echoing and bouncing off dimensions. She watched as it vanished, just to appear again. She saw a series of triangular images in the air, interlocking and spinning, faster and faster.

Smile put the small key in a shimmering keyhole. Pure energy and white light flooded the room.

She saw Kate, glowing, walking down a lonely Paris street. A dark figure in a severe black suit walked with her. It all phased back inside her eyes. The golden chain and the key vanished from Smile's hand.

He tapped her head gently.

'The fish-head god said the lock is in you. That's what he told me when he came to Friday Nights Music Club. It will open when you find what you need.'

The image of Kate lingered, it made her feel sad. Almost absently, she spoke. 'How cryptic. They aren't real gods, y'know. It's probably just a light show and a fish-mask.'

'Does it really matter?'

His eyes phased to a tonal purple. He whispered in Asanti, *'We are adrift but our place is the vast ocean.'* Music filled the chamber, and it felt like there were hundreds of suns powering the Room itself.

They slowly rose into the vast Room, faint pinpricks in the sea of snow. They grew sleepy as they ascended, hands lightly holding each other, lost in their private worlds. Until finally, the brilliant White Room dimmed, losing colour, and the music slowed and stopped.

Demorn awoke on the cold floor, her head throbbing with the power of the connection, remembering only vaguely who she was or where she was, filled with a light and peaceful heart.

4

She was aware of something in the shadows, a low piteous moan. The massive room was empty and startlingly cold; her breath misted in the frigid air.

Her hand was already on the pistol strapped to her leg. She slipped the bone ring back onto her finger, grimacing slightly as the needles of ice pierced her.

There was a rustle behind her. The girl who was once her girlfriend stood there, a profile in the vast room's cold, grey light. She was Bone, with a blue college jacket slung over the raw skeleton. She wore a long blonde wig and she had a thin golden bracelet wrapped around her left wrist.

Demorn looked at the face but there was nothing to tell Bone Kate apart from all the rest. The jacket and bracelet was less a sign of affection than making her wear a name-card. How stupid it all seemed now.

'How did you follow me?'

The girl spoke, her voice dry and distant, an echo of who she had been. 'Is this where you came from . . . ?'

It never worked. How many times had she brought the girl up to the penthouse, tried to play happy family. How many times had she held the girl in the dead of night and felt nothing, except the knowledge of how she was faking it?

Demorn knew exactly what the telepath had felt inside the bedroom. She had felt death.

She answered, 'No.'

The bone girl said, drawling, 'I've walked all night, I can still feel you, even when you took the ring off . . .'

'That's because I'm the only flesh in miles. Do you remember Chicago? Do you remember the Winter Park?'

The drawl. 'Chicago . . . have I been to Chicago?'

'Yeah, you have. In another life.'

Demorn dropped the bone ring on the floor. It struck the concrete and pinged.

The Bone Girl that had been the only true love of her life stared at her with hollow, angry eyes. And then the creature seized forward at her, soundless, hungry and totally damned.

Demorn let her get close, then she ripped the pistol up at the last moment, and squeezed the trigger, her hand shuddering with the impact as the Athena bullet blew away the Bone Girl's skull.

She went up to the body. The wig was blown to pieces, too, exposing dead Bone, like the countless numbers she had killed and would kill. Just a monster, mad and violent.

Tears flowed freely from her green eyes, and she slid her purple sunglasses on, letting the world take on a different hue. Just a monster, mad and violent. Demorn smiled to herself, despite everything. Who said you couldn't cry for monsters? It got fucking lonely in The Grave.

She ripped the bracelet off Bone Kate's wrist, throwing it into the corner. She reached into the blue jacket, taking out a scented, soft pink envelope.

When she closed her eyes she could see the vivid sun shining on the window, the hum of the cars outside, even the scattering of oddballs and suits sitting close to them — and Kate, her messy, lovely blonde hair pulled back, absently trying to a read a boring sci-fi book on her iPad, sipping at her coffee.

Like a movie, Demorn replayed walking to her table, Kate looking up with casual politeness, smiling in response to Demorn's opening about trying to get through the same boring book with the same grim determination. The warm, smiling face changed and the movie stopped, and Demorn was back looking at Bone and a shattered skull and nothing but sad echoes.

Demorn turned away, tearing the envelope open. It was a photograph of her and Kate standing by a bonfire at night, huddled close to each other. Kate was enclosed in an electric blue parka, wearing an incongruously cute short skirt, holding onto Demorn's waist tightly. Demorn was wearing a black Spider-Man shirt she still had, blue jeans, and a green Russian Army jacket she'd burned.

The fire lit up their smiling faces. The light around them was blurred. Over them, a giant UFO hovered, about to explode into deep space, taking up almost the whole sky in the photograph, huge glowing engines lighting up the circular craft.

Written in black pen in Kate's neat confident handwriting in the corner, was US AND A UFO!! FUCKING HELL I LOVE U Demorn! XXX

Demorn put the photo back in the envelope, and put it in her leather jacket. She pressed against the cold metal wall.

She realised the Spire wasn't humming; it did not seem to have a heartbeat. Maybe the craft had died. Everything was worse on this reality, it was to be expected that the crash was terminal in The Grave. Maybe that was why the White Room was gone, leaving only this empty expanse of blank metals and frigid floors, shorn even of the feeble advertisements.

Demorn felt the tattoo on her arm suddenly burn with a vicious fire, and the white scar on her face was slick with fresh blood. She felt the fresh scent of flowers in the wind. She could feel the spray of the sea of Firethorn. The Goddess, she breathed. As she watched the shattered skeleton of Bone Kate crumbled into the floor in front of her. The blue jumper lay over the bones.

She wrenched herself off the wall, following her instincts and the scent of flowers. The corridors of the Spire merged and twisted around her. Demorn put on her black-and-white death mask, feeling the patterns mesh into her, giving her both strength and a cold savagery in the soul itself.

She felt the Goddess before she saw her. One moment there was nothing but blank corridor, then suddenly she saw a black cape wrapped around a prone figure, pressed against a charred, burnt out tree. Demorn rushed toward her.

The Goddess looked up, and for a moment Demorn felt time stop, horrified, for beneath the shifting glamor the Goddess was undead, too. But then, magic burst through the decay and Demorn saw the visage change back to that of true beauty and power, despite the terrible wound from the sharp sword rent in her stomach, staining the black cloak.

The Goddess spoke in classical Asanti, *'This world is a disease and it infects all of us, Princess of the Sword, mortals and gods alike.'*

Demorn bowed. 'It is a cursed place, my Goddess. I thought you were not worshipped here.'

The Goddess laughed lightly, at odds with her wounds. *'Ah, brave sister in your scary mask. Don't view them through this crazy prism. They were not so different to you, before the end came.'*

Demorn's eyes rested on the glowing sword in the gut. 'Yeah, I had like a five minute window I guess. One coffee and some light chat about a book and a comic-book movie neither of us liked very much. Then the whole place went nuts.'

Demorn knelt as she spoke; she could feel the natural warmth of the Goddess.

But then she brushed her hand against the porcelain hand of Alodin Mars and there was a coldness which was totally unlike what she'd felt before.

'Something is very wrong, isn't it?' Demorn breathed.

The Goddess closed her flaming eyes. Her hand glowed and she grunted as she tried to drag the mighty sword from her stomach. The handle blazed and electric currents flowed up her arm, effort coursing across her features, but the blade did not budge more than an inch. The exertion left the Goddess looking exhausted.

'It's just Death, wielding his sacred sword. It happens to us all, we must return at last to the refracting prisms, weakened by the Fracture, flickering before the Fall . . .'

Great waves of emotion flooded through Demorn, leaving her trembling before the power of this lethal, falling god. She wasn't even conscious of what the Goddess was transmitting, flung headlong into a sea of energy from which there was no escape or respite.

Demorn took off her mask, tossing it on the floor. Her face was fully healed; she wore no scar. She felt loose and young. Her eyes glowed. Information flooded into her mind, and she felt an empty vessel being filled by an ocean of raging waters.

The Goddess smiled and she seemed to rise into the air, no longer dressed in armour, but in a pink robe. Lights danced around her. Briefly she seemed spectral, then suddenly as real as flesh and blood, her cheeks crimson.

Demorn looked down. The corpse was there, shed like a shell. In her hands Demorn held the jagged sword, still slick with blood.

'Do you see now, Sister? Do you see the story and the dark road? You doubted the Sword, and in your doubt the blade left you. Even in victory, in triumph, you wandered far from your home, you walked the terrible valleys of the dead seeking your heart.'

Demorn gasped as the terrible sword slid into her breast, the magic coalescing, her grip tight on the Goddess's hand as the blade sunk in deep, deeper than it ever had in all these years of meting out Justice to the evil.

'Do you see now, Demorn?'

Demorn looked up and she saw more than one face, more than one Goddess floating above her.

She saw the shadowy Last Breath of Firethorn, half present for a flashing moment, then gone. She saw a teenage girl with messy, long brown hair and hands that flowed with purple energy, dressed in '80s clothes walking through a bustling mall. She saw Alodin Mars, the armoured Goddess, patrolling a battlefield, soaked in the blood of her enemies, carrying a mighty spear.

And then Demorn saw the dancing spirit at the centre of it all, light pulsating out in waves, a fire at almost the heart of everything, consuming the others with an image that was everything at once, a mirror maze of complex rhythms, vibrating ceaselessly.

'I see too much,' Demorn murmured, turning her magic eyes away.

Alodin Mars held Demorn's with her cold hand. The images faded. 'It is reborn as it ends, Sword Princess. In lightning, flood and fire. Mourn nothing.'

Demorn got to her feet. She wasn't sure where she was. Weariness flowed through her body and mind. 'What ends? This world? Just fucking end it.'

The Goddess slapped her hard across the mouth, splitting Demorn's skin open with the stinging blow.

'All things are temporary. Life is no more permanent than love. Immortality is just a slower version of dying. Your bones are as brittle as the vows we make and break.'

Demorn wiped the blood from her lips. 'I wasn't talking about love. You seem depressed. You didn't talk like this in Firethorn.'

The Goddess sighed as she looked slowly at Demorn, who felt naked without her mask. 'I'm sorry for hurting you, Asanti born, who has already felt the harshness of the storm.'

She brushed her cold hand across the bleeding lips and they healed. The Goddess sighed. 'But there is so much more blood to come, and you must leave this cold place of bone. It was not meant for you.'

Demorn nodded, looking at the cold metal floor. She knew it was true. 'I've been selfish. I left the Innocents, I left my brother . . . I even left Firethorn.'

There was a youthful, familiar laugh.

Demorn looked up, feeling hopeful.

Leaning against the wall was the same wiseass Goddess from the grotto garden in Firethorn. Last Breath, in her black clothes, eternally seventeen and bored, wearing pretty pink lipstick.

'I'm not much into the whole sin and forgiveness thing, love. I'm more, just don't get your ass caught . . . most important, don't feel too bad about it all.'

Laughing, Demorn said, 'What happened to . . . her?'

The Last Breath looked at her with amused, wise eyes.

'Little Miss Majesty? The all powerful, all bossy, Warrior Goddess? The dimensions are at war across Reality; she can't waste time in graveyards.' She shrugged. 'So here I am.'

Demorn looked around the Spire. It felt lifeless and cold, the heart and soul gone out. She put her hand against the wall. 'The White Room has finally died. Ah well.' Demorn pointed down the hallway to an anonymous white door. 'We both died in the crash. Me and my brother. I found the bodies myself, a year ago, through that door. Nothing went right in The Grave, no Asanti got out.'

The Last Breath was uncharacteristically quiet.

'You took it a long way for a crush, Princess, showed a ton of crazy heart. Personally, I find it outrageously cool.'

Demorn walked into the huge, empty room. There was no pulse. The entire heart of the ship was dead.

She said, 'It didn't feel so cool. No matter how much I lie to myself, our five minute coffee wasn't that good. It wasn't worth this. I shouldn't be wasting time here either. The Spire was hurt much worse than on Babelzon. She was never going to fly again.'

The Last Breath looked at her with cool eyes. Her voice was light as she gazed up through the torn ceiling, into the ravine, and the blue sky so high above.

'You're such a moody hero! But there's a few different ways to get off a cursed rock.'

Her hot hand brushed over Demorn's heart, feeding and taking a piece. They began to blur and glide toward the distant sky, phasing through the air, more than flying.

They stood on the edge of the ravine, back where Demorn had started. The wind was cold.

The Last Breath laughed, the wind whipping her dark hair around. She looked wise and beautiful.

'You worry too much, Princess, what's the worst that can happen? This whole place is about to blow up anyway.'

In her fingers a dark flame flickered. 'We're just trying to get you out before it ends.'

Demorn sighed. 'What's so special about me?'

As she spoke, her golden crown flared up over her head, glinting across the twilight, making it all seem that much more melancholy, for so much was lost.

The Last Breath phased in and out of the shadows, only half there. Her light hand brushed Demorn's shoulder.

'What do you want to hear? That we saved you for your enchanting eyes?'

Demorn smiled. Her tattoos burned on her skin, hurting. 'I know what I am. A killer.'

'With enchanting eyes and beautiful hair. The Reality War is beginning, this was just one front.'

'You're leaving,' Demorn said.

The Last winked and gave a half bow. 'Strong heart, steady hand, Mighty Princess. Don't do drugs, eat apples.'

Demorn's eyes blazed. 'It's just a game, isn't it?'

The Last raised her eyebrow. 'To me? Of course. To other god-like things that aren't me? It's so deadly serious they have to make it a game.'

She smiled with a vivid happiness. 'Say hi to Wrecking Ball! Personally, I can't wait to see this depressing world blow up!'

The Last Breath vanished. In her place, for a moment that seemed to span eternity, there was a shining girl-woman with many different faces. Light erupted through the ravine from a miniature sun; a great wave of heat and light permeated all things for just a moment, filling Demorn with a warmth she had not felt since Firethorn.

Slowly it all faded back to cold, there were no more Goddesses, there was nobody but herself, alone by the yawning chasm.

Demorn was filled with an almost total disconnection. She felt surrounded by ghosts and omens. She sat by the edge of the ravine. The wind howled, feeling so empty, missing people who hadn't meant enough to her when they may have meant something, and now never would.

Demorn felt sometimes she almost knew the truth. She knew this awful spell of the Dead had infected everything. Space would be no protection from the insane magics which had erupted on this fallen earth. There was no Asanti above in the twilight sky, there was no Xaniath Hive to flee to, and the Spire was dead. It was all gone.

Her invisible watch buzzed, flashing a pink smiley icon. She flicked her finger across it, and the pink glow was replaced by Smile's golden teeth.

'Hey, Demorn, I just know you're thinking depressing thoughts out there in the dark. Take a look in your pocket.'

She fished out the power card Smile had given her in the White Room. The card glowed a hot, dark red, blocking out the sadness and the apathy.

Suddenly *she knew*. Somewhere across the desert, in a burning city, Wrecking was stirring things up in his near invincible manner, like some unstoppable Mystery Boss in one of his video games.

She said, 'Y'know, just prior to this little adventure, when I even lost the connection to my card game, I was thinking of finding a studio to record a truly definitive solo acoustic album to sum up this dark night of the soul. I figure I've got enough material.'

'Heavy, Sis. Only problem being, you hate modern music and often say only Sinatra can do saloon songs properly.'

She smiled. 'That's true. But anything beats watching cheesy horror movies alone in my bedroom.'

He squealed in delight. 'OH MY FUCKING GOD! HOW DEPRESSING! You actually own an acoustic guitar don't you, Demorn?'

She smiled ruefully. 'Sure do. I raided a store. I've even got a couple of choruses about lonely hearts.'

Smile laughed, softly saying something about trying not to go mad in an insane world. But the connection was always jittery in The Grave. His golden teeth vanished last, leaving her alone again.

Demorn saw a tiny dot on the horizon. The Xaniath ship. She grabbed her bag from the Jag, thoughts flashing across her mind as the ship drew closer.

The street shootout was always there, if things got too deep and serious. That was the thing about living in the dark dimension. When everything fresh and wholesome was dead, you had little left to lose. When Hollywood didn't even produce mediocre remakes of classic movies to complain about, when static had replaced the meaningless TV talk shows that had spread across a thousand channels all day and night, when the world didn't even have real people anymore, you had so little left to lose.

She thought of the Tyrant, up there somewhere, probably watching it all on satellite.

Demorn felt better to have somebody to loathe.

The Xaniath ship was above her now, blowing her hair wildly and scattering desert grass across the plain as it descended to the desert floor like a good old fashioned UFO.

Idly, Demorn wondered if the muscly guards would start to warm up to her on the flight to LA, and she reminded herself not to be too much of a bitch.

5

The ship flew over Los Angeles, light flashing through the smog and the thick smoke, the city sprawl invisible from this height.

The Xaniath ship was spartan, black and grey walls with bunk beds. It wasn't a deep space vessel; the big one must have been back in the hideout.

Or crashed and burnt out, escape route blown. The telepath had disappeared up a thin ladder, mind-murmuring something about an observation port above, seeming to want to be left alone. Fine, honey.

The two human guards oiled and checked their weapons, chatting in vague terms about some home they had left behind, but mostly about hitting the ground hard in LA.

It buzzed Demorn, and she stayed with them for a little while. They didn't seem too brainwashed. They mostly left her alone as they made small talk between themselves about LA, every once in a while glancing at her body with a detached, almost professional interest.

Demorn changed her bloody, torn up clothes while they spoke. She dressed in tight black war-pants, jackboots, her leather jacket and a fresh X-men t-shirt. The Athena gun in a leg holster. Knives, her gossamer whip, and extra goodies were hidden across her body.

'I always find this part fun,' she said. 'The whole stockpiling of weapons thing. I get so keyed up. Who knows what will happen, hey?'

The biggest guard laughed loudly. Demorn sat back, relaxed, and in the zone.

After a few minutes, the telepath called. She went up a narrow metal ladder to the cockpit. It was a two seater, and she sat down.

'When I was young, fresh off the boat, Tony took us to LA for a week.'

The woman's voice floated through her head.

This isn't your world or the city you remember.

She looked down at the smoke and the lights glowing beneath the cloud cover.

The smoke briefly parted and she saw the vast city for the first time. In that moment she thought she was looking into Hell itself. Burning orange lights blazed around a great vacant abyss that swallowed entire souls and hearts and memories into the bottomless pit.

She closed her eyes, very distant from the here and now. She could feel Tony's arm around her as they drove in his black Porsche through LA, the wind whipping in her hair as they sped alongside a vast golf course where he'd played a few rounds with old movie stars.

The sun was warm on her face and the air was dry. Tony told her what it was like to stroll those links with real legends, and she could still hear the mixture of pride and happiness in his voice. Classic songs played and Demorn sang along, so happy, just learning all the words. She'd never forget that sunny day no matter what happened afterward.

Her voice was soft. 'No. Different world, but same city.'

She opened her eyes and it was no longer Hell but something else entirely. The ship had descended through a layer of the smoke, and she could see the immensity of the place. Unlike Skull City, which hung always in a twilight melancholy red, LA was ablaze like a forest fire of a million multi-coloured lights.

The ship travelled fast across the sprawl. She could see smoking power plants and huge wire fences and burning buildings. Small arms fire shot from the lit darkness, flickering in the darkness.

They fight and kill each other as if there is nothing else to fight.

Skull City was in many ways easy to control. Bones controlled the city since Dead Day, they had flushed out everything else real fast. All she had done was keep the Bone on a tight leash.

But LA . . . They didn't really care who they were shooting at, they were just shooting. It was living, breathing chaos.

The woman looked at her with those sunrise orange eyes. *Did you come here often?*

Demorn smiled grimly. 'No, not often. Just special occasions. LA was a hot zone.'

Flashback a few years.

She was lying in a cool air-conditioned room in some motel, Smile beside her, trying to grab some sleep before the ride home, hearing sirens down Sunset. She'd taken a shoulder shot on a hit job the night before, a couple of mid-level Las Vegas lizards who thought they'd made a statement by stealing secrets from Tony.

They were dead now and the breach was contained. The tape was tight around her as it mended the wound. Smile's mask danced across his face, cartoon tears leaking onto the bed-sheet. She hated bringing him but the job had called for his unique set of skills.

It wasn't bad to have his company. She held his hand tight, whispering, 'It's so alive it's dying,' as they played the same classic Sinatra songs from years ago, low all through the night, gone by dawn.

Flash to now.

The ship was flying much lower to the ground. Demorn's bionics flickered in her eyes, drawing closer to a major build-up of light and activity in the rapidly approaching distance. The place drew into focus. Big fences, some choppers, jeeps and armoured vehicles, a lot of steel clustered around blocks. USA flag flying high and proud.

OK. She said, 'We're headed to an army base?'

All will be made clear.

Demorn gave a dry laugh. 'Make it clear now then. I don't do Army. Army is a slow, dangerous bleed-out.'

She felt for the Athena gun resting on her leg. This might not stay so friendly between her and the peoples of Xaniath after all.

The telepath raised her finger slightly.

TIGER EYZ seized the Jade Hotel 27 days ago. Wrecking was sighted there.

Ahhh, the Jade Hotel. It glistened like a magic tower amongst the fiery chaos of the city, the same mirrored surface as the one in Babelzon. Even with the purple starlight dimmed down, it was a strangely comforting sight in a war zone. She wondered if they had a beautiful restaurant at the top where clones sang and she met Tony for lunch every Wednesday.

The telepath glanced at her with those strange eyes. *Your mind is strange and loose. This isn't your world. It's just another hotel chain.*

'Thanks for prying, honey. How well do you know Tiger Eyz?'

I had a contact there, a believer in the Hive. He told me about the legend of Wrecking and he has seen him.

Demorn sighed. 'Great. So am I the only person who thinks this is just one really big, obvious trap? Tiger Eyz were nationwide gang players, and they reacted BIG right on Dead Day, tore shit up right from the jump. It was almost like they welcomed it. I killed dozens getting out of Chicago . . . you could say it got a little personal.'

They were almost in hover mode outside the hotel now. The craft started to descend. Everything about it felt bad; her instincts screamed each foot they descended.

She thought about the last no exit street and the big empty that came afterward, swallowing everyone and everything. She thought of the dark flames flickering in the hands of the Last Breath. Was she real, and not imagined? Was it all going to blow up anyway?

Demorn saw a proudly waving flag and their insignia scrawled over it, inside and over the stars and stripes.

Did it really matter who she faced in that last street? It could be aliens, it could be Bone, it could be Tiger Eyz, it could be who knew what.

I'm still talking to Tiger Eyz — they need us as much as we need them.

She looked the telepath straight in the eye. Demorn drew her Athena gun out of her leg holster.

'Careful when you say *we*. Sometimes not even I know what I need.'

They are as desperate — this will work.

Demorn smiled as the craft neared the ground. 'Don't try and sell me, telepath. So we take the meet and hope they know Wrecking? We do it knowing Tiger Eyz would happily shoot us in the back and slit our throats while we sleep.'

. . . yes.

'What a plan.' Demorn grinned her scary grin.

'Don't turn your back, telepath, and don't sleep.'

She went downstairs to be with the soldiers. Some telepaths could read all the minds they wanted, and they were still so dumb about people.

6

The Raaiq telepath lowered the craft.

Demorn could see the main square; it looked empty, dark buildings on all sides. She saw the big guns atop the hotel, unmanned.

Demorn kept her eyes on the rapidly approaching tarmac.

She remembered all her favourite songs, her best lovers, her top three movies. It passed by in a flash, like always. The old game.

Beatles, Sinatra, the Winter Park kissing Kate, freezing cold to the bone. Audrey Hepburn movies at midnight. Cheesy, classic sci-fi shows from years ago. The image of Asanti exploding into nothingness, searing her soul.

A collage of moments she called on when she felt death close enough to smile at it. Something exploded through the window, a wash of blue light. It didn't matter what. It was too late to pretend this wasn't end game.

She looked at the two soldiers. They looked on edge and robotic, eyes glazed, huge arms gripping their huge laz cannons tightly. Nobody was looking covertly at her tits now. There was no more small talk. They were on remote. Robo-dolls for the Hive. Turns out the telepath did make them go meat puppet, Demorn thought dryly.

The craft landed on the tarmac with a bump. The men were up, and the laz cannon was whirring. The hatch began to open. The telepath cut through her like a butter knife.

I hear bad things.

Demorn slid down a final mind-wall so she wouldn't have to hear anything, just feel numb.

• • •

The first thing she smelled through the door was smoke and the first thing she heard was screaming, deafening and awful. The whole city was screaming as it burned to death. Then the BUDDA BUDDA vibration from the soldier's laz cannon as they rushed forward and through the hatch, flash colours flickering over her face.

The telepath was still shouting words of caution in her mind, but for Demorn they were the faintest whisper, bounced echoes off the soldiers.

But for Demorn it was just a dance, the only real dance left in town. She was firing Athena bullets on reflex. Her wild heart was on fire. There was no doubt, no questions, no fear.

Who cared what came next?

She heard animals growl, and she turned to run for cover. A huge robo-cat took down one of the guards, his huge cannon still loosing off rounds while the mechanised creature tore his throat out.

In slow motion she shot at his handler, a thin trashy kid in garish clothes, who died, looking surprised with a bullet between his eyes. Incredibly, the soldier got up, blood spurting from his neck, the laz cannon still grinding. She slid into cover.

Suddenly, the hotel entrance was filled with a score of dead gangsters, blood pouring from their eyes and ears, some stumbling as they screamed. She watched more drop like flies. A wave of pressure passed over her, assaulting her sinuses, passing as quickly as it came, stripping the mind-shield away.

Fuck, Demorn thought. The telepath is exploding their damn brains. Heavy. She launched herself into the entrance, firing at those still breathing. Somewhere behind, she head the growl of more robotic cats. They wouldn't be fazed by a mind wipe.

She flung herself behind the reception desk, arms running with blood. Her black Spidey t-shirt was soaked red. She'd taken refuge in the lobby of the Jade Hotel, holed up behind the reception desk.

These damn Tiger Eyz had lived in style. It was velvet carpeting and beautiful fish tanks and discreet mood lighting in here — they'd lured her right into the honey pot. The monitor screen was a wavy screensaver of a luscious French model in revealing poses, flashing beautiful cleavage and bee-stung lips.

Demorn looked through the hazy laz-fire smoke to the ship outside, the hatch now securely closed again, inert on the tarmac.

The Xaniath woman was finally quiet. She didn't have a headache. People weren't keeling over with their brains exploding. Good. So much for peace talks.

Two gang members came barrelling out of the lift, shooting randomly. Demorn cut them down cleanly with two bullets, then dropped into cover again.

She dropped a spent clip out of her Athena gun and slammed a new one in. All around her, were the bodies of the dead. She kicked at one body that looked too damn young.

How the hell had the Hive got it so wrong? Was the telepath playing some weird death-wish angle or was she really just a naive, clueless chick way out of her depth? If she was in a casino, Demorn would have put ten grand on the former. It was awful hard not to have a little death wish in The Grave.

A low strong voice came across her earpiece.

'Hey, killing machine, you still breathing? They rushed you.'

He was out somewhere in the courtyard; they'd been separated by the horde.

'Yeah, babe, it got to wetwork. Not even scratched. You?'

His voice was gruff, 'Ah, I got a nick or two, luv.'

She heard the shudder as the laz cannon fired off a sequence of bursts into a bank of jazzed up cars. Then a dark, booming laugh as the cars exploded into fiery chunks of colour and fury.

She could hear pain behind the laugh. He'd been hit too.

'But I've nicked a whole lot more.'

She smiled. 'I bet you have. Off the telepath chain, hey?'

He laughed with a chortle. 'Yeah. Surprise, surprise, her bodyguards know more about guns than her.'

She heard movement from the first row of slot machines and she squeezed off a few shots. Bodies fell.

'So much for the meet and greet. What a fucking bust of a peace conference.'

He chuckled. 'Yeah, I never bought into all that.'

She looked out again at the ship, inert on the courtyard, shut down.

'She's your boss. Do you reckon she will fly away and leave us behind?'

Just a tiny pause. 'Probably not.'

'Why?'

Another pause. 'We haven't got much left back there. The Hive is a burnout. She's desperate.'

Demorn glanced at the bodies. Flashy bandanas, knife-blades, cheap guns. Desperate peace talks that turned into desperate raids. They were all so hungry, so desperate, everybody left in this screwed up world.

She held up the thin arm of one of the dead gang members, a teenage boy with acne and pasty white skin marked with all over pock-marks, probably from needles of cheap, bad Mirage.

Just a dumb kid. But even junkie gangster kids had dreams, maybe them most of all. Well, his mirage was over; it had led here, to an Athena bullet in the skull.

Ah well, there were worse ways to punch out. It wasn't like Demorn to get sentimental about her enemies. They didn't get that way over you.

There was a sudden, hurting howling across her mind, a red dragon burning so brightly it hurt her eyes. The tattoo across her abs lit up with burning pain, as the telepath screamed: ***THEY ARE POSSESSED WE'RE ALL DEAD DEAD FIND THE ROUTE FIND THE WAY OUT—***

The vicious shout cut off almost as soon as it began, lacing the inside of her brain with the mark of wildfire, an image of the red dragon stinging her mind.

Shining eyes still spinning, Demorn looked at the corpses behind the desk and across the foyer, still and quiet, actors in a silent movie of violent deeds.

Her skull ring flickered from chalk white to blue, on and off. Demorn's stomach dropped a tiny bit. For in this land, the dead so often woke.

She whispered into the earpiece, 'What the hell was that? You saw the dragon too, hey?'

His voice was calm. 'I felt something big. Who cares if she's dead. She's the bitch who sold us all on this ambush. But she's not pulling my chain now, maybe not ever again.'

Demorn smiled grimly. The bitterness of all slaves. In their shoes, she'd be exactly the same. 'Can you move?'

A grunt. 'Not much. I only got half a leg left.'

'Solo run for the prize then.'

He chuckled. 'Looks that way, killing machine.'

It was always the best way. The fastest, the most free. But solo run to where? Where was freedom?

His voice came back, less blurred. 'I just took a real serious painkiller.'

The THUMP of his gun outside, blowing up more cover.

'I can hold them off the ship for hours. You best finish them. Maybe there is something in there for us.'

She closed her eyes and nodded. Yeah, they were committed now. Better to clean the nest. Don't leave anything behind.

'Buy me an hour, man. Let me save us or die.'

He laughed in a good way at that one. She shut the connection down.

It was eerily quiet in the lobby now. She could hear the bubbling of the fish tank on the opposite wall, and she heard sugary pop music playing through the earphones of one of the dead Tiger Eyz. They had died listening to some truly forgettable Top 40 bullshit.

Working on hunches, she configured her watch and scanned for signals. Skull City had been a dead city ruled from her Skull Tower, but LA was different.

LA was random and filled with gnashing, wailing things that wouldn't die clean.

Connections popped up all over the place. There was one close by, in the hotel's gaming room, a glistening teleport portal that was literally throbbing with the power of full connection. That was the ticket out of here.

Twenty seconds of playing around with the wireless connection convinced Demorn she needed manual access. She flexed her legs. She felt good. The scratches were just scratches. The blood was mostly somebody else's blood.

In a flash Demorn was up and moving, sliding across the counter, finding cover along the wall. No shots rang out and she moved fast across the trail of dead bodies.

She roll-dived into the gaming room, entranced by the blurred lights of the main gambling floor. She came to the first row of bright slot machines, hearing a loud ringing sound. The lifts opened, and a creature burst out, robotic grey and feline sleek.

Demorn thought of robotic jaguars. It ran with perfect soundless grace, flickering past the bullets she shot, and was upon her in a second, metal teeth clamping on her.

The teeth struck her hip. She tumbled backwards, hitting a pink sea of Xmas lights. Was it even that close to Xmas, Demorn thought incongruously, as lightning crackled across her skin.

She flipped away, landing on a smooth section of ground, her hand and wrist avoiding a jagged chunk of glass by luck alone.

The robotic incisors had taken a piece of flesh. The steel jaws released her when she hit the lights. The robo-jag landed on its feet and spun around, snarling. She drilled three Athena bullets into its skull from a foot away.

The damage was extensive, but for a moment she didn't think it would be enough. You could never tell with robots.

She smashed a quick kick into its glaring dying eyes with her boot. The devil red eyes stopped blazing.

She noticed a weird mixture of blood and circuitry on her boot and on the mashed face.

Jesus, I've always liked jaguars, Demorn thought. It took a special kind of asshole to take the time to turn jungle animals into robots.

She could feel the blood, slick beneath her torn pants. But there was no time for pain. Another lift opened.

More. Gotta be tigers, Demorn thought. They call themselves Tiger Eyz, after all. Kicking on a pure adrenaline surge, she jumped up and over three slot machines, her mind focused on the blinking access port.

She felt it before she saw it, a pink-black crystal energy star hanging like a mist around a buxom Cleopatra gambling machine, the naked beauty surrounded by cherubic elves, disturbingly adult in their poses.

She heard loud growls behind her and spun firing. As the black and pink cloud absorbed her, she noted with a strange satisfaction that the two robo-cats leaping gracefully over the machines were indeed tiger themed.

She could see the red blazing eyes of the charging metal pack, she felt the death about to happen, she saw the bullets leave her gun. The energy star encased her in pink-black lines, changing everything in one blinding flash.

7

A complex pyramid of pink lights shone above her.

Demorn was fully awake and alert, but she kept her eyes shut. Her hand sought her pistol but there was nothing in the holster.

Soft electronic music was playing, a soothing voice murmuring over it. She didn't know where the portal had taken her.

She felt metal across her throat, humming, only millimetres from her skin. Vibro-knife. Cute, this was some ol' skool shit. Demorn liked ol' skool.

A male voice with a soft accent said, 'I know you're awake.'

She opened her eyes slowly. 'Makes two of us.'

The first thing she noticed about him was his kind eyes in a face filled with scars and pain.

He smiled and withdrew the knife. 'Well you're not one of them, anyway. That's something.'

Demorn got up cautiously. She wasn't soaked in blood. She felt fresh. Above her, the pink-blue energy star winked into nothingness.

'Yeah, it's something. Thanks for the pick up.'

He looked embarrassed. 'No problem. I recognised your signature, you're kinda famous. Skull Princess and everything.'

He wasn't far past twenty, dressed in a worn fatigue jacket complete with badges. If not for the scars he would look much younger.

'The portal has a heal up. There's a few still operating throughout LA.'

Old school, she thought again. They were in a cramped room filled with a mishmash of trinkets. A bed mat was rolled out. It smelled of boy.

'What's with the kamikaze gang kids just begging to die? Mind-controlled? Some kind of zombie hybrid?'

He looked away. 'A little worse than that, I'm afraid. The others can tell you more.'

Mystery time, Demorn thought, as she folded her legs beneath her, getting her bearings. Time for the movie to go black-and-white. Time for her to go all detective.

'How many have you rescued through these portals? How many soldiers you got left?'

He could not meet her eyes. She could see under the jacket how thin he was, emaciated. This was just another rat hole, this wasn't freedom.

'You're the first clean one to come through in six months. There are only five of us.'

Clean one. Interesting choice of words. Demorn saw a tiger patch on his jacket and tensed, hands casually flicking to her gun holster.

'Are you Tiger Eyz?'

He laughed. He pointed to a small stuffed tiger mascot in the room. 'I was. A lifetime ago. That's all gone now. Tiger Eyz is dead; what you saw above is a perversion. May her ghost ride the wind with wild eyes.'

He crossed his fingers across his chest in some archaic gesture.

Great, she thought. It's some cult religion.

A sad country song starting playing on his radio, a song she had known in another world, another time. It was so strange to hear it now, in this room.

'How did you get here alive? Why not the rest of your little gang?'

He looked toward the ground, then up. He took off his fatigue jacket. She saw his whip-smart body, no fat. Across his chest were deep red welts, from what looked like thorns. The marks covered his entire upper chest, carrying around to his side.

'Wrecking marked me with his flail. He gave me strength. He saw a purity of spirit the others did not have.'

She looked at his ruined face. She had a horrible feeling.

'Did the Wrecking Ball do that to your face?'

The man nodded. His eyes lit up a weird blue. 'By his own hands he gifted me with power.'

She nodded slowly, face unreadable. Great. So Wrecking Ball was borderline psychotic, and so was this guy. Well, Wrecking Ball could die with the rest of this crazy planet. She swore she'd slice his damn arm off herself before he set his damn flail against her skin.

Demorn smiled her happiest smile, feeling the opposite inside. 'Well, aren't you guys a kooky bunch. Why don't we meet your friends?'

The man nodded, putting his shirt back on. Together they left the small room.

'Where are we anyway?' she asked. They walked along a shadowy corridor lit by low phosphorescent green light. She had tried to get a reading on her invisible watch, but it was disconnected.

There was a sense of unreality to everything, a mixture of antiseptic hospital-style order that thinly overlaid a basic insanity.

The tunnel opened to a bunker HQ with panels and giant screens. Across the main wall a computer map of the USA fed a sea of electronic red into the darkened room. A few tiny blue spots were scattered across but the red feed ate into the room, blinding her to everything else and feeding her a sense of dread.

'I get it, the world's dead, the bad guys won,' Demorn said. 'You should turn it off, it's depressing as hell.'

He ignored her, talking in his vaguely helpful way. 'The blue spots are portal points, like this one. Dimensional pockets, into the safe zones.'

As she looked around the gloomy room, she felt entombed. How safe do they really feel, she thought.

'They were created in the Cold War, decades ago. Our President spent billions. Now it's just a place to hole up. There's a few scattered around the States.'

Demorn shrugged. 'We didn't have one in Skull City.'

He looked up at her with dawning comprehension.

'You don't run Skull City from a pocket zone?'

Demorn almost laughed. She waved her sparkling ring hand in front of him.

'I'm the Skull Princess, hon. I've got tricks of my own to help me survive. Now, maybe it's time to speak to your boss.'

He looked embarrassed.

The red screen cut out. All that was left were a few specks of blue dancing on the dark.

A chair spun round from the big screen. A blonde woman sat there, her figure curvaceous and beautiful, dressed in a long gown. An ornate ruby necklace hung on her breasts, glowing. A dark shock of black ran through the platinum blonde hair.

Alex smiled, flashing perfect teeth.

'Why, Princess, don't get angry at the help. We're all just trying to please and serve you.'

8

'Alexandria,' Demorn snarled. 'Why can't you stay dead for longer than five minutes? I always think of you more fondly that way.'

Alex fluttered her eyelids and walked towards her. Despite her harsh words, Demorn couldn't help but admire the way her body looked, all curves, long eyelashes and big boobs.

'Aw c'mon, Demorn, let's play nice and make this one of our Team-Up Adventures.' She purred. 'I like those.'

Demorn let her come close. She always forget how hot and classy this woman was, how good she smelled . . . the lust she awoke.

Demorn murmured, 'Those team-up adventures usually wind up with us shooting at each other, Alex.'

Alex laughed and brushed her hand across the Princess's neck.

'Ah, but you have *such* a bad memory, Fearless Leader. Sometimes we kiss and we touch . . .'

Demorn lightly slapped her hand away. But some of her wanted Alex to keep touching. She'd always had a soft spot for hot blondes.

'Yeah, they're the team-ups I'm talking about.'

Alex laughed innocently. 'I don't hold grudges in matters of the heart. I'm quite sure you shot me more times than I've shot you.' She traced her fingers across Demorn's neck. 'You being such a quick draw an' all.'

Smiling, Demorn caught her hand. She looked Alex in the eye.

'You've always been pretty fast yourself.'

Alex smiled and brushed her hand through her hair in a fast motion.

'To business, then! The Innocents sent me. You've been gone too long and your brother is worried, bless his heart.'

'He managed to triangulate a likely location to this pocket dimension.

Turns out he's good at what he does. I've been here four weeks, buttering up the local superhuman.'

Demorn nodded. She knew better than anybody how unreliable the time-scale was between parallels.

'So you're not an alternate version of the Alex I know back home? Like the nice, loyal version, who doesn't sell the mission out to the highest bidder?'

Alex fluttered her eyes. 'No, it's me, dear. The Innocents didn't survive on this world. I've been busy . . .'

Demorn was watching her close. 'Well, at least I know who I'm dealing with. I guess we *can* call it a Team-Up.'

Alex smiled warmly. 'Cool. You want to split and meet the boss?'

An enormous dark hulking figure came into view behind Alex.

If the creature was human, it was only barely so. His face was scarred, a sneer rippling through dead scars on his grey skin under the shadowy light.

Demorn went for her gun. The other woman waved her hand.

'Nah, he ain't the boss. Or a baddie.'

Alex placed her white hand across his bare, enormous chest and the creature smiled.

'He's my Guard Dog. I don't leave home without him.'

Alex caressed his huge, ripped up chest with her delicate fingers. The monster looked down at the beautiful blonde with a savage love.

Alex flicked a silver coin through her fingers.

'That's my brother's coin,' Demorn said, surprised.

The creature snarled at the Princess with a barely concealed hate, but Alex just shrugged. 'Yeah, he said to bring us to you . . .'

She flicked it to Demorn who caught it with quick fingers. It was warm to the touch, the faces and names upon it ever changing. Demorn's eyes blazed as she turned the coin in her fingers.

'... Across the span of universes.'

Demorn looked up and saw wild, vivid Goddess tats strewn over the skin of Guard Dog and Alex. Suddenly she realised they had bonded as full soul-mates, as per Innocent tradition.

'It's such a dangerous world we've wound up in,' Alex purred.

A dangerous world. An incongruous image of Kate sitting in the winter sun in Chicago talking about music and comics echoed in Demorn. Then it was suddenly Kate bleeding out in her arms, blood in her strawberry blonde hair.

Demorn wanted to think of something else. She wanted to get out of the Grave. She was utterly tired.

'I haven't bonded with anybody here,' she murmured.

Alex touched her lightly. 'Good. It's a cursed place.'

Demorn remembered the guard outside, with his blown up leg and his muscles and his huge laser gun. Had it been four weeks? Had he gotten back to the ship and gotten away somehow?

It all felt so unlikely. She hoped he didn't die hating her. She hoped it was quick and he didn't feel much.

'Hey, stop drifting so deep, Fearless Leader. You're the one who is supposed to lead us home and save everyone. Wrecking Ball, the World's Greatest Superhuman, awaits you in his throne room!'

Demorn came back to the moment, checking out Alex's voluptuous form in the black gown.

She said archly, 'I've seen what "the world's greatest superhuman" does to true believers. It was nothing I remembered from his games.'

Alex pouted and brushed her body close to the Guard Dog, who growled unpleasantly at Demorn. 'We all pay a price, dear. Even favourites.'

Demorn placed her hand over Alex's and the coin. 'I'm sure your heart is all cracked inside when you cry yourself to sleep at night.'

Alex looked at her with innocent puppy dog eyes. 'Maybe it is, poppet.'

Demorn smiled despite herself. The silver disc lit up, covering Princess, Alex and Guard Dog.

Demorn glanced at the boy, left in the shadows.

Alex said, 'The kid can stay. He's the welcome doormat. Depressing and moth-eaten, but so earnest. It's great advertising.'

The three of them flashed then faded away, leaving the boy with the scarred face in the shadowy blue-lit room, alone at the end of his world.

Demorn opened her eyes to a blaze of light.

They had come to a bedroom of great luxury with gold bedspreads and lavish oil paintings on the wall. The air smelled of fresh gardenias, and a trace of subtle perfume.

Demorn didn't know anything about art but she knew it was classic stuff, genuine treasures. It put her trashy movie posters and action figures in the shade.

'Cool stuff, hey?'

Demorn saw Alex under the golden bedspread, the cover pulled just over her full breasts.

'Are you actually lying naked in bed?' Demorn asked dryly.

'Are you actually not a 70-year-old crone? Because that's how you sound.'

There was a grunt behind her as Guard Dog snarled his gruesome laugh.

Demorn raised her eyebrow.

'Well, I guess I'll leave you two love-birds . . .'

Alex laughed fully.

'Don't be silly, dear, Guard *Dog* is my BFF.'

Demorn smiled despite herself. She'd never known Alex to be shy about her conquests. She had never seen her bond so deeply.

'Of course, Alex.'

Alex fluttered her eyelashes and the sheet fell down a little farther.

Demorn barely controlled the impulse to blow her a kiss as she left the room. Guard Dog stayed behind, transfixed by his sexy master, growling his savage affection, a slave to her forever.

This is why I keep my heart light, she realised. People were filled with passion and desires that ran so deep. Demorn had just as much, maybe more. They ran through her like a fire, the flames barely touching the walls that lay inside. She knew well the bliss the lips and body of another could bring, but in her soul, with Kate gone, she flew alone. There was no sense in bitterness or anger, nothing to own in anybody else, when all things passed beneath.

Demorn could hear distant country music as she walked through the beautiful home. The walls were carpeted and everything felt warm and secure. She felt longings for a peace she only vaguely recalled.

She came to the main lounge room, a stunning white room mixed with splashes of black and pink. Cream carpets, classy leather couches, huge buffalo heads on the wall. An electric fire sparkled in the fireplace.

A black scimitar hung in the air, slowly circling.

It was a deep, mirrored blade and glistened with a strange, magical darkness. Demorn saw herself reflected perfectly in the black mirror. She saw herself without the scar, worshipping some different, more savage god.

The darkness was rimmed with a rain of fire. The sword seemed to hum in the air itself. Everything faded into the background and all she cared about was the dark promise of its power. Her heart began to burn, and she felt the power seeping into her, not evil, nothing as simple or clichéd as that.

It was smooth and liquid and unlike anything she had tasted in all her years of wandering and killing.

As she got close, she saw that the blade had markings upon it. There were chips in the edges of the blade, and congealed liquid.

A deep male voice spoke. 'It is the blood of a cruel god, you know. A cage of souls. I beheaded him with the Scimitar, myself.'

His voice was warm and friendly. Strangely, her hand did not fly to her holster.

Softly, she said, 'I've seen the Black Scimitar before, but only in video games. And deep in them, so deep it was like a dream.'

His touch upon her arm was warm and dry.

'The fact you see the Black Scimitar with your naked eyes tells me that you are the one that I have sought in my visions and prayers.'

His eyes were a beautiful diamond blue against dark tanned skin. His face was brave, not a trace of weakness or defeat in him. Between his sparkling eyes there was a brush of gold dust. She had seen gods walk before. Her magic eyes could see the shards of divinity.

Demorn fell to her knees without thought, body trembling at the sheer power of his touch.

She whispered, 'You pray? But you are a god yourself.'

Wrecking brushed her chin with his hand. 'Yes. But a god of War . . . and the War is lost. Rise, Princess of the Sword, we are equals in these ruins.'

She looked up and he was smiling.

'Who won?'

Wrecking shrugged and waved his fingers. Behind him, the electric fireplace swung open. The skeleton of a huge humanoid figure hung there. Metal spikes were driven through the bones. The skull was separated from the body. Pieces of the Black Scimitar lay in the cracked skull.

'I'd say I did better than he did.'

Demorn was physically stunned when she recognised the charred evil symbol seared into the bones. Her fingers crossed her breast in an instinctive warding gesture known across dimensions.

'The body of Zaltuth!'

Wrecking winked. 'Don't worry, Princess. His soul and essence are banished to the deepest hell. These hollow bones are just something to impress the ladies.'

The electric fireplace swung back into place. The room was strangely quiet. The country song played low, giving an undercurrent of emotion.

His muscled chest was bare, an ornate tattoo across the rippling muscles. Wrecking gripped the dark scimitar by the red handle and his abs clenched and ripped. As he moved, she saw dark, foreign script stencilled on the underside of his arm.

Damn hot, she thought, in an abstract way. Curious, Demorn reached out and touched his arm, feeling the blue tattoo upon his warm skin.

'You wear the marking of the Goddess . . .' Her eyes danced with possibilities. 'Are you one of us, Wrecking Ball?'

Wrecking looked at her, the Dark Scimitar in his hand. With her magic vision she could see his power, the raw god-born magic filling his body and soul.

He broke into a friendly grin, speaking in fluent Asanti. 'I have travelled so many worlds, under so many suns. Different names. Alodin Mars was a friend, a kindred spirit, the spear to unite and defend so many.'

Demorn felt as if her entire spirit was aflame. She choose her words with care. 'I lead the Innocents now. What's under the altar in our temple?'

He looked at her with glazed, ruby eyes. She saw for a moment a flashing image of the Burning Cavern, floating inside the mountain in a sea of white stars. The very birthplace of the Innocents!

'A Red Box Edition Dungeon & Dragons rulebook. That you stole, if the grapevine tells true,' he added.

Demorn giggled, smiling brilliantly. 'It could just!'

'You wrote down seven new Club rules inside the cover. I saw them one drunken night.' He sounded sad. 'No, I can't recite them. I was just passing through, doing a favour for a friend.'

Demorn relaxed slightly, laughing.

'That's okay, I don't mind hiring off the books. We *were* all pretty high the night I wrote those rules down. I think of them more like a guideline.'

She pointed towards the ceiling and the dead land beyond.

'Serious though, if you actually killed the cruel god with the Scimitar, how come . . .'

'How has the world gone so wrong?'

'Kinda.'

His diamond eyes flashed. It seemed to her that some of the warmth of the room faded. He seemed to grow taller, even more magnificent and defiant. An old fashioned Renaissance-style black vest partially covered him. She saw shimmering images of him that seemed from centuries past: Wrecking upon a black ship that sailed between the stars, glittered enchantments upon his brow.

A giant red sun glowed on his powerful body, and Demorn realised he was young by the eternal laws, born under the magic star that most wizards merely dreamt of. She saw his true power was still emergent, vast and ominous in the near future.

Then they were no longer in the lounge room, but looking at a wasteland of the dead, and Wrecking hovered in the air above it all, grey light upon his proud face.

A chill ran through her spine. He carried a mighty flail which glowed with a cruel orange light in the broken twilight, the metal chains charred and burning.

Before him, a mighty lizard beast, some creature sprung from some deep cavern of the Earth, struggled to stand upon its twisted gigantic limbs.

The gigantic figure of Zaltuth lay strewn across the grey stony plain, beheaded.

Red energy flowed from the fingertips of Wrecking Ball, setting alight the dark, tattered robes.

The lizard beast rose, screaming a torrent of frustration and grief at its fallen master.

Wrecking ceased his energy fire.

He swung his mighty flail. Thunder crashed above and jagged lightning crashed downward from the clouded sky above as the metal spiked balls struck the beast, laced with his savage, holy fire.

Wrecking Ball smashed and smashed the flail into the creature, his face shining and eyes blazing, his body soaring into the air.

Demorn understood Wrecking was a true god of war.

The giant creature howled a final death cry and slumped to the ground, dead at last. The beheaded body of the dark god was crushed beneath the weight of the lizard.

Wrecking descended to the ground. He lifted up the shattered body of his dead enemy. His shining face was exultant.

Demorn heard a horrible moaning screaming in the distance. Wrecking looked to the horizon with diamond eyes.

She saw what he saw. A countless sea of walking abomination, skeletons and zombies, decayed flesh and Bone, shuffling through the wasteland, all the levels of nineteen hells spewing forth its rotten spawn.

The sun above burned blood-red and fire was falling from the sky.

A deep despair tore at her heart.

They were so tiny in the scene of things, just leaves falling in the dying autumn wind. Wrecking Ball flickered away from the land of the dead, his defeated enemy in his hands.

9

Demorn came back to now. Her head hurt. The room was warm. She was sitting upon a white leather couch, her legs tucked beneath her.

A warm mug of tea was beside her. She took a long, slow sip.

'You won, you killed him.'

He had put a thin black robe over his muscled chest. Her eyes glanced over his rippling muscles with a rare hunger, a gentle stirring of fire over the ice inside.

'Why do you call me Wrecking? Is it from the games?'

'Yes,' she answered without hesitation. 'My brother and I played them.'

'Ah.' His youthful voice was strangely sombre. 'I don't understand the games. I've never played them.'

'It's just a bit of fun. People glamorise what we do. It happens to me back in Babelzon. Surely you don't mind?'

His laugh had an edge.

'What is it we do?'

He looked at her with ruined eyes. Demorn realised something was wrong, very wrong. If this had ever been a game, it had long since turned insane and deadly.

She deflected. 'What do you prefer they call you?'

He grinned, raising his hand, red energy pouring off his fingers.

'I've forgotten what my friends called me. It was a lifetime ago.'

The chandelier above them started spinning, from slow to fast, a glistening mirror ball, that suddenly dropped from the ceiling. She jumped back on reflex, her hand going to her gun, but the scene had already changed around her.

She was swimming in a huge hot bath, wearing a slinky red swimsuit. The mirror ball spun above but the room was far bigger — if it was the same room at all — filled with a mixture of beautiful woman and men, mixing and chatting under the party half-light, many of their features vaguely familiar as if from a dream.

The ceiling flickered with constructs, diagrams of the planet, information nobody was paying attention to.

Barely clad models swam in the water around her, beautiful bodies brushing her fingers with their wake. Demorn felt a feeling of elation and freedom, almost foreign to her, as she floated in the hot water. She saw Wrecking floating above the pool, his eyes closed.

She swam to the edge of the bath, her fingers touching the stone side. It was daytime, the sun was pouring down. The doors were flung open to the sun-garden, friends were gathered around, having drinks, exchanging pleasantries and anecdotes.

Wrecking was dressed casually, sitting amongst them, talking deeply with a thin, geeky young man with black rimmed glasses, dressed in a green cashmere sweater. Wrecking looked up at her and smiled.

She got out of the pool, noticing that on the pool bottom there was the marking of a curved black sword. Time phased. The sun-garden was in twilight now. The men and women wore ballroom masks that were tinged with madness. She felt she could see the future in the water, in the perfect grace of the models.

She was back in the room with Wrecking. The lights flickered. Things felt real. He placed his hand against the fireplace. His skin crackled with strange red energy, mixing with electric blue flames.

Wrecking picked up a book from the coffee table. Demorn was surprised to see she recognised it. A massive hardback edition of a famous comic book.

'Cool comic. Nice taste. I didn't know you read them.'

He said, 'I met the writer at a party in San Diego not long after it came out. It was the end of the last millennium. They were all taking drugs that barely affect me, looking for the Next Big Thing. I remember the night so perfectly. I was bored at the party, bored of the whole scene.'

'Was he a friend?'

'No, he was somebody I barely knew. I can recall what he said perfectly. He told me I would like this book. He said it was the kind of thing I was always talking about. Fresh ideas. New characters. Weird thoughts.'

Wrecking threw it back down on the table; ran his hands through his longish hair.

'He said in one of my games that's all I talk about.'

She saw his veins charged with energy. He was fit to burst.

'My games! Can you imagine? I'd never read one of these damn comic books in my life.'

Demorn said coolly, 'You have to cheer up, amigo. Somebody else wrote your scripts, they bought your likeness rights. Just accept it.'

She pointed to the massive tome. 'Did you like the book in the end?'

His smile was distant.

'Yes, but I only read it after everybody died. I went back to find them in the end, after Zaltuth was killed. But the whole town was dead. It was just a lost sick carnival.'

For a moment Wrecking almost faded away. She thought she saw another much younger boy, beneath everything.

Wrecking no longer held the Black Scimitar. The blade softly spun in the air. His large frame had sunk into a chair. He look charred and empty, his humour gone utterly.

Are you as powerful anymore, Demorn thought. With the world above this fortress an insane tomb.

On impulse, she gripped the scimitar, feeling the buzz of power run through her heart.

The room flickered to almost total darkness and the electric fireplace was a single candle blowing in a cold night. It was a gigantic, cavernous room. The roof flickered translucently, showing the sky was on fire with mad gods fighting, tearing into reality.

There were entities in the vast room, no longer fully human. She could see the trails where their physical shells had cracked. And with her burning eyes, Demorn saw the savage energy angles they had formed, some final stand against extinction, a series of equations these humans turned demigods dreamt would grant them some sort of victory against the Plague God. It was a horrible future behind the Pale Suns, the end of dead-end short cut experiments to crack the mortal shell . . .

Demorn shuddered with the foreknowledge that it was not victory that awaited them in the sky above. It lasted only a single fraction of a second, where she saw them all, some still mostly human, others already fuel for their divine leader.

And then the angles coalesced into a stream of energy and Wrecking took it, throwing it against Zaltuth and the dimension itself, gorging his power on their fuel, their sacrifice.

Through it all Demorn could hear a single continuous scream piercing her mind. It had neither sex nor personality, but it was infinite and knew only terror.

Nausea caught her as the visions vanished, and the scream become a moan, then a sigh. Wrecking caught her, pressing a hot mug of scented tea to her lips. The tea made her feel better. Her sickness faded.

'Touching the Scimitar could have killed you, Princess. It has destroyed so many.'

She looked at him with huge, blazing green eyes.

'I don't die easy. I never have. What went wrong, Wrecking?'

'We awoke chaos. I tore down too much of this world to destroy the Plague. Now his ghosts own the Grave.'

Demorn shook her head.

'No, not with that. What went wrong with their spell? The people you had brought here. They're not just dead — they are gone, I saw them disintegrated.'

He went quiet, seemingly lost in thoughts.

'Who were they? Who were those people at the party?'

'Dead friends. Writers. Actors. Directors. Enemies. Traitors. Innocents. Thieves. They were many things. For a while I was winning this war, Demorn, though never by much. I helped form the Organisation. A coalition of sorts. A bulk ward against the Plague God . . . and even more terrible things I glimpsed in my travels. The fame helped then.'

Demorn smiled blankly. She saw the whipping marks across the boy by the portal. She remembered the whole world was dead.

'I bet it did.'

He grinned suddenly, cares seemingly washing away like magic. 'Is this what happens after the Final Battle in my games? Zaltuth vanquished, while we sit beneath a megaton of force fields and magics, and undead monsters wander across the ruins. Is that the victory you were promised when good won?'

She laughed wryly. 'Not exactly. But I never really believed good vs evil was the real battle, anyway.'

'Tell me, Princess, what do you believe?'

'That there's too much evil for the good to handle all by themselves. Sometimes the neutrals have to lend a hand.'

He chuckled. 'Ah, the neutrals. You are one, I presume?'

'I'm a hired sword. I'm whatever the buyer wants.'

Demorn sank back in her chair, green eyes glittering.

'Once in a while though, I take a personal moment. A vacation. It didn't turn out so well this time. And yet, here we are. Still alive. Alex made it through to me. Maybe we can hustle out.'

Wrecking pointed to the fireplace. His voice was wry. 'Maybe. You know, for all my organisations and secret bases, I've never thought I was *supposed* to win. My enemy was always stronger, vastly older . . .'

He rubbed his perfect face. 'I often barely escaped with my life. I remember the Snake Labyrinth . . .'

Demorn nodded. 'We played that game a ton. He seemed so strong. In *Escape from the Snake Labyrinth*, the Plague God's minions owned my ass for days. I was lost in the darkness of that dungeon. You seemed so much younger than him . . .'

Demorn's voice trailed off, lost in a childhood world of computer battles so distant now.

Wrecking's hand rested on her shoulder. As she looked at him, she now saw that around his neck glistened a spectral diamond, glowing eerily, lighting up his profile with an intense white light.

Demorn gasped, flashing her fingers in a reflex warding sign. *'A Spectre Gem!'* she breathed in Asanti. *'From the treasure pits of the Plague.'*

His fingers brushed the sharp gem. 'His legacy no longer has a hold over me. I never take this off. It was my first true victory over Zaltuth, the first prize that I took from him.' Wrecking's voice was vague and distant. 'I learnt things in the Snake Labyrinth that no game or story has ever known.'

'What does it do?'

His diamond eyes seemed to dim and his voice was far away, younger.

'The Gem can hear the secrets of those disintegrated into dust. They bite and hiss, restless phantoms, telling tales.'

There must be so many on this world, she thought. This grave dimension.

'What do the phantoms say?'

He looked at her, eyes shining, proud. 'That ancient gods do not truly die. They howl in the Void. That we long to return to a Source that has forgotten we exist. They scream that your homeland is run by a Tyrant who burrows so deep for secrets. They say so much, Princess.'

A strange horror came to Demorn, some dread awareness of a bitter, bleak death with no return, strung on the gallows, haunted by a thousand years of loss, unable to sleep, and the iron rattling on her legs . . .

'I can still feel him, I can taste his breath,' she whispered.

'The Plague Himself does not truly perish, he lingers in the rotten souls of all. We carry him, Princess, we keep him alive. He is buried deep inside an iron prison of ancient design . . . five hundred trials from rebirth . . . but we carry him, all of us.'

Demorn exhaled softly. The horror faded. She could hear the comforting hum of the electric fire. The perfumed air gave the room a soft, fragrant peace.

She smiled sweetly. 'That's heavy, but let's not forget he's rotting in a fucking soul cage. I hope he stays inside long enough for me to get off this damn rock.'

10

Wrecking Ball looked deep into one of his paintings. It was of purple glass pyramids in a grass meadow. It looked peaceful, universes away from the charnel house above them. Rain started pouring onto the pyramids. The picture became alive.

Demorn could feel the rain on her face, the sudden heat of the sun that burned through the clouds, shining on the purple pyramids, stunning reflections of multiple rainbows that shimmered in the air like a mirage.

Wrecking kept his gaze on the painting, his fiery eyes spellbound. Demorn walked softly across the room, as it became a meadow of deep green grass, the pyramids rearing up before her. Wrecking floated in the sky.

'I don't get what you did to the kid back there. It's probably your way of keeping the humans in line, but to me, it's just cruel.'

Wrecking turned away from the beauty of the image, and the room phased back to normal. She could see the power surrounding him, she could feel it, bleeding into the air, overriding the air con. The room grew hot.

'Tiger Eyz are far crueler. You don't know the damage they have done, and how they did it.'

Wrecking Ball pressed a finger to the right side of his temple. 'They're brainwashed, you know. Programmed. It was a cult for years. There's a huge clinic under Los Angeles. I hung out there with a lot of movie stars for awhile.'

Demorn laughed. 'Yeah, I know, doing drugs that barely affected you.'

Wrecking flexed his arm, muscles rippling. She saw the red shadow of his mighty flail, shimmering in his right hand. 'I've broken the mental conditioning in the boy. He's almost sane. It wasn't easy. But it won't matter now.'

She couldn't help a playful smile. I can spot somebody on a death trip, Demorn thought.

'I guess it won't.'

Wrecking Ball looked at her with searching eyes.

'The death spells poisoned the skin of this world like acne. There will be no New Genesis here.'

Demorn flicked a gossamer thread down the palm of her left hand. 'I've lived in The Grave for two years. Of course I know that.'

He was very handsome, but Demorn knew he was not quite sane.

'Yes, sad. This is my home, Demorn . . . my fortress, my people, my world. All poisoned and gone. It makes me laugh, Princess. After all those battles across all those worlds, this is where the endings to all my stories led.'

She shrugged. Flashbacks to playing computer games in Sub-Babel with Smile, before Innocents, before Mexico and what the doctors did to him.

'Don't be so depressing, it doesn't suit you. I loved your games when I was young. None of us knew where it would wind up. It was about the adventure.'

His voice rumbled. 'And how I loved the adventures. But what makes you think I hold the key to exit this Hell? Why wouldn't I have left, too?'

She kept her voice completely neutral. 'Maybe you hate to lose. Or maybe you are chained here.'

She heard him laugh and his breathing shifted. The Wrecking Ball formed fully, an orange ball of power, the spiked metal, charred smoking chains.

His voice was murky as he turned away. 'I didn't expect the famed Princess of the Swords to be so relaxed. I have never been some God of Mercy. I am a God of War.'

Her hand was on the katana handle. 'And what was he? What was Zaltuth?'

Wrecking Ball looked at her with eyes that were almost completely blood-red. With a dreadful knowledge, she suddenly knew what had infected him.

His voice was hazy. 'He was Walking Death itself, he was the Plague. I drove the Black Scimitar through him, when he would not bow to me. So arrogant and coveting his power, I violated everything! I am the very reason why death itself roams this world. I AM THE WORLD KILLER I AM—'

You're completely insane, Demorn thought. With perfect timing, she spun the thread at him, flicking it noiselessly across the short distance, expertly winding the chain around his neck, fast and clean.

His hands went to the blessed gossamer. Her green eyes blazed with a godly fire.

She tugged fiercely and the gossamer thread bit, choking him, crackling with electric holy symbols, twisting him onto his knees.

She fired three shots into his heart, straight through the thin robe. She saw the skin break and bleed. His diamond blue eyes shattered and his body contorted.

She held his gaze, watching the holy bullets kill him.

'I'm not some ignorant waif, you arrogant asshole,' she whispered. 'I can see the Raaiq infection on you. They have poisoned you. How did you let that happen?'

He laughed, the blood soaking his black robe. His eyes were bleeding. 'Hardly anybody knows about the Raaiq. I've carried her taint for a year. I wouldn't have expected you to see it, Princess.'

'Well, I've got magic eyes and I've been around,' she said coolly, the gun trained upon him. 'I've been to their home world, I've worked for them. They can only infect those they love. They are a dying species because of it. You would know this! How could you be so stupid?'

He looked at her with desperate, hungry eyes. 'Because I loved her. I can burn out this filthy sickness, I've lasted for months.'

'You've lost perspective. You're falling apart, man,' she said grimly.

She had seen the Raaiq virus before, most often from a distance. The cases were extremely isolated, but all the endings were the same. Blood-fever, insanity, deranged violence, a mercy killing the only sane exit. A normal person could last a few days with Raaiq infection, perhaps a fraction more at peak fitness. How long could a god last? What damage could they do?

Wrecking Ball laughed loudly. The golden bullets were visible in his flesh through the torn robe, already working out of his body.

'What will it matter if I can't beat it? What will it matter to this dead world?'

Demorn jerked on the gossamer thread. 'It matters because we need to get back home. How do I get back?' she shouted, sick of it all. 'Just answer me or I will kill you now!'

He opened his palm. Upon it lay a golden coin. Her brother's coin, changed by power. From silver to gold. She saw the melting face of the Goddess inscribed upon the gold, frail light spilling from the ruined face.

Wrecking let it fall upon the floor. His hands glowed red and he seemed to fight off some of the effects of the sickness. His voice was clearer.

'This Goddess Coin gave passage to your friend. A powerful item for a club of gunslingers and thieves.'

Demorn kept her voice neutral. 'You were one. It's a club relic . . .'

Wrecking nodded, looking sleepy. The face was melted. 'Worthless now. The power of the coin is spent. Your brother gave it to Alex; it was a one way trip. That's how desperate they are, Demorn.'

At some level the bullets had done damage, but Demorn could see that already he had stopped bleeding and the skin was no longer harmed.

She doubted even blessed bullets could truly kill a being of his power. She wondered if the damage was only to his mind.

He looked up at her with his desperate vision.

'Kill me, Princess, kill me before I scorch this world. It's all I dream about now. Somebody wiser than me can help you—'

She aimed and pumped a bullet directly into his forehead, without any emotion save contempt. She took five more shots, closing herself up tight inside. Demorn thought of the dead Raaiq woman on the vessel outside, the telepath queen on a death trip who didn't care anymore. She thought of her bodyguards, all dead now, how they had spoken in hopeless tones about a Hive that was destroyed and burnt out behind them. Everything behind her felt like cinders.

Demorn knew then that it was all preordained, there was nothing random about this cycle of dying, this journey to the ruined god.

She saw a stunning painting on the wall. It was the two of them, a tender image of Wrecking and his alien chick, floating in a gondola down a murky river. The woman was in a flowing turquoise dress and her voice-box glinted in the light. She was smiling, his arm wrapped around her. Her orange skin sparkled off the water. They looked so happy, so invincible.

Demorn wanted to believe this was before it all went crazy, she wanted to believe they had had a few good years, that the love was worth it, worth the Raaiq infection. But the painting showed the skies above them were red, and the more she looked, the more she knew. It had already gone to hell. They were just two more fools killing time in the aftermath of Armageddon. It was as bad as sleeping in the same bed as Skeleton Kate.

A shiver ran through Demorn.

His head slumped toward the carpet. Demorn moved forward and caught him by the hand.

Gods don't really want to live forever, she thought, nobody does. She took the Spectre Gem from around his neck.

With a twist of her wrist, she flicked the gossamer thread from around his throat, snapping it back into her sleeve.

Wrecking Ball crashed to the floor.

Demorn shot the picture out, bullets shredding the image of the couple until she could not tell what had been there.

11

The Spectre Gem reverberated in her hands, powered by death.

Kate pounded through her head.

I'm gone, Demorn, I'M GONE I'M GONE I'M GONE.

Painful. Soaked in dirty blood, ghosts rubbing against the Pain Locket, visions of the Clubhouse, Kate dead in Bone City.

I'M GONE I'M GONE I'M GONE.

Demorn staggered, almost falling to her knees. She refused to collapse. She gripped the nearby couch, focusing her magic eyes on Wrecking Ball. She wasn't sure if she imagined it but spirits seemed to issue from him, multi-dimensional, red angled shapes, slowly solidifying back to normalcy.

The echoes from the Spectre Gem faded. The ghosts died.

His inert body shimmered inside the black robe. It seemed to grow smaller.

She crossed to the body, turning his face. A teenage boy looked up, wearing a very different face from Wrecking. Sixteen, seventeen at most. His body was no longer bronze and muscled, but very white, dwarfed inside the magnificent black robe.

His right eye was a stunning ruby colour, the other was covered with a digital black eye patch. It was impossible to tell if this was the same being.

The boy drew the robe around his thin, hollow body. Golden bullets popped and burst from his forehead, falling to the ground. He smiled weakly and caught one of the golden bullets with thin fingers. His chest was heaving.

'Magic bullets,' he said in a child-like voice.

'Yeah. To kill magic things.' Her voice was calm. 'But the Athena gun won't kill anybody still truly blessed by the Goddess.'

He staggered to a couch and fell onto it, seemingly exhausted beyond measure, his voice ragged as he tried to crack wise. 'Lucky for me, then. I guess somebody is looking out for me.'

Demorn slid the gun back in her leg holster, watching him with cool green eyes. 'It takes more than luck to survive these bullets.'

Jesus, what had happened to the fucking indestructible Wrecking Ball? She felt frustrated and angry. I felt so close, Demorn thought with a sudden, savage bitterness. I actually thought we were going to get home.

She saw an old looking Chinese vase on a stand nearby, and picked it up and smashed it into the wall above him. The kid looked up, almost cowering. It just fed her more frustration.

'This whole world is lost *and I needed him* . . . not some whiny adolescent.'

She grabbed his robe and slapped him across the face. The teenage boy sprawled back on the couch, his chest heaving.

'What the hell are you! Is Wrecking still in there?'

He held a hand up to shield himself. 'In some ways, this is still him, just another part!'

Demorn sneered. 'Yeah, the weak bitch part.'

She sighed, her magic eyes searching him. Flatline. 'You don't have the power, you're not blessed like him.'

'Blessed?' He laughed with a strange bitterness, his words clipped and precise. 'I hope not! I'm a godforsaken atheist, dear!'

She slapped his face again, knocking him to the ground. 'So was I, until the Goddess bled her raw power into me. You taste that kind of juice, you stop being so clever about everything.'

His lip was bleeding. He pulled the robe around him and combed his hair.

'You're Asanti born, aren't you?'

He talked scatter-gun fast but eloquent, 'Try to understand, Princess. I don't care about the mythologies. I don't care about the debates of what the Fracture was. I'm aware that it's almost entirely artificially generated. But I can help you, even in this form.'

'How?'

The boy got up and went to the white wall, his fingers flicking across an invisible panel. 'I haven't been back here for awhile. Wrecking doesn't give me much screen time.'

A small safe opened outward. He brought out a small black leather bag and rummaged through it. His voice was quick and intense. 'You know Wrecking from his games, I assume?'

'Yeah. They were huge in Babelzon.'

A slight pause. 'Ever play *Return to Chaos*? It was one of the last.'

'No,' she said slowly. 'I'd stopped playing by then. The whole Wrecking franchise turned into endless fighting games; it wasn't my kind of thing.'

He smiled, but his ruby eye was sad. 'Well, that's why you don't know who I am.'

He tossed her a shining item, and Demorn caught it. It was a set of crystalline teeth, weightless in her hand, glinting from silver to black.

She could feel the powerful, dark magic shuddering off it. The Dragon Teeth. It was something Wrecking had worn in the early games.

She remembered the blood-red sun glinting off them when Wrecking had fought his long, bloody way through the Mirror Pools in Fate-town.

'Who are you and how the hell did you get this?'

'I'm the star of *Return to Chaos*. The central character.'

He kept going through the bag, his body suddenly shimmering. He was suddenly a normal looking boy in his late teens, dressed in a dark blue hoodie and casual jeans. He didn't look pathetic anymore, just young and less obviously terrifying than the burning demigod.

He shook her hand in a business-like fashion.

'I'm Jason Alequin, the kid who created Wrecking Ball.' He sighed. 'I wanted my codename to be Azure Sorcerer, but it never took off. Such is life.'

She was curious. 'You created him? How?'

Jason swept his hand across the room, seemingly indicating much more than this stylish lounge. 'My family were War Game designers. A mixture of sorcery and genetic construction. Slightly unpleasant, very lucrative.'

Demorn felt uneasy.

'I never liked the business much. Or my family. But I inherited their talents nonetheless. My specialty was character design. I kept the mazes and the death-traps stocked with engaging characters.'

He brushed his fingers against the white wall. A screen buzzed into being, Wrecking Ball locked in battle with a slithering green, electro-dragon. His long hair splayed in the wind, and his eyes blazed purple fire as he swung his glowing Ball into the shimmering green skin of the dragon.

'Now, Princess, you tell me, is that engaging?'

The dragon's spiky tail raked across his back, ripping the thin black robe to expose a complex tattoo wrapped around his torso.

They tumbled through the sky. Wrecking Ball ripped through the electric tail with one mighty hand. The burning, charred flail smashed again and again into the dragon.

The boy waved his hand and the image vanished.

'It looks totally wild,' Demorn said.

Jason laughed softly. 'Thanks. He was a labor of love. Wrecking won that fight, by the way, it was his debut scene. He saved a civilisation. The world fell in love with him. It put the company in a whole new earnings bracket.'

She looked at the necklace, glinting. 'These are priceless.'

Jason laughed bitterly. 'Except you can put a price on them. A price that makes you so damn rich you can buy pocket universes and build digital palaces to escape the end of the world.'

She looked at Jason sternly, her green eyes flashing. Demorn ran the old training exercises on herself, but there had been no breach. He was not trying to hypnotise her with mind-tricks.

Whatever else he was, this boy was no telepath. He was playing a very open game.

Demorn put the Teeth in her mouth, her body shuddering with magic, but she held on to his eyes, not sacrificing her soul to the Teeth's power, but mastering the flow, riding the wild current.

The flashing Black Scimitar was in her hands.

The boy moved back slightly. The dark blade sat in her hand, almost weightless, and so deadly. Demorn felt the tattoos upon her skin burning as exotic magic flooded her system. It gave her a weird clarity.

'You make your mind up fast, Demorn.'

Demorn smiled her scary smile as the magic ate into her blood. 'It's how I stay alive. I remember that scene. Wrecking versus the Electric Dragon Xaminua . . . or at least some version of it.'

'That's because Wrecking games were reflections of his real adventures!' Jason grew animated, gesturing his excitement. 'He went to so many worlds. Wrecking Ball went *so far out*, Demorn. He was exactly what I wanted him to be. I took him further than any character we ever had.'

She lowered the blade. Her heart still beat rapidly. She didn't know what to believe. 'I don't get it. He's a character you made? That's fucking heavy. So why did Wrecking turn *into* you when I put a bullet in him?'

Jason sighed. 'Desperate times. All those fighting games . . . a whole decade of them . . . It's not just the Plague God who was confined to the soul cages of the Iron Jail.'

He looked at her with dispiritedly sad eyes.

Her stomach dropped. No . . .

'Wrecking was captured, too. Tortured inside their Prison.' His voice drifted away, and the boy was slumped against the trophies, lost in private dreams and nightmares.

The crackling of the electric fireplace was the only sound in the room.

Vague memories stirred again of Smile playing those fighting games well past midnight, the light from the console images spilling over his face. It made her feel sad and slightly sick.

'Who's they?'

He rubbed his forehead, looking exhausted. 'The Ultimate Fate you fear so much. The Pale Suns carry its banner.'

Jesus, Demorn thought, her hand unconsciously clenching into a fist. The Pale Suns. She had almost forgotten them, so lost had she become in this world of skeletons.

'How would you know what I fear?'

The boy smiled, his ruby eye glistening. 'You're in his games too, Princess.'

Her heart went cold. 'I don't see how. I never met him until today. Wrecking was just a myth to me.'

The boy raised his hand over the wall. It became a glistening, electronic pool of water. 'You've made it this far. You're wise enough to know time reflects both backwards and forwards. It's all ONE MOTION AND MANY RIVERS FLOW INTO THE WIDE OPEN SEA—'

She moved toward the white wall, his words flowing dream-like and space-age through her mind. She heard music that she had never known, rhythmic hip-hop that seemed familiar and maybe she had heard it in some dark club with beautiful boys and girls so long ago.

The wall phased between blank white and the pool of crystal clear water — Demorn saw her face in the reflections, wearing the purple glasses, the thin scar long down her right cheek.

Wrecking Ball was beside her, his arm wrapped around her waist, his face happy and hair longish. She smiled, and kissed him on the lips.

Demorn laughed despite herself, her fingers brushing her skin, realising with a shock her mask was still on, and it now looked exactly like her face. The wall shimmered and the image vanished—

'I know enough to know that I don't know enough,' Demorn said. 'I just need to get home. I can still help Babelzon.'

Jason smiled. 'Do you really think you can save them? Or do you just miss your comfortable bed and the bevy of supermodels you call soldiers?'

Demorn sneered. 'You best stay out of my personal life. I've seen Gods die by Asanti blade. It can be done.'

Jason pulled a doubting face, his voice sarcastic. 'Sure, like when your dear brother sliced up an old Iron God who had rusted too long in the void? Is that what you mean by gods dying?'

Her blood ran colder still. How did he know such things? The old suspicion. Was there still a plant in the club, something beyond Red Morning? Or was it something else even more sinister? Did he speak to the God-Kin lost in the frozen void?

She flicked her hand dismissively. 'Believe what you want. This debate is boring me.'

He said, 'The Plague was beheaded and physically dead when his spirit entered the Prison. He sank deep, and remains inside the cage. But Wrecking Ball had raw power through the roof. He fought them every step of the way, he never fell far inside the traps. His Cell was only two levels from this reality. Still, they got their hooks in plenty deep.' The boy added delicately, 'He's made some . . . questionable decisions in his travels.'

Demorn *felt*, rather than saw, a small shape skipping and moving across the couches and surfaces of the room.

Her hand went to her gun but the boy smiled, his face lighting up, as a shadowy white shape leapt into his arms. 'Ah! Kaylin!'

Demorn's green eyes blazed and she saw a ghostly shape, writhing in his arms.

'Oh Mercy,' Demorn whispered, backing away. 'It's a Panther Ghost Cub.'

'It,' he said pointedly, 'is Kaylin, my life-friend.'

She could see the white cub now, playing energetically with the boy as he placed the cat in his backpack, the beautiful feline face rubbing thin whiskers across the boy's neck.

'You're insane, their mark will follow you beyond the grave, you've doomed yourself.'

Jason smiled. 'You really don't understand, do you? *I'm* the one who sprung Wrecking Ball from the Iron Prison. Kaylin found his scent from an entire Reality Level away.'

There was a strange wisdom to him. He didn't sound so young after all. She was pretty sure Smile would understand all this. But Smile was far away. Demorn realised she needed to believe in all this, right here and right now, if she was to get back to Babelzon.

'I understand that you live in a very complex world, kid. A lot of angles, games within games.'

He patted the cat's shimmering white fur. 'I've died in-game, Princess. I died in the first rescue attempt, before we got it right. My fallback was Wrecking Ball. I'm slip-streaming his DNA base. I built him after all.'

He held his arm up. 'A few skin scrapings. After a while, it doesn't even hurt, you forget most of what happens . . .'

Demorn blinked. Time shuddered. She felt a flash of hot warmth upon her face, falling through the air entangled in battle — the sound of the running river, and the huge, blinking, rose image of the Goddess rising above her — as she fell to her knees in the marshes of Firethorn . . .

The image passed, but the warmth of that sun slowly faded from her skin. She brushed her fingers against her cheek but it was ice cold.

She realised that somewhere in the last thirty seconds she had put her mask back on. Her distorted death mask leered out. The dragon teeth shuddered with dark magic.

'I'm just looking for a ticket home,' she said.

He grinned brightly.

'You've touched the Spectre Gem. That evil old jewel knows the ways out of the Grave. The rest of the key is in you already.'

The room blurred, the electric fire replaced by an endless succession of mirror mazes stretching to infinity points.

'The membrane is weak here, and you've been sliding through it all your life, Princess.'

'Stop saying that. Call me Demorn,' she murmured.

The gem around his neck shone a spectacular vivid orange, and for a second she was falling, not down, but upward — tossed without control into some starless ocean of space, spinning across parallel sheets of glass, her fingers and hands smashing against the merciless planes of reality.

She tired to speak, but there was only silence, as her lives circled around her. A succession of plush hotels and dead marks, beautiful people caressing her body, cash in the account, soulless skeletons in designer clothes, some with flesh, some Bone.

The glint of a bloody katana as she fought her way out of Chicago, a cruel smile upon her face.

The universes glinted, she saw faces of familiar friends who become strangers, names she didn't know anymore. She saw Toxis falling into an electric chasm in slow motion, her beautiful body hurt and bleeding, blood eyes pure red — replaced by a horde of blonde girls in short summer dresses. They changed into identical beautiful brunette women, kissing her mouth and body.

Demorn could feel the pleasure and the pain as one as she floated through it all. She blinked, and saw a long line of bridges burning all through the night. She walked on, a lonely ghost in the deep night, sometimes with a hand to hold, but mostly just the road for company, singing a few favourite songs softly to herself.

Demorn could feel the ice leave her heart. She felt the chill of all the Bone burn away. She was so free, everything open and aching.

Demorn gasped for breath, shocked at the weight released from her body. She opened her eyes. She had been crying, her face was wet with tears.

The goddamn ice ring sure was a bitch of a burden. Demorn wiped her eyes dry, and got up.

A huge purple sun hung in the black empty sky, a shadow of colour in the void where no other stars shone. There was no sound.

Jason stood beside her, looking at a glistening holo, the backlight throwing his form and face in profile. He seemed older now.

They were standing at the foot of a long stone bridge. The ghost panther cub was far more solid now, pale yellow eyes peering curiously at her, white fur shimmering. She watched it cautiously.

Huge pyramids surrounded them, floating in the void, weird ancient hieroglyphics blazing with neon light across the stone surface. This is the real fucking deal, Demorn thought.

'This is the otherworld,' Demorn breathed, 'the Sky of Multiple Heavens.'

'You know your pseudo-religious mumbo-jumbo,' Jason said, laughing gently.

Not all the pyramids were attached to the ground or to each other. Some were attached to hunks of floating rock; some hung eerily in the deadness of space.

A huge glistening battlement was built along the side of the Chasm. Massive granite stones emblazoned with holy symbols and the machinery of war. Spears stuck out from the stone and huge skulls adorned the top of the battlements.

The cub leapt gracefully from the backpack and prowled around the stone path before running down the great stone bridge that lay under the battlements and into the abyss.

Demorn walked to the edge of the broken bridge. She looked directly into the Chasm, heart leaping into her throat as she gazed into an endless abyss that sucked at her soul.

Demorn saw the restless energy sea, blue and green waves clashing in the dark tombs of the world.

She saw the sea rising, a vast tidal wave of energy and power from which there was no respite, no refuge. A howling sound cut across the silence, like a mighty thunder.

A hand came over her eyes and dragged her from the precipice. She shrugged off Jason's grasp and looked to the sky.

A red and blue train roared along a iron railroad that magically appeared in that starless sky. The air seemed to vibrate and roar and the noise hurt her ears and her mind.

'Is that filled with all the souls going to the Nine Thousand Hells?' Demorn said, and she was only half joking.

Jason laughed, almost shyly, his hand fluttering around his throat. The awful sound slowly faded away into a distant rumble which sounded like a warning. The iron railroad slowly disappeared behind it.

'I don't know where that train goes.' His voice was soft as he looked down into the swirling energy storm. 'But I know that the Chasm is the end of everything.'

Deep burn marks lay across the stone bridge. She kneeled and touched the markings, the wounds seemed fresh and charred where the bridge was broken. Her arm burned slightly, where the golden band had once been.

Her eyes blazed and she could see the markings upon the battlements, too, markings of a fire that had seared the neon symbols. The scripting was strange and unfamiliar, but the longer Demorn studied it, the more she understood, codes written in buried languages, holy prophecies of dead worlds.

Jason whispered, 'Across the Chasm lies the land of Night Gods.'

He was shrouded in shadow, no light shone toward him. For a moment it seemed he had grown far larger and more powerful, a tall, strong profile against the encroaching darkness, some sort of saviour . . . but then she blinked and all she saw was the same young man, a wistful expression upon his face as he looked over the Stone Bridge.

She chuckled. 'What happened to the brave atheist I was talking to?'

He pulled a face, focusing on her, the vague look still in his unsettled eyes. 'Call them night gods, call them dark entities, call them forces of nature . . . call them whatever you want, Demorn. There is some real raw fucking power here. It always impresses me. It's the worship that puzzles me, the whole prayer trip. It's the same as worshipping a neutron bomb.'

'Is that what they are to you? Weapons?'

He pointed to the floating structures in the violet sky.

'The things that build those pyramids don't care about our prayers. We're just meat in the charnel house.'

Black lightning crackled from the purple sun, searing the barren land beyond the stone bridge, the arcs twisting in the cold sky. The wind suddenly cut through her.

Demorn smiled. A thrill ran through the dark mask. A shadow of some terrible future drenched in blood and battle. 'You are so goddamn deep it's depressing. Where to from here?'

He shrugged, pulling his jacket close against the cold wind. 'Your legend is distant, a whisper to me, Demorn. Perhaps you are already lost. But across the Stone Bridge, in the wilds of Dark Heaven, you may find the exit you seek.'

Nothing really grows in the land of death, Demorn thought. Not legends. Even they die here.

As she watched, the dark wasteland across the bridge became filled with those same dread images she had seen with Wrecking, bad fever dream memories on the edge of her mind. With terrible, ancient purpose, a legion of Bone and decaying undead walked across the dry plain. Demorn could see the corrupt fruit in their souls, swollen with negative energy and evil.

She turned away, sickened.

Demorn untied one of her black wrist ribbons, and threw it into the Chasm, watching as it swirled into the maelstrom of wild energy, until it became invisible even to her blazing eyes.

I'm not ready to follow Toxis, she thought, as the chasm ate the ribbon. I'm just not ready.

She looked back over the wasteland. The zombies and Bone had vanished, everything was dark and empty.

She looked at the floating pyramids, hovering above. She could see the icon of Wrecking, his image and glowing spiked ball emblazoned into the stone.

Jason gently took her hand. 'You ready?'

'I'm just imagining the aliens who built these pyramids. I mean, have you ever seen a pyramid an alien didn't build?'

Jason laughed. They flickered off the stone bridge.

12

Demorn stood in a pungent, thick forest of green leaves. Her mask was off. Jason was gone.

The forest stank of rich perfume, peppermint and lilac and scents she had never known. She heard the distant crashing of waves upon a shoreline, but it faded, an echo in her mind, like old songs from favourite bands you had forgotten.

She walked through the quiet wood, only half aware of who she was. The lilac stung her mind. She stopped before a perfect pine tree, growing by the side of a crystal clear lake.

Fire burst out, orange fire encasing the tree. The water steamed. The heat was intense on her face.

Wrecking stood by the edge of the lake and the forest. As he stepped from the shadow, she saw that he had changed. His skin glowed a darker hue, and diamond blue eyes shone. He was dressed in a thick red robe.

He laughed, deep and rich. Around him the forest burnt in purple and orange flames.

'You won't burn here, Sword Princess.'

Demorn looked nervously at the flames, feeling the heat reflected off her skin. 'Why?'

'Because this is my Heaven, my birthing place. I do not wish to harm you.'

Wrecking rose above the crystal water. She could see a reflection of Jason in the pool, his image growing more distant, spinning deeper and deeper into the water, until all that was left were smooth ripples.

Wrecking lowered his feet in shallow water, touching her brow with his warm hand. 'He is just a skin to shed.'

Rain started to fall in the forest, refreshing to her sweat-soaked body. It felt like each drop was a wave of peace, lulling her to some soft destination at the end of a long road. The flames died in the forest.

Demorn came back to herself. Her hand went to her holster but it wasn't on her leg. This is astral travel, Demorn told herself, her sharp mind fighting the magic.

'We all have so many skins, don't we? So many lives,' he murmured.

Demorn caught his wrist, cool and collected.

'Hey, Mr Mystical, stop with the New Age crap. Start talking straight to me!'

His hand caught aflame and he laughed. The universe flashed. She felt herself stretched across a great divide—

Icy wind.

Demorn opened her eyes and she was above a mighty rock cavern through which a stormy sea tore, smashing against clean rocks with a violent fury, smashing again and again. Her mouth opened in amazement. Shivers ran down her back. She knew this cavern. She knew that angry sea.

A tall, solid man was sitting on the rock. He wore severe black clothes and a dark glass crown lay upon his head, spiked and terrible. As she got closer, she could see the glass was covered in sprays of blood.

It was the Dead King. She looked toward the distance and the world wasn't dead; there were tall, green trees and people scattered across the shore.

A white fort lay in the near distance, a red flag snapping in the strong wind.

'Firethorn . . .' she said, and a delicious shiver ran through her. It seemed to her the water was a healing balm as it shot up from the cavern, drenching with an achingly icy freshness.

She looked closely at the Dead King. He was younger and more solid than she remembered. It's because he's still alive, Demorn realised. He hasn't died yet, not in this moment.

She sat beside him on the rock, peacefully.

He said, 'I can always bring you Home. I can always bring you back.'

'How . . . this happened years ago? I never remember long . . .'

His lips brushed her forehead.

'Because you gave your soul and heart away, Princess. Away to the cold ocean, to the wars you fight, to the cruelty of others.'

His fingers enclosed her hand. She pressed it to her, feeding off the energy. Emotions flooded her, the good kind, the Saturday morning cartoon kind, killing all the emptiness inside, all of it. She felt peaceful.

'If we sit here long enough, we can watch Firethorn fall and rise and fall. We can watch Varangians and Ice Dragons and wraiths all come to the White Fort. We can watch you be the hero who saves your people time and time again.'

Demorn felt like crying as she looked at the wild sea.

She said, 'I gave my heart to vengeance and I'm not done yet.'

'The weight of a Skull Ring is a terrible one, Princess. I told you to beware it.'

'You told me too late. I wanted to bring my girlfriend back. I don't really care about anything else.'

The Dead King nodded, smiling. She could see the white shadow on his tanned skin where his Ring had been.

He said, 'I'm born in magic. Enchantments lie heavy on me. To one such as me, a Skull Ring is a powerful trinket.' The King paused. 'But you, my Princess of the Sword, my dear Demorn . . . you flicker between two worlds, two lives. Under the magic sword, and the flashing eyes, you're a mortal soul, bound to go beneath. The Skull Ring will cage you and ensnare you. It will doom you.'

Demorn pulled a face. 'Yeah, I can bleed, and die. So what? So can all the rest. I've saved Firethorn for years, both before and after your death!'

He slammed his fist into the rock, shattering it. 'Obey your King! LEAVE HERE! LEAVE THE DEAD WORLD AND LEAVE THE SKULL RING!'

Demorn sneered, getting up. 'My *Dead* King. I have seen your Fall. I wear the Crown now.'

He looked at her, his composure broken. Her heart beat fast as his piercing black eyes scanned her deeply. 'It is true . . . I see . . . the promise of your Golden Crown.'

She felt the Crown appear on her head; she felt the power flooding through her body, untainted by ice or the death spells of The Grave.

'It becomes more than a promise, my King. I tossed the witch from the filthy coven that the White Fort became in your absence.'

He turned away, back to the wild sea again. Three black ships sailed toward the shoreline. The Dead King watched them with wistful eyes. He spoke with a defeated tone. 'So you killed her then.'

Demorn spoke sharply, 'I did. Why did you allow it? You were a man of great power, you must have felt her witchery upon your soul.'

The Dead King was philosophical. 'She was what she was fated to be. And we had love in our way.'

Demorn rolled her eyes.

'I have said what I came to say, rising from the graves of memory, to sit by the White Fort by the Sea. *Listen to me, Princess of the Sword.* Toss the Skull Ring into the Chasm. Walk away from the land of the dead. Walk away from the memory of lost girls.'

She laughed with genuine surprise. He looked at her, and his severe, stern face held hardly a shred of hope.

'Just give up and go home, pretend nothing happened. You really are an absentee father, aren't you?' Demorn shook her head. 'You don't even understand. I'm trapped. The Skull Ring is the only thing that's kept me alive so far.'

She watched him slowly stand. The earth trembled. In the corner of her magic eyes, she could see his glass crown flashing. His stern, handsome face was rotted, and the terrible spiked glass crown was drenched in crimson blood.

Xalos blazed into her hand, shimmering purple flames.

'Pass beneath, my true King, do not dare become my enemy,' she whispered.

He held out his decaying hand. It contained a shimmering glass globe of light, the interior covered in thick, swirling mists. She took it from him, cold to her touch. The King vanished.

And then an inexorable slowness, the image of the blowhole, and the White Fort faded into white. And she felt truly alone.

Demorn knelt by the side of the crystal pool, her fingers trailing in the cold water. The humid forest was around her again.

She held the small globe in her left hand, shrouded in mist. Xalos had vanished, there was not even an echo of its passing. Perhaps she had dreamed everything, lost in the deceits and powers of the gods.

Wrecking looked down at her with a smile in his eyes.

His hand shone red and he sent a wave of energy into the pool. Space and time shattered and they shifted again, landing back on the other side of the stony bridge. Wrecking stood over Jason's crumpled body.

Demorn said, 'So you take turns dying for each other? That's just weird and dysfunctional.'

Wrecking grinned. 'It's a game. We bring different things to the table. I know the legend of the Sword Princess well.'

'My legend?'

'You come with your blazing sword to those in need. You bring vengeance. You kill bad things. You vanish.'

Demorn smiled as she gazed into the abyss, letting the spatial emptiness and the distant churning waves of energy fill her blazing eyes. 'Sometimes it's a gun loaded with holy Athena bullets.'

She shrugged and looked toward the dark lands, at the lightning sheeting from the violent sky. 'But this world isn't saved. Not even close.'

Wrecking laughed. 'This world is damned and ever will be. Even the Heavens are corrupted, leaking dark, twisted magic. It will end soon, rolling into extinction or some endless eternal prison of the damned.'

He sighed with a sound that was almost lust, the shadow of red energy flickering in his hands. This crazy damn god was looking forward to some last suicidal battle, Demorn realised.

'But did this world even call you, Princess?' he said, his deep voice rumbling. 'Or was it something *you* needed? Did you come here on your own mission?'

'So what if I damn well did?' Demorn snapped.

I know what I needed, she thought. She had known it since she had arrived on Dead Day. She needed another five minutes in Chicago. Five minutes in the coffee shop with Kate, before the screams and the TV and the whole world went crazy. I needed time to say real things, time to not just to talk in clichés about things I don't even care about.

She remembered the pathetic image of Bone Kate in her wig and blue jumper, Demorn's golden necklace around the skeletal neck, holding her tightly at night, pretending everything would be OK . . . pretending the skeleton understood all the delicate things she told her, deep into the lonely night.

She looked into the snow globe that her father had given her. The mists parted inside the globe. She saw the black ships upon the blue sea. She saw Kate when she was very young, just a girl really. Long blonde hair ran across her face.

Kate was surrounded by black robed figures, tall, thin and senatorial. Their faces were skeletal. Kate smiled and laughed with them, chatting as the black ship approached the harbour. She wasn't afraid of the skeletons. She had always sailed with Death upon the wide, empty sea. She was dead, always dead.

Demorn was crying. She flung the globe into the abyss, heard it smash against the sheer walls before vanishing into the dark.

'I lost my girlfriend. I wanted to turn the clock back,' Demorn said quietly. 'You don't know how long it is since I held her for real.'

'It's true,' he said. 'I don't know your heart, or what led you here, and your followers after you.'

Demorn caught a far away glimpse of Alex and Guard Dog, sorting through distant ruins, a snide sneer on Alex's face.

His voice rumbled like the thunder from across the stone bridge. 'And yet I know many other things. I know the Dark God is locked away, trapped in a distant hell. He will not rise to face the Ultimate Fate.' His glance seared into her. 'I know you are the Princess of the Swords, drenched in blood, worthy of worship.'

Demorn laughed. 'Worship. Wow. That's a stretch. Are you flirting with me?'

She felt a surge of energy in him. Wrecking took her in his powerful arms, flinging himself high into the air. His eyes were shining as they rose higher and higher.

'The chaos we unleashed upon this dimension is accelerating. Breaking point is upon us. Even the Heavens are being torn asunder!'

They soared upward, his burning energy feeding into her body, eating into all her thoughts. She felt clean as she looked downward.

Jungle had enveloped the stone road and the other side of the Bridge, swollen green vegetation spreading to the battlements before it withered at the abyss. The chaos of the Dark Land lay over the stone bridge, where it was all bleakness.

'I could change the whole world, Princess.'

Her heart stilled. 'Can you cure them? The Bone?'

He laughed and his diamond eyes were on fire. He surveyed the grey land beneath. He started swinging the ball and chain. It hissed with static and electricity.

His voice rumbled with deep thunder. 'I do not bring resurrection to the fallen. I bring a fire that would clear the forests and the cities to start anew.'

She felt weightless. The great spiked ball swung faster and a sheet of red lightning blazed from the black sky, searing the ball and then cascading downwards into the dead lands.

With a thunderous shout the angry god threw his mighty flail at the ziggurat of Zaltuth, a grey shaky pile of stones, with the face of the Plague God carved miserably into the side.

The red lightning smashed into the giant face of the Plague God. Wrecking roared his approval.

She shielded her eyes as the red waves of inexhaustible energy spiralled from the sky and his weapon, the ziggurat crumbling when charged waves of arced crimson lightning hit it, before exploding in a fiery ball so sudden and so powerful that Demorn felt the feedback of the energy wave flood through her, flowing from the skies into herself.

He cried out with a savage passion, 'I have killed you, Dark One, Plague Walker, Zaltuth of the Thorn Isles! I have destroyed you and I take what was yours!'

He roared with laughter. His body grew hot. He screamed chants in some primal, ancient language she did not know. The Goddess tattoo burned a wonderful blue on his huge tanned arms, merging with his wild godly sorcery.

He's gorgeous, she thought. Her own tat echoed upon her skin with a painful hunger. The shadowy ziggurats transformed into polished, elegant pyramids of his own design. Bizarre visions of Heaven reconfiguring in his moment of glory.

Wrecking looked at her, his eyes glazed as the energy wave soaked into him. Both their bodies shuddered with the power of the energy flow, while the stormy skies flickered with arcs of lightning.

He's triumphant, Demorn realised. Even if the world is a charred ruin, he's triumphant.

'There is no turning back now, Princess. I shall cleanse this world.'

They kissed savagely, his hand gripping her hair semi-roughly. She felt up his toned body. For a while she didn't care about anything. For the first time in years, she was alive.

They began to drift toward the ground. There was no need to hide in front of him.

'Your fire burns through lies,' she said in Asanti. 'You cured yourself, didn't you? You actually burnt out the Raaiq virus.'

Wrecking smiled, and she saw a shade of normality in his maddened, luminous eyes.

His voice was clear. 'Victory has cleansed my system. The boy had said it might. I was past caring.'

'Did it end badly? You and the telepath?'

He was watching the last of the elegant pyramids form. 'No. It just ended. I took her from the ruins of her craft, she stayed with me in the first months of the Dead . . . I did not want to hurt her. After a while . . . it seemed like something real. We were both very lonely.'

Demorn waved her fingers, sighing. 'She was damaged. The Raaiq are an enclosed species. To be lost without her partner on this damned rock . . . it would have been a living hell. She was a stronger woman than I thought.'

'Did she save your life?'

Demorn smiled grimly. 'She exploded the brains of everybody else, so yeah, she helped.'

Filled with a strange peace, she walked to the edge of the bridge, looking into the abyss howling beneath them, the angry electric sea.

'It's moments like this where I can still pretend it's just about Good versus Evil, Love versus Hate. It's nice to be simple for a moment, stop thinking in angles.'

He steadied, his body seeming to have absorbed so much power as to be filled. 'Sometimes it can be simple. Will you travel into the Wild Heaven with me now, Wandering Princess?'

His diamond eyes seemed to see into her soul, looking for the answer that lay within. She averted her eyes. Charming and powerful though he was, nobody deserved to know all those secrets.

She turned from the abyss and looked into the dark lands. She could feel the wild calling her, clawing her up inside. 'I need a favour.'

Wrecking chuckled. 'So brave, asking favours of a god.'

Demorn looked at him with sharp pride. 'I'm asking as the Leader of the Innocents.'

His eyes glistened. She wondered how much or how little Alex had told him. She felt his interest flare as he murmured beneath his breath, some strange variant of Asanti, an old, dead dialect. '*I have risen far above my Temple form . . .*'

Demorn caught his arm. His skin was hot. She felt the Glass Crown flare upon her head.

'Yes, and this will release you from the final vows, Mighty One.'

She took the Black Scimitar from the scabbard, and tossed it to him. It spun beautifully in the air and Wrecking caught it easily with one strong hand.

'It's your blade, your war,' she said. 'I just need Xalos back.'

'How did you lose your sword?'

She shrugged. 'Time passed. It burnt out. It went away, capricious and unpredictable as any magic sword.'

He was smooth. 'What have you been using?'

She flexed her hand. 'My backup blade. I've killed plenty with it.'

He nodded. 'Of course you have. You're the Sword Princess, after all.'

He raised his left hand. A lurid triangular symbol was written upon his palm, eerily similar to what lay on Sinatra's hand, years ago in Vegas. A red energy star formed within the triangle, and his hand bled. Emotions flooded her. The triangle of light flooded her eyes and mind.

She was on a cold beach long ago, kissing somebody special. Long black hair and mysterious eyes. A name she could not place. Her heart aching with regret for a person she would never see again, a name she would not ever remember.

Her voice against the cold wind, it's a Quest . . .

The fire was warm and enveloping. She caught glimpses of herself at fifteen, with the hazy neon of Babelzon shining on her face, as she sat in a small room, listening to old Beatles' songs.

Life cut forward, Demorn sat laughing and singing with the Innocents on Music Fridays, reaching the crescendo of "Hey Jude", a glimmer of something magical in the air, her brother's face lit with a Smile . . . before that too passed.

Kate floated topless in her old apartment, her long hair partially covering her breasts, the sun strong across the room. Cartoons were on the TV and Kate was saying nobody has ever loved me like that, baby, nobody, looking like a star from the 1960s movies . . .

Gnawing black vision. An awful silence. Demorn lay on an ice-cold floor.

With clinical interest, she watched a single flickering flame in the near distance. She tried to struggle across the freezing surface.

She was tumbling inside her own memories. He appeared before her, a spirit that was almost entirely fire. She knew her magic eyes saw him truly. She saw how nothing in him that was simply evil or merely good. He was as dangerous and constant as life or death, he was change, he was the wrecking ball which could cleanse entire systems, creation and destruction.

He spoke eloquent, trained Asanti. *'Tell me. How did you lose the Sword, Princess?'*

Through gritted teeth, she snarled. 'I showed Mercy.'

The flame came close to her. She could feel the magic vibrating off him. She could see his beautiful face, without care, just pure wanting.

'Mercy? From a Sword Princess?'

'Yes,' she whispered. 'But she's dead, and it's over.'

His burning hand touched her head. The terrible cold stopped, utterly. She gasped. In her heart she felt an aching pain.

In her mind she heard a slow Sinatra song, the one playing on the day Kate left for Paris, right on the edge of her memory, eons ago.

He was taking all her memories, taking all her loves and hopes — he was in the Jade Hotel with Tony, as White Lion looked at her with a sneer.

He was talking to the Dead King on the seashore as the witch gazed at her with covetous, hungry eyes.

He saw Kate surrounded by the crowd of robed undead, bearing gifts to the Skeleton King—

Everything stopped. Wrecking stood before her in gleaming red armour. The Skull Ring lay in his hand, shattered and broken.

'Where did you get this, Princess?'

'I killed a witch for it. It makes me sick, but it kept me alive in The Grave.'

His hand pressed against her breast, the ring gripped tight. He pulled hard on her shirt. He dragged out a bloody silver thorn, holding it delicately in his fingers. Demorn sighed with an awful pain.

'You would never really have been free. The Skull Ring is old, bad magic that carries a sting. It infects the spirit.'

Wrecking threw the bloody thorn away. He pressed his hand against her chest. Her shirt was ripped but the skin was unbroken underneath. The ring felt lifeless and depowered on her finger.

'Is it gone?'

'In this dimension. If you get home, cast the physical shell away.' He cocked his head, expression kind. 'Was she an Innocent? Your true love?'

Demorn smiled. She hadn't heard anybody use the phrase true love in a long time.

'An Innocent? By association. She dated one for long enough.'

He laughed lightly. The world was filling in around him, building like a jigsaw puzzle around the cold, blank dark. She saw the dark bridge and the bottomless abyss behind him. They were crossing to the other side, but slowly, and each step felt like an age. Sometimes Wrecking looked like a god, sometimes he looked like Jason.

'Did she dance in the Temple? Did she swim in the Lake and swear to us?'

Us. He had pledged allegiance like every other Innocent. He had given a chunk of his soul, kissing Alodin Mars, dancing with the women, drenched in blood-painted charms, swearing deep promises inscribed upon his mind and spirit.

Demorn felt shy. 'She danced with me . . . but she was her own girl. Kate didn't swear to anything. She didn't like killing. She didn't like guns. She just stayed in the Clubhouse sometimes and slept in my room.'

He was quiet. 'When I was an Innocent, we weren't all soldiers.'

Demorn wondered how long ago he had trodden the halls of the Temple. She was no historian, but she wondered what had changed. Each incarnation of the Innocents formed around the leader.

Red Morning had been an assassin, a spy in some former life. And, it turned out, a traitor. She hired people with ice in their veins.

Demorn was a Princess of the Sword, drenched in blood, born for war. Her colonels were like Alex, killers on gossamer chains.

'Did you lead us?'

He looked at her kindly. 'No. I could not have walked away then. I was an ally, a friend.'

There was a howling in the Chasm. A ferocious wind screamed from the abyss. Her frame trembled as the air whipped harshly around them. Wrecking closed his eyes, levitating slightly from the ruined bridge.

Her katana flew through the air, soaring out of the abyss. Demorn caught it, icy in her grasp. The handle was black and adorned with skulls and miniature hearts.

It had the same lightness, hissing and glinting in the air, as she arced the blade through the air with a deliberate casualness.

'I release you from your vows.' He waved his fingers. 'Your shirt was torn. You look sexier in black.'

Her clothes rustled. She was dressed in the kimono of the Midnight Clan. Her jacket and t-shirt were gone. She hadn't worn the kimono in so long. She felt so damn clean.

Demorn bowed deeply to him, grateful. 'This is awesome.'

Wrecking placed his hand upon her shoulder.

'I lost this world, Demorn. I need you to be my vengeance, in this world and the next.'

She smiled. So many wars. 'That's never been a problem for me.'

13

Demorn walked over the rubble, turning her back on the abyss. The purple sun became a weak orange one, shining wanly through a grey sky.

The bridge was half ruined. She could see the river running far, far below. Demorn cried out as ice shards suddenly ate at her heart, worse then ever before, more powerful, then gone.

'It's the real world,' she gasped, her hand going to her breast, almost tumbling to the arid ground.

'Real as it gets, Wanderer. You are no loner protected from the undead, but you live again.'

She looked at Wrecking. It was strange seeing him in the light of a normal day. His earthly form was powerful and graceful. He looked rugged and handsome, slightly older, his hair cropped shorter than it had been in Heaven.

He was encased in red and black armour that carried his hulking form with controlled ease. His great flail glinted in the weak sun, charred fire swirling around the grim metal.

He smiled and pressed his hand to her forehead. Warmth possessed her. Most of the ice pain melted away. She felt almost normal, the cold ache fading.

'Thanks.'

'Perks of having me on the mission.'

Her green eyes flashed past him. The huge temple jutted out of the arid landscape. Jagged spiked teeth rose from the crumbling entrance. She saw Guard Dog trudging across the arid, lonely field toward the temple entrance.

The ground around him erupted and skeletons burst from the dry earth, surrounding and attacking his massive form.

She ran toward Guard Dog, the wind hitting her face, her black kimono and blade cutting through the air. Leaping over the small rocks and outcrops across the plain, her heart seized with adrenaline and excitement.

Like a blur she was upon his enormous figure. Guard Dog roared and snarled, his huge, muscled forearms swinging hard and heavy at the skeletons, ripping any asunder that he caught.

The Dog looked at her, his grey, scarred face weary from the miles and the sun.

Directly in her path, an Admiral Skeleton erupted from the dry sand, a jaunty purple hat upon its head, long curved sword in its bony hand. It singled her out and attacked, the death face carved in a macabre frozen smile. She could feel a wave of sorcery in the air, hearing it in the maddened cackle of the animated Bone.

She ducked the wild swing, and took off its head with one slash of her katana. Satisfaction flooded her.

Guard Dog snarled. Recognition and dislike flickered dimly in his animal eyes, even as his huge hands ripped apart another skeleton. The huge blue monster bellowed a guttural cry of victory and anger.

'Nice work, punchy.' Demorn casually gestured to the dead Admiral. 'I got the boss,' she said sassily.

Guard Dog growled. Demorn playfully spun into the air and slapped him hard twice across the face, a wild smile upon her as she landed gracefully back on her feet.

Veins bulged on his blue skin. He threw his massive bulk at her. Laughing, she flung herself backwards into the air, half-toppling the giant with a rapid-spin whirlwind of kicks.

Demorn was completely happy. Out of nowhere she heard the hiss of a bullet, nicking the back of her hand, disrupting her flow.

Rattled, she fell heavily to the ground, barely avoiding a huge fist from Guard Dog who swung, howling with pleasure at seeing her fall.

Demorn twisted away and looked up to see Alex emerge from thin air, a small pistol trained directly on her head, dressed in an arctic white jumpsuit.

Alex was sardonic. 'Little Princess has got herself a flashy new set of teeth. You sure look adorable for a monster.'

Guard Dog guffawed.

Demorn said, 'I see you've finally gone full invisible for the battles, Alex. Now you can really let your puppy do all the heavy lifting.'

Alex smiled tightly. 'You slapped my Dog. Only I get to do that, you ungrateful cow.'

She fired twice.

With a quick turn of her wrist, Demorn deflected the bullets with the katana blade.

Alex smiled savagely, firing as she shouted, 'Can you stay that fast forever? Doubt it!'

Red lightning blazed around them. Demorn saw the flail flash in the sunlight. Guard Dog was smashed brutally to the ground, a huge red energy wave enveloping the area with a suffocating force.

Demorn leg-swept Alex and quickly brought her blade to the girl's throat, pinning her.

Spread across the dusty ground, Alex smiled sweetly, her fingers still curled around the gun. 'You've got some hot moves.'

Demorn didn't shift position. 'Hotter than yours.'

She glanced at Guard Dog, squashed into submission with Wrecking's great flail of energy.

'Nice rescue attempt, Alex. Looks like the two of you were headed outta here, minus me.'

Alex fluttered her ice blue eyes. 'Sorry. Instincts took over. Competitiveness. General loathing. That kind of thing.'

Demorn moved the blade a millimetre closer to her neck. 'Sometimes I think you should have stayed dead, Alex.'

Alex poked her tongue out. 'I never stay dead. God, stop being so judgemental! You're not so perfect. You never gave me back my signed Beatles album, after all, and you've had it since Singapore.'

A sly smile stirred on Demorn, she could feel herself blushing. 'I'd forgotten about Singapore.'

She sheathed her blade, and released her death grip.

Alex smiled sassily, getting up, dusting off her clothes, tossing her gorgeous blonde hair back proudly and with more than a hint of contempt.

Demorn noted the white, lattice skull insignia on the ebony handle as Alex spun the gun back into her leg holster.

'You carry a Tyrant gun?'

Alex laughed richly. 'Just as arrogant as ever, Demorn! 'Cause only you could possibly be the single, famous Innocent? Well, things change. I've got a full dance card these days. I'm keeping the Club afloat while you've been off chasing ex-girlfriends.'

Demorn's eyes didn't waver from Alexandria's as she spoke in a flat tone. 'Or more likely, you're one of his pets, and he gives you presents like a good bitch.'

Alex walked away, flicking a single insulting finger in the direction of Demorn.

'Think what you like, Mighty One. I've beaten the Tyrant Run ten times in two years. I got famous. All the boys loooove me.'

Demorn smiled. 'You've never had a problem with the boys loving you.'

Alex pouted. 'Just give me back my damn signed Beatles album, or I'll kill you in your sleep.'

That's the only time you could kill me, Demorn thought with an icy hate.

Guard Dog growled, following Alex across the ruins, toward the jagged Serpent Teeth.

The sudden impulse to cut Alex down blind with the katana leapt up, fanning across her emotions like a brush-fire. Demorn fought it down, controlling the images playing like a short, violent movie in her head.

Her heart was beating so fast. Where was her self-control?

Wrecking put his burning hand on her shoulder, his soothing force flooding through her, the red rage softening.

'It's the black magic of the Dragon, feeding into you and through Xalos. My gifts are not for the weak.'

'I'm not weak,' she said defiantly.

Wrecking looked deep into her eyes. 'No, you're very strong.' He paused. 'Braver than you are wise, Sword Princess.'

Demorn sheathed her katana. She gazed upon the Serpent Teeth, and the figures of Guard Dog and Alex. 'There was a saying in the Club. Wisdom is what losers get.'

She smiled, moving her fingers in ritual warding. 'But it wasn't my saying. It was somebody who's gone beneath now.'

She looked up in the sky; night was coming. She could see the cold stars shining down on this dead world. All around them lay the arid plains.

In the dim distance she could see the bridge, flickering like a bad graphic in a video game. She saw one of the skeletons wore a plain gold wedding ring. She took it from the broken finger. A shiver went through her, to think they had all once been human, with their weddings and rings and arguments and happiness and sorrows. Demorn tossed the golden ring back to the dry earth.

She still had the golden coin in her robe and she ran her finger across it. She could feel the disfigurement across the face of the Goddess. Her finger tingled with small, sharp pains, a constant reminder that no matter what the distance, strung out across universes, she was bound to the Clubhouse and the Cavern temple hidden inside forever.

Demorn looked at Wrecking with curious eyes, flicking the coin across her hand in a quick motion.

'Y'know . . . Alex is an impatient one. It's not like her to have waited two weeks.'

His quick eyes watched the dancing coin.

With sudden grace, he snatched it from her grasp, the air warm from his powers. She laughed, her own fast reflexes still a jump behind his.

'The LA jump portals are damaged and unreliable. She got to my mansion, but couldn't get out. There's too much feedback. It's an epicentre of the sickness, a place of the damned.'

She laughed. 'LA. How fucking clichéd.'

His voice was low. 'Maybe, but it's true. I have been into the Pit itself. I have seen into the dark heart of everything. The markings were upon us all, before the spells reversed and the dead roamed this grave world. Zaltuth had followers amongst the highest and the low, drenched in his foul symbols, their souls wrapped in chains. It is how he still clings to some kind of existence from the Iron Prison.'

His hands glowed with red power, and his eyes had become lasers. He looked at her, but Demorn was quite sure he was seeing somebody else entirely.

He tried to recollect himself. She saw the strain.

'Alex got to my mansion, but couldn't get out. Too much feedback.'

'What happened to Rebecca from the Forest?' she asked quietly in Asanti.

He ran his hand across his face, the metal bracelet digging deep into his tanned skin. His red eyes glittered through the haze.

'How do you know about Rebecca? She wasn't in the games . . .'

Demorn spoke lightly. 'She was in one. I played it Asanti when I was a child. It was a side mission, a long way from the main story. You saved her from slavers.'

He smiled sadly, murmuring something soft in a language she only half knew from her travels and time spent on The Grave.

She journeyed with me. And when the storm wind blew hard, I took her to safe shores.

The ground in front of them shimmered. The granite slab captured a ghostly image of a girl with dark hair and a shy, pretty face, running alongside Wrecking Ball, as he blasted a savage amount of energy from his eyes and hands.

I had forgotten her . . .

Demorn placed her hand on his hand softly, which was warm to her touch. 'Come back, Wrecking, you don't need to remember.'

His eyes cleared of the redness and the image upon the rock faded.

'You know of Ultimate Fate, Demorn. You whisper of some great Being beyond us all, even the Gods, obliterating who we are and what we knew. How can you know so much, mortal child? How can you know?'

A sadness passed through her. Asanti knew, she thought. Before the destruction and the years of exile, Asanti knew, her home so far gone now.

Demorn looked at Alex, in close conversation with Guard Dog, the two of them arm in arm.

'Enough back story,' she said. 'If we escape the Grave, let us talk of the future and the past then.' Her eyes glinted. 'But if we die, we die like kings.'

He nodded in agreement, their hands finding each other. The tattoo burned on her arm, and she felt whole for the first time since Kate died. Or was it when Toxis plunged into the electronic abyss?

She didn't know anymore and she almost didn't care. Everything was raw. Demorn took a deep, cleansing breath.

She chuckled, giving Wrecking a friendly shove.

'You like Alex, don't you?'

He nodded. 'She has her virtues.'

'Props for noticing, lover boy. Alex might be a head-case, but she's got a warm heart. And a lovely ass.'

Wrecking was deadpan. 'She doesn't hate you nearly as much as she makes out.'

Her magic eyes focused. Alex and Dog were outlined against the gleaming Serpent Teeth. She could make out the imperfections and markings on the great fangs. She wondered what dark mysteries lay behind the cruel fangs.

'Oh, I know that,' she murmured. 'I'm their Fearless Leader. The best of them keep it ice cold or love-hate. She bothered to come find me, nobody else did.'

Sometimes, I find her quite beautiful, Demorn thought with a sigh.

'Lets go fight for freedom and all that jazz.'

Wrecking laughed. 'I thought you were trying to escape, Princess.'

Demorn's green, gleaming eyes grew narrow in the dying sun.

'In the Grave, freedom is escape.'

14

The four of them stood before the Serpent Teeth, dwarfed by their immensity. The Serpent looked ominous and evil, heavy lidded eyes set in red leathery skin.

Demorn imagined the serpent awakening and roaming through the restless night. She caressed the handle of her katana.

Guard Dog hurled his massive fists repeatedly at the Teeth. The crystalline teeth did not bend or break as his hand slammed again and again into them.

He howled in frustration. His great fist bled.

'Stop hitting it, Dog,' Alex said, disinterested and bored. She peeled off one of her studded gloves and examined a crimson fingernail. Guard Dog snarled and stalked away, brooding and sulking.

'Comments, Holy Princess?'

'Brute force won't be enough. And I'd rather you just call me Demorn.'

Alex smiled. Wrecking floated through the air toward the Teeth. Thunder rumbled in the sky but no lightning came.

Specks of red flashed through his fingers and played over the sharp crystal Teeth.

Wrecking spoke, his voice far away. 'The Serpent roamed this world centuries before me, bringing chaos and disorder, before slithering into the deep darkness with its secrets. Zaltuth Himself drew the beast from the Dungeon, and struck it down with his Holy Spear.'

Demorn's eyes flashed and she could see a great scar in the surface of the serpent, just as she could see the magic heat in the god as he caressed the leathery skin.

'Zaltuth sealed this crypt for centuries, entombing its rotten secrets, and was worshipped absolutely until I rose to prominence. When I killed Zaltuth, the Dungeon rose from the sands, as the prophecies read . . .'

Demorn rolled her eyes. Gods were so vain about their myths.

'Screw the history lesson, JUST HIT IT.'

Wrecking nodded. He swung into the Teeth. The sky exploded in an orgy of lightning . . . there was cracking and a small sliver fell from the crystal Teeth.

He swung again. Red lightning blazed from the sky. Again. Again. Again.

Wrecking turned to them, his face flushed but he was laughing. Blood ran down his hand.

'I can batter through the spells protecting the Teeth . . . but it will take days. I will be weakened for some time.'

Demorn looked over the arid field behind them. The bridge was invisible to her eyes now. They were on such a hostile world.

'I need you on full power when we go into the Dungeon.' Her green eyes flashed and she could suddenly see writing and codes within the crystal. 'Hold on.'

'What do you see, Holy One?' Alex purred, sliding close.

Demorn snapped, 'I see a nosy chick who should get her paws off me.'

Alex giggled. 'OK, grumpy.'

Demorn could see much with her magic eyes. The Teeth blazed with words and secrets, and the longer she watched the more she saw.

'I see my name. I see all our names. Alexandria, me, Wrecking . . . even Guard Dog. In a loop, over and over.'

Alex pulled out her revolver and shot her full clip at it. The Teeth tinkled and sparkled as the bullets hit them and bounced off.

Demorn raised an eyebrow. 'Surprise, surprise, they're resistant to bullets,' she said dryly.

Alex snarled, 'We aren't even born in this damn universe. Why the hell should we be part of their stupid legends and rules?'

Their names blazed bright red, then burned away, leaving the images of four palms, red and bright.

Alex sighed, frustrated. 'Can't you see it's all a trap?'

Demorn looked over the grey plains. The Sun would set soon. The vast hordes of Bone could stumble across their path at any time.

'It's a trap we are already caught within.'

She walked up to the Serpent Teeth and placed her hand against the cold crystal. Her face lit up with a pink glow, energy coursing through her body.

Alex looked at her with hatred, flicking her long blonde hair contemptuously. She waved one of her gloved hands, the metal studs flashing in the dying sun.

'Dog . . . touch the Teeth.'

Guard Dog did it, his scarred face dumb, watching Alex for her reaction. Her lips tightened in a small smile when he was unharmed.

Wrecking drifted toward them. Alex looked him hard in the eye. She didn't seem intimidated or in awe of the god at all. Demorn wondered what had really gone down between them and what deal had been cut. Alex had always done things her way; she didn't bow to anyone for longer than it suited her.

In a curious way, she was the perfect Innocent to have in a damned place such as this — unsentimental, selfish and wholly ruthless.

Alex flashed a perfect smile and took off one of her studded gloves and pressed her hand to the Teeth.

Wrecking floated to the Teeth.

'Why can't you see it?'

He looked into Demorn's green eyes.

'I don't have the magic eyes of the Goddess. This was in no prophecy.'

He touched her face with his hot fingers. She was struck again by his beauty.

'Only you see with her eyes, Demorn. You alone in the universes.'

She chuckled. 'Maybe. There's a lot of universes.'

Wrecking placed his palm upon the crystal Teeth. There was a cracking sound from within and the serpent head vibrated. Demorn's hand slid to her katana handle; Alex went for her gun.

None of them could remove their hand from the crystal, they were melded together, vibration binding them to the Teeth.

Guard Dog howled plaintively.

The Teeth cracked again, sickeningly. She saw more blood flowing from Wrecking's hand. He grinned savagely, his eyes pure fire. Red energy gathered around his body.

The Teeth splintered with a horrible cracking.

Wrecking moaned, the great flail almost falling from his hand, charred smoke issuing from the chain. His muscles tensed and hardened. The Serpent Teeth began to open, as the great wrecking ball struck again and again.

His blue eyes were fogged with pain. 'His final trick, the evil bastard . . .'

With a titanic effort, Wrecking ripped his hand away from the crystal and smashed through the Teeth, the mighty flail burning as he struck with inhuman strength, shattering the crystal.

Wrecking fell, half-slumping to the ground. Crystal protruded from his hands. Demorn could see shards of the Teeth in his bleeding stomach.

Wrecking smiled ruefully. 'Zaltuth god-mined the entrance. He blocked the escape route from this world, when he sealed the Serpent in . . . he didn't expect you to come, Demorn, he didn't expect that.'

Alex was watching impassively, her eyes flicking to the dark entrance. Guard Dog stood mutely beside her.

Demorn grasped Wrecking's hands. His blood was hot and burned her skin. His eyes shone bright, then dulled down to embers. She felt the magic teeth inside her mouth tremble with a dirty power as his blood stained her kimono. Demorn did not care, she never cared for herself when it was one of her Innocents in pain.

'Will you die?'

He smiled and for a moment he phased to Jason, his young face haunted by all the darkness and despair he had seen. But it lasted only for the briefest of moments.

Wrecking again lay within his dark cloak, his expression defiant as he fought back the crystal pain.

'Probably not, but I can't stay much longer. I have to return to my Heaven . . .'

Demorn kissed him impulsively, hard and passionate on the mouth. She gave him everything in that one moment, her love, her heart, her hope, gave it all to him for however far that would carry him. It was the only way Demorn knew how to feel. She couldn't do halfway, that wasn't her style.

'Remember Rebecca,' she whispered into his ear.

When it was done and their moment was over, she looked into his eyes and they were brilliant and blue.

'I will. Catch you in the game, Demorn,' he whispered, his eyes so terrible and kind.

Her eyes glistened with tears.

Then he was gone and all she held was his robe.

Alex spoke from behind. 'Well, aren't you just his faithful little piece on the side?'

Demorn got up, carefully keeping her burning eyes averted. 'It's just us now. Don't make me kill you, Alex. This could be our most legendary team-up.'

Guard Dog smashed through the broken Teeth, stripped of their power now. He shattered them like glass. He howled something guttural to Alex.

'He's so cute. Dog doesn't even worry about traps,' Alex said half-fondly.

Demorn rolled her eyes. That requires a brain, sweetheart.

She drew Xalos and whispered a small prayer to the Goddess, for luck, for victory, for a swift passage to the Shadows, if that was her Fate.

She took the bizarre black and white death mask from her robe and pulled it across her face, feeling the rich, death magic feeding from the air itself. From the burnt out corrupted ruins of this world, the souls that had perished lingered as tainted ghosts of themselves. She took a little part of their pain. She wondered if she took some of his, too.

Demorn smiled grimly, her heart black as the depths of hell. She saw Alex move the fingers of her left hand in some small ritual. There was no such thing as a non-superstitious Innocent.

'Put your gun away, Alex,' Demorn growled, 'this is a Dungeon Crawl.'

Alex nodded in agreement and drew a long flickering electro-bowie knife from the sheath on her thigh. Jesus, she was so beautiful.

Demorn stepped through the broken Teeth into the dark of the dungeon, every sense alive. The katana was singing a dark song of death, and her head was a messy web of blood and shadows.

Acknowledgments

Huge thanks to Chuck Dixon for his advice and help.

So many thanks to my editor, Jaye Manus, whose hard work has been of incredible assistance.

To Kim at Deranged Doctor Design for their awesome cover designs and professionalism.

And to Patchie, who kept me company on the long nights. We love you.

A lifelong lover of classic movies, Conan stories, and comics, David Finn lives with his girlfriend in Sydney, Australia. *Demorn: Blade of Exile* is the first book in the Asanti Series. Book Two, *Demorn: City of Innocents*, coming soon.

Please direct all business queries to darklantern@gmail.com

www.demorncafe.com

www.ingramcontent.com/pod-product-compliance
Lightning Source LLC
Chambersburg PA
CBHW071256170626
46809CB00001B/243